FAME & LOVE IN NEW YORK

ED SANDERS

FAME & LOVE IN NEW YORK

TURTLE ISLAND FOUNDATION
Berkeley 1980

ISBN 0-913666-32-7 Trade Paperback $7.95
ISBN 0-913666-31-9 Trade Clothbound $17.95
Library of Congress Card Catalog Number 80-52239

Fame & Love in New York is published by Turtle Island for
The Netzahualcoyotl Historical Society, a non-profit foundation
engaged in the multi-cultural study of New World history
and literature. *For further information & catalog, address:*
Turtle Island, 2845 Buena Vista Way, Berkeley, California 94708.

Book Design: George Mattingly, GM Design, Berkeley,
in collaboration with Eileen Callahan, Hipparchia Press
Cover Design & Titles: George Mattingly.
Typography: Abracadabra, San Francisco.
Illustrations: Ed Sanders. *Cover Montage:* Arthur Vitols.

CONTENTS

Part One:
BEETHOVEN'S DESK

Part Two:
THE SEARCH FOR HART CRANE'S TRUNK

Part Three:
THE BALZAC STUDY GROUP

Part Four:
J'ACCUSE

ILLUSTRATIONS

*The author would like to thank
and to dedicate this book to certain friends—
to Gus Reichbach for the ticket to the Philip Glass concert;
to Ralph Martel for helping resolve Milton Rosé's biography;
to Margaret Wolf for her insight into the underside of the Brooklyn Bridge;
to my agent Carl Brandt;
to Carol Bergé for her kindness in 1974 when this book was begun;
and most of all to Miriam & Deidre Sanders.*

FAME & LOVE IN NEW YORK

Fame & Love in New York
is set in New York City
in the near future,
with technology
slightly more advanced
than it actually is.

—Ed Sanders

PART ONE
BEETHOVEN'S DESK

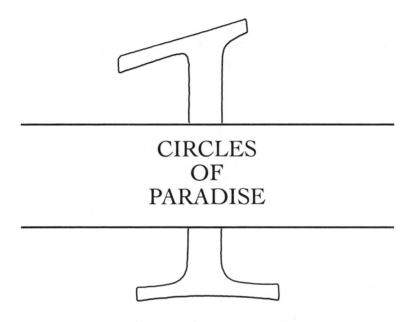

CIRCLES
OF
PARADISE

The furor had begun, oddly enough, with certain foreign news-papers, who railed rather sharply concerning the initials of his wife carved into the desk top near a game of X's and O's. The furor spread to New York. The blah blahers of the American art magazines, ordinarily enervated to the point of being riverine, suddenly found themselves suffering spasms of wrath. It was difficult to analyze the swelling of it, since certainly there had been infinitely more outrageous things occurring in the uni-verse. And real anger, as injected from without into the world of art, by critics, had been absent from art reviews for most of the century.

Indeed, the furor threatened the whole delightful tradition imposed upon art publications by that great poetic palindromic BAOAB of art-write—the BAOAB of Baudelaire, Apollinaire, Frank O'Hara, John Ashbery, and Ted Berrigan. These men wrote the brilliant but placid exegeses of Apollo, but in our time, the anger flared like the widening nostrils of a pissed taurus. Anger at works of art seemed suddenly IN, and *Circles of Paradise* had become the primal target.

The *Gorp* and *Urge*[1] reviewers had apparently huddled in a midtown restaurant over their response to the painting, the sentences of their reviews were so symphonious.

Gorp chuckled chortlingly: "Milton Rosé has done the impossible. He has created a work of art which has raised a mode of public anger not seen since the good citizens of Paris rioted during a performance of Stravinsky's *Le sacre du printemps* in 1913. And it's about time. Except this, that Rosé fully deserves the glops of anger that are flying around his face, for he has taken what many detractors view as his elementary urge for the Tawdry, capital T, into new paths of anti-glory, and has insulted the worldwide millions of Beethoven fans by emplacing Beethoven's legless composition desk into his new 'destruction/construction'—as Rosé haughtily describes his recent pieces—called *Circles of Paradise,* which opened at the Hammerbank Gallery two weeks ago. Questions are thickly clawing the air over the circumstances whereby Rosé acquired the priceless treasure and particularly whether fraud . . ."

"Fraud!" Milton Rosé shouted, barely able to hold the photocopy of the article in his hand. "It cost me 75 grand! Money I should have given to Citibank for my overdue loan payments. That desk is genuine! It has to be. I had it authenticated! Where do these cobras get off!?"

Thus anger bounced into, and from, the reticulations in peoples' skulls, from critics to artists, and artists to critics.

Milton was elated of course to have made both major newsmags the same week, but saddened at the same time that

---

1. *Gorp* and *Urge*, weekly publications that had arisen to challenge *Time* and *Newsweek.*

neither had been a cover story. In moments of cynicism he said he didn't care what was written about him, as long as they got the acute accent on the final vowel of his name correctly placed. In the mode of citizens surfeited with controversy, Milton had years ago become a controversy addict. He loved that "self-face flash," the sudden encountering of one's own countenance boldly emblazoned in a widely read or watched medium. In this regard, Rosé was not far removed from the type that rushes back to headquarters after the press conference about the impending riot, in order to watch the 6 o'clock news, dialing from channel to channel to feed back upon the coverage.

Through fast-dial, one could wear out a channel selector every few months, but oh, it was worth it! True feedback, that glorious rush, was to switch suddenly, say to channel 7, and to see one's face fastly babbling, defending one's position, or announcing grave strife in the wind, and then to pray that channel 4's coverage is not being run at the same time, and then, when your visage fades, and the commercial for Ultrabrite begins, you switch breathlessly to 4 to seek further self-face-flash.

The magazine *Urge* said as usual about the same thing as *Gorp* about *Circles of Paradise,* except that *Urge's* Adjectival Injections, or A.I.'s, as they were known in the chatmag trade, had injected a differing plethora of descriptive ire into the sentences.

Let us now discuss the specifics of *Circles of Paradise.* What was this painting, this assemblage, this destruction/construction that was causing so many nails to fall from the fingers of critics? The outer frame of *Circles of Paradise* was of flat pressed steel. It was huge—shaped more or less in the form of a truncated ellipse, with a vertical maximum height of nineteen feet and a horizontal width of ten. To stomp out the huge metal border, Rosé had used the facilities of the New Directions Steel Plant in Pennsylvania, owned by the rock band J'Accuse.

This steel frame was the enormously blown-up likeness of the very needle head used by Betsy Ross in creating some of those famous early American flags. The pits and scratches in the needle's head, made almost garishly large in the blow-up, were etched upon the pressed steel.

Near the summit of the needle frame lay a rectangle of

3

white linen with a star scissored from the center. To the dismay of conservatives the steel in back of the star had been tinted a faded rosy hue. When word came forth that the strange frame of the destruction/construction was Betsy Ross' alleged needle, right away critics accused him of bad history, that Ross had had nothing to do with the design of the American flag. As to the pink star, rightists spread the legend there was a burnt flag stashed somewhere in the work. Rosé was grossly alarmed over the rightist lies, for nothing harms the pocketbook of an American artist more than being thought a traitor.[2]

Rosé was on a lecture tour when a dealer in Copenhagen first offered him the desk. How thrilling it was to own Beethoven's very own scriptorium, next to which, prone on the floor, the great composer had worked on his final quartets and symphonies. "I also work supine!" Milton exclaimed. And it was so—Rosé loved to paint in a kind of breast stroke position, which was why his ornate canvases were so much more busy near the edges, and why the interiors, the parts out of arm range, seemed sometimes so stark. There was a blue head print on the edge of *Circles of Paradise* capturing for art lovers unto the supernova where Rosé had passed out while at work, bonking a fresh blue expanse with his noggin. Rosé then surrounded the cheek/sideburn/hairy temple smear with one of his favorite motifs (like the arrows of the early Joe Brainard)—a nice white oval-shaped dotted line.[3]

It was a beautiful little slant-top desk Beethoven had used, of dark walnut, with circular brass candle brackets built out on the left and right sides. The scriptorium was lidded, opening upward, revealing a storage compartment which could be locked through a brass fixture on the front shaped like a rose—a fact fraught with symbolism as far as Rosé was concerned. There was another small open shelf at the bottom of the desk beneath

---

2. The rumor, started by an ultra named Hunk Forbes, head of the American Security Command, was that Rosé had obtained one of B. Ross' actual flags, and had, prior to torching it, used it to clean his head after the noggin nod-out noted above.

3. We shall see later how the dotted line motif, so dear to Rosé, was used by the partisans of the C.T., that is, the Conceptual Threat.

the lidded compartment. At the base, of course, were the four three-inch leg stubs, which had apparently been originally severed by sawing, perhaps by the Big B himself.

Rosé purchased the desk, convinced that it had been used extensively during composition of the Ninth Symphony, and that one of Beethoven's specially bound 16-stave notebooks had been found in the lidded compartment, filled with notes for the planned Tenth Symphony. The price for the sketchbook and desk was out there in orbit, but worth it to Rosé, who computed there were exactly enough pages for the border of the projected destruction/construction. Right in the dealer's own showroom Rosé lay upon the floor, sketching feverishly using Beethoven's very desk, finalizing the plans for the great work.

His musicologist friends at Princeton had examined some of the note pages and had adjudged them to be genuine. That was part of the problem with the desk, for, since the musicologists had authenticated the notes, Rosé never subsequently thought to question severely the scriptorium.

There began to appear open speculation in the gossip columns that the desk either was a fraud or that it had been stolen. Several European collectors had sent angry notes to the *New York Times,* such as, "I have the *real* Beethoven secrétaire, and it is *nothing* like the cheap fake esconced in Mr. Rosé's tasteless collage." The *Times* assigned its crack art-theft team to the case, and by the end of a month had blown a few grand in room service at the various European Hiltons, but nothing conclusive could be determined about the desk.

"Maybe Beethoven used several desks," was one route Milton was possibly going to take.

Quite belatedly he hired experts to examine the desk. He secured a so-called Scroll of Authentication from the dean of European art experts, one Count Claudio Volpe. Rosé himself had blown up a drawing of the desk, made while Beethoven was still alive, to life size, and had gone over it nick by nick. It had seemed to be the same piece of furniture, although, to Rosé's symbolic grief, the brass lock in the drawing was not in the shape of a rose, but then maybe someone had broken the original, looking for Beethoven's personal effects after his death, and had replaced it.

5

As a matter of fact, the number of letters claiming owner-ship of the *real* desk of Ludwig von B., made Rosé wonder if perhaps someone were not pulling off the old Viennese Desk Scam— "Oldest con game in the world," as William Burroughs would have chuckled, remembering the pieces of the *real* shroud in which Jesus was placed in the cave, which millions of the faithful have purchased for the last 1000 years at least.

To get back to the description of *Circles of Paradise*; there was an open top'd 9-foot J. Broadwood & Sons pianoforte, an exact replica of the Broadwood sent to Beethoven in 1817, situated within the huge needle-head frame, with its 88 ivory keys positioned at the bottom of the painting. Like the desk, the piano too was legless, and the lid had been removed, revealing the piano strings, which had been marvelously warped by Rosé into wavy ripples.

The strings were made wavy according to the patterns of a computer printout of the resonating vibration curves of each of the strings two seconds after a B-flat major chord was struck. Using a photographic blow-up of the patterns, Rosé bent and stretched each string to match the printout, and glued them permanently to the piano frame. Then each string was painted with a thin shiny blue line, each line of a slightly differing shade of blue. Critics, many a clandestine painting patter among them, loved to run their fingers wantonly over the ripply blue strings. Is there a thrill more sublime than a crypto painting pat?

One of Rosé's rules for his destruction/constructions was that every free surface had a covering of canvas, upon which the master might ply his legendary brushwork, and *Circles of Paradise* was no exception. Rosé's stroke methods were studied in many college art departments, where, aided by computer analyses of the pressures, widths, lengths, curves, and the emotive evocations of his strokes, students worshiped the brainsurgeon calm of his masterful hand, his "language of personal concoction."

It's when you computer analyze the brush strokes of a painter that you determine the level of greatness.[4] Such was the

---

4. "There've been only five," Milton told his lecture audiences, "whose strokes can withstand the embarrassment of blow-up analysis."

6

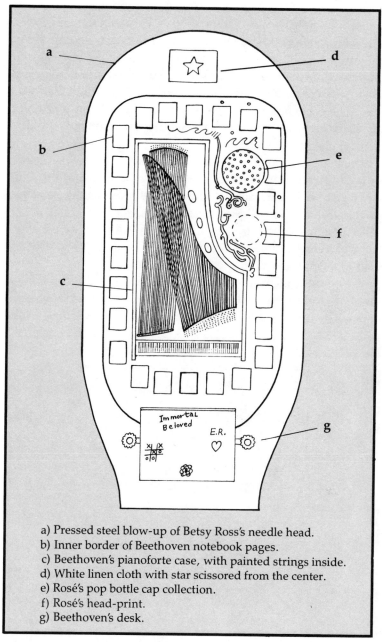

a) Pressed steel blow-up of Betsy Ross's needle head.
b) Inner border of Beethoven notebook pages.
c) Beethoven's pianoforte case, with painted strings inside.
d) White linen cloth with star scissored from the center.
e) Rosé's pop bottle cap collection.
f) Rosé's head-print.
g) Beethoven's desk.

founding principle of a major modern school of art criticism. That was fine with Milton Rosé, who confidently considered himself the finest brush man of all time. He could not glue pages into a scrapbook without chuckling over how some computer in the future would swoon over the marvelously fluid swoops and curves with which he squirted the glue upon the page. "Blow up my brush strokes 100 times, and weep, o aeons!" he challenged.

The challenge was accepted. Brush Stroke Blow-up Analysis I/Brush Stroke Blow-up Analysis II, were courses in the curricula of the best schools.

Where the pianoforte case was incurving, that is, at the upper right side of the frame, Rosé had glued his youthful Cub Scout pop bottle-cap collection upon an 18th century globe of the earth. Oh how the critics sneered! Also sneering were avid cap collectors, who noticed with dismay how Milton had ruined some extremely valuable 1952 strawberry soda caps by driving nails through them affixing them to the globe.

The desk of Beethoven itself was situated directly below the pianoforte keys and below the lower border of notebook pages. The upper portion of the desk rested on the canvas, and

the lower part upon the steel needle head, the leg-stubs inserting into holes drilled in the steel. (See diagram of *Circles of Paradise* on page 7.) And then, directly scratched on the slanted desk top were those last straws for Beethoven lovers: that slightly lopsided heart that looked as if it had been hastily cut while the teacher was out of the room, plus the half-completed game of X's and O's, and Evelyn Rosé's initials.

The painting was signed, at the lower right, in his unusually large fashion, with his coat of arms, gold background with two bars gules[a], pocket watch melted silver, and three fire-wielding hamadryads vert in the chief[b]; tressure[c] of fleurs-de-lys alternating with rain crows and azure pirogen.

---

a. Gules, the color red; b. The chief, the top part of the shield; c. Tressure, a narrow inner border.

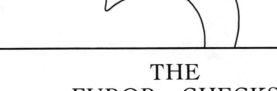

THE
FUROR = CHECKS
FORMULA

The City of Vienna, upon reading of the sacrilege in *Urge* and *Gorp,* immediately sent a letter of complaint to President Kennedy. In addition, an entity of irate humans known as the *Beethoven Society of Yonkers*[5] picketed outside the Hammerbank Gallery with battery-powered neon lollipops bearing Beethoven's

---

5. Who could have predicted the rise of Yonkers, with its city block-sized warehouses now in demand by artists, designers, bankers cum surrealists, as the Ultimate Lofts, catapulting "YoHo," as it was affectionately known, onto the front pages of the magazines? Don't laugh, better YoHo perhaps than the art colony of Houston, known as HoHo.

hirsute head and the flashing logo, repeated in cycles, "For Shame! (green), For Shame! (yellow), For Shame! (blue)."

Rosé didn't really care if Betsy Ross had actually shown George Washington how to cut a star from cloth, or that the critics were outraged that a game of X's and O's had been cut into the walnut lid of the desk, for if they could not ascertain the message he was presenting on the question of cultural inputs, then to hell with them. So, during the initial phases of the furor, Milton was serenely content. His faith was in the formula,

$$FUROR = CHECKS.$$

Had not his entire career been played out in sore contention? And had not the money never ceased to flood?

But, when President Kennedy's cultural affairs assistant called the Hammerbank Gallery to inquire, Milton Rosé knew he had to make some sort of response.

It was at this time that Rosé first learned there was something truly dangerous to his career lurking in the controversy. He decided to hold a press conference, figuring he would attract a fantastic crowd, since the matter seemed at the top of current cultural news. He was wrong. An 11 a.m. conference, featuring coca leaf champagne and a lunch afterwards, drew only three reporters and no TV crews to the Hammerbank Gallery. One of the reporters left promptly upon determining there would be no admission of fraud or guilt by the artist. What a disaster! For there can be no self-face-flash when there's no camera present in which to implant the images of self-face-flash. Never had the six o'clock news seemed so devoid of meaning.

Part of the tribulations of genius is the necessity on occasion to stand on top of the Empire State Building and chant through a P.A. system to the crowds below, "Je suis Ra! Je suis Ra! Je suis Ra!" There is a variation of this that requires a modest version of Je suis Ra to be intoned at the dinners and banquets given by a genre of rich and grouchy art patron and matron of inestimable value to a great artist. How? To bring to fruition the mystic formula, "cop the symbols / cop the mon / cop the power /

cop the wall," a powerful tetrad Rosé was wont to chant for the unification of mon/power/sigil/wall.[6]

You can picture, if you will, the Clancy Brothers singing, to the tune of *Risin' of the Moon*, "O th' coppin' of the wall, o th' coppin' of the wall . . ."

Rosé had not experienced difficulties for years selling multiples, destructions/constructions, or indeed anything at all, so had not anticipated trouble dealing out *Circles of Paradise*, the work of a year. Both *Gorp* and *Urge*, however, had paid careful attention to the fact that, whereas Milton's works usually sold out at least by opening night, on this occasion the opening had come and gone, with nary a nibble.

Therefore, Rosé flew down to Washington for a whirlwind round of dinners with the military-industrial-surrealist-banker conspiracy, to shore up the dikes of wall and mon, the stability of which kept his art from plummeting in price. "The prices!" Milton moaned, waking up from a recurrent nightmare, "the prices!" Dreading, as any artist must, that the price tags'd be scribbled over with hideous new low discount Columbus Day red tag sale prices, or that museums would suddenly store his work in racks in the basement near the exit signs.

Rosé strained to enjoy these dinners. You know how early in your schooling or career the apothegms of those you trust you receive like drops of wine from the Grail, and how throughout subsequent years you are reminded of them, and feel affection for them, no matter how stupid or unfounded their texts will have been shown to be? So it was with Milton Rosé, who heard someone say when he was beginning college, to the effect that, "Nothing makes a banker happier than to dine with an artist who enjoys his money."

Now deep inside, Milton didn't believe that—he was sure there was only one thing to make a money lender happy: foreclosure; that and the metaphor of stripping armor from the slain. Nevertheless, Milton felt it necessary to dine with them.

---

6. Cop the Wall. To Rosé, this meant grabbing off for his work the maximum amount of wall space in galleries, museums, and villas all over the world.

After all, did he not have a certain pride in America, the country where he was allowed to poke fun at will at the institutions of his choice, and which paid him handsomely for the honor?

You might call them "Am-Chauv vectors," those barbed comments in praise of his country, that he strove to inject into the dinner party conversations in D.C., trying to overcome the negativity surrounding *Circles of Paradise*. Oh Lord, does everything at last come down to, "We won the war"?

Milton generally won favor, especially among those present who'd purchased in the past the destructions/constructions or The Shaped Foot Multiples.

This mention of one of the most successful editions of multiples in history suggests the need for a general description of some of the main projects in the career of M. Rosé. As to multiples, artists will thank him forever. Everybody has known all along that the true game is to establish a precedent whereby the price of the multiples of a great artist will equal the price of a single large piece. You dig, muh fuh? Milton did it—his multiples were priced according to his major works. So, as of plucking green from the pecunia patch, this meant that a multiple, say of fifty units, provided the green of fifty single works.

We have no space here to catalogue Rosé's career, which is already too well depicted in the many thick art books now on the coffee tables of the world. But the following seem the highlights:

1. *The Moon Leg.* Rosé had beaten out 1000's to gain the commission from the National Endowment for the Arts, to construct the first sculpture on the moon. The result was known rather sarcastically as *The Moon Leg*. For, what Mr. Rosé chose to erect upon lunar soil was a 250-foot-tall aluminum leg—supporting Rosé's contention that it was the marvelously muscled human leg, and not the brain, that had trekked civilization forward.

2. *The Shaped Foot Multiples.* Rosé's only known venture into eroticism, and they sold like the 1st cancelled stamps brought back from the moon. They were shaped of canvas, and were exact duplications of the right foot of singer Mel Tormé. Oh what labor Rosé wrought in painting the inflections of the sing-

er's foot upon the cloth! But, where was the eros? On the inside of each foot, which was a mere shell of a foot, which could be viewed via a curved telescopic lens stage built into the top of the ankle. The insides of the feet, particularly the tarsus and the toes, had been cunningly transformed into the interiors of igloos, where fantastic fornications among tiny replicas of well-known American politicians could be viewed. These were not crude little dolls getting after it, but when you looked at them under the telescope, it was as perfect as a production from a CIA porn lab.

3. *Homage to the Food Chain.* This insured Rosé his international reputation. It was a 400-foot-tall, 500 ton, green frog bearing a mysterious Mona Lisa-type smile upon its mouth, from which by the way, dangled a 150-foot-long red fishing worm, which it was in the course of swallowing. Located high in the Santa Monica Mountains near the Pacific Ocean, it was most mystical to round a certain curve of the freeway, late at night, and to confront *Homage to the Food Chain,* all lit up like a Bel Air estate, the strange aura surrounding the green frog no doubt caused by the floodlights reflecting off Rosé's wondrous fountain which bubbled out of the top of its head and spread out on all sides, giving the animal that suitable wet and oleaginous appearance. Most startling, however, was the motorized worm, which whipped this way, then that, in apparent protestation over the half-completed chew-job.

4. *The Martian Football.* One of Milton's first destruction/constructions, following on the success of *The Moon Leg.* All the world had been touched by the first sports activity on extra-terrestrial soil, that first game of touch football played by the spacesuited men and women on the Martian landing zone. The football, signed by the President, was handed over to Milton for suitable enshrining in a destruction/construction. Stop off and see it at The Smithsonian sometime.

5. *The Burnt Bank Multiples.* In these multiples, Rosé reached his summit in pleasing divergent minds. The series was inspired by the decade-long rash of burning and looting of bank branches

by humans of all persuasions. *Everybody* was doing it; even a few bank owners were caught looting their own firms. It was Bank-burn Chic. Rosé constructed scale model duplications of burnt-out banks as they appeared in official police photos. He selected 25 banks from scattered sections of the country, which were published in an edition of 100, at a price of 35,000 dollars per set, the entire edition selling out weeks before the opening. The Left loved the work, in that it was truly inspirational to gaze upon such blows against capitalism; the Right loved the work, believing the bank burnings to be fit punishment against the banking community, long known to be under the evil control of the International Illuminati Imperium. Oddly enough, however, *The Burnt Bank Multiples* were purchased for the most part by bankers. They graced many a board room, where a mere gaze could provide a dazed banker with fresh energy to make the mon, and with firm resolve to prevail against the Godless and unpatriotic forces of bankburn.

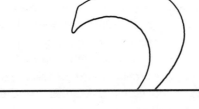

THE SECRET PLIGHT
OF MILTON ROSÉ

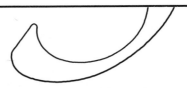

Milton's dining with the rich, the grouchy, those weighted down with the safety of the democracy, was extraordinarily successful. The "whaps" of being slapped on the back by well-wishers faintly bruised his clavicle. No doubt the praise of the center-right and the military-industrial-surrealists, with their promises to continue purchasing his works, should have sent him into ecstasy.

But it didn't.

Such banquets gave him the opportunity to try out new personae. You should have heard him discussing Kierkegaard, anarcho-People's Republicanism, and theories of suicide, leaning against an Oldenburg soft fireplace in which teak logs were softly aflame, sipping the rarest from solid gold Helen of Troy breast-shaped goblets and Groin of Ajax beakers, after candied duck sprinkled with 500-dollar-a-gram rock spice brought back from Mars. Lord, was he witty—his fluttering tongue thrilling all with the peccadillos of the painterly, while at the same time inserting anecdotes of tragedy and calamity about artists such as could make the art matrons weep and the art patrons sniff.

But oh how he was tired of it all—these osculations in the abyss! He was tired of repeating the tale printed on the back of the buck: American Art = Novus Ordo Seculorum. He wanted to turn his back on them all, the left, the right, the center, yet he could not, for Milton had a secret burning within him, which, when understood, explained somewhat his inconsistent behavior in matters of politics. A gnawing gnash-worm of fright ate at his mind around the clock. For this artist, so at home with the titans of bankerly mon-rake, was equally on friendly terms with some of the most notorious radicals of the century.

The question of Rosé and the radicals is difficult and obtuse. One thing is certain, when it came to the theory and practice of social dislocation, Rosé was elegant—too elegant. His ingenious plans for halting the subways and jamming the bridge lanes with burning dirigibles—his mass laughing gas dispersal system design, were not too well received by the guardians of social order.

He was trusted by the various underground armies, squads, and cells. They would plot in their bug-proof plexiglas domes and bounce their ideas off Rosé, who never urged, never really deprecated (unless an idea involved gore), but rather served as editor of possible plots, and a fine editor of rad-plots he was, for the era had seen marvelously cunning radical activities under his editorship.

"After all, what of it?" he asked himself. "They can't indict you for chit-chat."[7]

---

7. Important in circumventing conspiracy laws, was the Chit-Chat Principle, which made law in the sense that it established a definite bifurcation in intent, separating chit-chat from "serious" conspiracy. Pleading the Chit-Chat Principle kept thousands out of jail.

To Rosé, the thrill of the following configuration was almost sexual: $0°$. That is, picture a zero, the zero denoting a hot conspiracy, say the one wherein the radical unit known as Air Weather schemed to chopper-lift 100 tons of oil spill sludge and drop it on the New Jersey cancer belt petrochemical plants. Next picture the degree sign, $°$, at the upper right of the 0, as this: $0°$. The degree sign was Rosé, who liked to get just that close, and no closer, to the zero orb of a conspiracy, so as to absorb some of the inspirational energy of the radicalism, without, at the same time, absorbing any of the jail terms. And never, swore he, would the degree sign enter the conspiratorial zero.

His troubles came about from his association with the Heartbreak Hotel Brigade. Then the $°$ definitely entered the 0. The Heartbreak Hotel Brigade began with one of the most elevated and ethical mandates in the history of art. Its purpose was to monitor art auctions, galleries, and private collections to make sure the original artist or heirs received a just percentage of the resale price of works of art. It wasn't easy, and gradually the Heartbreak Hotel Brigade shifted from being a collection agency to a sort of enforcer squad. The Heartbreak Hotel Brigade was a part of the Barrel Generation[8] and was connected with the Diogenes Liberation Squadron of Strolling Troubadors and Muckrakers.

---

8. The Barrel Generation. It was proof that "Art triggers life" that a work of art, namely Arnold Biblon's monumental sculpture, *Homage to the Burning Barrels,* should have created a lifestyle. Biblon had always been greatly impressed by citizens of the Bowery who, in the wintertime, hover near rows of burning barrels filled with packing crate wood from nearby loftfirms, on Houston Street and The Bowery. He fashioned a labyrinthine work out of soldered-together barrels, hundreds in all, which he somehow got the City of New York to erect in a vacant lot near the real burning barrels. Local kids quickly discovered that the long barrel-tunnels in the mammoth sculpture could be crawled in, so it became used as a social club and as a meeting place for lovers. A group of impoverished poets discovered it also, and moved in, becoming the Barrel Generation. With development of solar heating systems, and an apparatus known as the "vibra-shower," it was possible to live in a barrel quite comfortably, and stay as clean as a fresh-washed radish. From the Barrel Generation was born the Diogenes Liberation Squad-

Gradually too, the anger of the H. H. Brigade on questions of economic justice overwhelmed their pacifism, and they increasingly turned their attention to social dislocation. It was nothing more or less than the primitive urge that hundreds of thousands feel, to rush into the offices of Consolidated Edison and spray the premises with ack-ack after a light bill increase.

Leaders of the Heartbreak Hotel Brigade confided to Milton they were going to kidnap key officials of AT&T to force a nationwide 25% rollback in telephone rates. Something, a quirk of irresponsibility, made Rosé approve. Perhaps it was the 1500 dollar phone bill just received in the morning mail, that caused Milton, *horribile dictu*, to aid a project possessing the direst possibilities. What if something went wrong and executives were offed? Would not the voice of weeping children and wives follow Rosé forever? Somehow, a vision of ultimate justice to be enacted against the phone company prevented such a line of thought in the artist.

After the plans to kidnap the executives were well under way, Rosé was pleased to ascertain that the utmost precautions were being taken to avoid violence. He inquired as to the living quarters to be provided to the men and women, once they'd been 'napped. The hiding spot was to lie in subterranean SoHo tunnels, under West Broadway and Spring Street in fact, but Rosé discovered they were exceedingly sparsely furnished from the point of view of comfort.

Rosé thought it important that if the exigencies of social dislocation made it necessary to 'nap executives, the precedent

---

ron of Strolling Troubadors and Muckrakers. Tourists came from all over the world to hear the Squadron recite its hours-long memorized epics which they delivered while residing within their barrel-hive. The strolling muckrakers would walk about the city, sometimes wearing their barrels, serving as walking newspapers, declaiming news and scandals often left out of the dailies. The finest investigative reporting, as well as the best poetry, of the entire era, came out of the Barrel Generation. In time, the Barrel Generation housing complex grew too large for its vacant lot, and when the city tried to sell the superstructure of the Brooklyn Bridge (vide, *The Search for Hart Crane's Trunk*) the Generation moved the housing project down to the pediments of the Bridge.

of comfort for the 'napped should be established at once. Thus, he offered to design interior decorations for the underground facilities.

The walls of the Heartbreak Hotel, as it was called, were filled with early Rauschenberg. As tempting as it had to be, Rosé resisted putting any of his own works on the walls. He designed especially comfortable "killing time" furniture for the Hotel, since kidnapped executives might have to be held in the same bedroom for weeks or months. His kitchen facilities were a marvel, with wine vaults, veritable walls of copper kettles, skillets and soufflé pans. His oversized walk-in freezers were stocked with European game and provisions worthy of a J'Accuse album party.

Rosé thought that this single act would be his sole contribution to the Heartbreak Hotel Brigade. But the Brigade, in the normal up and down mon-configuration of an underground group, fell into fiscal plight, and came to him for help. "But, you said that all you ever wanted from me were the decorations for the Hotel," an exasperated Rosé whispered over tofu at the Bed of Nails restaurant.

"Surprise! April Fool! Where's the mon!" the angry leaders of the Brigade whispered in response.

Milton got off lightly, agreeing, after pleading a crushed cash flow, to supply a major painting a year to them, the most recent being the magnificent triptych titled:

MAXIM GORKI HANDING OVER A ROYALTY CHECK
TO V. I. LENIN TO FURTHER THE CAUSE.

One problem in dealing with far-left groups is that you can't be sure if you're dealing with Red Brigade or Red Squad. Is the firebrand chatting before you a true dedicated communard, or an agent of the Office of Naval Intelligence? Milton realized this most sorely, and feared greatly after designing the Heartbreak Hotel. His one abiding terror was that of being labeled a traitor on defense department computers. That was the reason, as part of a continuing program to avert the bony finger of "Traitor!," that he had used Betsy Ross' needle head in *Circles of Paradise*.

It was what they call a double bind. He wanted the seven

years such as would make him unindictable to rush past as one big gulp, yet he knew that seven years would lead him unmistakably into the hoariness of biologic phasing.

Returning to New York from the Washington dinners, Rosé was faced with the greatest tribulation of his life. Total dry-up of the cash flow. Nothing was selling. No one was expressing serious interest in purchasing *Circles of Paradise*. Was it the price tag? Certainly not; the Smithsonian had paid 500 thousand for *The Martian Football* construction/destruction, and *Circles* was priced at a mere 400.

In desperation, Rosé turned to the Heartbreak Hotel Brigade. He signed an encoded agreement with the Brigade, at a cost of 25% of the retail price of *Circles of Paradise*, contingent on its sale within 30 days. The H. H. Brigade promised to flip heavy pressure on the media, particularly on *Urge* and *Gorp*, and on President Kennedy's cultural affairs assistants, to get them to ease up on Rosé.

A deputation left at once to interview leading collectors and museums in Europe, using appropriate cover stories, to determine if a conspiracy was afoot to crush the reception of *Circles of Paradise*. Careful attention was paid to the accumulation of a list of possible purchasers. "Don't worry, Milton," the Heartbreak Hotel Brigade assured him, "Just give us 30 days, and your malfiscality will be but faint traces of angst in current pleasures."

But money a few weeks in the future is no cure for the dreaded dry gulch of shekel-less sand in which Milton Rosé was crawling.

THE
MORN OF
IMPECUNIOSITY

The implications of what you create in just ten minutes of brilliant inspiration, wafted aloft by the wings of genius, and scratched with haste on an empty box top, may take ten years thereafter to bring to fruition. Thank God, Milton Rosé knew that well, otherwise he would have been overwhelmed by his morning swells of ideas.

Hypercreative individuals sometimes get tossed here and there among abundances of projects that screech for attention. What a plague upon the pocketbook are 10,000 screaming plans, none of which gets brought to fruition! Milton knew that well also, and his solution was to get fanatical about one particular project among the many—in his case, it was the series of de-struction/constructions such as *Circles of Paradise,* each of which were fulfilled on a grand scale, with no expense spared, and up to a year spent on each. But, to spend a year on a single work of major art, that could also spell pecuniary disaster. Milton knew about that snare also, but it was simply solved by one of the great fiscal operations devised by artists in our era, that is, the fiscal device known as "framing the stages." First you sign and enshrine in a nice Kulicke frame the envelope containing the original sketch or idea; then you frame the first stage or sketch growing from the originality; then the second sketch, then the first execution, then the second execution, and then you have the Final Work to frame or to empedestal. Considering mon, you work geometrically from that first doodle on the envelope, be-ginning say, at 1000, and then going to 2000, 4000, 8000, 16,000 and by stage six, say you are pulling in for the Final Work sixty-four thou, but you have all those other stages as pecuniary pad-ding!

Each morning of his life, fresh with sleep, Milton Rosé's bulging brow produced a veritable gush of ideas, and he felt guilty if he didn't write down as many as he could catch from the gush.

They were not only ideas for multiples, sculptures, paint-ings, prints, and destruction/constructions, but ideas for C.T.'s, inventions, novels, poems, furniture, short stories, plays, build-ing designs, movie treatments, hair styles, new species of trees, and investigative articles.

He had a tape system, triggered by a foot pedal, so that if, say, he were at work on a destruction/construction, he could speak the idea into the system without halting production.

Often, he was embarrassed at his idea flow, and tried to stifle it. He did not let others know, even his gallery man, Sig-mund Hammerbank. He dated each idea sheet, prepared a neat index folder, and filed it in its proper place in a bank of filing cabinets.

Why, one can ask, did not Rosé publish his stories and novels—some of which were bordering on excellence? Well, Mil-ton had a belief, most strongly held, that success in literature

23

might eat his painterly fame, and spit it out in demi-fame. He didn't want to appear to be spreading himself thinly, so the 700 short stories, the six novels, and the 13,212 poems in his filing cabinets would await the astonished archivist who some day would prepare his post mortem papers for cataloging.

Rosé woke on the morn of impecuniosity, and the first idea hit him as he was reaching with his bare foot, patting the cold parquet floor for his slippers. He jotted it on one of the pads he kept beneath his pillow, "Idea: a romantic short story, in which Lucia Joyce and Samuel Beckett actually decide to have an affair—they marry and live out their life in the quiet of a Dublin townhouse . . ."

Milton dated the note sheaf and trotted to the short story cabinet to file it. No sooner was the cabinet door shoved shut, when "Oh no!" he groaned, "a poem idea!" Thank the stars it was not one of those hundred-section time consumers, but a graceful little item of unrequited eros dedicated to his wife, Evelyn, tossed off and in the file cabinet in fifteen minutes. Then it was time for breakfast.

Breakfast was as fitful as usual; he was interrupted even as he was sitting down by a plot for a novel, and, arranging his silverware by his plate seemed to trigger an idea for an invention: The Anti-Painting-Molester Homing Manacle.

On the napkin he quickly sketched a prototype of the Anti-Painting-Molester Homing Manacle:

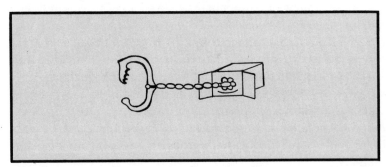

This idea actually possessed great business potential. Around the world in recent years had been a wave of slashings and punch-outs directed against art treasures. In the system Rosé designed, a painting would have a pressure plate mounted on the back of the canvas. Whenever a sharp object should impinge upon the surface of the painting or whenever sufficient pressure should be applied, the box containing the Homing Manacle would spring open and the Homing Manacle, utilizing heat-seeking mechanisms and laser guidance, would dart forth and seize the culprit's leg.

With a sigh, Milton rose from the breakfast and walked to file the napkin in the inventions cabinet. The tendency of people with filing cabinets to "file and forget" made it unlikely he would ever proceed with development of the invention.

Resuming his breakfast, Milton was chewing his croissant, and noted the curved way the arch of crust in the center lifted from the main part of it, so he sketched a plan for a new type of aircraft hangar. Then, while he stirred his coffee, a Negative Capability spasm (see footnote page 72) hit him, and he let slide an idea for a new and better logo for CBS.[9] Such guilt! He never failed to feel it when he did not jot down an idea.

After breakfast, Milton trotted into his work studio, and lay down immediately to work on a painting, one of his Moments in History equestrian series, this one titled:

GEORGE SAND, AFTER AN ELEVEN-HOUR WRITING PERIOD, RIDING OFF TO MEET HER LOVER.

And thus began his work day, stretching 14 hours, the so-called "Rosé Rondel" so admired or envied by fellow artists. Few had his private phone number, and so when the phone rang, he knew it was one of three people. He hoped it was his agent, Sigmund Hammerbank, announcing that the Smithsonian had purchased *Circles of Paradise.*

It was not. Rather, it was the bank. He was a number of months late on his various mortgage and business loans, and they warned him if some arrangement were not made at once, today, they would be forced to go into court to grab up his synagogue/loft.

---

9. Ever since Milton learned that NBC had paid 500 thou for the design of a new logo, his head had swarmed with possible network initials. Again, all 378 ideas went into the filing cabinet.

Rarely did Rosé moan. Now he moaned, facing the first full crisis of middle age. Not since he had broken up with Evelyn had such a calamity engulfed him.

He was totally out of money. Even carfare. It was the sort of calamity that can sneak up on an optimist like Rosé, who would ever stare at the calendar, convinced tomorrow will bring a thatch of checks. For several weeks his accounts had been attached. As soon as money came in from sales of multiples, or from resale percentages provided by the Heartbreak Hotel Brigade, the mon was sucked from his Citibank accounts to pay his debts.

He was penniless in luxury. He was like someone who, in a flight of arrogance, decides to split from a top rank rock group, in a squabble, say, over whose song will be the lead tune on the next album, and then, upon calling his accountant to get some money, discovers he's in the "five Rolls Royces and a can of spam" situation, and plummets into instant poverty.

We mention a can of spam, because that was what Rosé was left with as he contemplated his barren cupboard, preparing for a lunch of spam and matzoh fritters.

Worse than such an ignoble lunch was that his normal flow of work on paintings and destructions/constructions was halted by the angst of penury. "It's all the fault of my Business Empire!" he shouted. It had been a disaster, he well knew now, to have tried to set up a business empire, yet creative people all over America had been doing it, so why not he?

There are many, no matter how soundly financed they are, whose business empires are more fragile than the coprogenous spheroids shoved along by a Lamellicorn.* So it was with Milton Rosé, whose paint brush and welder's torch were pure gold, but whose skills in business were minimal. As soon as he'd get a little cash stored, he'd invest in something, usually one of his own ideas, and poof! the mon'd disappear.

After a number of years, he did fashion, after much trial and error, a business empire of sorts. In this book, we shall examine the modern Creative Business Empire, the first being Milton Rosé's.

---

* Egyptian Dung Beetle.

His agent Sigmund Hammerbank's advice had always been, "Buy a pizza shop." According to Hammerbank, a pizza shop was a marvelous part of any Creative Business Empire; you could suck a freshet of mon from it in times of horrible pov, or you could hide several freshets in times when you had a freshet or two to hide. Therefore, Milton opened the world's first "Spin Art Pizza Stand."

The reader will have seen spin art booths, say, at school carnivals. A piece of paper is attached to a disc which rapidly spins. Using the type of squirt-containers one finds in restaurants for squirting mustard and catsup on hamburgers, you squirt various colors of paint on the rapidly revolving piece of paper, and la!—instant spin art. In the Spin Art Pizza, the pizza dough, properly flattened and rounded, was placed on a spinning griddle, and the customer squirted hot, melted cheeses in bright colors from an assortment of nozzles, which spread upon the whirling dough in delicious mouthwatering profusions of abstract expressionism.

A brilliant idea but a fiscal flop, for Milton was embarrassed to associate his name with such an endeavor. Again Hammerbank had words of wisdom. "Don't hesitate to have some tacky components of your business empire, Milton," he expostulated. "I call it the 'grabbing of gauche-cash.'"

Another aspect of Rosé's Creative Business Empire, at first a success, then a failure, was Cover Story, Inc., a p.r. firm specializing in setting up cover stories—not in the intelligence agency sense, but magazine cover spreads. You'd be surprised who among the rich and famous hungered for, yet seemed denied, the prize of coverism. They paid dearly, but it was another enterprise Milton kept hidden out of embarrassment, fearing the sneers of brother and sister artists. Sigmund was right when he counseled Milton, "Look, Miltie, if you can't trumpet an empire, you're bound to fail." Some other aspects of Milton's empire:

1. The Electric Banana Sleeping Hammock. With the knowledge that electric blankets are a cheap method of getting an edge on high winter heating bills, Rosé created an entirely enclosed wintertime sleeping hammock, the replica of a giant banana, with heat-

ing coils inside, and a zipper to zip the occupant inside head to toe.

2. Coke Burnout Warning Transponder System, Inc. A warning buzzer occurs when over 20,000,000 brain cells have been destroyed; concomitant message from tape-loop, "Slow down, slow down, slow down," is played to the owner.

3. Medical Equipment: The Comic Strip Band-Aid. Milton initially had great success with a line of adult comic strip band-aids, starring Gilbert Shelton's Fabulous Furry Freak Brothers, but the market had actually been ripe for kiddies, and Milton watched in disgust as Johnson & Johnson sailed to market with Donald Duck and Fred Flintstone bandages.

4. Laser Sculpting Tools, Inc. The one profitable enterprise in the Empire.

Milton would make a bundle on the Electric Banana Sleeping Hammock, and then blow it funding the Coke Burnout Warning Transponder System—for who, however the device might be hidden on his or her person, would want to be known to be wearing such a device?

Rosé meditated upon his Empire. Was there something that could be sold immediately, today, to raise some green?

A shudder, almost a convulsion, passed over him, as he realized it would take days. He glanced over at the cabinets of his ideas, his eyes stopping at the elegant rosewood five-drawer console holding his novels. Would the greatest artist of the era have to stoop to peddling for quick bucks a novel?

With tears in his eyes, he dialed Sigmund Hammerbank, to beg him to hasten with the campaign to sell *Circles of Paradise.*

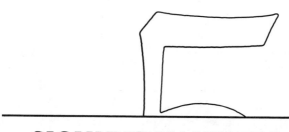

SIGMUND HAMMERBANK—
PRINCE OF
PRINCE ST. REAL ESTATE

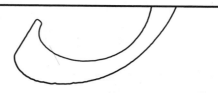

To most careful observers Sigmund Hammerbank, the owner of the Hammerbank Gallery, was lecherous, cruel, despotic, falsely forlorn, lupine when normal/loup-garouish when coming down, smelly, his personality ping-ponging between hate and grouchy friendliness. His love of money, he would have sworn, was so refined as to have matched that of a Nelson Rockefeller buying an expensive Max Ernst-made sleeping bed, but, on the street, the word was that you had to guard your loose fillings lest Hammerbank try to hook them out with a dirty fingernail. Sigmund would have been hurt had he known of such opinions, for he thought himself to be sentimentally profound, an old softy, kind, tearfully gentle, you know: sniff! sniff! oh tempus fugit!—it was not, however, the sniff of tears, but of auld lang coke sniff.

Hammerbank was the author of the famous homily of art dealers: "Sooner or later we all get into real estate." And did he own the real estate! "I never saw a building I didn't want to own," saith he. Some wags called the Prince Street area Ham-Ho, so much did Siggie control. As of his own pad, Hammerbank lived in a quintuplex in an historic iron-framed building on Spring Street, the ground floor of which was the Gallery. The quintuplex was grandly celebrated in the chatmags as the ultimate in Woodlands of Weir chic. The five floors of former sweatshops had been truly transformed. Most famous of aspects was the five-story fireperson's pole Sigmund had installed down the middle of the quintuplex. Many a self-destructive drunk had nearly snuffed themselves streaking down the brass. A diamond-crusted sampler on the wall near the top of the pole read:

If Fried,
       Don't Slide

,

placed there after a famous ballet dancer slid down the pole upside down and in the middle of the slide began to feel coke-hairs tickling his hands, and therefore let go, and totaled himself at the bottom.[10]

Hammerbank's bedroom on the sixth floor was in the shape of a pyramid, for reasons, as one might guess, of harnessing the pyramidal energy beams. Sigmund slept with his head exactly in the midpoint of the highest energy field, on the anal-

---

10. Who could have predicted the national attention riveted on the runaway problem of coke-hairs? For those mountaineers still ignorant, coke-hairs are those small imaginary cilia habitual coke-snerkers sometimes swear they see and feel growing out of the palms of their hands.

ogy that if one could keep one's Gillette razor blade honed sharp at the center of a pyramid's energy field, one could keep one's mind honed Einsteinedly brilliant sleeping there.

There was a genuine Roman tile bath in a chapel off to the side of the pyramid, with extremely erotic spigots, from a N. African take-it-out-by-night-quick mafia archeological expedition.

The basement under the Hammerbank Gallery was occupied by a highly classified operation known as the Ecce Puer Chicken Farm, about which the less said the better.

On the roof of his building there was a hot air supported dome duplicating the shape and hue of a vanilla cone with chocolate sprinkles; in fact, a magnificent example of Milton Rosé's SoRoof inflatables. This translucent contraption contained Hammerbank's famous roof garden which produced most of the vegetables for his Bed of Nails Restaurant, through a tax shelter called Tar Strand Organic Products, Inc., operating roof gardens all over SoHo, Tribeca, BrookHo and YoHo.[11]

Whereas the fiscal empire of M. Rosé was undersubstantial, the Empire of Sigmund Hammerbank grew with each day's schemes.

HAMMERBANK'S EMPIRE

1. The Hammerbank Gallery

2. SoHo/SoHoNo Properties, Inc.

3. Sub-SoHo Properties, Inc.
   (Specializing in "loft" space for artists in abandoned subway tunnels.)

---

11. It was a sight for sore sniff-nez to see Hammerbank himself tilling his roof gardens, yodeling instructions from roof to roof, his white goatskin bibbed overalls wet with sweat of honest toil. The Bed of Nails Restaurant was one of his persistent money makers, where New Yorkers could experience 4-star thrills by reclining to dine upon more-comfortable-than-you'd-imagine beds of nails. Hammerbank had bought the entire edition of Milton Rosé's Bed o' N's Multiples, a collection of 25 lounges made of 1000's of roach clips protruding from body-sized concrete grids. These roach clip lounges were the cause of long lines outside the restaurant of big appl'ers wanting to celebrate the mystery of Jansenist/hedonist asceticism via banquets of ouch.

4. The Bed of Nails Restaurant and Bakery

5. Tar Strand Organic Farm Products, Inc.

6. The Ecce Puer Chicken Farm

7. The Beef 'n' Art fast food chain
   (now defunct, but a continuingly marvelous tax scam.)

8. The Eat, O Moo Moo, Eat! Cattle Feeding Company,
   Omaha, Nebraska.

9. Theatre Groups Promotion, Inc. (Promoting the trend of "live in your own theatre" lofts; for, if you can encourage the creation of say, 5000 theatre groups vying for the same 1500 loft-theatres, rents will bound into the sky.)

10. The Hard Edge Zig-Zag Elevator Company. (Manufacturing a far-out elevator that meandered upward — I mean, why go straight up?)

He was, in brief, one of the greatest business humans SoHo'd ever supported. Alas and alack, he was a cokaholic, but one of those who hides it in Dristan mist bottles. He controlled his habit behind the following formula: "I never snort before I make some morning money, at least a thou . . . And I never take a drink until I log a Tom Mann Two."[12]

Ironically, Hammerbank helped set up special screening laws to weed out the uncreative in the various new residential sections of New York devoted to artists. Typical of this was the New York State SoHo Credentials Committee, an entity virtually created by Sigmund. That was where the mon fiendishly was to be raked, in figuring out complicated (and expensive) ways of circumventing these laws.

He formed, for instance, the *Wallace Stevens Society* of bankers and insurance executives, each member filing affidavits attesting that they worked at least two hours a day on painting.[13]

---

12. Tom Mann Two. Referring to author Thomas Mann, who, or so Sigmund had read somewhere, worked two hours per day, year in and year out, writing his novels, turning out at least 1000 words per morning. This data was of a religious nature to Hammerbank, who substitued 1000 dollars for 1000 words.

13. As argument, the N.Y. Bank for Savings commissioned a market study on New York painters which determined that the average

After a lengthy court battle, the *Wallace Stevens Society* won residency in the area. They founded their famous Bankers' Painting Club, where the businesspeople, amidst closing down deals and exchanging insider stockmarket tips, engaged in "painting business lunches" standing at their easels.

Milton Rosé respected Sigmund Hammerbank immensely for his ability to rake in the sheks. And Hammerbank truly thought Milton Rosé to be a great genius—and sorely hankered for the art history books to treat him, Hammerbank, lovingly as the benevolent life support system for a great artist.

On the other hand, Hammerbank thought all artists essentially crazy—and ripoffishly dumb in pecuniary matters: "Take my money then confuse me!" he felt was tattooed on every artist's forehead.

At the same time Rosé felt all art business was run by "yuk yuks and arr hars"—with Hammerbank being a friendly exception. And of course each thought the other entirely dependent on him.

"Without me he's nothing," Rosé boasted.

"Without me he's nothing," Hammerbank boasted.

Hammerbank loved to sit all alone with Rosé's art, preferably in a darkened room, to meditate. To Hammerbank it was better than any dope, save one, ever devised. He was greatly troubled by the hostile publicity generated by *Circles of Paradise,* a work he swooned to meditate upon late at night in the dark gallery. But it was attracting the attention of the Feds, and that could conceivably impinge upon his chief money source, as speculator in rare powders.

Hammerbank had difficulty grasping the problem. There was a half-inch thick manila folder of adverse articles on his desk, yet the opening party had been so placid, it was hard to believe there was a controversy. Hammerbank sat there, thinking of the opening. He loved such events, not for their substance, but for those glorious moments at their close when he

---

amount of time consumed per day in actual painting was slightly above two hours. "It's the Tom Mann Two!" Hammerbank exclaimed when the bank president told him of the survey.

33

could throw people precipitously from the premises. He adored that thrill of instant riddance.

You couldn't have predicted the furor at all by observing the art-flock baaing that night. And, after 50 years of remedies by gallery owners, people *still* refused to look at paintings at openings. Even so, with a worldwide controversy swirling around *Circles of Paradise,* one would have expected at least *some* would have stood in front of it for a few minutes.

Not that there weren't quick glances at it by the wittily wealthy and the wealthily witty, who spewed to partners little catticisms, like, "A carved heart in Beethoven's desk, really! Pardon me, but that's rather crude, if you can monitor my zone, muh fuh."[14]

Instead, it was buttockry that garnered the attention of the throng. For it was, as the newsmags bellowed, the Year of the Tattooed Buttock: everyone wandering around the opening exhibiting ornate pictographs on quivering derrières—many with fetching translucent panes sewn into the buns of their Levi's—men, women, even children, and shaved lap dogs with their owners' names or caricatures haunch-inscribed. Several soy futures men with clear panes in the rears of the conservative suits strolled circumspectly at the edge of the crowd, revealing sedate "'tock-'too's"—as the buttock art was commonly known—to querying eyeballs.

So, the opening party did not add to the furor, nor did it quell the furor. It was a glop of spinach. President Kennedy had been invited to attend, but was held by crises in Washington. Three cabinet officers graced the set, and a drove of U.S. Drug Enforcement Administration officials stood about, staring at the half-naked revelers. But that was the extent of the political puissance present.

The *Circles of Paradise* party had finally ended, the Gallery

---

14. Muh fuh. Oh how that word, at once so euphemistic and at the same time so powerful, had gained in usage and acceptance. Even on the late night talk shows; and a fervid tool when used by radio and television Christian revival ministers. "Rise up, o sinning muh fuhs! and grasp the TV sets in thine hands.!"

was silent, and Sigmund Hammerbank sat, lips curling with anger, exhausts and belches singeing the air, looking out over the polished floors with throw pillows out of kilter everywhere, a meadow of plastic champagne glasses, 100's of throwaway coketubes scattered around like jack straws, and cigarettes stubbed into the varnish—some poking perpendicularly out of the shininess, forming interesting patterns on the floor slats still faintly stained with machine oil from the generations of sweatshops occupying the floor.

Sigmund removed his white patent leather cowboy boots in the total calm, revealing his socks, always an unpleasant sight, though none but the eyes of Zeus could view them in the darkling dank. The condition of his socks was a quirk of his personality, for he would normally be wearing several thousand dollars worth of clothing, exotic perfume, and diamonds, but whenever Hammerbank, upon entering certain health food restaurants, or visiting certain religious cults, or even visiting his bootmaker; whenever he had to remove his white patent boots, with their fashionable wear and tear giving them a frayed birchbarklike appearance, all eyes would be averted in slight disgust at copping a visual on his socks, which afforded to a spectator's sensibilities a grayly griseous, not to mention wanton, stretch of wet silty streakage festooned with strange cocoonlike bumps and a sort of mirage effect when light tried to reflect off the oily weave.

And the smell—with regard to the smell we shall use the technique, so dear to Cicero, known as preterition, that is, we shall float hawkishly high over the subject with kidnapped voice.

With boots removed, Hammerbank crawled over to the space beneath *Circles of Paradise*, wiped away the cigarette stubs and the disposable snort straws, and sat there in the lotus posture, staring through the demi-gloom upon the Art, and a strange peace began in his toes and spread through his muscles and bushwhacked his mind. As for his hand, it too crawled, knuckles rising like inchworms and pushing the fingertips forward, across his stomach toward the divine altar, where for hours he engaged in the cherished calisthenics of whack-whack.

35

Dawn blushed shyly above the rooftops of SoHo before Hammerbank could pull himself away from the ecstasy.

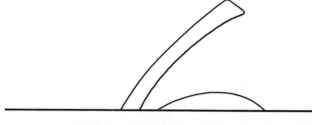

THE SECRET LIFE OF
SIGMUND HAMMERBANK
SPECULATOR IN RARE
GRANULAR SUBSTANCES

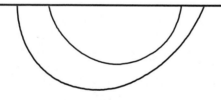

It was the installation of elaborate telephone code-scramblers
between his Gallery and his offices in Beirut, Mexico City, Bo-
gotá, and Martha's Vineyard, that aroused the curiosity of the
New York Police Department. The attitude was this: "Here's a
guy that's supposed to be an art dealer and he's sending out
messages in obsolete Japanese codes." The chief questions in
the officers' minds were:

   a) what the hell is going on? Espionage?

   b) can we get a piece of the action? (if it's not espionage)

c) when and where will there be, immediately subsequent to a transaction, a room full of relatively unguarded cash?

In addition, one simply does not call one's dope smuggling vessels the Niña, Pinta, and Santa Maria, and not attract the attention of the DEA.

This trio of vessels was Sigmund's fleet, used to bring powdery wares up the Western Mexican coast to Santa Barbara, and to bear, say, guns hidden in plywood consignments back South.

The DEA, and even some elements in the mafia, considered naming them the Niña, Pinta, and Santa Maria, just a bit too un-American, and the decision was made to flip some heat on Sigmund.

Therefore the N.Y. City P.D. assigned one of its Barrel Generation undercover agents to live in a painted barrel outside the Hammerbank Gallery, and to monitor all incoming/outgoing traffic. The Barrel Generation narkos, or bung-shoes, were the natural successors to the beatnik narkos that once stalked Rienzi's Coffee House on MacDougal Street attired in sandals, berets, sunglasses, copies of the Partisan Review, beards, and shoulder holsters; and later the hippie narks attired in Elton John tee shirts, tie-dyed Levis and American Indian stash bags. The Barrel Generation cop soon set up his barrel outside the Gallery, where he quietly resided, occasionally expressing his Oscar the Grouch impressions when a passel of tourists came too near or, sin of sins, dropped money into the barrel, bonking him on the head.

Rosé knew very little, or cared to know very little, about Hammerbank's dealership in powders, and knew Hammerbank's key associates in these matters only as employees of the Gallery. These associates were one Sadie Newcombe, and one Louie the Chop a.k.a. SoHo Lou a.k.a. Louie Livermant (as an adept of the cruel practice of hepatomancy).

Sadie was Hammerbank's electronics ace. She debugged his scrambler lines once a week; in fact, she set up the scrambler code that he used. The system she devised translated Sigmund's businessman's babble into a tough all-but-forgotten WWII Japanese numeric code, after which it was scrambled and mixed in with 16-track unreleased Beatles tapes. At the other end of the conversation, it was retranslated automatically via computer into Hammerbank's deathless words.

She was an expert in poisons, a store of knowledge from her days with Defense Intelligence. It was she who had developed the use of the so-called Conceptual Threat, the innovative creative method of warnings used by criminal rings servicing the artistic community. Hammerbank loathed violence, and tried to utilize gunless and knifeless business procedures, in the manner of the old LSD Brotherhood, so he was more than eager to use the Conceptual Threat.

Of the many business affairs she handled for Hammerbank, one of the most important was that of snuff buff. That is, she hung out at city and federal courthouses attending murder and felony trials, listening for gossip and rumors about impending investigations. We do not have to emphasize how she was always on the alert for the word "Hammerbank" in chit-chat about grand jury targets. She was a welcome friend around police precincts; she drank in police bars and she crashed a lot with the N.Y.P.D. Art Theft Squad.

Sadie Newcombe's front was as a tracer of the sequences of ownership of SoHo buildings or loft floors.[15] Sadie's cards were plastered all over New York:

SADIE NEWCOMBE, LTD.
Structural Genealogies
115 Spring St.

---

15. It had become the rage to know your loft's genealogy, as it were; to know in sequence what had occupied the loft/sweatshop from

In her years of employment, she had made almost a million dollars for Hammerbank in the so-called Lear Jet coke-ratio hustle. When the money-to-cocaine ratio in one country was, say, 5/4, and in a second country, at the same time, it was 6/4, she rented a Lear Jet and flew the circuit a few times, like a merry-go-round: buying the coke in country A, flying to country B, selling the coke at a profit, taking the money back to country A, buy more coke, spew off to country B, sell it, and back to A with the mon, and so forth. It was dizzying to arrive at the same country fifty times in one week, but it kept her boss in a calm frame of mind.

Her loyalties were already shifting away from Sigmund Hammerbank at the time of the squabble over *Circles of Paradise*, and Sigmund's business affairs began to suffer as a result. For instance, his cattle feeding business had recently crashed due to the strange malady known as the Morris the Cow Syndrome,[16] but, had the salient information been supplied to him in time by his employees, he could have gotten his cash out.

Though it was kept hidden from Hammerbank, it was all over SoHo that she just about had enough capital to open her own Gallery and Coke Complex; her only problem likely to be that of trying to find a suitable site not under the control of Hammerbank, who was certain to evince a lupine vindictiveness against Sadie.

Like Milton, like Hammerbank, Sadie too had her secret life. She was a key coordinator for the Heartbreak Hotel Brigade, and shook Milton to the roots when she showed up to

_____

time immemorial. She checked old bank records, and early century transfiles in city archives-warehouses in QueensHo. She usually was able to secure enough info so that wealthy lofties could sport a wall devoted to old photos and letterheads and logos of the various businesses that had once occupied the pad.

16. The Morris the Cow Syndrome. University of Illinois Agriculture scientists had utilized techniques of gene splicing to improve the intelligence of cattle, thinking that a more intelligent cow would be a fatter cow. This plan backfired when Sigmund's entire herd, their awareness heightened, that is, aware of their impending conversion to hamburger, balked at becoming fat, refusing to eat any feed grain except Bulgar wheat.

handle the negotiations whereby he agreed to supply them with a major painting a year.

It was when she met Rosé under different circumstances, not just as Hammerbank's assistant, that the possibility of romance occurred. Since he had broken up with his wife, Evelyn, Milton had lived as a compulsive loner, plying his 14-hour Rosé Rondels with unflexing severity. His personal life was outrageously ascetic, though he pined for the days of torridity. Men and women still come on in great numbers to artists of renown with offers of instant gratification. Some there were who offered to have a baby with Milton, as if a time machine had taken them back to 1955 Provincetown. Milton turned all offers aside, for he could not keep from thinking of his "immortal belovéd," now finishing medical school, and facing a brilliant future after fourteen years at the shadows of his side.

Yet, meeting Sadie in her secret life caused him to stare at her personality afresh. Was she not a wonderful woman? She too, looked upon him with loving eyes.

But something occurred which cooled the romance as it had barely begun. Sadie had a delicate balance in her life, balancing a

> *life of thrills*
> *life as employee of Hammerbank*
> *life as secret operative in the Heartbreak Hotel Brigade*
> *life as Loft Geneologist*
> *life as Hangout Route Diarist.*

It was her life as Hangout Route Diarist and Rosé's response to it, that spawned the trouble.

In recent years the Hangout Route Diary had been the literary rage. The basic position of the Hangout Route was this: "Why tell our stories to the Balzacs of the world when we can write them ourselves?" Sadie Newcombe had begun taking copious notes when she was 16, and now had ten volumes ready to polish for Random House.

The Hangout Route Diary business was profoundly frightening to politicians, to artists, to writers, and to the business community. Famous people had release forms that new lovers

were asked to sign, to prevent Hangout Route from being published later on.

Hangout Route still meant martyrdom to the writing desk,
for the public would not purchase forever mere lists of licked
limbs. Sadie accepted that painful fact, and slaved fiercely to
polish her licked limb lists.

They had not yet lain down to fuck, but almost, when Milton asked her to sign a Hangout Route Release Form, guarantee-
ing that she would never write about their affair.

"Milton, I'm your friend," she replied incredulously,
"How can you ask me to sign a Hangout Route Release Form?"

Rosé knew of her contract with Random House, and insisted. She ordered him out of her sub-SoHo loft, and the romance chilled to its former tepidity.

Sigmund Hammerbank's other close associate, Louie the
Chop a.k.a. SoHo Lou a.k.a. Louie Livermant, was an enigma
wrapped inside a mystery folded inside a dipshit. He was what
they called in the early '60's an Animal. Weightlifting kept his
body in shape for those occasions when Sigmund needed a
bodyguard. He was hopelessly loyal to the Hammerbank Gallery and to its owner and artists. Louie the Chop viewed Sigmund Hammerbank as a religious leader, and a genius. If
Hammerbank suffered a memory lapse, Louie would contend
that Hammerbank was deliberately forgetting as part of some
cunning game plan.

He lived in a dream world. One of his fantasies was that
Hammerbank was really some form of secret agent for the government. Otherwise, he thought, why all the fancy telephone
scrambler equipment? And since Hammerbank was obviously a
cop, did that not make him, Louie, a cop also? Louie always
wanted to be a police-one, but there was the matter of his 13-
page FBI computer arrest record.

Louie had one outstanding physical feature, a nose with
nostrils enormous at the entrances; a young chipmunk easily
could have hibernated in one of them. For jokes, Louie sometimes inserted broom handles in them; it was the sort of natural
gift that you can use innumerable times for winning bets in bars.

His nose had one quality apparently unsusceptible to scientific explanation—it was nearly unerring in nark-sniff. He was like a pot-whiffing canine at a JFK cargo hangar, so infallible was he in pulling a dowser's wand scene on undercover police officers.

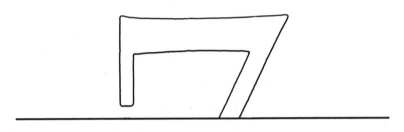

CONCEPTUAL
THREATS

On the morn of M. Rosé's fiscal calamity, they lay in slightly grungy weather-leathery bumhood inside their swirly-painted oil drums outside the Hammerbank Gallery—the trio of Barrel Generation poets. One of them was the DEA/N.Y.P.D. undercover narcotics agent, who was sleeping with one eye open, so as to monitor incoming traffic into the Hammerbank Building. The undercover nark had been outfitted rather conspicuously with a luxury barrel. It had a little TV set built into the upper edge, as well as a battery-powered refrigerator built in the bottom beside the foot-warmer. (Partisans of the Barrel Generation usually kept their barrels in an upright position during the day, some affixing lids for privacy; but at night the barrel was tipped over and anchored for an easier sleep.)

Shortly after twelve, Sadie Newcombe and Louie the Chop returned from a futile morning spent trying to snag some Federal Grand Jury minutes from one of Sadie's court reporter friends.

"I tell you, Sadie, the only way to get the information out of him is to hit him with a C.T.," Louie insisted.[17]

Then Louie Livermant, revealing his 96% accuracy in cop-sniff, spotted the trio of sleeping Barrelies. Well, it's the little things that count in gumshoeing—and by habit Louie leaned down after experiencing the mysterious shudder that told him "Cop afoot! Cop afoot!," and noted that one of the sleepers had his eye open, and furthermore, there was a light humming sound coming from the barrel. Leaning down even closer, Louie could have sworn he was hearing the bellowing vox profunda of Sigmund Hammerbank issuing forth from inside the barrel. That meant only one thing: there was a bug monitor unit in the barrel, and the cop had forgotten to tune down the channel from Sigmund's office.

Louie and Sadie rushed up to Siggie's office to report the data. Hammerbank had only one reply: "Hit him with a C.T., tonight."

Sadie and Louie quietly stripped and walked into the sauna together, breathing rapidly out of handsized oxygen, then nitrous oxide, bottles. Sadie and Louie loved C.T. planning sessions, involving as they did getting high, great sensual comminglings (idea-triggering, they told each other), and running great hilarious C.T. ideas up the coca flagpole.

Five hours later the C.T. plan was ready to go.

They borrowed part of their Conceptual Threat plot from *Circles of Paradise*—namely, the white dotted line around Rosé's headprint where he had fallen asleep during the painting.

They waited until 3:30 a.m., when usually even the most jittery Barrel Generation partisan was soundly asleep, and stole quietly upon the street to the side of the barrel.

---

17. Conceptual Threat.

Sadie drugged him, slipping a time-release capsule of pharmaka between his lips, a binary Incontinence/Fear drug which would engender bladderial incontinence, combined with mild paranoia, beginning at 8 a.m. Her experience with the incontinence spansules was that they often caused a rolling snowball of fear in the subject. That is, when the subject found itself bewetting itself, it often took fright as it somehow sensed impending danger; then real fear would arise; the fear augmenting the incontinence, the incontinence becoming uncontrollable, and the wetting subject waxing totally afraid.

While she administered the drug, Louie the Chop painted the white dotted line around the drugged officer's head. Next he applied a local anesthetic to both of the subject's hands, and enacted the Vegeburger Threat. They did not, in any way, harm the hands, but rather proceeded to make melted swiss and alfalfa sprout sandwiches on top of them. They added good 17-grain Bed of Nails Bakery bread, making sure the hands were securely affixed on the inside, tying them around with the cloth strips so that if the subject should roll over during sleep the sandwiches would not fall away.

They left a note nearby announcing that the fingers of the agent's hands would soon wind up in the vegeburger vat at the Spring Street Restaurant.

Before they split, Sadie pried loose the micro-console hidden in the barrel, containing some 15 monitor speakers able to receive broadcasts from various microphones planted in the quintuplex. Even as she yanked, one of the speakers was sawing with the soft snores of Sigmund Hammerbank.

Then they parted. Louie went home to BronxHo, and Sadie to her former subway station loft, where she worked 'til dawn on her Hangout Route diaries, for she did not want to burn Random House, or to cause any unseemly delays such as to crimp any possible paperback bidding war.

The next morning the barrel was gone. And a trail of micturitious splotch-blotches led liquidly down West Broadway, ending in a phone booth, where no doubt the officer tried to call his control, and where for hours thereafter there awaited for anyone so dumb as to have closed the door when calling, ig-

46

noble and nose-damaging suspirations from the wet floor, that common, muggy big apple smell of wet paper bag mixed with unwashed hamster cage.

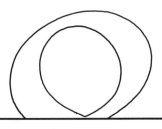

COUNT VOLPE
AND THE
ETRUSCAN THUMBS

COUNT CLAUDIO VOLPE, ART HISTORIAN,
REGAL SURROGATE OF
THE CROWN JEWELS OF RUSSIA, VICEROY OF
THE U.S. CONFEDERATE GOLD HOARD

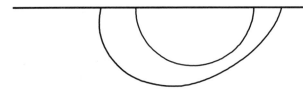

You wouldn't have thought that the worldwide production and distribution of cocaine would have been controlled by one Italian art expert living in graceful lonely eccentricity in a villa by the mouth of the Tiber. But it was so. "No way to get coke without cutting in the Count." That was the adage recognized everywhere as reality.

"It was the gosh darnedest thing," an art dealer friend of Hammerbank remarked. "You could be in some box canyon in Peru, 50 miles into the forest, closing down a deal for some spare coca leaves with some farmer, when the whopa-whopa-whopa of the helicopter would be heard, and some agent of the Count would land and wouldn't even bother to get out of the copter, she'd just open the door and hold out her palm for a mon cut. You'd find yourself ducking down to rush under the blades for mon-forkover, praying that the Count wouldn't add your thumb to his collection."[18]

Count Volpe was 6 foot 9 inches tall, and looked a lot like Gabby Hayes, except that his hair, nearly knee length, acquired by asstime a tail-of-Trigger bushiness, and had the consistency of thin yellow-white straw. He dressed in black: black shirt, black tie, black vest, suit, socks, and shoes. He was strange indeed, his mind being a flood-zone, access to which was blocked by the sign, "Bridge Out." Get too close and you'd wind up on your back like some poisoned insect at the wet edge of a Fly Agaric mushroom. The Count had his humane side also. For instance, he was responsible for bringing the mafia, or maf-org as it is known on all the computers, into the fore as sponsors of art and artists. He was responsible too, for preventing, on the part of maf-org, any more lamentable incursions such as the Oldenburg caper.[19]

No one knew his age. Wrinkles and circles of tiredness were banned from his face, but somehow nothing could prevent the image of a vulture after a flood about to dip down into the eye of the dead pony from determining one's overall memory of the Count's facial expression—his kill-ya-for-a-candybar countenance. But perhaps we are being unfair, for he was, after all, a proven partisan of Beauty, as witness the fantastic museum-sized art collection at his villa.

It stumped powder merchant buffs and investigators the world over how Count Volpe ran his empire. It consisted of this,

---

18. The Etruscan Thumbs. The Count had a hideous collection of thumbs in his favorite meditation spot, an Etruscan tomb where, in a burial urn, he stored his collection, seized from those who'd burned him.

19. The Oldenburg caper. The sad maf-org plot to corner the worldwide Oldenburg market by obtaining, by violence, threat, and rip, every single work by the artist. Maf-org went so far as to burn down part of the Museum of Modern Art as a cover for removing the museum's horde of Oldenburgs.

in brief: two hours of nonstop mouth-spew per morn. Had Hammerbank known about it, he would have exclaimed about the universality of the Tom Mann Two.

Still in his dressing robe, the Count sat down in front of an elaborate double-tiered semicircle of phone speakers, 24 in all—looking a bit like a recording engineer sitting in front of a 24-track console. The Count could thus talk with 24 voice-sources at once. The electromagnetic revolution had supplied him with some neat gadgetry, enabling him to carry on the 24 simultaneous phone conversations without, at the same time, any of the voices hearing any response but the Count's specific words directed at a specific voice. The Count's two-hour work-day was structured as follows:

1. The first five minutes, to get the unpleasantness over with quickly, was devoted to violence:

    (A) commands for thumb-gathering
    (B) the threatening of relatives of burners by:
        (a) crude violence
        (b) creative violence
        (c) New Age threats (as, say, leaving deceased animals with cultic charms attached, on doorsteps)
    (C) the ordering of offs, and listening to off-reports
    (D) the destruction of law enforcement investigations
    (E) the ruining of careers of nosy public officials.

2. The next hour was spent in a babylonic din of 24 simultaneous conference calls to 24 countries over 24 scramblers. With each conference call averaging around five people, the Count therefore could be closing down deals with as many as 120 people at one time. This was the secret of his success, being able to handle, without taking any notes, such a plethora of the details of coca leaf marketing at one sitting.

3. The last 55 minutes of the Count's two-hour spew was spent tapering out of it, wrapping up the details of his decisions, after which the Count's day presented itself as 22 hours of hedonism, art-work, and voluptas.

And where, pray, did Sigmund Hammerbank fit into all of this?

Well, first of all, he wanted to climb up the powdery ladder of the Count's organization. His scheme was to grow creatively and contiguously, but not pissoffishly, alongside the Count's operations, in order to convince him that it was he, Hammerbank, solely capable of handling the desperate needs of America's artists/filmists/writers/designers for sniff-flash. His eye was on the West Coast markets also, particularly Hollywood, where the words Energy Crisis meant only one thing: Coke Famine. There he would have the best of both worlds: he could fill their walls with the paintings of his clients, and fill their nasal passages with Volpe's mono-colored white mural.

Little did Hammerbank know what Volpe had in store for him. Hammerbank wanted Hollywood, but the Count was going to offer him Finland. He was going to activate the so-called "Russian frontier porn line." For decades it was a lucrative business to sell erotica in the small towns along the Russian frontier, mainly in Northern Japan and in Finland. The porn trickled into Russia, disguised in bindings alleging the contents to contain scientific or agricultural treatises, whereas in reality it was smut.

Count Volpe was going to utilize the same principle, but he was going to deal out, not smut, but coca leaf chewing gum, phonograph records, and fancy black market jogging shoes. Soon the Count would ask Sigmund to sell the Hammerbank Gallery and move to Finland to head up the operation.

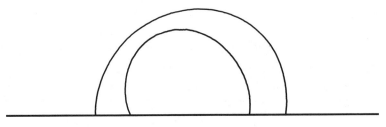

FOOTSIE
SATCHEL-SINK
TO THE RESCUE

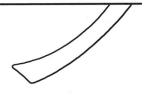

While Sadie Newcombe and Louie the Chop were holding their
C.T. planning session, and Milton Rosé paced his loft/former
synagogue in fiscal angst, Hammerbank was trying to make his
morning thousand, so he could take his morning snort. Seven
times already that morning the pitifully plighted Milton Rosé
had called. The city marshal, Milton announced, had tacked up
notices of auction on the front door of his synagogue/loft, and it
had already made the afternoon gossip columns. Rosé was
ready for sedation, and artists all over New York were chuckling
with happiness.

Milton stood in his beautiful former synagogue on Eldridge Street, with its high metal peaked roof and fieldstone exterior, barely able to blink away the tears. What sculptor would hoist her works on Milton's block and tackle soon? Or, would a maf-org disco disgrace these hallowed premises? Or a boutique?

Worse than that possibility, Milton hated the gossip of his peers. Not that there were open guffaws from brother and sister artists—it wasn't that crude. But there *was*, nonetheless, always that outburst of amused surprise when a staid member of the painterly community, ever thought to be on a pecuniary peak, should have been shown to have been wrecked on the shekel-less shoals. From his colleagues, Milton masked everything, even his morning idea-spew problem, not wanting it said, "It comes too easy for Milton."

To his credit, Hammerbank was doing his best to deal out the treasure, for it was his reputation too that was in danger. One of the first things he'd done after the scandal was to raise the price of $400,000, anticipating reward for the formula, FUROR = CHECKS.

The Heartbreak Hotel Brigade was striving mightily to deal it also, and Hammerbank rather reluctantly kept track of the offers they managed to attract. On the surface, the offers seemed to arrive with frequency, yet everyone soon changed their minds. The originally firm, but later infirm, offers had come from The Grateful Dead (still going strong, and now owning $350,000,000.00 of coastal real estate); the Proustcork® Writers Silencing Systems, Inc. (fronting for the Balzac Study Group); and the Future Farmers of America Investment Trust (having gutted the Teamsters, the mob moved onward).

Sigmund Hammerbank was brought to Pity by the condition of his friend and client. But what could he do? He told Milton he'd buy *Circles of Paradise* himself, but, well, there were those reverses he was experiencing with regard to his Nebraska cattle-feeding business, and certain building sales were not going through as expected. So, Sigmund himself, while not exactly feeling a pinch, was feeling as though a giant friendly roach clip were grasping his life in its ivory arms.

Rosé was so desperate he seriously was considering donning a wig and a fake mustache and carrying an easel to Washington Square to do some of those five dollar pastel sketches of tourists.

In the last of his seven calls to Hammerbank that morning, Milton had truly stunned his agent. Hammerbank, while worshipping Rosé as an artist, was not fully aware of Rosé's morning spew of short stories, inventions, movie treatments, poems, and logo designs. Nor was he aware of the morning sketches that Rosé had framed over the years and which were now stored in a tunnel beneath West Broadway. The conversation went like this:

Hammerbank: "You mean, you have 23 years of fully executed morning sketches stored in a tunnel under your loft?" (Pause) "Well, what are we talking about—the total—I guess it's something like two or three hundred sketches, huh, Miltie?"

Hammerbank was thinking, "Hey, well, maybe I can buy these up from this turkey for a few thousand, hold them, and then, ten years from now, heh heh, sell them at auction . . ."

Rosé: "No, Sigmund, I have a terrible problem on my hands. You see, for the last 23 years, I have been executing 25 sketches per morning, and I've framed them all—it's a terrible storage problem; I've got them stacked in what appears to be an old creek bed, and they stretch about a block under West Broadway."

Hammerbank still did not grasp the problem.

Hammerbank: "Wait a minute, how many sketches do you have stored, *exactly?*" He could not believe that Rosé had spent thousands on frames that were never used. "You didn't say, Milton, that all these drawings were in frames, did you?"

Milton: "Yes." And, with a note of embarrassment in his voice, "The last time I did an inventory, there were 186,875 framed sketches down there."

Hammerbank's voice became cracked at these words; he was unable to respond when Milton urged him, his voice racked with sobs, to hurry up please on a cash flow solution.

Hammerbank was unable to speak because of the terrible new burden Rosé had imposed on himself. Better not ever to have mentioned the sketches! For if the art world should discover that Rosé held a six-figure total of unsold sketches, the market value of his other works might plummet disastrously. Could the Western Hemisphere absorb 200,000 sketches, even by a major artist? Was there that much extra space on the dining room walls of the wealthy? In fact, very likely the only wall space available for such a glut was that horror of the modern artists—the space above the beds in motels!

Hammerbank's opinion was that it was just as if you'd discover in an attic somewhere about 600 copies of the first edition of Apollinaire's *Alcools*. Better you burn about 500 of them, and sell the rest at orbital prices. But, could the art dealer urge his client to destroy, say, 175,000 framed sketches, the work of 23 good years, and have the client still remain a client? That was the question. And that was what had caused his voice to crack.

Well, the threat of malfiscality hyperactivates the hyperactive, as they say, and so it was for Sigmund Hammerbank. Within the hour, he made his morning thousand, snerked his morning snort, and then, in a fast 20 or 25 thirty-second phone calls, he closed down a long-standing real estate deal that turned the old police property clerk's office on Broome Street into an artists' condominium which he would slyly name French Connection East, after the 100 million dollars worth of seized French Connection case heroin sneaked out of evidence lockers by corrupt narks.

Thirty minutes after closing down the deal, a courier arrived with a satchel full of 750,000 virtually untraceable dollars. The new owner of the building was so hidden by paper companies as to be unknowable, and the money was as tax-free as skim from a gambling casino in another solar system. Hammerbank made efforts to relax for a few minutes, as he opened the satchel wide, not in order to count the money, but rather to remove his white boots and his griseous socks, and to place his raw appendages down into the satchel for one of those pure thrills, that of sinking one's tarsals and toes down into crinkly curlings of loose cash.

It was during this footsy satchel-sink that Pity began to overwhelm the art dealer's mind. He thought of his friend Rosé about to toke up the ghastly bitterness of bankruptcy. And his mind considered the wonderful painting *Circles of Paradise*. He was at a loss. He considered taking a few days off, and flying the great work down to his Mexican hideaway, just to stare at it. But what if it gets ruined? he asked himself. A soft vacuum cleaner by Oldenburg had melted one summer in Death Valley where Siggie had brought it for meditation. A triptych by Ralph Martel had been storm-spattered to shreds in a similar situation down in the Peruvian forests.

But it was now more than meditation in front of it, for *Circles* was becoming part of his soul. Did not a human need something Numinous to which to cling? In fact, beginning with the long meditation period in front of *Circles of Paradise* on opening night, he had begun formal votive activities in its presence, but did so holding a towel in front of his groin, having in mind a strange theory of molecular memory, that is, of great art somehow being able to "remember" what occurred through the ages in its presence. And Hammerbank certainly did not want a painting in some distant century to relate to a querying computer that he, Hammerbank, archon of art, had on several occasions engaged in whack-whack while staring at its panerotic pinhead, piano, and secrétaire.

It was at that Moment of Pity when Hammerbank decided to take 400,000 dollars out of the satchel and buy the painting for himself, not however forgetting to deduct the usual 50% commission. But he decided not to tell Rosé that he was the purchaser, partly to spare his feelings, and partly not to set a precedent of such heavy bail-out. Never let your client believe you're a sucker, was one of Hammerbank's ruling principles.

Then, to his mind, came the Solution. He would give the painting to the Count! What a great idea! "It's gotta curry favor," he exclaimed. "He told me himself he wanted to open a modern wing at his villa! And besides, he'd have to accept it! He was the one who authenticated the desk in the first place!"

"It's mine, it's gonna be all mine!" he continued, meaning, of course, the noses of America, when the Count let him take control.

He leaned down into his data console,[20] and said, "Louie,

---

20. His data console. A most ingenious carved desk into which

56

please get Count Volpe on Scrambler 14. Try him at the Mt. Ostia villa."

With his opening sentence, Hammerbank offered *Circles of Paradise* to the Count. "I should like to present to you one of the great treasures of our age . . . ."

"*Circles of Paradise,* no doubt," the Count broke in. "I thank you very much. It's a great work indeed." Volpe knew all about the problems the work was having in finding a purchaser. "But who," he continued, "Mr. Hammerbank, is to pay the artist?"

Hammerbank responded, "I thought I'd pay for it myself, without, as I'm sure you'll understand, letting the artist know the donor's name."

"How noble of you," Volpe exclaimed. "Naturally you will allow me to contribute an amount equal to yours?"

Hammerbank protested.

"No, I insist," the Count reiterated. Hammerbank stared at his thumbs, not wanting to risk a pissoff.

"Of course, Count Volpe, of course."

Hammerbank was not thinking as quickly as he might have, otherwise he'd not have given the Count the opportunity to say the following.

"There's only one matter remaining," said Count Volpe. "Am I to assume you're giving the artist the full 400 thousand, and not deducting your 50%?"

Hammerbank's lengthy silence told the Count the answer. One simply cannot lie to the Regal Surrogate of the Crown Jewels of Russia. "No," said he, "I had planned to deduct the commission, and to give him only 200 thousand."

Brushing aside the possibility that Hammerbank might

---

were built TV surveillance screens of his rare powder stashes, a stock market ticker tape, the phone scramblers and a bank of phone lines, a hot line to Umberto's Clam House, a pull-down auto-inflatable couch for moments of sensual unification with visitors, a small swan-headed pissoir, a microfilm viewing unit, tape recorders, a video cassette system, a microdot photomaker, an oven, a laser manicure/pedicure machine, a liquor cabinet, a voice stress lie detector, and a small microwave french-frier (not for eating, but Hammerbank found that one of the finest coke spoons in the world was a thin overcooked french fry).

have tried to burn him for $100,000.00, Count Volpe replied jovially, "Splendid! That means each of our shares will be $100,000.00, a mere 30 seconds of my morning labors."

"Quite," was all Sigmund could think to say, still staring at his thumbs.

The conversation continued in a sort of self-congratulatory coca-rapid mode. "It's such a pleasure to aid a great artist in need."

"Yes, Count, o yes."

At last the Count signed off, and Sigmund called Milton at once. "Hi, Milton. Yah, I think we have a buyer. This time it's certain!"

Milton's tears began to dry at once. "Hotdog! Zowie!" were his utterances. "Uh, who is it, Sig?"

"Huh?"

"Who?"

"Yes, it's a European collector. It's q.t. city, muh fuh, understand? He's that glorious combination of Hapsburg and rare powders, if you can scan my zone. But it looks certain!"

"How long do we have to wait for the mon?" was Milton's next question.

"I think it's gonna take at least 90 days to get the check, " Hammerbank replied, his feet still twitching inside the satchel of bills, "But you can probably get some mon from the bank this afternoon via a letter of intent, which I'm sure the buyer's attorney would supply for you."

There was only one other matter which might block the sale. "What about getting *Circles* back for retrospectives, and for servicing?" Milton wanted to know.[21]

Sigmund assured him that the buyer would definitely allow the painting to be returned for any major retrospectives, and that at the end of a suitable period, he would allow access for patch-up.

---

21. Rosé insisted on personally servicing his destruction/constructions, for you could never tell when something might fall off or become unglued. He even created a service manual for each major work, so that the aeons thereafter would know how to maintain the piece's perfection.

There were sighs, and thanks, and exclamations. They both hung up at once, and uttered unfortunate epithets.

"Fucking punk," Rosé muttered.

"Fucking punk," Hammerbank muttered.

Rosé had been too proud to ask his agent to send him over some carfare, but proceeded instead with his spam and matzoh fritter lunch.

The remainder of his 14-hour Rosé Rondel was spent in glorious creation. The only reminders of the hours of malfiscality were the rims of his eyes, slightly sore from the welling of tears.

Already he was venturing on a major new project, the most important of his life. He was singing a poem. Not his own, but the Atlantis section of Hart Crane's *The Bridge*.

He was running his voice through a seven-part harmony voice-splitter, which made his single note sound like a seven-person chorus.

Chanting the poem, he became so excited that he began once again to pace back and forth. There were tears again in his eyes, but this time the tears of ecstasy. "Oh, how holy it shall be," Milton Rosé cried into his tape recorder.

PART TWO

THE SEARCH FOR HART CRANE'S TRUNK

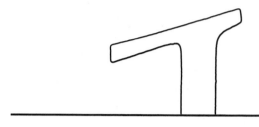

FITZ MᶜIVER
COMES TO NEW YORK

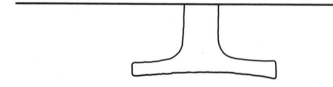

I was on a case involving some stolen Balzac manuscripts, and I had the perps[1] wiggling in wet ophidian gnarls of guilt and malice—a group that dared to call itself "The Cénacle," a term used by Balzac to denote a certain highly motivated and idealistic group of artists, writers, and thinkers. The group that had stolen the manuscripts is of course now internationally famous under the name, the Balzac Study Group, but while I was on the manuscript case they appeared to have been nothing more than

---

1. Police slang for perpetrators.

a really sly quartet of book rooks[2] who, for the last six years, had been borrowing the themes, apothegms, ideas, plots, character-izations, and energy, not only from Balzac's life, but from about 65 of his novels, and had "translated" the mooched matériel, without crediting Balzac of course, into modern circumstances, the result being a string of six-figure best sellers.

I was working the case for a private source who had been ripped for the manuscripts, which the Balzac Study Group had apparently been using as votive relics to rev themselves up for scriptation sessions. I took the opportunity, as long as I was in New York City anyway, to attend the convention of the Society of American Archivists, for whom over the years I had done a lot of work tracking down an occasional grad student, an occasional scholar whose sweaty palms seemed glue-drawn to expensive and rare literary relics, and even an occasional archivist sinking into the back alleys of the book rooks by leaving town with a Dylan Thomas letter or two, or some hand-corrected pages of Joyce. I'm not sure what it is—but the compulsions of manu-script thieves are as deep and dire as any forbidden passion in a Victorian novel.

I found time somehow in the midst of attending the con-vention, and closing the case at the same time, for my quarterly tour of N.Y. City bookstores, a rare afternoon of supernal thrills, my lungs seeming to perk up and to thrive, inhaling that fine Limited Edition book-binding grit and the close but excellent, almost dopelike, but possibly unhealthy from a long term point of view, N.Y. bookstore air. But groovy, that ancient jazz players' word, is ever the appellation for the bookstores of N.Y. I started uptown with the slipcased leather bindings of 57th Street, and meandered my way downtown through bookstores new and rare, in the direction of the 4th Avenue and lower Broadway stores (where incidentally one of the perps in the Balzac Study

---

2. Book rooks: slang among investigators in the field of stolen manuscripts, as denoting a kind of common amateur manu/rare book/ letter thief, often a marginal literary person who desires, although his or her own career is in ashes, to stay close to the action, in the manner of the failed watercolorist who cowbirds as a real estate tycoon in an art colony.

Group had a cover job) located to the east of Greenwich Village, and north of SoHo, and west, to be sure, of BrookHo, and way to the south of YoHo. Once inside the second-hand stores of 4th Avenue, it was almost like a visit to a shrine in the Himalayan hills, as I healed my psyche for several hours by standing chin to toe against the world's most complete collection of editions of William Cowper; and yea, even engaging in a kind of bookstack frottage: rubbing back and forth across a row of Mark Twain first editions in a tall wooden stack that seemed to loom out of sight at its highest shelves near the ceiling.

Finally, I strode into the Village itself, along 9th Street, to visit the store of an old World War II buddy of mine, Jack Barnes, who owned one of the oldest and finest rare book stores in the area. Jack's store had for many years been named Thoth's Beak in the Eye of Time, but the horror of the image of the title had been brought home to him one night in a dream, when Thoth's beak seemed dabbishly to explore his, Jack Barnes', *own* eye, so the next day, as soon as the micrograms had worn off, Jack changed the name to Lantern of Knowledge.

I figured old "Shrapnel Faced Barnes," as we called him once, would take me out to dinner, and maybe some drinks, a sniff of coca leaf, who knows, some thrills, to liven my wires burned sullen by the long Balzac case on which I had been occupied almost exclusively for eight months.

I hadn't seen Jack Barnes for several years, although I must say I had read enough Surveillance Summaries of his private conversations lately to last me a lifetime. Most unfortunately, Jack had become a peripheral suspect in the Balzac manuscripts theft, and I'd had to put his private conversations under watch, scaling down the outside wall from his roof to a bedroom window ledge, ouching my shins on crumbly West Village brick, to plant what we call a surveillance chip (more on surveillance chips later) against the pane to pick up his talk from the vibrations of the glass. Moralists will ask huffily, "You mean you'd surveillance chip one of your best friends?" In answer, I can only say that I learned 35 years ago that the exigencies of a case may cause you to have to put a stake-out on your own mother, as she showers.

As I said, I hated like hell to surveillance chip my ole war buddy, so I hired a security cleared colleague to handle the actual transcriptions of the tapes, and I myself only read the summaries, in which way I avoided the embarrassing duty of listening to the sounds of a close personal friend. Believe me, you never know what sort of hideous personal practices a friend may engage in, until you Surv-Chip® her, or him, or them.

Jack had been one of those soldiers returning laden with booty. Many of them had brought back porcelain, gold, weapons, paintings, rare coins—but not Jack, who, if you believe the legends (and I do, having helped him to secrete the packets into old issues of *Life* magazine), arrived in N.Y. in 1945 with a batch of Goethe manuscripts, liberated from an underground bunker that Goebbels had built near Munich. Goethe was exchanged for gold, which he used as a down-payment for the Lantern of Knowledge building.

The Lantern of Knowledge was a small two-story structure from the 19th century, the bricks of its walls bearing patterns of darkness, the charred signs of fires perhaps from even an earlier century. The window ledges were of smooth marble, supported on the undersides by puffy-cheeked Neptunes carved in limestone; and finely carved Neptunes they were, obviously just about to blow some snorts of dominance upon a surly sea. The building was a blessing to behold. It stood like a pristine relic amidst the chrome-and-crud decor, the fast food shops on every corner, the minicopter pads on every roof, of the new Greenwich Village.

Jack Barnes, and his wife Mitalia DeLynn, a retired ballet star, lived on the second floor. Also on the second floor was a room called the "Archives Staging Area," where new acquisitions were catalogued and indexed and sorted.

The ceiling of the store on the first floor was almost 14 feet high, the shelves packed floor to ceiling with first editions, storage drawers of literary relics and letters, display bins of corrected galleys, et al. In fact, an inordinately large section of the store was devoted to book galleys. Jack, and many of his customers, felt that book galleys, when properly studied, reveal a great amount about the character of an author. How carefully did the artist proofread its own galleys? Did they hesitate to re-write inadequate sections, risking the ire of publishers who always insert monetary penalties for costs beyond a certain percentage of corrected lines? Did the artist let slip changes, sentence inversions and elisions, inserted at the last minute by sneaky editors? I agreed with Jack, who said the exigencies of modern haste-write, even in geniuses, is such that any writer who doesn't add corrective clusters, and mark black ink on at least 25% of the first galley's lines is a hack. When you browsed through the galley bins at Lantern of Knowledge you realized, according to Jack's rule, how many hacks there were.

Looking through the front window, I chuckled, noting that Jack was just as quarter-biting as ever. When customers walked from darkened aisle to darkened aisle in Lantern of Knowledge, they pulled on a dangling light string, and *please*, the little cardboard signs imprecated, when you split one aisle for the next, pull the string behind 'ee, huh, muh fuh.

Far to the rear was Jack's desk, built upon a platform of polished planks just of a sufficiently imperious elevation so that, while not appearing overly hostile, it would allow the owner an occasional sweep of patrolling eyeballs for the intimidation of book goniffs.

Two items were on the platform, a small printing machine, and a large desk of the type they call a "plantation" desk, with wide vertical slots at the back of the top, suitable in Jack's case for alphabetical ordering of items for his literary catalogues. I always admired the fact that Jack, even in this era of instant printing, still printed his catalogues by hand. He did not even use an electric mimeo. Ever tight, Jack had once totalled the figures, concluding that printing by power of biceps and forearm would, with the new 500 dollar a month utility rates, save him in the course of a lifetime augmented by body parts, pacemakers and transplants, somewhere in the upper four figures for his endeavors.

Jack was typing his fall catalogue, even though it was the hottest part of the summer.

The catalogue at which he was awhack featured the love letters of poets and novelists. In great measure because of Jack's catalogues, exchanges of love letters had become a raging literary fashion again, with the most unlikely individuals (bad poets with extensive high-culture love lives) soaring into the *Times* bestseller box via postmarked passion.

Much of Jack's success was due to his honesty. Honesty could be rare among modern dealers who have only to purchase old ink from antique auctions, and then acquire a handwriting machine, in order to turn out signed first editions of Henry James. I always figured that Jack's probity was due in great part to a desire to pick up top security clearance in the event of another war. Why did he bother? Some of the biggest crooks of all time have the most exalted access to the nation's secrets.

However much his putative honesty helped Jack's sales, there is nonetheless a secret, shrouded with a "bodyguard of lies" or at least a hedgerow of hype, to account for the success of catalogue industrialists. The secret is that people are out there by the millions psychologically addicted to purchasing from catalogues. They will order stuff from crisply depicted lists which they would never in a million years obtain seeing it propped in the raw in some bookstore's front window. There is a genre of pithy, nigh on to epigrammatic, writing style necessary to rare book catalogues. You have to be able to lip-moisten the reader of the catalogue, to cause the reader to enter what might be termed a "Book Trance," a sore anxiety which whelms prudence of pocketbook, and which implants a sore urge to order the item even by telegram in fear that others afflicted similarly with Book Trance will beat the buyer out. Such is the potency of Book Trance that a ridiculous price will be paid for something like Vachel Lindsay's annotated hymnal or Dylan Thomas' autographed shirt. In fact, the price as considered in the mind of the Book Trancee will seem reasonable, even cheap, and the slight scratching sound, so dear to artists, writers, rare book dealers, *et alii plurimi,* of a rich person hastily writing out a check upon a desk, will be heard.

So, I stood for a few minutes at the front window of *Lantern of Knowledge,* watching Jack whack away at the stencils in the dim store's back. Occasionally he would glance up from his plank-plinth to scan for book-clip. The smell of stencil correction fluid ever subtly wafted from the typewriter across the store and out the door, mugging my nasality. He paused now and then when he had made a mistake, to pull aside the protective screen of clear plastic which keeps the typewriter from cutting the stencil too grossly. Then he could gently abrade the type with the round end of a paper clip, brush correction fluid upon it, blow it dry in an instant, replace the plastic protection sheet, and whack onward. Jack would chuckle each time he began to type. I speculated that he might be bemirthed *pro tempore* over the fact that all over America the targets of Book Trace were right then relaxing at their summer retreats, sunning in Europe, groveling in sand, moping in mountain rains, whereas, in just a few weeks, they would be returning to their desks, to their archives, to their scholarly stacks, with fresh fall budgets causing them to sweat with the urge to type out requisition forms for new acquisitions. It would be then, the labor of Jack's August, that they would find Lantern of Knowledge catalogue #147 awaiting them.

As part of his fairmindedness, Jack released his catalogues according to postal zones, so that the catalogues would arrive at Trance Targets everywhere in the country on the same day, allowing all equal access to telegraph wires, cablegram channels, ship-to-shore frequencies, special delivery stamps, and even to airlines and buses, in order to beat out the opposition.

For Jack, the thrill of thrills awaited him—something only a cataloguer can ever experience. After many a night of whack whack whack typing descriptions of items, and stapling catalogue sheets together, and sorting into postal zones, and after many a fleck of drool bewetting a stamp back, at last to relax in the several days after a catalogue has been issued, and then to be beseiged with telegrams, ardent phone calls, special delivery imprecations, and even airplanes landing at LaGuardia releasing anxious librarians bearing chaotically annotated copies of the catalogue and blank requisition forms from their respective comptrollers—such was the thrill to come for Jack Barnes!

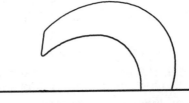

ART ARCHIVES
AND SWEAT-BROW
"I'M A MAILER MAN" BILL

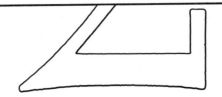

Finally I entered the store. Jack greeted me most affectionately, but I must say that in between the bursts of affection and war years sentimentality, Jack did manage to turn again and again for a few karate-like études upon the typewriter keys. Nor was it rude, for he was only obeying a principle rule among bookstore owners typing their catalogues: that even if the ghost of Edgar Allan Poe should walk in through the cracks in the floor with a few unpublished manu's to sell, don't let that deter you from finishing the day's work of rare book lists, or of wrapping the book shipments before the post office closes.

Jack honored me by actually stopping his typing for the

70

first few minutes. Were I a visiting poverty-stricken poet with some Ginsberg postcards to sell, the clacking, as we haggled over prices, would have continued without intermission.

He called his wife to tell her I was in town, and we decided that the three of us would spend the evening at Scythia, the latest rage among the brilliant, a restaurant equipped with a heated pool and a Scythian Hemp-Seed Sauna.[3]

It wasn't long before our conversation veered toward the growl-whine of strafing planes, and the plonf! of OSS parachutes opening over Northern Italy during War Two.

Barnes and I were vividly reliving those few terrified hours when, after our parachutes had been hidden and we were strolling into the village, we were picked up by the Italian police. I remembered all too well how Barnes, during the interrogation, was standing rather apart from me, almost finger-nail-paringly standoffish in my opinion. His knowledge of Italian was far superior to mine, and I was afraid he was going to pull his own version of Picasso denying knowing Apollinaire in front of the judge, or, more basely, that he was about to act out the old Tonto/Lone Ranger joke, where the Lone Ranger turns to Tonto when they're surrounded by hostile Indians, and says, "It looks like we're surrounded," to which Tonto responds, "What do you mean *'we'*—white man?"

Such was my pained state of mind, when the first of the archivists entered the store. I recognized him immediately as the dean of American archivists, Arthur J. Adamson, Chief Archivists for the University of _____ Library. A tall, skinny Athens-of-the-South type draped in tweeds, with a smoker's cough, Adamson was universally known in the trade by the name "Art Archives." So afraid was he of TB, he wore his tweeds even in the summertime. Art Archives ran Total Data

---

3. Hemp-Seed Sauna. A passage from Herodotus began this million-dollar franchise operation—a restaurant/pool/sauna hemptent, bringing a taste of Old Scythia to modern SoHo. For the etiology of this franchise goldmine, see the author's work, *The Grid.* Just as the right solved the problem of what to do with the world's apricot pits, so the left has put to use the previously unused tons of hemp seeds: burn 'em in your Scythian sauna.

operations on a great number of twentieth century authors; and I mean *Total Data!* He had been the first to bring "case officers" into modern Archivistics, many of them burnt out intelligence agents, each of whom resided as a "desk officer" responsible for a specific data-target, usually a living or recently deceased poet or novelist, regarding whom the tracks of information were still fresh and fruitful.

As soon as Art Archives walked coolly into the store, Jack dropped me out of his attention-gaze as if I were a second edition previously thought a first, and began to discuss with Mr. Archives an esoteric matter regarding an archives investment they were jointly pursuing.

Of course the reader knows that it had become the Age of the Archivist—the age of new methods of data retention,[4] with everybody therefore hesitant to let anything fall into final catabolism. Archiving was a thriving growth industry. The weekly news magazines spoke of the New Archives as at last making history accurate. It was such a data-retentive era that one could have predicted the growth of Data-Retention Chic, a fine age which saw the birth of the Archives Swap Meet, but an eminently nervous age in which the Keatsian "negative capability"[5]

---

4. Witness the silly computerized "brainpower-augment" headbands which people were wearing on their noggins like the hippies of the '60's.

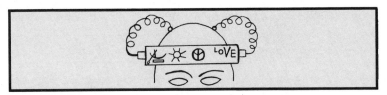

5. The creator of the phrase Negative Capability of course, was John Keats, in a letter of Dec. 1817 to George and Tom Keats: "Browne & Dilke walked with me & back from the Christmas pantomime. I had not a dispute but a disquisition with Dilke, on various subjects; several things dovetailed in my mind, & at once it struck me, what quality went to form a Man of Achievement especially in Literature & which Shakespeare possessed so enormously—I mean *Negative Capability*, that is when man is capable of being in uncertainties, Mysteries, doubts, without any irritable reaching after fact & reason—Coleridge, for in-

could not assert itself among town archivists, or the thousands who stored their archives on computers, or the federal intelligence agencies who used the Age of Archives as a cover to open up files on the dead as well as the living. Archives Shelters, fashioned in the mode of the old concrete nuclear defense shelters, gave the cement industry a big boost, and middle class families vied with one another over the opulence of their ever-dry family-history storage facilities in the back yard.

In the case of young literati, there was a tendency for a poet's first book to come in at around 200 pages, and his or her associated archives, from college years alone, to arrive at the purchasing point in air freight cartons containing at least 35,000 pages—with every shred of paper saved, of notes for poems, of notes congesting the notes, of first typed drafts from the congested notes, of second drafts from the first, third from the second, to the nth from the $(n-1)^{th}$; of novels begun at 19 and abandoned at 20, of batches of letters from friends—all to reveal that mysterious hoard of scriptation known as juvenalia, inside of which somewhere, like a skylark, all of a sudden the flights of genius lift aloft. A dealer could buy a jumble of juvenalia say for ten grand, then store it upstairs for a few years in the Archives Staging Area, and watch its value soar with the fame of the author.

It was nothing for a poet, even before its first book, or even its first NEA grant application,[6] to have fully typed and indexed lists of its personal archives to mail to the university archives

---

stance, would let go by a fine isolated verisimilitude caught from the Penetralium of mystery, from being incapable of remaining content with half knowledge . . ." When applying *Negative Capability* to Archivism, it projects the possibility of actually *throwing something away!*—a concept akin to murder in the minds of some of the new Aggressive Archivists.

6. National Security Agency study done for the Post Office indicated that the White Blizzard, NSA's code name for the five or six million pieces of grant-funded poetry magazines shown to be passing through the postal system at any given moment—that the White Blizzard was increasing in size, weight, and number, such that the Post Office, the computers alleged, would finally be choked into silence in May, 2017. Was it a secret Communist plot?

department willing, in the mode of the "gambling archivist," to buy in early.[7] Sad it is, o muh fuhs, to report the archival hubris of young literati, not to mention old, placing six or even, in a couple of cases, seven-figure tags on their archive boxes before the ages of 22 or 23, or in the cases of late beginners, of 47 or 48.

The Age of Archives was heaven for the glut of young citizens with Ph.D.'s in history; archiving absorbed all of them in a big data-midden gulp. It was the greatest data-growth surge since the inception of clay cuneiform merchant inventory lists in 3500 B.C. Off raced the Ph.D.'s to mine the slag heaps of eternity, the dryasdust data-middens of big city storage facilities, the aged electronic tapes of the heretofore boring past, the mountains of the microfiches of malarky, the pale footpaths of the industrial miserly tycoon, of the murderer, the mirthmaker, the militarist, the mighty, tucking them all goodnight forever in the filing cabinets of fame.

The reason for Art Archives' visit was immediately apparent. Art and Jack Barnes were working together to pick up cheaply[8] all poet William Szabo's notebooks, letters, manuscripts, and so forth, without, they prayed, hipping Szabo to the trip.[9]

---

7. "Buy in early." A crude phrase, but used by archivists in the Casino Poésie of potential fame and worth. There was nothing so horrible as to have purchased the youthful archives of a poet who later, in middle age, became a real estate baron.

8. Cheaply, but not too cheaply. Luckily for Archives Data-Targets, it was part of the mythology to appear to place high value on the Data Target's work, so in Szabo's case, notebooks were fetching a base rate of $450.00 per 75 pages, and more if there were literary comments or rough drafts of poems contained therein. However, had Szabo become hip that he was a clandestine Archives Data-Target, he could have taken that droll stroll, so dear to citizens of every persuasion, down large bill lane.

9. Jack had originally called me in on the case, offering substantial per diem mon. The purpose seemed to me to be reprehensible, so I turned it down. They wanted to begin a supersecret project on selected poets, called *What the Bard is Really Like*—taping them secretly in their homes during the same two-week period while at the same time making movies of them in their most intimate circumstances, using the top secret Stare-o-Rooter® surveillance cameras, to create an archives for all

74

It was a phenomenon called Archives Gambling, as of Gertrude Stein collecting the young Picasso; you couldn't be sure at the time if the young man painting at the Bateau Lavoir were truly a part of the Titian Time-Track. Both Art Archives and Jack Barnes were fans of Szabo's verse, and felt he was just a few years away from permanent insertion into the bardic section of the Titian time-warp.

Art and Jack were within a most ticklish phase of Operation Szabo, taking secret depositions, using a court reporter, about his life from family and friends. Such a stage, even with bribes flowing to the dependents, will usually hip an Archives Data Target to the targetry. A disaster to the Archivists, for if you let the data-targets know you're collecting their papers, then, with the collusion of their friends, they can fiddle up the price. Therefore, you usually hold off taking depositions until you have grabbed up the available manuscripts and papers at rock bottom prices.

Lately, with the prices rising and the Age of Archives fully upon us, there has been occurring a price-fiddle known in the archives trade as the *Letter Loop*. The *Letter Loop* is often a project of younger, pecunia-famined poets, for whom, money matters aside, the *Letter Loop* will have lifelong educational benefits.

Let us say that four young poets write each other each day for fifteen years, at the end of which time it will be likely that at least one of them will have reached a lofty reputation. With each of the four writing three a day, you have as a scriptorial total, 12 letters × 365 days × 15 years, and the resulting *Letter Loop* will overflow the file drawer.

Allowing for inflation, let us say that at the end of the fifteen years, the letters go for fifty each. Therefore, as of moolah,

---

time exposing the barren bagel of reality, answering the ageless question: "Are poets any different from the rest of us while showering, shaving, vibrating themselves, and mumbling nigh the pillow?" I had an opportunity to hip some of the 50 selected poets to the trip, and the case was blown open, quite a scandal as it played in the columns of *Gorp* and *Urge*. I had not, until now, as I stood in Lantern of Knowledge, known they were interested in Szabo and were still apparently working on *What the Bard is Really Like*.

you obtain $12 \times 365 \times 15 \times 50$, and you're again upon one of those droll strolls down along green grab creek.

Of course, for more instant cash the *Letter Loop* can be carried on, say, for a year, or even for a few months, and then you can head for the rare book/manuscript dealer, but be sure to keep the letters chatty, highly opinionated on literary matters, theoretical, full of erotic gossip, extravagantly learned (always sprinkle the texts with Tibetan, Sanskrit, Greek, Hebrew, French, Russian, Gaelic, German, Italian, and Chinese phrases), and don't forget to include at least four or five poems with each envelope. It is obvious that the *Letter Loop* is a great educational tool for the American Poet—for if you're in a wit race, you read more, think more, create more, and imbue your bardery with more of your mind.

—o—O—o—O—o—O—o—O—o—O—o—O—o—O—o—

As Jack and Art Archives were plotting their Al Fowler campaign's finality, the second archivist entered the store—another legendary man in the Age of Archives by name of Sweat-Brow "I'm a Mailer man" Bill, fresh out of the subway over the Manhattan Bridge from BrookHo, where he had been conducting raw research on the life of his career's Data Target, novelist Norman Mailer. Sweat-Brow was a short, chubby, energetic human, his forehead e'er sweat-suffused like a watertank in a dank cellar. Such was Sweat-Brow "I'm a Mailer man" Bill's vigor working the data-midden that his shoes, no matter how new and expensive, always bore the cruel scuffs of zeal, the soles of them curling up like the 9 p.m. hick town sidewalks of legend. Even Sweat-Brow's detractors, legion within the jealous congeries of archivism, had to admit that, in gathering information from hostile or hesitant sources, he had no peer.

Sweat-Brow "I'm a Mailer man" Bill's Data-Target, Mr. Mailer, had a house at 142 Columbia Street, Brooklyn Heights, N.Y., an address and area of waterfront Brooklyn, overlooking the high cenotaphs of Manhattan business, that is important to the main freshet of this tale. Sweat-Brow was so supernally frenzied in his pursuit of Mailerana that once at a drunken con-

76

vention of archivists he had gone to a 'tock-'too[10] parlor to have "I'm a Mailer man" ornately inscribed beneath the clear plastic 'tock-'too panes of his otherwise scholarly tweed trousers. He was not quite drunk enough not to have noted, just before the laser needle was due to grave, that the Data-Target, with its residual homophobia, might have considered the 'tock-'too portal'd too close to Sodom's hirsute harbor for dignity's sake. "Never cause unnecessary ire in the data-target" being a principle apothegm of archivists, Sweat-Brow "I'm a Mailer man" Bill opted instead for a private kidney-'too, which on occasion he sported for the eyes of skeptical brother and sister archivists, who challenged him, "C'mon Sweat-Brow, there's nothing on your kidney but a roll of fat! If so, prove it!"

Sweat-Brow allowed nothing to stand between him and the Data. He was not afraid of anything. He'd stand all 5'4" tall in front of a sneering data-target, ask his questions, sweat, and wait "'til the end of time" for the full and correct answers. He was the founder of the Aggressive Archivistics school of modern data-collectors. His motivation was this: why wait for the diaries and notebooks and letters of the Great One to be examined only *after* the Great One takes the stroll down Off Alley, as of thanatos? For, after bucket-kick, the archivist usually has to rely on heirs and relatives and their weird whims as to what is suitable for transmission to the ages from the Great One's personal papers. There was a sampler above Sweat-Brow "I'm a Mailer man" Bill's desk in his office that bore the following legend: "Hopkins' two sisters burned his Spiritual Diaries."[11] In reply Sweat-Brow wrote "Aggressive Archivistics focused on a living data-target is the only way to circumvent relatives," the opening sentence of his famous doctoral thesis, since become the founding document of the Age of Archives.

That's where Sweat-Brow's and my own concerns coincided—dealing with the problems of one-on-oneing it with a living data-target; the main problem being the puke problem.

---

10. See page 34 regarding 'tock-'toos.

11. See entry on Gerard Manley Hopkins in Untermeyer's *Lives of the Poets*.

Or, perhaps I'm being a bit too cynical. Sweat-Brow Bill would argue that, in terms of quality and quantity of usable data to be obtained, if the data-target is of your own generation or perhaps a generation older, then the data is 100 times of better *quan-qual*, to use one of Sweat-Brow's Aggressive Archivistics terms. What Sweat-Brow did not address himself to in his famous Ph.D. thesis was the above-mentioned puke problem. That is, what is an archivist/sleuth/historian, living by the principles of Aggressive Archivistics, to do when he or she finds out what an artist/writer is *really like?* Penetrating the smoke screen that all writers put up around their private lives: when you have tapes of their bedroom chatter, can you still maintain the halo-garlands of your prior impressions about them? The puke problem —so troublesome to intelligence officers tapping leftwing Hollywood stars sitting in their jacuzzis of cocaine soup, as well as to the Aggressive Archivist, not to mention to a lowly gumshoe such as I, with his pocket packed with surveillance chips.[12]

I know. I remember one summer weekend with a friend, helping her till her EaHo roof garden, and Milton Rosé's synagogue/loft/studio was below us. At her urging, I planted a couple of surveillance chips, dangling them by string down upon the window ledge at an open window. I found out, in a mere two hours, all that I ever wanted to know about the private life of the great artist, whom I have always admired, and who was then in the midst of a horrible battle with *Gorp* and *Urge* magazines over having used Beethoven's writing desk in a montage. It seemed that Rosé was to begin to haunt my life, one of those lentuchs of leisure whom one can never seem to avoid in a life of

---

12. Surveillance chips: small devices, looking like tiddly wink chips, color-coded as to their broadcast frequencies, which were placed wherever needed, able to pick up the slightest mumble or whisper, broadcasting the mumble to the so-called Surv-Box,® or surveillance monitor box, which could pick up broadcasts from over 100 different colors of surveillance chip, over 100 different channels. After ten days the surveillance chip could, upon broadcast command, spontaneously melt and assume the appearance, should the surveillance target subsequently discover it, of a piece of bubble gum stuck there by some rude person or other.

thrills and creative pursuit, encountering them in the strangest places, at airports, at parties in Kazakstan, at conventions, at spas, again and again and again.

|'"|'"|'"|'"|'"|'"|'"|'"|'"|'"|'"|'"|'"|'"|'"|'"|'"|'"|'"

Back to the Lantern of Knowledge bookstore. As Sweat-Brow "I'm a Mailer man" Bill entered the store, I noted that he was wearing his "data-jacket," which was wired with exceptionally sophisticated recording and video equipment, disguised equipment usually reserved for the boys of national security. In his cartridge belt resided several packed tapes of interviews with the proprietors of the grocery, liquor, magazine, and pharmaceutical stores frequented by Mailer. Sweat-Brow was as happy as a bard in a field with a flashlight jotting down quatrains after a nightingale's dusky solo.

Art Archives and Jack Barnes asked Sweat-Brow, almost at the same time, how things had gone in BrookHo. "Well," he replied, "you know how a data-target'll sometimes just for the heck of it slip you a bunch of nonsense nodules until you uncover what you need. Mailer's grocer was an agéd specimen who made me wade through his war diaries before granting me M-data, but he had a memory that would bring tears to a tape recorder eager to hear minutiae, if you can scan my zone, muh fuh . . ." Here Sweat-Brow paused to smile over how much of the times his language was. "And to the point, he mentioned that he has an aunt who owns a house on Columbia Heights Street—not too far up the hill from the grey granite buttresses of the Brooklyn Bridge—and not very far from Mailer's house, which is on Columbia Street, a different street by the way, but in the same neighborhood. Anyway, he told me something you might be interested in. It's not my field of course, but . . . ."

"But what?" Art Archives asked, rather too eagerly in my opinion, especially granted Art's lofty position as Archivists' Archivist. Jack was behaving much more in line with the m.o. of a cool collector, pretending not to listen, and even karate-clacking a column of epigrammatic descriptions about a couple of James Dickey's love letters for catalogue #147. However, as I monitored the position of Jack's good left ear, I noted that, as of a radar antenna, it had rotated itself in the direction of the conversation. As cunning as ever, Jack, as cunning as ever!

A good archivist can "sense" in the manner of a dowser finding water under a hill, the impending arrival of important data, or of relics, letters, or other archival accretions. So it was with all of us, as we sensed the imminent advent of information which might bode well for a quick sprint up Mt. Mool'.

"But what?" Art Archives repeated, again a bit too eagerly in my opinion; but again, A. Archives had not been trained, as Jack had been, in clandestine interrogation techniques, so I could forgive his drool-trill.

At last Sweat-Brow "I'm a Mailer man" Bill replied. "He says there's a trunk in the basement of his aunt literally packed with what appear to be Hart Crane's personal possessions—a bunch of letters, old books on American history, magazines, some notebooks, clothing, and so forth." Sweat-Brow paused and mopped his forehead. Gees, you *had* to pay attention when someone with the reputation for sleuthery like his fed you a data-trail. An outsider, however, would never have figured that out, judging from the shellac-eyed reactions of Jack Barnes and Art Archives.

Jack, whistling softly to himself, as soon as the words "trunk . . . literally packed with what appear to be Hart Crane's personal possessions" hit his ears, began to type with renewed ferocity on his descriptions of the James Dickey love letters. For his part, Art Archives, softly replying, "Really?" with an incredible tone of nonchalance, and stifling one of the most feigned yawns in the history of modern archivistics, slowly began to run his fingers along a packed shelf of Creeley, spotted that it was alarmingly close to the Hart Crane shelf, and veered at once ten feet to the M's, and began patting the thick rows of Mailer, which was fine with Sweat-Brow, who was drawn magnetically to the same shelves which he began to scan, chucking each book on the underside of its jacket as if it were the chin of a child.

I could sense that the scene was waxing flambantly phony. No one obviously wanted to take the lead in pumping Sweat-Brow about the trunk. One thing was certain: the air of nonchalance was fraudulent. I'm trained to watch face muscles. The motion of facial musculature, slight as it may be, is useful when interrogating a data-target. The faces of the two literary gentlemen had twinged like the haunches of a spotted Holstein quaking for fly removal.

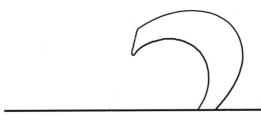

THE TWAIN OF
TWITCHES DID IT

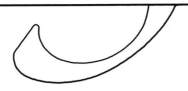

Yea, the concomitant twitching of the two faces, that of the cataloguer, and that of the archivist, convinced me at once that I had
a case on my hands. I was upset that I had not switched on my
pocket recorder to catch Sweat-Brow's assertions. Then I could
have later performed a Holo-Lie® Analysis on the tape.[13] Jack

---

13. Holo-Lie® Analysis. This technique created a three-dimen-
sional laser image of various components of the sound patterns of the
subject's voice during key questions. The Holo-Lie® looked like a long
gnarl of interwound cords—a twisted 'resonance-strand,' the lies being
determined by certain pits, and patterns, and unusual bumps and dis-
tortions in the holo-strand.

began to type most frenetically; I figured that since he was such a tightwad he was doubling his work in order to feel free for some later chore. What chore? Obtaining Hart Crane's trunk. I'd bet my surveillance chips and the chip monitor-box on it.

I was beginning to float into ire. It became apparent at once that Barnes had forgotten entirely about the dinner invitation, and the memory-skeins of our shared youth no longer were marching from his mouth. I fondled the surveillance chips in my pocket, fantasizing about his bedroom chatter, wondering if ire was going to cause me to chip him.

Jack kept on typing like an A-head in the middle of an all night epic. It was *so* obvious that a veil of larceny was being lowered upon the case. What did he think I was, a moron? I decided then and there to time-track both Jack and Art Archives, and to perform a Morality Analysis on each of their behavior patterns as they scrambled to possess the putative trunk.

Finally I asked what no one seemed to want to ask. "What's the woman's name, Sweat-Brow?"

"Marta Alonzo," he replied.

I thought of my friend up at Columbia, who was one of the foremost scholars on Hart Crane. The library owns much of the source material for the various biographies of him. I could have called up my friend and picked up a lucrative assignment to track down the putative trunk, assuming that their budget had a few coins left for such a contingency operation.

I glanced at Jack Barnes, a good disguise man in the OSS let me assure you. I pictured him coming on to the aunt as an antique dealer eager to purchase the groovy old trunk, while feigning a total disinterest in its worthless contents. I pictured him saying, "Yes, Mrs. Alonzo, we'll even cart away the useless junk inside the trunk for you. Or, maybe we'll find some postcards with old postmarks. That way we could raise the total price for you. Picture postcards from the early part of the century are worth 40 or 50 cents apiece, you know. That way, Mrs. Alonzo, you won't have to lug the papers to the compactor yourself."

(•) (•) (•) (•) (•) (•) (•) (•) (•) (•) (•) (•) (•) (•) (•) (•) (•)

Sweat-Brow soon headed back to the Hilton to sort his data, to develop his film, and for his final shower of sweat removal of the day. As he left, I considered the strong possibility that Sweat-Brow was attempting to insert meadow muffins into our data-streams. Perhaps he held some obscure grudge against Jack Barnes or Art Archives for some crime committed while all were working the literary data-midden. Literary cataloguers are particularly prone to data-midden transgressions. I sensed that Sweat-Brow could rationalize acquiring the trunk for himself on the ground that Hart Crane and Mr. Mailer both carried out great portions of their creativity in the area of the Brooklyn Bridge, or in Brooklyn Heights, and in fact lived only a few blocks, in their respective decades, from each other, and had been inspired by the same BrookHo roofs and buildings.

I figured that at the very least Sweat-Brow might have cajoled his way into the grocer's aunt's basement, using the old meter reader con, or the boiler inspector routine, or the telephone repairman hype, or the assessor scam—techniques dear to the bugger or the tapper. Why then had he mentioned it at all to Barnes and Art Archives? To taunt them?

It could have been archives hubris, that sense of arrogant triumph to which one working the data-midden will fall prey on occasion when they have just reeled in a bundle of weighty data.

I knew that Art Archives was staying at the same hotel as I, so I offered to share a cab with him. That way I was able to slip him some surveillance chips, one in his tweed vest watchpocket, one in his pants, and most importantly, one I was able to stab into the edge of his shoe sole. It wasn't often a surv-target changed his shoes in the middle of something exciting, a principle unearthed by the intelligence community who came to trust shoes as safe surveillance chip repositories.

I tried, in the meantime, to gauge Art Archives' state of mind about the trunk. It was, he told me, strictly ho-hum. Too ho-hum, in my opinion. "Come on, now, Art!" I enjoined him. "Aren't you at all interested in finding out about it?"

"No sir," he replied. "I have too much to work upon as it is."

"Yes, but what about the pecuniary aspects of it?" I

coaxed. "You know what a Crane boom is on now, with the space program using the Brooklyn Bridge as a logo, and quotes from Crane painted on spacecraft."

"Yes, you have a point. But I am so damn busy! I tell you, if you get involved, call me, and I'll help you. You and I have worked together on many projects; we can trust one another."

Sure, Art, sure, I thought, thinking how he had tried to listen in on the private conversations of James Dickey, Anne Waldman, Phil Whalen, and other bards. Only the truly trustworthy, like myself, I thought, should listen to such conversations. "Well," I replied, "you've got me there. You know I'm also in the midst of a big case. But if anything comes up, I'll surely get in touch with you, Art."

He invited me into his suite for a drink, a further opportunity to Surv-Chip® him, which I accomplished in so many locations that there was no way the strayest mumble could escape my ken. It was interesting that in his room Art had set up a large screen connected to an archives microfiche retrieval system. This was sort of a teddy bear for Art, who, by punching codes upon a set of keys, could retrieve images instantly of his favorite archive items back at the library at home. Images flashing upon the screen were as a palliative prayer of permanence just before gulping the sleeping pill and donning the jam-jams. Sure, Art, sure.

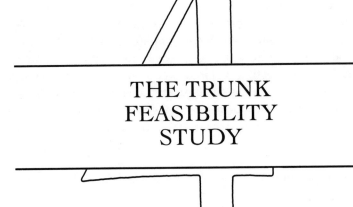

THE TRUNK
FEASIBILITY
STUDY

Once free from Art Archives' suite, I knew I had to prepare a
Trunk Feasibility Study. For this, I cabbed down to the reading
room of the New York Public Library. I ordered a stack of biographies and essays on Hart Crane, on the history of the Brooklyn Bridge, and on the neighborhood of BrookHo Heights.
When they were brought to my table, my mind went into a stu-
dious fog, and two hours quickly passed, zzzt zzzt, during
which I dictated a report and later dropped it off to have it typed
with the service I'd been using on the Balzac case.

I discovered that Crane had lived in at least four places in the same small neighborhood of Brooklyn Heights from 1924 to 1930:

1. 110 Columbia Heights
2. 77 Willow
3. 130 Columbia Heights
4. A "tiny basement apartment," in or near
   130 Columbia Heights

I learned that young Hart Crane had moved into a house at 110 Columbia Heights Street just before Easter of 1924, about a year after coming to New York from Cleveland. He lived off and on at the house 'til 1926. Number 110 was a very fashionable address and had once been owned by Emily and Washington Roebling. Mr. Roebling had been the chief engineer and driving force behind the construction of the Brooklyn Bridge in the 1870's and 1880's. He had become afflicted with several ailments, including the bends, during construction, and throughout the latter years of construction was forced to monitor the project from an observation post in the very house in which 45 years later Hart Crane received his visions of the Bridge as a symbol of the friendly synapse of American civilization.

110 Columbia Heights had been bought by the Roeblings in late 1873. The house lay on the block between Pineapple and Orange Streets, on the West side (the river side) of the street. It bore a deep garden in the back, which extended out over the top of a carriage house and stable built below the brink of the steep incline. The carriage house fronted on Furman Street at the edge of the wharves. The back is now blessed with an altered vista, the major portion of which is the roadway of the Brooklyn-Queens Expressway.

I was excited, reading that during Roebling's time there were brick sidewalks on both sides of Columbia Heights. Oh boy! Were they still there? I sure hoped they were, for I needed some healing thrills for my data-trampled ocularity. It was when I began to skim some books about the history of the Brooklyn Bridge that I began to get excited about this case on its own merits rather than merely because of my slighted feelings. One of the ironies of the private investigation industry is that it often attracts people with sensitivities easily piqued and pained; which can be a disaster in a career furnishing endless put-downs, phone hang-ups, painful schemes, grief by the bundle, and the distress of trapped humans at every turn.

I was impressed with the historical stature of the Brooklyn Bridge. I was anxious myself to walk upon it. Dang, I must have driven across a hundred times in my life, but had never strolled, testing the contention of a historian that "to be on the promenade of the Brooklyn Bridge on a fine day, about halfway between the two towers, looking over the harbor and the city skyline, was to be at one of the two or three most soul-stirring spots in America, like standing at the rim of the Grand Canyon."[14]

I'll believe that, I thought, when I see it. After all, is not the area beset with marauding muggers in souped-up minicopters (the mopeds of the New Sky), and with the rebellious hive-like communal housing complexes of the Barrel Generation?

I kept on the watch, in the books and essays, for any rumor that Hart Crane had stored somewhere any material which was subsequently lost, especially in the neighborhood of Columbia Heights. I quickly learned that Crane's habits were sometimes so turbulent that there well *could* exist a stray trunk or two. I learned for instance that he kept his letters in a trunk, as in a letter from the summer of 1925, Crane writing to Waldo Frank from his summer vacation: "Dear Waldo: I'm awfully sorry about the Jimenez translations; they are locked in my *trunk* at Columbia Heights in my letter file."

There was at least *one* instance where he abandoned trunks, which perhaps was part of a pattern. In October of 1926, Crane, working on *The Bridge*, was living in Cuba on the Isle of Pines, and after a hurricane, decided to return to N.Y. In his biography of Crane, John Unterecker notes that he took back to N.Y. "only his manuscripts and such clothing as would fit into one suitcase." Abandoned were the "remains of his wardrobe,

---

14. *The Great Bridge*, by David McCullough, p. 548, an extremely interesting account of the bridge's construction. He was speaking of course, of a time when a stroll across the bridge was upon air not so foully septic, and before the advent of minicopter muggers.

two trunks, and many of his books. His 'texts', those books he still needed for his work on *The Bridge,* he set aside for forwarding to wherever he might hang his . . . hat."[15] It was obvious to me, reading that passage, that Mr. Crane had a habit, as he completed sections of *The Bridge,* of leaving behind, perhaps in deliberate obfuscation, the historical references no longer needed. What a trove, I thought, if Crane's historical references should be found in an abandoned trunk! As valuable perhaps as Melville's books, or Charles Olson's library, in providing exegetic focus.

I noted that in early September of 1928, H.C. was again living in a house in BrookHo, apparently a rooming house, at 77 Willow Street, a block away from Columbia Heights, and just around the corner from where I later located Mrs. Alonzo's fine little house.

He stayed at 77 Willow until circa December 1928, when he traveled to London, and France, 'til around August of '29, when he returned to N.Y. In September of the same year, he was working on the Cape Hatteras, Quaker Hill, and Indiana sections of his poem. He wrote to Caresse Crosby, who was publishing *The Bridge,* on 9/6/29: "I am working like mad since I've found this apartment where I can keep my own hours." The apartment was located at #130 Columbia Heights, on the same block as #110, where he had begun his poem five years previous.

He was at #130 Columbia Heights on December 26, 1929, when he completed the final line of *The Bridge.* A week later he moved. I wondered if it was at this time that he may have left a trunk with Mrs. Alonzo. It would have been in keeping with his deportment, I reasoned. He was done with his resource texts and notes for the poem, so he could safely store them somewhere. From his letters, it was obvious that Crane had been going one-on-one with T. S. Eliot, whose *Wasteland* had just appeared, in a contest of bardery. It seemed appropriate somehow that Crane might have deliberately occulted his source material in the contest with Mr. Eliot. One thing was certain, in my opin-

---

15. Unterecker, *Voyager: A Life of Hart Crane,* pp. 457-58.

89

ion: Crane was the ultimate winner, for you'll not find "April is the cruelest month" stenciled on any spacecraft's hatch.

On 1/2/30, H.C. moved to his "basement apartment"—a tiny place according to his biographers. There he stayed until the following summer. Around July 1930, he moved his possessions from Brooklyn to the Gaylordsville, Connecticut home of a close friend, Eleanor Fitzgerald, the business manager of the Provincetown Playhouse in Greenwich Village. Crane's belongings remained at her house until long after his death and her own. I noted in a letter to Allan Tate during the summer of 1930 that Crane was studying Dante. "My summer seems like a blank to me right now," he wrote. "Perhaps my study of Dante—the *Comedia* . . . will have been seen to have given it some significance."

Did that mean, I wondered, that Crane had written something on Dante that summer? Notebooks? Perhaps that was in the putative trunk. I had noted too that Crane had seriously considered, as a future writing project, a "poetic drama on Cortez." That also, as far as I was concerned, was a dandy candidate for inclusion in the putative trunk. My mind was afire: manuscripts on the Divine Comedy, a drama on Cortez, and then there were the missing letters from his mother, Grace; add to that a "letter file" of letters from his famous friends, some unpublished poems, journals, plus the reference books. Oh Boy!

The summer of 1930 he had given up his basement apartment on Columbia Heights, and when in the fall he returned to N.Y. he was beaten down by the Mallet of Pov. Depression / No Job / No Mon.

On December 12, 1930, he split to Chagrin Falls, Ohio to visit his father, and to help with Christmas rush in the family store. I could find no indication that Crane ever returned to N.Y. A Guggenheim Fellowship enabled him to visit Mexico in 1931, and he was on his way back to N.Y.C. in April of 1932, when on the 27th, he jumped at noon into the water.

By the time I'd made my final dictation on the Feasibility Study I was about as excited as I'd been about any case since my first big operation in '48, when I'd been hired on the Howard Hughes

90

war profiteering case. But then, you're always sentimental about your first case.

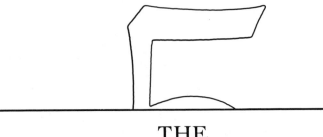

THE
STARE-O-ROOTER® INSERTS

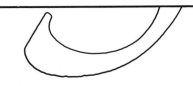

After the Feasibility Study, I must say I still did not have a final determination on the trunk's probability. Nowhere, for instance, was Marta Alonzo's name mentioned in the 15 books I had consulted. On the other hand, I had to admit that a Trunk was *possible*. During a five year period, Crane had spent time in at least four apartments and rooms in the same several-block area. He had a proclivity to abandon possessions, and he lived quite a drunken, boisterous existence. And he did form close friendships with various women. But that was it.

I was thinking these things over, when I had a flash of inspiration. I called a friend at BrookHo Intelligence, another old war buddy, to see if he had anything on a Mrs. M. Alonzo who lived on Columbia Heights, or maybe Willow Street.

"Marta Alonzo?" he asked.

I told him yes. It was then that my pal at BrookHo Int. began to speak with a muffled voice as if he were cupping the phone. "She's gonna have, sometime soon, I'm not sure when, a National Security watch on her house. Sometime this week. Jeez! we've been busting our hump putting together a chronology on her for the Mayor's office. We're not sure what it's all about, but it has something to do with the Mars Colony project."

It took a bit of reminding him of the several favors he owed me, after which he grudgingly promised me a computer printout of the chrono on Mrs. Alonzo. Now, I owed him.

Next I called my friend at the Columbia University Library, but I was careful not to blab the putativity of the Trunk. I asked if there existed, in theirs or in any other collection, any notes or drafts for a verse drama about Cortez, or if there were Crane notebooks on the subjects of Dante or the *Comedia,* and if Grace Crane's letters to her son had ever turned up.

I hate it when people whom I'm trying to question start to pepper back with stress-questions. And that's what my friend began to do. Had *I* any knowledge of a Cortez drama? What's this about Dante? She was so obviously trying to build up tension that I thought I was going to have to hang up on her. One thing was clear—Hart Crane was a priority item in the new budget, and whoever should offer them any Trunk was fixedly due for a droll stroll down past the pecunia patch.

This conversation only inflamed my interest in monitoring this case. I left my room, whistling down the hotel corridor, the dried coke and spatters of weary travelers mixed with ammoniate cleansing fluid and the burns of ashes on the plastic-fibered dark green rug sporting patterns of pineapple slices, all causing distress to my feet. For, so sensitive were the soles of my Surv-Silent® shoes to the untoward vibrations of crunch, that a wave of displeasure rippled up from my ankles.

I paused near the ice machines, listening to the almost si-

93

lent and muffled "splurps" as the machine spat fresh cubes into the questionably white, nigh to grey, ice compartment. I turned the channel of my chip monitor to Art Archives. Ugh, my ears were attacked, as I dialed the volume much too loudly, and picked him up overwhelmed with the noises of archivistics.

Instantly, I knew that the case was moving much more rapidly than I had anticipated. Art was in the shower, but my surveillance chip was near enough to pick up his song of lavation:

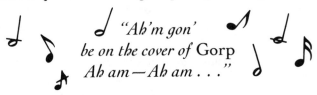

"Ah'm gon'
be on the cover of Gorp
Ah am—Ah am . . ."

which over and over he intoned, more or less, especially less, to the tune of "Camptown Racetrack five miles long, do-dah, do-dah."

I knew that this was a situation worthy of a Stare-o-Rooter® insert, so I reached into a tiny carven jade perfume bottle I carried in my watch pocket beside my surveillance chips. I pulled the Stare-o-Rooter® out, and plugged it into the Stare-o-Rooter® monitor box attached to my wrist watch, pushed the button, and the tiny monitor screen elevated itself up from my wrist to a height of 3½ inches.

The Stare-o-Rooter® required only the tiniest of fissures or cracks, or series of fissures and cracks (if more than one layer was to be penetrated), through which one could rooter it into a room. Once the Stare-o-Rooter® was rootered within an enclosure, a trained rooter-worker could maneuver the Stare-o-Rooter® into a virtually invisible position, so that one could observe upon the wrist screen outside what was occuring inside.

Arthur Archives, coughly of smoker's lungs, and thin as a roll-of-dimes, emerged dripping from the shower into the archives room. So afraid was he of tuberculosis that he showered with his woolen scarf still upon his neck and upper chest, and as he emerged it was wet and clingy upon him. It is one of the tribulations of Stare-o-Rootering® that one is treated to the spectacle of a subject after a shower inspecting for piles with a

THE STARE-O-ROOTER®

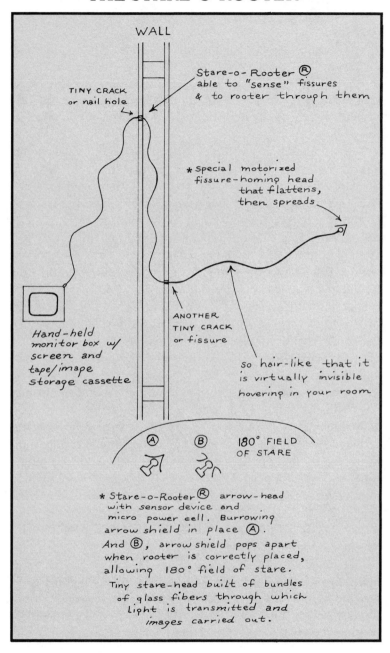

WALL

Stare-o-Rooter® able to "sense" fissures & to rooter through them

TINY CRACK or nail hole

* Special motorized fissure-homing head that flattens, then spreads

Hand-held monitor box w/ screen and tape/image storage cassette

ANOTHER TINY CRACK or fissure

so hair-like that it is virtually invisible hovering in your room

Ⓐ Ⓑ 180° FIELD OF STARE

* Stare-o-Rooter® arrow-head with sensor device and micro power cell. Burrowing arrow shield in place Ⓐ. And Ⓑ, arrow shield pops apart when rooter is correctly placed, allowing 180° field of stare. Tiny stare-head built of bundles of glass fibers through which light is transmitted and images carried out.

hand-held mirror. Thankfully, he soon had satisfied his poste-
rial curiosity, and was vigorously attendant to the business of
archives.

I heard, disgust pickling my ears, Mr. Archives start to
read various drafts of a press release announcing the recovery of
the Trunk. You would have thought, listening over the Surv-
Chip,® that Mr. Archives were running for mayor, so frequently
was his own name mentioned as the discoverer of the priceless
trove.

I wondered how complex Art's plans were to achieve his
goal, so I moved the Stare-o-Rooter® around the room, "parsing
the pad seg by seg," as it is known in the trade. I could see that
Art's operation was pretty thorough. What they call a Harvard
Outline of the project was taped to the wall, filling around 25
pages, extending through Roman numeral headings, I, II, III,
IV, V, . . . to XCVIII, with sub-headings (A, B, C . . .) packed
with details of the operation. A quick scan of the Outline informed me that he had ordered Psychological Assessments to be
prepared on the grocer, on Sweat-Brow Bill, on Jack Barnes, on
Marta Alonzo, on Hart Crane, and on the several librarians in
the country with big enough budgets allowing them to enter a
bidding war for the Trunk. And also he had ordered a Psychological Assessment on *me!!!* Boy, was I angry!

I noted also that Archives had rented a silent minicopter
with whisperfeather rotor blades, so as to hover above Mrs.
Alonzo's house to take layout snapshots. I caught in the Stare-
o-Rooter® screen the chit from a mountain climbing shop, indicating that he had purchased metal shoe-cleats, pitons, climbing
rope, and an Alpine hat. I don't know to this day what he had in
mind: perhaps it was a contingency plan to human-fly down the
side of her building, or perhaps to lower himself into the basement via a dumb-waiter shaft that had, as I later noted when I
was in the basement myself, been sealed for years.

I could see, at section XCVIII of the outline, that Art was
going to visit the Trunk surreptitiously that very night. I bothered no further with Art Archives, and withdrew the Stare-o-
Rooter,® coiling it back within the alabaster-capped jade bottle. I
went next up to the roof of the Hilton, where I took a chance that

I could pick up Barnes at his house down in the Village. With only a small amount of fiddling, I tuned upon his soft voice. I could not fight off a twinge of guilt, as I invaded the sacred privacy of one of my closest friends.

You see, throughout the Balzac manuscript case, I had adamantly refused to listen to his conversations. Instead, I had hired someone to listen to the tapes, and to make only the most concise summaries of the discourse, and gave instructions that the summaries were to contain only those sentences that perhaps could pertain to some aspect of the manuscript matter. Guilty I felt, yes, but again I always felt guilty, even surv-chipping some heinous banker redlining the poor.

I'll confess it: I always wanted to monitor Barnes' privacy. It's a sickness you get when you're well into a career as a snoop. The greeny elixir of the most private data a person has to offer, i.e., pillow talk, ever whelms my sensitivities. And hadn't he burned me, his oldest friend, for chow and a hemp-seed sauna, just to chase the Trunk of some obscurantist from the 1920's?

It was soon clear, listening to Barnes from my spot upon the windy grit of the Hilton roof, that he was planning to pull a rip on the Trunk. That upset me greatly. Sentences like, "She sets no value on it . . ." and "Won't let anyone in," provided clues to me that maybe Jack had already visited BrookHo to try for a peek at the treasure. Or maybe, (as another part of my mind butted in to try to rescue Barnes' good name), maybe he just wanted to check the Trunk before making a big offer for it? "Yeah," I said aloud in reply, "then why is he renting a van and a hand-truck?" Barnes was making a crucial mistake: he thought that Mrs. Alonzo did not know what was in the Trunk, an error whose importance will become apparent later on.

Just before the Surv-Chip® went silent, I heard Barnes apparently dictating a letter into his cassette, addressed to a librarian, mentioning a "special new find" in twentieth century literature, and that sealed bidding on the find would begin in the fall. That did it. I swore to myself then and there, that if he broke into that poor widow's house and offed that Trunk, that I was going to file the most scathing report imaginable with the Defense Department, so that Jack Barnes, in the event of war, would not get security cleared enough to gain access to a mop and pail.

You know how when you tune into someone's private conversations to check for a conspiracy, some of the things you hear, no matter who the source is, will fit into the paradigm of the putative plot. So it was with Jack and Mitalia Barnes. I would have sworn, listening to their bon babble, that they had brought Sweat-Brow "I'm a Mailer man" Bill into their schemes, or, as another part of my mind reminded me, more likely he them.

They mentioned him several times, which was natural, since Sweat-Brow had been the one to have posited the Trunk's existence. It was the words, "I wonder how much Sweat-Brow can lift?"—uttered by Jack to Mitalia, that triggered my fears. To this day, I don't know what he meant. All I know is that Jack definitely was planning to break into Mrs. Alonzo's basement that night at 12:30 sharp. Wow! Both Jack and Art were planning a sneak-look around the same time! Was it a coincidence? At the time, I thought it was a cabal. In the worst case, maybe Sweat-Brow, Art Archives, and Jack had joined in cahoots. It didn't really bother me if they had—but my feelings were really hurt if they had not bothered to *cut me in!* Of course, as I considered at the time, it was a testament to my morality if they should not have offered me the action—no doubt they thought me much too elevated in ethos to entertain a lowly trunk-rip, or an exalted trunk-rip for that matter, or any trunk-rip, or any rip at all. It was a small consolation—and an inadequate one.

Faith, I hated to place a surveillance chip on Sweat-Brow Bill, principally because another bubble of misconception would surely pop. I left the roof and walked again in my Surv-Silent® shoes upon the filth-crunchy rug of the hotel corridor, and paused outside Sweat-Brow's door, my stomach pancaking back and forth with anxiety—you never know what sort of misconduct you will encounter when you first tap into someone's private life-stream—hauling the Stare-o-Rooter® from its jade encasement, eyeing the ceiling air vent as a possible insertion point. As I rootered the vent, the voice monitor began picking up Sweat-Brow's sad, plaintive voice singing what sounded like "Ave Data!" or rather, "A–a–vey Da–a–ta!"

I hastened to insert the Stare-o-Rooter® within the room, and as soon as it was through the wall ready to stare, I began to search for him. First I maneuvered the stare-eye into the bathroom, thinking perhaps the "Ave Data!" was a song of lavation as had been Art Archives' "Ahm gon' be on the cover of *Gorp*." I scanned Sweat-Brow's bathroom, skirting the rather awesome supply of ointments, sponges, oils, shampoos, and cleansing bottles ringing the tub, but found him not within.

I withdrew the 'Rooter to the bedroom, and began to parse it seg by seg. Where was he? I wondered, just before the dresser top delivered me a profound shock. You know how at the Museum of the American Indian in New York, there's that little shrunken white man, about two feet tall, dressed in a tiny suit, perhaps a trader who had wandered into a village of shrinkers? Well, so it was that on Sweat-Brow's dresser stood what appeared to be a two-foot-high shrunken Norman Mailer. The homunculus-sized Mailer was attired most spiffily in a dark blue pin stripe suit and matching vest. The homunculus was crouched in a fighter's stance, but with a small half-filled glass in its left jab rather than a padded glove. Oh no, I half-groaned, half-laughed, could Sweat-Brow have offed Mailer during the day and somehow already freeze-dried him into homunculus-hood?

I wondered about it, then scoffed at myself. Had not Sweat-Brow for over twenty years shaken the tambourine of Aggressive Archivistics performed on "living data-targets?" He would be violating his own principles of data-middenry, should he have offed his subject. Besides, Sweat-Brow was not insane. "Yes," another part of my mind broke in, "but what if Sweat-Brow had discovered some hidden closet of information that had snapped him over the edge regarding his target?" I was trying to pooh-pooh that proposal, while I positioned the Stare-o-Rooter® just inches in front of the homunculus.

All at once, I understood the purpose. It was a shrine. I could picture Sweat-Brow Bill praying to it like the young man prayed to the Balzac shrine in the movie, *400 Blows*. With that in mind, I quickly located Sweat-Brow, who was locked in a cultic knee-grab grovel on the floor beneath the shrine. Either that, or he had fallen unconscious and needed a doctor. I turned up the sound on the monitor box, the better to pick up his soft mumbles. I fought away a shudder of disgust as I picked up his words. He *was* praying.

But not to Mailer. Thank God! It was, as I recognized, a Masonic prayer to the Architect of the Universe. I must say I was glad to be relieved of the proposition that Sweat-Brow was a hopeless sickie. In fact, as I then maneuvered the Stare-o-Rooter® around the room, there was something touching, even poignant, about Sweat-Brow's attention to the duty of data. Upon nearby shelves, he had begun uncrating the 116 volumes of raw data he was using to prepare his target's biography.

On whim I maneuvered the stare-eye again upon the dresser, to observe the contents of his pockets, which I had detected dumped around the homunculus. I wanted to see if Sweat-Brow used surveillance chips. I wiggled the S.-o-R. virtually on top of the "statue" and lo! I saw the Stare-o-Rooter® tip disappear into it! I chuckled, realizing I had been fooled. The Mailer model was a laser hologram projected from an apparatus affixed with suction cups to the ceiling. As I moved the 'Rooter around the laser holo-writer, I laughed as the Mailer-gram delivered boxerlike jabs with its drink hand, thrilling little holo-sloshes splashing down from the glass as he jabbed.

From his lowly kowtow of obeisance, Sweat-Brow arose with vigor, and began to pick up various volumes of his central Mailer data files, and tenderly to read through them. I rootered into a better position, and at last saw what I sought—Sweat-Brow's famous forehead! Surely it was!—furrowed with the anxiety of data collection. I could see most clearly in the survscreen a browlace of moisture beads just beginning to adorn his craggy skin. A beadlet dropped high from his eyebrow and total'd itself upon the binder containing Mailer's baby and grade-school pictures, and his report card photostats.

'Brow seemed energized by his spiffle through the Mailerana, and began at once the task of transcribing the tapes from his afternoon's foray into Mailer's BrookHo neighborhood. He used the recently developed "Plexus Transcription System," an invention which had greatly reduced the time required to transcribe tapes. Anyone who has worked the middens of dry-asdust knows the horror of tape transcription. In the Plexus System, the typewriter automatically picks up the most common words on the tape, using a sound sensor system—all the *and*'s, *the*'s, *a*'s, *of*'s, all common verbs and adjectives, and places them into phrases and sentences, leaving blanks for the remaining words the system, usually because the words were mumbled or garbled on the tape, does not recognize. The Plexus System automatically types this first version. The transcriber then can listen to the tape and fill in the blanks. It eased tape transcription time by a factor of four.

You may wonder why a lowly archivist like Sweat-Brow "I'm a Mailer man" Bill could afford such expensive equipment as portable wrist computer screens, the Plexus Transcription System, and so forth. For the answer, you have to understand Ironword.® It turned out that of all the problems facing archivists, one of the most distressing had been the condition of letters, notes, and drafts of novels and poems that had been typed using typewriter correction strips or fluids. These corrections, in just a few years, would wear away, so that the archivist or collector was faced with texts in which the original Freudian slip, or moronic misspelling, or upper-addled spasm of the writer, loomed through.

It was a particular pain for those charged with determining the final test of a work, especially if the author were dead and the work had not yet been published. Sweat-Brow became quite wealthy after he invented Ironword,® a permanent correction fluid. The scientists at NASA had said that a word corrected with Ironword® would last 15,000 years, and that corrected words would exist, like tiny bits of a typesetter's font, as metalloid hieroglyphic nuggets, long after the paper around them had weathered to dust. After Ironword®'s invention, the word had gone out to the writers of the world from their archivists, and the concept of the Final Exact Text was thereby saved.

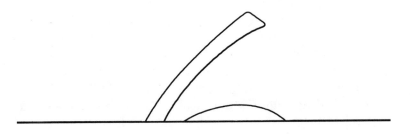

AN EXCURSION
TO BROOKHO

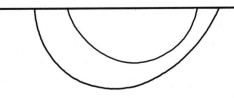

I ordered my automobile brought around from the hotel garage, and proceded to BrookHo, crossing by way of the Brooklyn Bridge. My first stop was to pick up the printout on Mrs. Alonzo from my friend at the Art, Safe, Archives, Division of BrookHo Intelligence. It was raining barrel staves outside. I was short on time, so I tried to read the report as I maneuvered through the narrow Brooklyn Heights streets. I discovered, reading the report, that Mrs. Alonzo under her maiden name had been a friend of Mr. Crane when he was writing *The Bridge.*

I popped in on the grocer, cunningly, just as he was closing, so he would be apt to talk in order to get rid of me. I used the insurance inspector routine, to which the grocer gave a co-operative smile. I found out the general location of the Trunk in Mrs. Alonzo's house. "Is it safe?" I wondered.

"Oh," he said, "the basement is very dry. It hasn't flooded in 40 years. You know, a number of gentlemen have been asking about that trunk. What is it, an antique or something?"

"Quite," I replied, giving him a look of shrugging eyebrows, tilting my face to the side, that said wordlessly, "Aren't some people coocoo and crazy?"

"Quite," he nodded.

I was able, without, I think, arousing his suspicions, to find out from the good grocer the time Mrs. Alonzo generally retired for the night. As with many concerned citizens, it was right after the 11 o'clock news.

After talking with the grocer, I felt an irresistible urge to drive past Hart Crane's old house. I proceeded north, along a street parallel to Columbia Heights, since Columbia Heights was one way going south. I turned right on Clark Street and proceeded the short block to Columbia Heights. There I was! But an ache of the heart I felt when I saw that the sidewalks were not of brick as they had been in the late 19th century. Then the biggest shock of all: Crane's old house, the home of the builder of the Brooklyn Bridge, was torn down!

You see, I had violated one of my own rules—against hasty scholarship. I had been so fevered that afternoon, skimming the books preparing the Trunk Feasibility Study, that I had neglected to determine if the house still existed! At once, I parked my car, donned a camouflage rain cape, and walked in the hideous chemical-suffused rain that only New Yorkers know, to the former home of the bard.

I stood midblock between Orange and Cranberry Streets on Columbia Heights, and lifted my face upon the building that had replaced the shrine of American Literature and bridge construction, the acid rain running caustic into my eyes. Oh no! I thought, as I stared up at a nine-story red brick building that appeared to occupy not only the location of #110, where he had begun serious work on his poem in 1924, but also #130, where he had finished it the day after Christmas '29.

What was worse to my nearly atheist mind was that the brick building was owned by the Jehovah's Witness religious sect, and I could see through the spatters hurting my eyes that the building was called Kingdom Hall. I bent down to read the cornerstone, and felt a shudder: Watchtower 1909-1949. Ee gads! I thought, the house of Washington and Emily Roebling, and that in which Hart Crane had held his visions of America, now torn down and replaced by the hawkers of Armageddon! For who has not been awakened some drear morn by the sect's pro-selytizers trying to sell you Doom-Is-Near publications probably printed on Hart Crane's very land. Why, O Jahweh, why?

I knew Mrs. Alonzo's house was just around the street from the site of Crane's apartment, so I hastened from the sect site. So narrow are the streets, so compact the buildings that I was standing at Mrs. Alonzo's front steps in a matter of seconds. Even in the rain, I marveled at it. What a beautiful house! No wonder such houses are of interest to historians and artists, who want to gauge how beauty of building was measured in the days before the rise of the chromium fist.

It was a tall building, of ivied brick, its porch painted mocha brown, shiny, perfectly adorned—a combination of wood, stone, painted masonry, and wrought iron. There were beautiful wrought iron railings on both sides of the front steps, and the glass of the vestibule door was protected by an iron grate of the same floral curlicues as the railings of the steps.

You could see Mrs. Alonzo's books—plenty of them on tall white shelves—through oblong window panes so old you could see the wavy ripples of antique manufacture. I contemplated searching for the Crane section of the shelves through my Surv-Scope.® I was afraid however of being thought a putative felon, so I hastened to the back of the house, to scout a path to the basement.

Suddenly I stopped. I had been so caught up in a gaze of admiration that I did not see the sign above the mail slot at the right of the front door. It was a neat *No Soliciting,* beneath which was another legend, this one handwritten, difficult to discern in the downpour. I darted up the steps, and bent down to read. "Especially antique dealers," it said. I nearly rolled on the pavement with delight, wondering if perhaps all three of the gentlemen had come to the door at different times posing as antique dealers.

The back of the house was such a pleasure, even in the rain! There was a neat garden, with flowers in the four coigns, and the loveliest tendrils of aged ivy on both sides of the wall, the central stalks edging perfectly the entranceway to the steps leading down to the basement door. I checked the lock in the Surv-Scope,® and saw that it would be a cinch to pick. I sketched the layout of the courtyard, a mnemonic device invaluable to night-sneak—for an area seen by day, by night seems vastly different.

ththth°°°:=:=:=:=:=:=:°°°ththth°°°:=:=:=:=:=:=:°°°ththth°°°:=:=:=:

I returned to my car, drenched in the N.Y. sky-drool, and drove down the street along Columbia Heights, which runs north to the base of the Brooklyn Bridge itself. I passed Middagh street, just past the Crane house site, where the street takes a sharp dive down a hill toward the bridge's stone pediments. I thought the bridge base very suitable for pausing to read the remainder of the BrookHo Intelligence report on Mrs. Marta Alonzo, so I parked near the Fulton Ferry Museum, feeling wonderful. Why was I happy? I who was wet, tired, burnt-out at 64, horny, fearful of heart disease, and bent down with 38 years of cases that however much I slaved on them, never somehow got fully closed. It was simple—I was happy because I had fresh data, in a fresh case that had beauty to it, that involved great poetry and American history.

Ironically I was parked right behind a recruitment van with *Go Navy* on its hoarding. I could see two hightowered ships being unloaded or loaded near Dock #2, beneath Pineapple Street, a sight which Hart Crane too, standing at his 4th story window, must have marveled upon in 1924. Before I began reading, I swept the area with my eyes: the van, the dark wet bridge buttresses, the yellow wood museum, the gulls braving the damp, the oil-dark harbor waters, the sheets of rain, the hill leading up to BrookHo. . . . The ghosts of ithyphallic sailor caps seemed to dance in the pediments' mist.

I won't bother the reader with the text of the BrookHo Intelligence report. I must say that it was very neatly put together. Archives and Historical Heritage Divisions were proliferating in police departments in major cities. Often as adjuncts to Art Theft, Safe & Jewel squads. The report was so well constructed that it read like an article in Mr. Sanders' high flying quarterly, *Journal of the Lives of Poets in Verse,* which features biographic poems about poets.

I almost wept, reading the report, for a past I knew was probably extremely tawdry when it occurred, but the story, arrayed in a computer printout, seemed pure, pristine, holy of love, full of idealism.[16] Mrs. Alonzo and Crane had been very intimate in the '20's. He would visit her, exhausted after nights of Cutty Sark and standing against the leather and sailor suits of waterfront bars. She had loved and cherished his memory for almost 60 years. Like a war widow ever grieving, Mrs. Alonzo wept daily for the sea-tossed bard, dead before his prime. Indeed before his prime, for was not Dante 40 when he began the *Comedy?*

She went down to the cellar each night to polish the Trunk, the report stated. That reminded me of a question I had neglected to ask the green grocer, and that was: "Why was the Trunk kept in the basement?" I could read between the lines of the report, and came up with the age-old answer of jealous spouse. Marta Alonzo probably married a guy who treated Crane's memory like some high school sweetheart whose picture he would have scissored from his wife's high school yearbook.

With the printout was a note from my pal in BrookHo In-

---

16. Of great use in preparing the report obviously, had been old N.Y.P.D. Red Squad reports of the '20's. Included in the BrookHo Int. report for instance, was a 1925 Red Squad Surveillance Memo in which Mrs. Alonzo was featured. Crane was a friend of Eugene O'Neill and of writers like Isidor Schneider, which was suspicious to the boys of the Red Sq. Crane apparently visited Mrs. Alonzo's house after a party in the Village attended by Paul Robeson, O'Neill, Edna St. V. Millay, and other suspected rubicund perps of the era.

telligence, reminding me that the Trunk was scheduled for a round-the-clock National Security watch beginning the following weekend. He himself didn't know what was up; he had heard that it was somehow involved with NASA, and that President Kennedy had personally ordered the watch.

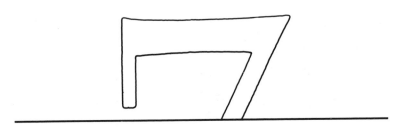

THE TRAP
AT THE TRUNK

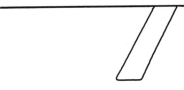

I felt I had only one recourse—I had to come out in the open. I had to game-plan both of them, Art Archives and Jack Barnes, to arrive at the Trunk that night at the same time. I had a scheme in mind for them. Barnes was already set to arrive at 12:30, and I knew Art was going also to sneak to BrookHo, but I didn't know when. So I called Art.

I told him that BrookHo Intelligence knew about the Trunk, and that the government was probably going to scarf it up. I could tell by his voice that he was as jittery as a poet before a reading. I had to be careful not to scare him away totally, so I told him about the National Security watch due in several days.

I told him the best time to "visit" the Trunk would be about 12:30, and the famous archivist agreed without a fleck of suspicion, although he put up a show of disinterest initially. "Uhh, I've made other arrangements this evening," he said. Sure, Art, sure, I thought to myself. Then he continued, "Are you gonna take a look at it also?" I had to laugh at Art's guileless transparency.

"No, Art," I said, "It's not my case. But *you* should probably take a real close look at it. It could easily be a fake. You may find it's just junk, and not want to bid on it. On the other hand, it may just be packed with national treasures."

I "molded his larceny," a term we use in the surveillance business, and webbed him into a plan I could control. It was so simple; I felt like I was in the middle ages selling a fake copy of the "casket Iliad" to a Bishop.[17]

"12:30?" he asked, as he hung up.

"Yeah, Art," I replied, "12:30. No need now to use your Alpine hat." I had fed him exact instructions to get into the basement, telling him I would see that it was unlocked, and clicked upon his startled silence.

It was the luck of a private investigator I guess, but as soon as I had finished my drenched stroll around Brooklyn Heights, and I was back in my car, the rain stopped, the sky cleared, presenting a beauteous dusk above the BrookHo waters. When I had driven across the Bridge, I had spotted a sign that read, *To Bridge Footwalk*. I wanted to see for myself what this fabled cable-webbed walkway could bear to a modern walker, so I parked again, and there strode I across to Manhattan, eyes ever trained to the surrounding sky for marauding muggers in stripped-down minicopters.

As I walked however, the fear faded, and the beauty enclosed me. I recalled Crane's letter about walking across with his friend Emil Opffer, "The ecstasy of walking hand in hand across the most beautiful bridge in the world, the cables enclosing us

---

17. *The Iliad*, born in a casket, which Alexander the Great carried on his expeditions, and a great rare book scam in the Middle Ages. (See *The Balzac Study Group*.)

and pulling us upward in such a dance as I have never walked
. . ." I did not feel the jubilance in quite such a fine tuning as
Crane, but it *was* pleasant. I could see what he meant, even with
the baleful air of N.Y. and the Manhattan skyline now resem-
bling a giant jawbone of square-edged fangs. It was the first few
minutes of peace I had known in fifteen months.

On the New York side, I walked through the large Barrel
Generation commune, a huge polymorphous array of living
quarters made entirely out of barrels. I admit I had a certain
prejudice against the Barrel Generation, based on newspaper
accounts. Walking among them, I must say my heart went out to
the Diogenes Liberation Squadron of Strolling Troubadors and
Muckrakers, who had moved their entire housing project from
the Bowery to the pediments of the Bridge in protest against the
city's plan to sell the superstructure to the City of Long Beach,
California. N.Y. politicians wanted to keep the roadway, and to
turn the air space above it into layers of housing and recreation.
If I were not so damn old as to have had trouble bending down
to enter a barrel, I would have moved right then into the Barrel
Generation complex while I finished my business in N.Y.

I guess a few sentences are in order, describing this heinous plan to ruin a great American symbol. The city had in mind
to turn the valuable air space into housing and recreational
strata, just as the London Bridge had once held elegant housing
in the 17th century, 'til it burned down. They wanted to create an
enclosed, all-weather roadway, air-tight so that exhaust not
sully the noses of those living above. Luxury co-ops would
adorn the bridgeway where now loom those beautiful stone
towers lifting the wingéd cables; above the co-ops would be a
huge shore-to-shore mall composed of tennis and swimming
clubs, minicopter landing areas, stores, fountains, a soccer field,
and an elevated marina (boats were to be lowered by cable to the
water below).

The figures were enormous, billions of rake-off were to be
raked. The attempts at fiscal chicanery by suppliers to the original Brooklyn Bridge in the 1870's and '80's were nothing compared to the slobber-mouthed thieves of now, igloos of coke-
bricks lining their nostrils, plotting at their smoke-hazed computer terminals.

110

Thankfully, millions of citizens became aroused. There were picket lines, and petitions signed by the strolling wooers of a half-century ago who spooned upon its walkway, remembering the Bridge when it was a tourist attraction rivaling the Grand Canyon; The Diogenes Liberation Squadron of Troubadors and Muckrakers used its Barrel City Commune as the staging grounds for protests, defying the torchmen to begin cutting the cables and removing the stones. A million signatures were collected by The 2000 Society[18] demanding the Bridge be renamed the Hart Crane Memorial Strollway (for Lovers and Thinkers), with all vehicles, save mass transit, banned.

Shortly thereafter, the superliberal Kennedy administration stepped in to quell the furor, and NASA announced its adoption of the Bridge as its official emblem. The resulting outcries against the bridge-killers grew so fierce, the speculators withdrew in grouchy self-justification back to computer card-strewn lairs, and the Brooklyn Bridge was saved.

+ # # + ¢ ¢ ¢ ¢ ¢ + # # + # # + # # + # # + # # + # # + ¢ ¢ ¢ ¢ ¢ + # #

I walked around BrookHo for several hours, visiting some of the saloons I imagined H.C. himself once had frequented, and then I returned to my car. There was a distinct "chip-rrrr," as we call it, a special sound of the surveillance chip indicating on both channels that Barnes and Art Archives were in motion, the signal strength such that I knew they were approaching, though still miles away. I had to move fast.

Mrs. Alonzo's house was dark, a clock striking twelve times from the library as I walked around the back, scaled a beautiful wrought-iron fence, and surv-shoed through the garden, the only sounds being a couple of squish-squishes as I oozed down the five or six wet steps to the basement door, to await the twain of shadows, the one beset with Hunger of Explication and Ownership and Moolah, and the other with Hunger of Catalogue and of Moolah.

---

18. An organization whose aim was the establishment of democratic socialist economic structure in the country by the end of the century. See *The Balzac Study Group* and *J'Accuse*.

I felt what Carter must have felt breaking the seals of Tut-Ankh-Amun's golden worm farm, as I vibro-keyed the door lock, and slipped into the basement. I donned special goggles and struck an infrared Surv-Flare.® I grew dizzy for a moment, standing at the bottom of the stairwell, on the very floor of the basement. Dizzy with triumph, for I had a little plan laid out for Mr. Archives and for Mr. Barnes. I was going to dart them with instantly-acting tranquilizers, as each should arrive, and then I was going to slump them in a pile on top of the Trunk and take photographs of them.

I had it totally planned. They'd pay dearly for the original negatives, or what they prayed to be the original negs. I'd use a blind-stopped mail box, and automatic telephoning equipment to handle the details, so that the operation would be totally untraceable to me. Even with Mrs. Alonzo asleep just on the other side of the ceiling boards, I could barely restrain my chortles, and cackles of conquest, in the damp, dank basement.

Then I saw the Trunk, standing upon an elevated platform of polished wood, as if it were on exhibit. How beauteous it was! It had a gently curving top, with a frame of narrow wooden bands that looked as if they had been sanded and polished only recently. On the sides were leather handles as well-oiled and free of decay as if the clock were turned back to 1924. On the top, between the bands of polished wood, were silver-colored panels stamped with what could have been the shapes of chicory blossoms, thin long petals with blunted saw-toothed tips.

I could see that the Trunk was not locked, and my heart ached seeing a small dusting cloth on a nearby footstool where Mrs. Alonzo must have sat in meditation but hours ago. I hungered to see within it, this Trunk that had become a symbol to me, of things just and honorable, as the Bridge must have been to Crane; his the Figure of Outer, mine the Figure of Inner.

I opened the lid, and began to rummage. It was obvious if it were real, that here was a treasure! With the Crane boom now occurring in American letters, the value of the Trunk was obviously in the high five-figures at the least. Even magazines like *Gorp* and *Urge* were jumping aboard the schooner. *Gorp*, for instance, had hired a computer to unravel the intricacies of *The*

Bridge, and had determined that it was more complicated than any other poem in history; the so-called Exegesis Printout, when paginated, came in at 918 pages.

I did not get to see much: a bundle of letters, the top of which I could see postmarked the spring of 1930; some books, a folio of papers with typing and voluminous corrections, and some clothing. I was just opening what appeared to be a Crane diary, when I heard feet walking the planks outside.

I glanced at my watch—it was much too early for Archives and Barnes to be arriving. I could blow my career if the grocer or Mrs. Alonzo should find me lurking by the Trunk. I monitored the surveillance chip frequencies for both of them, but by the humming and rrrr-ing of the chips I could tell they were in motion and some miles in the distance.

Oh no! Someone was opening the door to the basement! I lit a Surv-Flare® sufficient to illuminate the entire basement, and donned my goggles. I saw in the gloom the dim outline of a human. And then, I heard a squeak that repeated itself again and again. It was, as I saw when it passed the furnace, a padded dolly. And the human . . . why, it was . . . it was . . .

Milton Rosé! I must confess an instant urge to stun-dart Rosé, and to slump him over the Trunk along with the others, and photograph the tableau. *Gorp* or *Urge* might have paid me ten grand for a snap of their favorite smear-target unconscious at a crime scene. I saw at once they'd accuse him of preparing to glue priceless National Heritage literary relics onto a fourth class painting, just as they felt he had done when he attached Beethoven's composition desk to a destruction/construction a few months ago.

My mind naturally drifted, even in this tight situation, to the subject of mon, since I was just then plunging into a real estate project, The Golden Bard Retirement Colony, so I chuckled, inwardly and freely, over the thought that *Gorp* or *Urge* might provide me with a substantial portion of my share of the down payment.

Then I wavered, thinking wildly. First of all, I respect a mind permanently creative, and I knew first hand that Rosé, just

113

from the few hours my friend and I had surv-chipped him from the SoHo roof garden, was as creative in his private life as anyone alive. Why was he galumphing and clanking loudly in the basement? What didn't I know? Then, I could swear I saw a drool of happiness that shadowed down through the lux of the Surv-Flare® and spread silently upon the polished curved Trunk top. He was even humming softly, something that sounded like the Beethoven/Schiller *Ode to Joy*.

Did Rosé have legal claim to the trunk? If I tranq-darted a person removing his own property, I could find myself in the redwood tub of boiling felony for sure. Because, how could a world-class artist like Rosé put something like Hart Crane's trunk into one of his destruction/constructions if he didn't own it, given the controversy surrounding his career? And I was certain, as I lurked there in the shadows, that Rosé was not engaging in a larcenous form of literary collecting. He just didn't need the mon.

So, I waited; perhaps there were accomplices. He glanced at his watch, as if he too knew Art and Barnes were due at the pumpkin hour. He hoisted the Trunk upon the dolly, making considerable noise I must say, and vanished out the door. As he wheeled it through the rear courtyard, I could swear he whispered something that sounded like, "Good flight, O Mystic Lozenge!"

You never can tell, with creative people. I thought, well, maybe he was speaking to the Trunk that way, calling it "Mystic Lozenge," perhaps as if it were something to soothe the Divine Throat of Art. Then, realizing my chumphood, I figured out he had said, "Good night, Mrs. Alonzo," trundling the Trunk past her window.

o o o   o o o   o o o   o o o   o o o   o o o   o o o   o o o   o o o   o o o   o o o   o o o   o o o   o o

I left. I don't know to this day what happened to Art and Jack when they arrived. I should have left them a note—"Art and Jack, don't bother," but I felt it would have compromised my position. Later I learned that removing it by stealth had been part of the deal with Mrs. Alonzo. Rosé wanted the project totally wrapped up before *Gorp* or *Urge* sniffed a case. It wasn't for several days after the midnight in Mrs. Alonzo's basement that I had a chance to plant surveillance chips on Rosé.

Thereafter I monitored his telephone conversations with NASA officials in Huntsville, Alabama as they huddled over maps for possible locations on the surface of Mars for the secreting of the Trunk. Rosé's voice was weak with emotion when they at last located a suitable cavelike niche in the Martian mountains in which to hid the trunk. "This will be more alluring than the Inca gold!" Milton shouted. "The Ultimate Treasure Hunt! And how many thereby, in preparing for the hunt, will be turned on to Crane's poetry for the first time!" His eyes closed ecstatically, picturing rich literati, using back-hoes and cranes, prying boulders from crevice lips for hundreds of years.

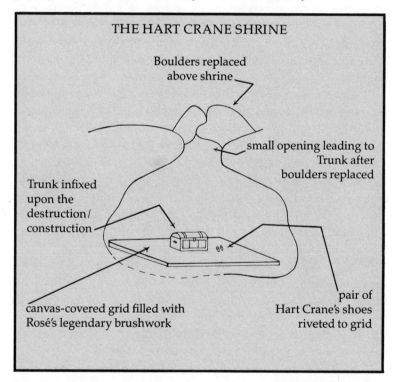

THE HART CRANE SHRINE

Boulders replaced above shrine

small opening leading to Trunk after boulders replaced

Trunk infixed upon the destruction/construction

canvas-covered grid filled with Rosé's legendary brushwork

pair of Hart Crane's shoes riveted to grid

To insure the greatest treasure hunt of all time, he knew it was necessary to work closely with the Kennedy administration and NASA. At the same time, he was concerned that his *own name* not get lost in all this hubbub, because he knew that after several centuries, long after his last body-part operation had failed and he was living with the worms, his name might become disassociated from the project. So, Milton began plans at once for a deathless destruction/construction, with The Trunk as its main component, and his name stenciled circumspectly in Ironword® across Trunk slats.

With most of his heart, Rosé prayed for a media turn-around in his favor. He looked forward to the week when the friendly covers of both *Gorp* and *Urge* would be devoted to The Crane Shrine. It was difficult to restrain a tear, so great was the thought of forgiveness from the weeklies.

Speaking of forgiveness, we can forgive Milton for more mundane considerations also, pertaining to strolls down cash cache creek. He pictured a Crane fashion boom. "Think of it!" he shouted, "There'll be Hart Crane haircuts! Male boutiques featuring Crane-wear! Maybe we can get J'Accuse to invent a dance called *The H.C.!*"

I checked around and learned that Rosé had wanted first to hide the Trunk aboard an orbiting satellite, but the Intelligence Community, still going strong, even stronger, after all these years, was afraid that drug-weakened Barfists looking for the trunk of a poet would begin boarding military satellites. They threatened Rosé with a very graphic C.T., or Conceptual Threat, and he planned elsewhere for a hiding place very quickly. He himself was afraid that someday, zzzzzt, Hart Crane's Trunk would fall sizzling like a fragment of literary tempura into the Earth's atmosphere, should it be hidden on a satellite.

My heart went out to Rosé and his vision of *The Bridge* as an ethical symbol of the outer space movement. The story of Crane's trunk had everything. It had love, a widow grieving 60 years for a bard; it had devotion, it had stealth and cunning, it had High Creativity. Ahhh, I was glad I had come to N.Y. for the convention of the American Society of Archivists!!!

I never found out exactly what it was that had hipped Rosé to the Trunk in the first place. A famous guy like that has access to data. He probably overheard it in a literary saloon. What I admired most was that Rosé had hatched the project in a single afternoon and evening. That very night he had contacted NASA, gotten tentative approval and had checked in with the White House. This was two days *before* he approached and closed down the deal with Mrs. Alonzo, so confident was the creator of his project.

One thing was certain—the search for Hart Crane's Trunk would pique human curiosity for centuries. With the bridge at last the symbol of American endeavor, emblazoned on NASA's orbiting farms, on its posters and stationary, truly the nation had found a worthy configuration of the Synapse of Outward Bound. And someday the Trunk, embedded in its destruction/ construction and dedicated to the love of Marta Alonzo, would be found. For its home, it would reside on Mars permanently, in the Hart Crane Museum, the first museum for the Sailors of Outer Space. Art and Love, hand in hand by the wires of the bridge.

PART THREE
THE BALZAC
STUDY GROUP

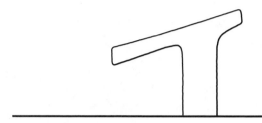

THE YEARS
OF BARDIATRICS

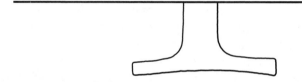

Ione Appleton began it. Ione Appleton had become one of America's best known poets during her mid-twenties, and thus could tour the entire bardic spectrum, from the biggest and most prestigious citadels of learning to the tiniest of junior colleges in the canebrakes of culture. It was a tail/snake/mouth scene—the fame begat the touring, and touring fame. She had been invited to give a solo reading at the St. Mark's Church when she was only 24—an honor that Homer himself might not have been granted. The age of flambancy is still very much upon us, and the candle in Ione's mouth was color-coded to the candle in her axillae as well as to the candles in her lower sections. All tallowed tips brightly burned.

Ione had stumbled upon a secret when she was lowly graduate student at Columbia. The Secret of the Apothegm. She had wondered as a child why it is that modern poets are so very rarely quoted in the course of conversation, article, or argument. Of course there was the so-called "gibberish factor," but that alone did not explain it. Ione discovered the reason one night as she slaved to complete her first book. The mimeograph machine was waiting patiently, and a just-banked NEA Grant was waiting too, held by the publisher, to pay for printing, staples, paper, mailing, and a publication party at Scythia. The reason was

◯ LACK OF APOTHEGMS ◯

There in her apartment, at 3 a.m., she made a vow whose fulfillment sent her name upon the bardic hoardings of recent poetic history. "I will be the most quoted bard since Pope!" she shrieked. "Apothegms! Apothegms! Apothegms!"

And even that very night, Ione began her Apothegm Notebook, into which she poured in the coming years some 17,224 ideas for the construction of sententious metrical maxims. She would take newspaper articles and rewrite them into verse, hoping to extract a fitting apothegmic sentence or two. In no time at all, her verse brimmed with ponderous, almost Biblical, but at the same time space-age, apothegms, metrically complex, and eminently quotable.

Yea, Ione Appleton was brilliant, with a bulging forehead like a painting of Beethoven, and the inspiration of reams of verse. She was tall and strong, full-figured, with long Egyptian fingers suitable to serve as sculptor's models for arms-&-hands hanging out of the Sun Disc, and a long flat aircraft carrier stomach considered a divine alluvium upon which grad students by the hundreds in obscure colleges everywhere desired to lie or lick supine.

Ione had barded around for nearly a decade, a practitioner of what might be termed *slash-&-burn bardiatrics*. Slash-&-burn bards moved from college to college, teaching and reading for a day, a week, a month, a term, and at most a year or two, after which they perforce moved onward. Ione developed it into a High Endeavor. Her ten-year slash-&-burn bardiatrics map looked something like this:

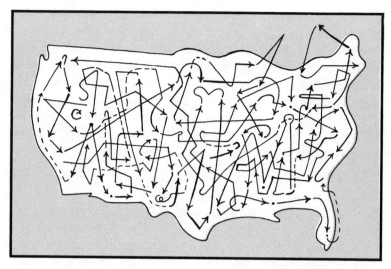

One can isolate fairly easily the eleven main elements of slash-&-burn bardiatrics:

1. *Stage presence*—it has to be excellent. When a poem goes out of focus in a reading due to micro-sleep, hallucination, or seizure of mental filing cabinets, the bard has to be able to ad-lib a flowing continuum 'til the text of the poem comes back into focus. The bard must, when the inner energy of the poem requires it, become a one-person ballet company, able to leap descriptively, to swoop low to the floor, to pace and twirl.

2. *Ability to emote.* Never must the voice drop intensity, except as part of a cunning stage plan. The voice will resonate with such intensity, it will often border on the trough of flip-out. The ability to cry on command of the text is important. The bard will be seen on occasion to quiver, and will grasp the mike stand to keep from falling in moments of abandon. Hysteria is not forbidden, *temporary* hysteria, to be as crisply turned on and off as a faucet.

3. *Identification with student rebels.* Were there still student rebels?—you ask. They came back by the millions, confounding all predictions, and Ione would get in close, without getting so close as ever to become the target of a grand jury. She could

speed-read student manuscripts, spotting weaknesses in a non-hurtful way, and encouraging strengths. She had many friends at N.Y. publishing houses, and when she located good writers she obtained contracts for their books. Her touch at landing gigs for new writers made her legend ever more secure. She was willing to discuss a manuscript even in bed, and many a young Apollo or Polyhymnia who approached her swaying Mayan hammock made sure, just in case, his or her unpublished novel were outside in the car.

4. *To write a continuous stream of poetry and stories.* "God, how does she do it?" is what she wanted on everybody's lips. She held regular, but mysterious, writing sessions about which she let slip details to her students. Her writing period was divided into five parts: during the early, fresh minutes she wrote her poetry; then she shifted briefly to notes for short stories; then she leaped to her diaries; then to letters; and last, in the minutes before concluding her writing period, she tossed off a review or an article for the *Times*, or for *Lives of the Poets*.

5. *To set up, and maintain in years thereafter, excellent relations with local press wherever she should bard.*

6. *To keep stature within the community of poets:*
    i. always in the back of the mind that call from Stockholm.
    ii. always attempting to become a poets' poet, but if the poets' poet role is denied, to know *ALL* gossip about approximately 800 poets. If you know in depth 500 recent and juicy particles of info about each of the top 800 poets, then that's a treasury for cocktail parties and faculty receptions, of 400,000 separate babble-units. Now, let's say there are 30 seconds to a babble-unit; therefore you've got over 333 hours of new gossip at any one time to impart to a listening ring of scholars.

7. *To juggle a hundred intense, jealous, querulous, demanding lovers in 50 towns and cities.*

8. *To obtain a reputation as instant mediator in marital disputes in far-flung English departments.* Ione might wind up debriefing a

heartbroken spouse as early in a visit as waiting for the luggage at Canebrake Muni Airport.

9. *To be punctual always, however wasted.* Ione would attend some total trash-out party, and she'd amaze the students, some of whom would place wagers on whether she'd make it to class. She might have partied all night drinking those devastating Tequila Leaf-Lashes (tequila, nutmeg, coca leaf wine and crushed ice) with her students, and lo! the rubicund wahwah pedal of dawn might have seen her partying still, and the class might all leave the party together, with Ione stumbling among them, to go directly to the lecture room. She would disappear, perhaps retching, into the bathroom, the stains of license bemottling her dress; yet, in maybe ten minutes, she would emerge, smiling, hair combed, eyes clear, firm-voiced, not a stain anywhere on her perfect attire, looking like a million dollars, scanning her lecture notes, ready to begin. Needless to say, practicioners of slash-&-burn bardiatrics liked to have their lectures scheduled in the mid-afternoon, to avoid the problem of the a.m. lecture hall pour-in.

10. *To develop "Real Estate"*—which in the parlance of bardiatrics, means to locate lots of fresh unburned-down colleges at which briefly to teach or to read. At this, Ione was matchless, writing on the average some 25 letters a week to far-flung schools.

11. *To maintain an outer glaze of rectitude:* to be solemn, to sit through boring banquets nodding, laughing and applauding at the exactly appropriate moments. That is, no matter how profligate, to appear substantial, and to face with dignity whatever outrageous accusation regarding one's deportment might filter down from administrative officials.

thththththththththththththththththththththththththththththththththththththththth

Obedience to these eleven precepts of bardiatrics kept Ione Appleton on the road for ten years.

It had not been her intention to go the slash-&-burn route, but whatever she did, she seemed to fall into controversy. Controversy is fine in this country, as long as you do not get political. So many professors of English, men and women, fell in love with Ione, and so many wanted to lie "supine on the floor of a narrow canoe" with her, as it were, that she held therefore a natural buffer of protectors.

But, for every person friendly to her, there were two that were opposed. We do not have here time to go into the incidents which made her career so scandalous, other than to say they were nothing more or less than common scandals to which bards have always been prone, such as: demanding to read her latest verse at somber academic parties, thus spoiling the mood; passing out in airplanes (she being the pilot and the Creative Writing faculty being the passengers); alleged public fornication; helping fellow bards to escape mental hospitals; booking readings the same night in seven cities; urging the bombing of banks; fucking her students; secretly videotaping clandestine affairs with university chancellors; cooperating with leftist secret societies; and affecting on occasion an exaggerated Christianity while bragging of bisexuality.

One big advantage of slash-&-burn was that Ione didn't have to waste time drooling on those in power for reappointment. Even so, it was always a cruel blow at the end of a school year when she learned she would not be rehired.

If her earlier problems were cultural, her later problems were political. She became radicalized. She was inspired in part by Michael Harrington and the Democratic Socialist Organizing Committee, and in part by the Diogenes Liberation Squadron of Strolling Troubadors and Muckrakers. From campus to campus, and town to town, Ione had observed the intense struggles going on for municipal power, for rent control, for food without profit, for universal health care, yet she was struck by the lack of national vision, of national nexus and interlinkage among those local groups.

She brought her politics more and more into her poetry and into her stage raps.

Although there were many, many political and cultural conservatives where she read and taught, they seemed more than pleased for five or six years at the gossip and spectacle provided by what they viewed as a silly, dronesome Byroness burning brightly. No doubt someday she would provide them with a marvelous suicide or flame-out, with book contracts aplenty thereafter for biographers, movie scripts on her life story, jobs editing her diaries, etc. When however, her new book, *Sonnets of Nationalization,* sold 100,000 copies (her average audience was 2000 per reading and those who know the size of normal poesy crowds will appreciate that amazing figure) conservatives rose against her, mumbling to the effect that human tragedy based on economic calamity would be lost to literature in a socialist world.

As if from nowhere, a flock of enemies began to claw her image. Conservatives sneered at her as a "compulsive loner," and brought up the old charge of homewrecker and enemy of the family unit, merely because a couple of lecherous Petrarch scholars had dropped everything and chased her around the continent. Certain Creative Writing instructors joined in, spreading exaggerated tales about her on the English Department WATS-line bard-gossip nexus. In general, there was a backlash against the emblem of the Ancient Greek Lyre—that poets should sing and perform. Barding-around bards were suddenly getting trashed in the news magazines. The sturdy apostles of dryasdust somber recitations shorn of unnecessary motion and theatrics pushed their case in intellectual quarterlies, using Ione's performances as the basis of their critiques. Little mind that her poetry was on the lips of an entire generation.

Ione put up a grand fight against this calumny, but she was little used to savage fray, and had always relied on personal friendship and charisma to melt away the fences of fuddy-duddy. She staked her case on gnosticism—that words, apt and melic and beauteous, would carry the day. And she might have won, except for several disastrous relationships with men carried out in the ninth and tenth years of her cycle of slash-&-burn.

Ione owned a cane, an exact replica of the thick turquoise-and-gold headed stick once owned by Honoré de Balzac himself; hers was of elmwood, with five-petal'd clusters of the stone around the top. When her career was at its summit, her cane seemed often as famous as she. It inspired a publication called *Ione's Cane,* a very successful poetry magazine in the government-funded White Blizzard during the century's final quarter. No one, however, connected her famous cane with Balzac's, not even any of the 1000's of professors and students of literature with whom she flocked. That single fact may have provided the burning coal in the ideational fennel stalk that later would inflame as the Balzac Study Group.

The cane was not just an adornment, for Ione was crippled. The circumstances of her crippling engulfed her in its own fame—a helicopter accident while hovering with her lover—a rock star named Billie Brigham—at dawn above Machu Picchu, stoned on Tequila Leaf-Lash, having in mind to clink groins just as the rubeous fingers of the sun were shining on the temple stone below. All should have been well, with the whopa-whopa-whopa of the copter rotor blades serving as sort of a rhythm instrument behind the fucking, except that Billie Brigham, normally so precise as the lead singer for Dark Pelt, nudged the stick, and the copter banked precipitously down upon the cliffs where he died. Ione Appleton's tragedy-tinged book, *Machu Picchu Sonnets,* sold so many copies that it qualified for insertion within the bestseller box in the Sunday *Times*, but since it wasn't fiction, and it wasn't "general," a third category box, "Metrics and Verse," had to be installed for the first time.

Her affair with Billie Brigham was the first of the disastrous relationships that led to her burnout. His rock group, Dark Pelt, was often in trouble with the law, and wrote some of their finest songs in prison. Dark Pelt members had served federal sentences for attempting, apparently as a publicity stunt for an album, to operate on the noses of Mt. Rushmore with an airborne high-energy laser knife stolen from the Air Force. The group later testified it was attempting to carve nasal passages in the presidential visages in order to blow "spirit coke" into them with an industrial vacuum cleaner dangling from a 'copter. It was a combination religious rite, publicity stunt, and album cover shooting session.

While there had never been any evidence to connect Ione

Appleton with the infamous Mt. Rushmore laser caper, university wags happily spread the rumor that she was staying with the band at a nearby motel in Rapid City, South Dakota at the time of the incident. Ione considered it beneath her to disclaim such a rumor; a mistake, since it fueled the campaign against her.

Not many months after the death of Billie Brigham, Ione once again embarked upon an ill-starred relationship. Ione had been given a singular honor by the Kennedy administration, to recite a poem at the White House banquet honoring the nation's first left/liberal head of the United Intelligence Bureau (successor to the defunct CIA). It was on the dais that she met a powerful bureaucrat in the field of Government Grants to Writers, one Mortimer Magoux. Magoux fell topsy-turvy in love with Ione. After Billie Brigham, Ione seemed ripe to fall into the clutches of someone as "safe" as Mortimer Magoux, and as powerful, for Magoux reigned supreme over 155 million dollars a year in gov't poesy-dole. Sycophants at parties would have given him an oral pedicure, had he merely nodded to his tarsals.

Ione accepted his love, but steadfastly refused to give up touring for a Georgetown townhouse and a vision of matrimony she had forgotten existed. So strong was his love that for a few months Mortimer Magoux joined her on the road. This forced him into the role of a "bardiatrics beau," a role he found most distasteful, since it gave rise to giggling anecdotes, and eroded his power as king of bard-mon. As he accompanied her from town to town, he nearly went insane with jealousy encountering the gaping flies of former flings awaiting Ione at the airports. "No more!" he finally cried.

But Ione refused again to leave her career, and Magoux sulked back to Georgetown, nursing hatred and images of chop-up where love alone had dwelled.

While the evidence is scant, many believe this august gentleman provoked a conspiracy, than which none is more heinous in the annals of bardiatrics. He provoked a Bardiatrics Dry-Up. That is, he intervened in Ione's career with purse-string power, and those on the bard circuit, themselves in need of a continuum of grants, gave sway. Her enemies, those wastrels of the WATS-line, began circulating carefully orchestrated rumors of a most baleful kind, whether for a poet, a novelist, a baseball player, or an intelligence agent: the taunt that she was "burnt-out." Shame of shame, "She hasn't written anything for *months*," the WATS-line wastrels sneered.

Almost immediately Ione began to encounter problems getting bookings—especially of the large fee variety, and her Grants-flow, which she had always used to pay her taxes, came to a dry gulch. She was soon stuck on the $100-a-night circuit, until that too was burned from beneath her. She struggled on-ward, enduring the Praise-the-Bard-and-Pass-the-Hat coffee house circuit, with its free orzatas and club managers trying to disrobe her in the washroom.

All at once she seemed to snap. She saw conspiracies against her where there were none. Although she had ample clues as to the culprits, she reserved much of her anger, even malice, for her true friends. She would stay awake two or three days at a time, lining her nasal igloo with stay-awake bricks, in order to remain on top of the situation, as if she still had to handle the mountain of paperwork, contracts, and itinerary de-tails of a famous poet on the road. The igloo of coke-bricks only increased her paranoia.

She drank more than ever. Her liver began to ache and to outline itself with throbbing fire. At readings she hurled insults at her audiences, always a sign of burnout. Her letters became chaotic and desperate when the opportunities for readings completely ceased. As with many conspiracies, the scope, the horridness, and the intensity of Magoux' evil-do did not be-come fully known until long after Ione had organized the Balzac Study Group. Her revenge, of course, which took years to ful-fill, was sweet indeed, and Mortimer Magoux, the reader should know, is now lucky he can get a job dicing tofu at the Spring Street Restaurant.

Nevertheless, Ione Appleton had to endure years of need-less suffering. There was nothing else she could do, so she re-tired quietly to her apartment on St. Mark's Place, determined to save her liver and to fight off the encroachments of the Worm Farm.

When she retired, Ione was a figure of great, burnt-out elegance on St. Mark's. She was nevertheless quite ashamed. She felt as if a whispering voice of reproach followed her down the street taunting her. As her turquoise-headed cane would plink the sidewalk, she could swear she heard a sound-mix of "Plink!" "Burnt-out!" "Plink!" "Burnt-out!" "Plink!" "Burnt-out!" "Pl . . . . ."

She was what is called by wags a "sniff-leper," with nasal passage and sinuses so ravaged by the Leaf of Lust that she was in need of some sort of medical nose-cane in addition to the Balzacian replica with which she plinked down the street. And her difficult breathing, especially on a rainy day, augmented the "Plink!" "Burnt-out!" sequence, creating "Plink!" "Snerk!" "Burnt-out!" "Plink!" "Snork!" "Burnt-out!" and so forth.

She stopped writing verse. She made much of her silence, as if the sections of silence were to be catalogued among her works. To be sure, she continued to maintain a nucleus of fans who viewed her as the finest writer of the century. She basked in the attention, ever the salve of the citizen with crashed career, keeping up correspondence with 200 or more of them, groin-gonging the best when paths should cross.

Her fortunes seemed irrevocably reversed. Nary a Grant loomed on the horizon, and when she bothered to apply she barely spent five minutes scribbling the application forms. She became the object of whispered anecdote, sometimes right in front of her, at the few parties she attended, and became the object of the hideous phenomenon known as "snicker-pity." God forbid you should stop writing for one second!

So when humans sauntered up to Ione at parties, and mumbled something that sounded like "Wha'ya-intah," and then departed with almost audible snickers, it was not the password of a secret society. It was rather the question, "heh heh, muh fuh, perchance art 'ou broken up upon the breakers of burnout in your career—snicker, snicker?"

Ahh, what writer has not had a nightmare about such a question? And to have to look down to the floor, dejected, circles of minus-signs surrounding your shoes like Fairy Rings, and you reply, voice hollow like a robot in an early sci-fi movie,

"Nothing. That's right. I haven't written anything for six weeks."

Thereupon, with a smile that conveys, "Ha, I thought so!" the brother or sister of the typewriter throws you out of sight, and walks away to pay attention to more worthy, more productive sorts, leaving you waist-deep in the cinders of failure.

After almost a year of retirement, Ione seemed destined for that horrible fate of the totally cashless bard: begging liberals for food money. Not so. When her last slash-&-burn check was gone, Ione hobbled on her canne de Monsieur de Balzac to the subway uptown where she obtained employment with a publisher. By so doing, she violated the POETS' SACRED OATH OF PREFERENCE:

> *"Hot Oil in the Eyes, O Lord of Bards,*
> *Bamboo beneath the Nails,*
> *Funnels of Hot Lead to Limn the Colon's Contours,*
> *Rather than to Work for Pay not Parlayed from Poesie!"*

Not only did Ione violate the POETS' SACRED OATH, but she actually enjoyed the months she spent with the publisher. She saved some cash, and rented a storefront on St. Mark's Place, near Avenue A, where she cleared a little room in the front, and lived in the back, designing what she called her "sculpted mammal sheathings," that is, a highly original line of dancing gowns, which were snapped up expensively by the clan of lusty damozels who, century after century, follow the ikon of torrid Terpsichore.

She settled into a pleasant routine, with hard work erasing her angst-strained face. She slowly restored her health, removing the igloo from her nasal passage, turning off the lightbulb inside her liver, and entertaining the tight circle of friends and fans that would pilgrimage to Avenue A to see her.

THE
DUCT TAPE
BOUTIQUE

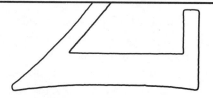

Ione's shop was located in one of those unique buildings with central steps upon an iron stairwell leading up to apartments. On each side of the stairwelling there was a separate small set of stairs leading down to two small stores, their entrances a few feet below the sidewalk. The steps were of worn stone, troughed with 90 years of falling feet, slomp! slomp! slomp!, of the burdened walking upward, downward, laden with laundry or groceries or books. One of these stores set below street level was the Duct Tape Boutique.

The Duct Tape Boutique? Yes indeed, the energy and brilliance with which she had conducted her ten years of bardiatrics, Ione applied to her store, and not much time passed before she broke new ground on the fashion scene, inventing a style of clothing combining haute couture with a hard practicality that made her little front room one of the most desirable showrooms in North America. To understand her success, we must first discuss a miracle.

Of all the alleged miracles of our era, one of the most important, but sadly neglected, is the miracle of the modern tape. Tapes exist which will help heal wounds, as well as others which instantly will seal the spewing of broken winter pipes frozen in the mountains and thawed beneath a butane torch some minus-20 morn. Tapes exist for emergency repairs of spacecraft in orbit.

Ione marveled at the miracle of tapes, and brought it to bear on modern attire. The result: Duct Tape Haute Couture. She chose the low-gloss silver-gray duct tape deliberately, as an implied philosophical statement. She could have just as well chosen to work with high-gloss gold tapes, or tapes of real silver, platinum, or those with all the colors of the rainbow.

In choosing duct tape, invented for use on heating ducts, critics accused her of dabbling in the old Marie Antoinette-dressed-up-as-shepherdess scam. Ione persisted, and won the market because of her skills as a collagist of abstract ribbings of duct tape arranged upon the edges of beauteous patches of cloth. The effect of her duct tape strips upon diaphanous silk, antique Italian needlepoint, and Flemish bobbin lace, some as old as 200 years, was as of a collage by Braque or Juan Gris.

In addition, the wealthy liked that combination of exclusivity that at the same time was earthy. By that we mean the attraction of "mini-ouch," the risky thrill, dearer somehow to the bemoneyed, of an occasional ouch of a nipple or of a crotch hair being grabbed by the gluey underside of a duct tape gown where the lace had permissively pulled away while they were dancing say, to J'Accuse's latest single, *The H.C.*, named after the poet Hart Crane, whose name of late had become a household word. Such is the ouch of life, relished in measure by the assured.

Ione charged as much as 2500 dollars for her formal duct

tape gowns, but her close friends enjoyed discounts amounting to as much as 97 percent. She performed valuable services *pro bono publico* also, as when she outfitted the *People's Choir* division of the Diogenes Liberation Squadron of Strolling Troubadors and Muckrakers with their famous all-weather Duct Tape Capes.[1] To see them swooshing upon Senate hearings to sing their 55-voice Anthems of Investigation, pulling their capes apart to reveal their famous Scrolls of Indictment, from which they'd sing, was a majestic sight.

After costume departments of museums began purchasing samples of Ione's gowns for their permanent collections, Bloomingdale's paid the Duct Tape Boutique its highest compliment by marketing a line of Duct Tape Apparel, including in addition to gowns and capes, a brilliant booty-garnering line of "boudoir canopies," offering the ultimate in leisurely dalliance to customers who could look up during moments of pleasure and see above them a complex web of tape and lace and shiny jewels and diaphanous silks. The situation became excessive when chains of discount stores in the midwest marketed duct tape halters and duct tape ski jackets and duct tape/denim aprons and duct tape/vinyl auto seat covers, and the like.

Ione did not rest with duct tape triumph, but marched back into ancient history to retrieve a cosmetic idea that was to change the appearance of the American head for decades to

---

1. Duct Tape Capes. Another fashion trendsetter; raincapes made of duct tape and plastic trash bags. The capes Ione made for the Diogenes Liberation Squadron of Strolling Troubadors and Muckrakers were veritable tents, with inside pouches for surveillance equipment and walkie-talkies. When public officials spotted from their haughty windows the close order march of the Diogenes Liberation Squadron in their wildly colorful hooded Duct Tape Capes, they would quail with belching malaise. Not long after Ione invented the duct tape/trash bag cape, trash bags began being manufactured in a variety of bright colors, and like the printed flour sacks of old, were soon being sold with printed designs. The two-dollar duct tape and garbage bag formal, "haute garbage gowns" they were dubbed, became a subject of great odium to small town formal shops, as haute garbage gowns were worn by millions at proms and homecoming dances across the land.

come. By this we mean the ancient Egyptian Festal Cone, and Festal Noggin-bund.®

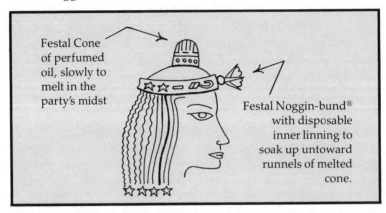

Festal Cone of perfumed oil, slowly to melt in the party's midst

Festal Noggin-bund® with disposable inner linning to soak up untoward runnels of melted cone.

In ancient Egypt, women at banquets and parties would wear atop their heads, directly upon the coiffure, what is called in the textbooks a "Festal Cone." The cone consisted of a shaped vertical elongation of perfumed mush-gush, sometimes with colored stripes running perpendicularly down from the summit of the cone to the hair. The Festal Cone sometimes bore striations, giving it in modern terms the look of the top of a wavy-edged Dairy Queen cone. This ancient mush-gush of sweetened oil slowly melted during the party, and spread in a luxurious stream upon the head and shoulders, oiling the skin, and even perfuming the upper attire.

Ione began to experiment with various greases and perfumes, until she at last developed a Festal Cone that would not melt until a temperature suitably above the normal body temperature was reached. She knew that men would be very interested also in Festal Cones, so she marketed a slightly smaller version for them, so that taller males wearing it on their heads through doorways might not leave untoward besmirchings of attar of opium blossom gush on the upper door frames.

Ione performed a noble service to her country, and earned at least a cluster of footnotes in its textbooks, by helping America overcome its oleophobia, or Fear of Gush.* Fear of Gush had

---

* Gush—the "u" pronounced as "oo" in foot.

been the major barrier to surmount in marketing the Festal Cones. Fear of Gush, a product perhaps of an earlier pilgrim/ puritan heritage, was nothing when compared to Fear of Gush Oozing in an Everwidening Path of Perfumed Paste Out Over the Top of a Freshly Shampooed Hair Style at the Formal Dinner Party! The answer of course was to make it a fad, so Ione herself began to wear Festal Cones at appropriate haute couture festivities, cutting a fine figure in a duct tape/trash bag cape and a duct tape/16th century lace gown, while people clustered about her marveling at the gracefully melting cone of cold cream, axle grease, myrrh, acacia sap, and distillate of lotus. Ione invented a hair style to be worn beneath the Cone, i.e., dread locks with tiny platinum stars on the lock-tips gleaming with solar-powered glow lights.

It did not take very many parties before the fad caught on, and the Duct Tape Boutique was selling Festal Cones hot-cakishly, and the country took a big leap toward the grand day of the eradication of oleophobia.

Ione also marketed a Disco-Cone® that melted at a much higher temperature, and did not wobble out of shape or fling drops centrifugally as the wearer twirled upon the torrid floors. Shampoo manufacturers went berserk with happiness—they owed plenty to Ione, for if you get your hair beglopped like a candle-dripped beatnik chianti bottle, out will come the shampoo in the shower the moment you get home.

Just three months after Ione's cones astounded the marketplace, she quietly sold the rights to a leading cosmetics manufacturer for a guaranteed 55 grand a year royalty for fifteen years. A more cunning routine had never been worked by an inventor. The company became convinced that Ione had developed a secret formula. An entire laboratory was assigned to examine her cones in order to determine the mystery components, and thus to avoid royalties. The lab failed. Ione said nothing, only agreeing during the negotiations that once the contract were signed, and the initial royalty prepaid, she would provide the formula. How shocking it was then when after she had cashed the first royalty check and had 55 little pieces o' green in her pocket with Grover Cleveland on them, she handed over a photocopied 1921 article from the *Journal of the Royal Egyptian Exploration Society,* suggesting the components of the Festal Cones, to which she had merely added her own trial-and-error discoveries, to wit, cold cream and axle grease.

THE CREATION
OF THE
BALZAC STUDY GROUP

The success of the boutique and of the Disco-Cones® allowed Ione a surfeit of free time during which she could brood on the past, and speculate about the future. She felt such blissful healing from her labors, and from the tender ministrations of her friends, that she looked longingly in the mornings at her typewriter, its metal cover powdered white with incinerator fallout, and near it the neat ream of cotton bond that had lain beneath the same mantle of grayness for almost a year.

Thus healed, she could turn again to her poetry. Since her burnout, she had not been able even to touch the binders and boxes containing her work. Now, it seemed as if from a vantage point on Mars she were reading the notes of a stranger, as she spiffled through her verse, much of which she had forgotten, and, coming upon it as if unknown, she was astounded with the power and worth of it. "They are my *Bridge*, my *Four Quartets*, my *Iliad*, my *Beowulf*," she wrote in her diary one night. She resolved that very moment to gather all her poems together and to polish the past. She discovered new works never before transcribed from notebooks, from diaries, and some on the flyleaves of books and on ten-year-old airline ticket holders. Altogether the poems were sufficient to put together a six-volume edition of her works, which she titled: *The Years of Bardiatrics, Vols. I-VI.*

She searched hard for a publisher, a task most difficult, the reader can guess, especially if anyone might have ever tried to place among nervous editors worried about the censure of the conglomerates who own most of the publishing houses, a six-volume collection of verse.

The chore was made even more complicated by Ione's insistence on a "guaranteed availability" contract. A Guaranteed Availability contract, very important to the modern poet, is one in which the publisher promises to keep the book in circulation for fifteen years. After many rejections, Ione Appleton located a publisher, and she was then almost totally at peace. Her life could end at once, or begin anew.

Almost at once, Ione Appleton felt that mystic tingling of the shoulder, which only the great-hearted seem to feel in great abundance. The tingling signaled a hunger to spend a cycle of years again shoving at the cumbersome Wheel of Change,

FOR A SHOULDER FULLY MUSCLED AT THE WHEEL OF CHANGE IS A HAPPY SHOULDER

Ione remembered well from her idealistic early cycle twelve years in the past. Of course, a reader whose mind is glutted with the galactic landfill may chuckle over the thought, but Ione Appleton felt a hunger for what might be termed Perfect Behavior. A hunger for purity, for entrance into a long tradition, of Plato, Plotinus, of Emmanuel Kant, of Hegel, of Ione Appleton, dancing through the skush and gush toward Eidos . . . It was a

140

chance to escape the ink-clogged capital "I" on the typewriter, to stand with that which is apart from the self: The Ideal, pristine, without flaw, toward which one might crawl, balancing a grail upon one's forehead—crawl, crawl—and then to feel certain flashes which tend to have been felt only in earliest youth, of the divine unification, subject and object, the object being the Platonic Forms. "With forms, through forms, and ending in forms," Plato wrote, and Ione wanted that very much indeed, the practice of using fragments of the Ideal to obtain it.

She felt the way that thousands of newspaper articles would have had you believe had been torn from the souls of the last three generations, leaving embers of malice and hopelessness. Not so with Ione Appleton, who against all odds determined to raise the torch of Good among the salvationless scum of money-grovel.

At the same time she felt a certain malaise at not having anything specific in mind when yearning to shove at the Wheel. And would not, she wondered, the Wheel distract her from paying enough attention to bread and cheese? Did not distracted hearts invite fiscal disaster? Quite sanely, she held fears that what had arisen to blight her career in bardiatrics might haunt her anon. Some of her fears were out of place, as is common in those who, their minds first ripped by personal tragedy, then by economic disaster, come out of both only to discover all the old petty problems they had forgotten existed while their big calamities were so burdensome. The petty problems naturally then reasserted their priority with false banners of importance; such were the banners among which Ione had to sort during her meditations.

How, she pondered, can Calamity be held a gnashing distance away? A question once partially answered, she believed, by medieval guilds. And why not form a guild?—she thought. She had only to call to mind the bottomless pit of distracting personal labor of such an endeavor to know its impossibility. But, why not form an informal society? Call it, say, *The Calamity Club*. She kept these musings to herself, and for weeks contemplated which of her friends might fit into her proposed *Calamity Club*.

It was during her days of pondering that Ione Appleton began, in her evening leisure, to study the life of Honoré de Balzac, a revival of a pre-bardiatrics interest. Many will revert to "pre"—that is, to concerns established prior to a cycle of years of burnout, in order to construct something green again upon the acorn of oblivion. Ione plunged wildly into the Balzac Question—as deep and murky with eddies as any that had ever puzzled scholars. What *was* Balzac? Was he a UFO insert?—Ione sometimes wondered. The Balzac question ranked among the big league questions, such as did Homer write both the *Iliad* and the *Odyssey* or either one, or from what Qumrun sect did Jesus develop his ideas?

She read as many biographies of Balzac as she could pick up in the 4th Avenue and lower Broadway used book stores— the English edition of Stefan Zweig's biography, and those by André Maurois and V. S. Pritchett, plus an old edition of *The Letters to Madame Hanska.* Of greatest interest were the novels, some of which, three to be exact, she had read in college, but there were 71 she had never touched. These novels shocked her soul almost as much as had the spiralling fall-down upon the ruins of Machu Picchu. After she had read fifteen of the novels, it occurred to her that there was little essential difference between literary lives of the 19th and 20th centuries, even taking into consideration that the latter is electromagnetic.

One morning Ione awoke after a dream in which Balzac had appeared in his white writing robes and had touched her forehead with his turquoise cane while intoning a series of sing-song sentences with hissing sibilants. Like most of her generation Ione kept a notepad on her bed table with which sleepily to debrief herself instantly after a groovy dream. Afterwards, she could lunge quickly back into the embrace of Somnus, content that if, like Rilke, she should have been visited with a deathless dream poem, at least the skeleton of it resided safe to face the tattered circuits of morning memory.

On this occasion Ione slapped herself awake, and spent hours piecing together the shards of the dream. As best she could reconstruct it, Balzac had sung to her the following lines:

Sum ut sum
Cogito ergo sum
Rebello ergo sum
Freak-out ergo sum
Je me consume ergo sum
Je me consume ergo sum
Je me consume ergo non existis tu

Ione recognized the biblical reference, *Sum ut Sum,* and the lines from Descarte and Albert Camus. *Freak-out ergo sum* she spotted as possibly a barbarism from the countercultural '60's. *Je me consume* was the Big B's famous outcry to his future wife, Eveline Hanska, when she seemed on the verge of rejecting him. The last line the Balzac apparition had sung, *Je me consume ergo non existis tu* seemed ominous to Ione. What did it mean? She hoped the message of it to have been, "Ware thou of burnout!" rather than, say, "I burned within myself with such a supreme art, that you might as well keep on making Disco-Cones,® my little confessional post-beat darling."

Whatever the message, Ione knew at once what to do with *The Calamity Club.* It would focus its attention on Balzac. If the modern New York creative human would only carefully study the life of Honoré de Balzac, she reasoned, she would be able to understand her metaphysical mire-in with highest insight. Ione might have gone so far as to say that ALL the pitfalls of modern life, with the exception of such events as being mugged with knockout gas by "air toughs" in hovering minicopters, could be avoided by careful study of the Big B.

"Belief in Balzac," she termed it that morning in her notebook, a devotion tempered at the same time by "Wariness of Balzac," for although the Big B's fawnings over heraldry and nobility could be forgiven as necessary to acquire data on elevated levels, a leftist like Ione could never have swallowed his affection for monarchy.

"The road doth fork in a coca leaf dawn," she wrote, "where only Balzac, particularly his mistakes, his foibles, his snobbery, commixed with a fierce knowledge of his survival techniques, can carry me forward in this treacherous century,

143

especially if I pick up the pen again." At this point in her diary, as the archivist who ultimately purchases it from her estate will see, her writing grew quite large and rounded with excitement. "For I know that *The Calamity Club* must intertwine itself with him. But, what shall it then be named? The Balzac Calamity Society? No! It has to be strictly scholarly—but what?" She paused, her forehead bulging in the dawn as she wrote then the four words that changed her life: "The Balzac Study Group!"

That was an early Friday morning, and when she re-awoke about noon, she had all day to scheme wildly about the Study Group. Quickly night arrived. Each Friday evening, carefully chosen friends were invited to gather in the back of Duct Tape for a quiet night of music, a bit of necking and affection, modest amounts of coca leaf wine, chatter, and the reading of works of literature aloud.

Ione had intended to continue searching for the perfect mix of friends to join her group, but the trio that Friday night, a smaller number than usual, seemed to fill every requirement— they were intelligent, interlocking, discrete, unafraid, creative, and all possessed highly developed senses of humor, yet amidst their laughs you could feel the outrage over the crumbly course of the civilization preparing to leave the earth like rats off the mooring rope of a scow.

During the evening, Ione outlined her idea to the three. "There would be studied four main Balzacian inspirations," she told them. "Number one would be his life, with emphasis on his loves and on the cultural milieu in which he wrote. Number two would be his manuscripts and galleys . . ."

"His galleys?" one of her companions broke in, "Whatever could anyone learn from studying a 19th century novelist's book proofs? Come now, Ione!"

In reply Ione said simply, "A careful perusal of the Big B's proofs is one of the most satisfying events in all of literature!" At that, she held up what would shortly become one of the most sacred documents of the Balzac Study Group, the first page of the written manuscript for *Illusions perdues*. She continued, "His written manuscripts too are treasures for study and contemplation. Much better to study a Balzac page for six hours than any

144

painting or photograph anywhere!" Her voice took on a bardiatric quiver of defiance. "It's mystic," she added, "and worthy of the appellation 'cultic'. I think a few months of our common study will bear me out—that Balzac's galleys and first drafts, just considering their physicality only, possess properties such as to heal any wounded psyche researching their profundity."

"The third inspiration will lie in analyzing the plots, characterizations and historical settings of the *Comédie humaine*. She who has memorized the plots and chief 500 characterizations of the *Comédie* is ready for triumph in our era!" When she uttered that last sentence, a tone of maenad-moan coming at the same time from her healed nasal passage, the rest of the group was on the edges of their seats in excitement.

"Finally," she continued, "we shall unearth his economics. I think we can learn plenty from Balzac's business records, his flight life-long from the debt mire. If we learn from Balzac's MISTAKES, we can face our era with a permanent, unwobbling safety! Belief in Balzac, it's as simple as that, my friends, so what do you say? Shall we form the Balzac Study Group, and take common endeavor against the Hideoma?"

All three stepped forward to press her hands in acceptance. "How long do you think this will take?" someone asked, "in order for our studies to prepare us?"

"It should take us several years," Ione answered, "just to read the 74 novels to one another, and to explore the outlines of his life. It may take us all the way to the time in our lives when we start getting purple with body-part scars!"

Without further discussion, all minds accepted the invitation. Ione motioned to them to join her around her writing desk. She flicked off the light, and lit a silver candlestick. She reached to the long shelf of Balzac, and brought forth a tome, which she opened at random and placed near the candle. All four began to stare as the candle's glow swept across the darkling typography. All else was gloom. Only Balzac's text seemed to dance in the light. So excited was the quartet, their hearts beating insistently, that an occasional huff from a nose disturbed the flame.

In the silence Ione placed her palm upon the book, and the others also, one by one, placed hands on top of hers. What a sight! The four fiery hands pressed fervently upon what was to be the bible of the Balzac Study Group, i.e., *Lost Illusions*, and then Ione's firm voice led forth, the others repeating after her The Balzac Study Group's

Solemn Oath of Initiation:

"I, Ione Appleton,
  I, John Barrett,
    I, Wendy Sark,
      I, George Plyght,

do solemnly vow to unite with my brother and sisters in this room in common struggle against the Hideoma,

> *to share our money and connections*

> *to live a life of honest daily toil, no matter what temptations lurk to thrill our loins or drain our pocket books*

> *to maintain absolute silence about the Balzac Study Group*

> *to uphold the Big B's spirit of Total Curiosity and Description at whatever cost*

> *to die to protect a brother or sister of the Group in danger*

> > *This I do swear in the sacred name of the* Comédie humaine.*"*

It was the portion of the vow to stick together even though a Black Hole should threaten to devour, slup slup slup slup, all the stars in the galaxy, that spurred the greatest emotion in the Group.

They agreed to meet each Friday in Duct Tape's back room, where they would begin at once to read aloud all 74 novels. Ahh, the thought of it! Nine hours of total isolation, 8 p.m. to 5 a.m., perusing the Big B! Oh, Balzac, loosen thy dancing hordes!

The very next day, the Balzac Study Group ordered micro-film copies of the leading newspapers and magazines of the last twenty years of Balzac's life. A careful raking of the feuilletons, the gossip columns, the garbage grids, as it were, would, the group knew, provide great information about the master. Balzac had been subjected to considerable chop-up and raillery in the popular press, and Ione was shocked to discover the ratio of caricatures to likenesses printed of him during his lifetime tally-ing at almost five to one.

FOUR HANDS
ON THE ALTAR OF
LOST ILLUSIONS

Who were these three humans crowding with Ione around the altar of *Lost Illusions,* who, as they lowered their hands upon the bible of burnout, ironically felt so uplifted, so full of hope, so full—dare I use the word—of Idealism?

First, the hand that lay most eagerly upon the open *Lost Illusions,* was that of John Barrett, a 39-year-old academician and playwright with a gingham café tablecloth for a career smeared with opening night candle wax, his satchel packed with half-finished plays like modern canvases with barren sections, and a career in Indo-European linguistics half-entered, half-neglected, so that rather than to know the whole, he had had to specialize and to speculate in an obscure corner of his profession to save himself. Mr. Barrett had charged into his career in the early '60's, determined to conquer with a trifurcation—first as poet, second as a composer of "Ballad Operas," and third as a scholar. What a disaster.

At first, it had been all quasi-glory. *The Pronunciation of Vowels in Imaginary Indo-Hittite Oral Epics* had been the title of his Ph.D. thesis, and well received it was among his colleagues. It was published on an academic press, where it sold a fashionably sparse amount over the years. In 1963, around the time of the assassination, his ballad opera titled *Glory of the Bomb Calf*, was a great success at the Luminous Animal Theater in the East Village.

The play provoked a controversy, which Barrett had wrongly interpreted as injuring his career when instead it was quite the contrary. Therefore, he skulked sullenly away from the theater and did not write another play for six years, by which time his career had dwindled to the point of starting afresh. Since he was an Indo-European linguist, his academic colleagues during the sixties had perforce gone along with his stagework, but as the century waned, they groused heartily against it.

Barrett persisted, however, and there were many off's to the off-off's prefixed to the locations of his productions: off-SoHo for instance, or the JersHo Community Playhouse in Bayonne. Barrett never forgave himself for allowing his tenured brothers to laugh him out of finishing a ballad opera in 1972 which had predicted that Nixon would fall. Even to the day of the Balzac Study Group, John could be heard uttering audible sneers at himself for quailing in the abyss, especially if the amount of the paperback advance for *All the President's Men* should come to mind.

By the time of the Balzac Study Group, Barrett's physique had phased to muttered morning mirror "ai-yi-yi-yi!"'s. His face flesh was beginning to dangle from his skull and there was a honeydew melon in an alcoholic gunny sack hanging from the midsection of his stoop-shouldered thin-boned frame. His despair was like a permafrost. Muscles to smile were never used. He was willing to place himself in Ione Appleton's hands as if taking vows for a monastery.

The second woman in the Balzac Study Group was Wendy Ann Sark, age 34, who has worn her hair in nearly knee-length tresses since her first Fugs and Grateful Dead concerts back in the '60's. Wendy's eyes have ever borne the bruised look of overwork and overworry. So outstanding are her eye rings, that when she has eaten too much for a few months, her friends kid her she looks a bit like a panda bear. When that occurs, Wendy rushes home in tears, to jog the panda away from her form, and to regain her normal slinky debauched look.

In her early youth, Wendy had been what they call a "tune freak," with many erotic attachments among rock musicians, jazz musicians, fiddle-&-stomp musicians, trance musicians, electronic musicians, Balkan folk musicians, chance musicians, street musicians, chamber musicians, Alpine yodel musicians, and others, indicating a subservience to that mysterious phenomenon known as the Secret Lost Chord of Lust.[2] Wendy later discovered the women's movement through an organization known as *Groupanon*, which assisted tune-freaks in analyzing and controlling the Secret Lost Chord of Lust. For a few years thereafter, Wendy Sark bent the other direction, to the Lost Chord of Hate, and subsumed her eros beneath the thought of offing the enemy.

By the year of the Balzac Study Group, Wendy had mellowed considerably. She had come to terms with her past, had made peace with the Secret Lost Chord of Lust, and was ready to face the future with great zest.

Wendy Sark had the ability of total recall, a "Videotape Memory;" she had only to sit relaxed after an event, and she could speak into a recorder, or a videocam, not only the dialogue, but most importantly, a brilliant debriefing of the facial expressions, what people were wearing, how they stood and gesticu-

---

2. The Secret Lost Chord of Lust, not so outlandish a concept as it might appear, since cats can be stimulated to erotic activity by *mi* of the fourth octave. The secret of the riddle of the attraction of nubile youth to expensive rock concerts, the Lost Chord is triggered through a series of notes struck in certain patterns and time signatures, combined with certain harmonies and powerful spinal/skeletal vibrations from hyperamplified bass guitars. Find the Lost Chord, and you're on the charts.

lated. Because of this, Wendy was sent by rock magazines to cover bands backstage, in dressing rooms and recording studios. She was the unobtrusive type, the sort that once existed, say, on the edges of the Surrealist movement only to surface years later with their bitter diaries and acid archives. Her hatred of the residual sex-toy-ism of the music scene made Wendy greatly feared.

"Who *is* this woman? Who let her into the dressing room?" the angry managers of the latter century "rock-a-bards" would exclaim when one of Wendy's sneering paradigms of naked rock dressing room lunch appeared in *Gorp* or *Rolling Stone*. She was so greatly feared she had to resort to elaborate disguises to get access to the rock-a-bards.

Wendy shared with John Barrett a desire to flame upon a scene spectacularly, to flip out with historic genius, or to flee barely alive in ashes. The romance of the burnout burned brightly in Wendy, but she had, as Barrett, a built-in safety mechanism that prevented it. She admired Ione Appleton's ability to go through, and survive, a genuine bardiatrics fry-down.

She had met Ione when Ione first retired in flames to St. Mark's Place and had just rented the Duct Tape Boutique. They were lovers for a few months, but by the time of the Study Group the eros had calmed considerably, and they could be in the same room without translating to their bodies that great quatrain of Sappho where in the presence of her lover, the *tromos*, the trembling, seized Sappho wholly, and the sweat poured down the sides of her chest, and her skin seemed greener than grass, and the menacing wigglings of the worm farm loomed so near.

The remaining member of the Balzac Study Group was George Plyght, a tall blond-haired gentleman of 45, fairly famous as a partisan of a literary genre dubbed "The Q & A of Anguish."[3] At the Q & A of Anguish, Mr. Plyght had no peer.

---

3. The Q & A of Anguish. Or, Stress Questioning, wherein the questioner begins probing, first gently, then firmly, into sensitive areas that cause the Q-Targets great anxiety. A marvelous way to dislodge data in the few minutes allowed at an after-dinner confrontation. In Stress Questioning, orchestration of instant, peppery, on-the-spot Q-Lists, is all important.

You could have called it High Level Stress-Questioning just as well. Plyght's hair was combed a bit like a combination of Chill Wills and Carl Sandburg, with a cowlick in the back like a docked pony's tail—a suspicious cowlick that might have been thought brought to the world through a curling iron, had not George Plyght such a reputation for naturalness.

On the surface, George was pure fluff—his fluffiness made him, oddly enough, an extremely valuable member of the Group, as will be seen, for it enabled him to acquire information of a peculiar kind unavailable to anyone else. George's family was extremely wealthy, with the highest social credentials. Everyone thought that therefore George was rich, but he had a most unfortunately icy relationship with his parents, who considered him a kind of lazy throw-back. His parents were the sort whom a child could never really please, who never let a fault pass, who continually accused him of inability.

When quite young, George began wreaking vengeance by asking the most embarrassing questions he could muster at family dinner parties. He would ask presidents and cabinet members the most *outrageous* Q's regarding military matters. His father, grooming him for eventual hegemony over the family conglomerate, was a "know everybody's weakness" man, and filled his son's mind with infinite tidbits on the foibles and economic scams of others.

It left its mark. Later, when swarms of creditors overwhelmed George, and he was forced to turn temporarily to journalism, his connections, plus the Q & A of Anguish, allowed him to obtain startling data at the highest levels of power. "George Plyght! The questions you ask!" many a society matron would exclaim at a bankerly banquet. George would sit quietly, his tape system inside his Sprint-Tux,® waiting patiently for the fine Balzacian moment when "brilliant controversy gave way to anecdotes."[4] It was then, when admirals, presidents, and corpo-

---

4. The Sprint-Tux®: George's only entrance into the Age of Invention, but very popular among busy nightclubbers who wanted to stay in shape. A tux with disposable tough Kleenex inner linings to soak up the runnels of sprint-froth as the joggers would run from nightclub to nightclub of an evening.

ration executives were adorning the skeletons in the closet, that George plied his stress questions. You'd be surprised how much they revealed in the security-cleared library of his mother and father, or recent history as it really had occurrred, and not as it had been typeset, videoset and hypeset.

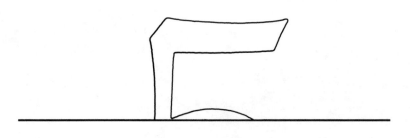

TWELVE PEARS
DOWN

Secret societies create their own slang. And so the Balzac Study Group. An anecdote such as "Werdet swears he saw him (Balzac) at Véry's eating a hundred oysters, twelve cutlets, a duck, a couple of partridges, a sole, and a dozen pears," produced the expression used by the Group, "That's all just twelve pears down." This expression had to do with their attitude toward last month's paperback advance.

As a surprise one spring day, Ione gave them each a white, cowled monk's robe, of linen, which she had copied from Balzac's own writing attire, without which he was apparently unable to fulfill his eight-hour nightly martyrdom at the writing desk. She even recreated the gold rope ceinture with its scissors and papercutting knife on the ends, to which, bowing to modern necessity, she added jewelers' magnifiers and coke spoons. The magnifiers were needed for close contemplation of the master's manuscripts, which were beginning to occupy more and more of the Group's time.

Whereas to the outsider the sight of the four sitting in a circle attired in their white robes, reading aloud *Histoire de la décadence de César Birotteau,* might appear ludicrous, yet so satisfied and glutted with inner glows were they, that full nights on end the Hideoma was beaten back, defeated, even forgotten. The road seemed paved with permanent gnosis, gnosis of the most exalted quality, gnosis inwoven with pleasure.

In just a matter of weeks however, it struck. The Mallet of Pov. A nadir of moolah was reached by all at the same time. Sales of Duct Tape apparel had faddishly fallen away. Ione was not due another royalty check from the Festal Cones for a few months, and so was like some fledgling rock star with a hit single and no touring act who watches the moolah river dry up overnight like a desert gulch. Wendy Sark had been employed at the famous Scruffle Alley Bookstore,[5] but had always felt a kind of moral gunge accruing, and had finally quit when someone had brought in fresh from the racks of the Lantern of Knowledge Bookstore, an offed armload of three sets of Ione's *Years of Bardiatrics, Vols I-VI,* barely in print a month. Meanwhile, Wendy had offended the rock magazines by providing a mental videotape transcript of her various encounters with the *owners* of the rock mags. This caused but the most minor ripples in the gossip columns, but lasting damage to her career as a musical mental videotaper. After all, are there not some things sacred, such as the privacy of the people of genius who own rock magazines?

---

5. Scruffle Alley Bookstore occupied a unique position among N.Y. bookstores, being the main warehouse wherein bookstore employees and junkies dealt out their books. Owners of stores often hovered outside Scruffle Alley in purring autos wearing fake moustaches and slouch hats waiting for their employees to sneak-haul the purloined booty over after work.

As for George Plyght, he was now reduced to staying home of an evening in order not to soil his last shirt and suit. Nor could he pick up his Bentley in the garage, for the maintenance charges were frightfully past due. So he hid in his apartment, the repair manuals for the Bentley on his desk. He would study them intently and then dart down to the garage after midnight to do his own repairs, but stealthily, for he wanted to keep up the good face among his neighbors, to whom good old George was as rich and affable and silly with his stress questions as ever.

The faculty tenure committee had put out the notice among assistant professors that there had been a sad slackening of the sounds of keys whacking at typewriters in their offices, and to please publish more books, more articles, more lectures. It was an angry Indo-European linguist, John Barrett, who had rushed into the chairperson's office to complain. An altercation ensued that resulted in a sort of combined quit-firing.

In the days that followed, with his first free time off during school months in many years, John tried to inflame himself enough so as to go insane. One of the hungers that made him now most bitter was that he had never given his all during his youth, never had burnt himself out at some great endeavor, but had pulled away just in time, and thus had bounced 'tween the triad of academic failure, failure as a playwright, and failure as hell-raising burnout. And now, with no job, he faced fiscal calamity.

"One thing is certain," he told himself as he entered Duct Tape for the regular Friday night meeting, "I'm one moth that's going to flap into the supernova and survive it!"

The others were just as mired in malfiscality as John Barrett, and it was a sad-faced Group that, sad one by sour one, trudged into the back room to don their gold-belted robes.

One of the first things the Group had noted in their readings aloud was how applicable many of the books were to current events. As soon as they discussed a character, immediately a New Yorker living now would come to mind. For the Napoleonic wars, you could insert Vietnam. As for the Balzacian horde of faces, those of Lucien de Rubempré, of Horace Bianchon, of Philippe, Joseph and Agathe Bridau, of Rastignac, Emile Blondet, Aquilina, La Rabouilleuse, and so on, all one had to do was to gaze carefully upon the streets of QueensHo, in the bistros, in the editorial offices of magazines, in the TV studios, in the loft-salons of creative N.Y., to find them. Everyone knew, for instance, a doctor who at least partially reminded them of the great Dr. Bianchon. Combine the partials, and you will have obtained a 20th century Bianchon!

Regarding the incident we shall shortly describe, each member of the Balzac Study Group in later years tended to grant to himself or herself an overemphasized role in its action. It began amidst great mumblings over the sad conditions of their bank accounts. They were hoping for loans from Ione to pull them from the mire. Ione, however, was as temporarily impoverished as they. Oh no! Was it time to beg again from rich liberals!?

"I have an idea," Ione began. "Why don't we write a book together?" Not a dour face lifted up excitedly at her suggestion. "Not a *mere* book," she continued impatiently, "but one inspired by the Master." Still no excitement.

Ione was undaunted by their glumness. "I think we all agree, that each novel and story we've read has such energy and universal significance that there *must* exist transformation equations by which we could shift it to the present. *Not a translation,* but rather a *transformation;* it's very important to make that distinction; otherwise we're nothing but shameless hacks."

"We begin with Balzac's characters, his situations, his historical milieus, his themes and plots, and we transform them with our own desperate genius *now,* almost 150 years later. You understand, we *mix* our genius, his and ours, and such a mix will cause our marks—moral, stylistic, and fiscal—to be indelible, all in our own time, while we are still alive!!"

While there was a stir of interest in the Group—their faces, at least, were lifted from the floor to hers—nevertheless no one spoke.

Ione continued. "Naturally, we've not going to tell *Gorp,* or anyone for that matter, that we're the Balzac Study Group. We'll stay totally anonymous. Furthermore, Balzac will never be mentioned. Our plots and characters will have such a life and brilliance of their own, that the critics, never too sharp in any case, will never discover our transformations. What do you say? You understand, I'm not talking about writing only one book, but ten or twenty."

At this, there *was* definite excitement, but none fully saw the contours of the torch Ione waved, so silence continued.

Ione could see that she had won her friends. "I think we should begin at once. Thirty days, and we'll have our first book. We'll be able to remain anonymous, earn a living, and any money left over we can use to help improve the lot of our friends, or devote to noble causes!"

"Think of it!" Barrett broke in. "We could set up a prize, call it 'The Balzac', which would be like a Guggenheim or a government grant, but would go to the truly deserving, to the Melvilles, clerks at the docks, to the Dickinsons, to the Edmund Spensers and Thomas Chattertons, to all those who might have starved to death, or have committed suicide, or died too shy to demand their place!"

Truly Barrett was ready, as he patted his suit coat pocket to see if his writing pen was at the ready. Ione did not burst his bubble of optimism by reminding John that not only had they no money, they had no idea as yet regarding what book they'd transform—nor had they contacts for contracts, nor anything really but grit and desperation. Instead, she turned to Wendy: "I think each of us is uniquely equipped to help. All of us are good writers, and our fields of information, while separate, intermingle. Wendy, do you remember when you and I were standing with Milton Rosé and President Kennedy next to the Shaped Foot Multiples? I want you to describe the conversation."

Wendy responded with a letter-perfect Q and A on the event, including the exact description of the Secret Service pins on nearby lapels.

"You see!" Ione continued, "each of our lives will allow access to the resplendent data needed to put this age upon the pickle fork of persuasion!!"

"Yes!" George Plyght interrupted. "How easy it would be, to distill the nervous chatter of our era, always with an ear for what our great companion calls"—here he paused, to savor the impending quote—"'dialogue, closely packed, nervous, pregnant, terse, and full of the spirit of the age.'"

This quote he delivered with an exclamation point at the end, so that the Group nearly jumped to its feet with approval.

"But what book?" Wendy spake, her voice a strange hollow drone, and it could be seen quite plainly at what tome her glazed eyes were staring. All turned toward the book, residing open on the Balzac Shrine: *Lost Illusions!*

"How cunningly we shall translate . . . I mean, *transform* it. How fiendishly subtle we shall be!" Plyght almost shrieked, as he sprang to the altar, the others close behind him.

The rest of the night was devoted to their inspired and cunning cryptotranslation of *Lost Illusions*. They worked steadily, sending out for food and coca leaf wine, till the next noon, when they collapsed in common sleep on the couches of Duct Tape, the floor strewn with tossed leaves of inspiration, the novel already plotted, and well on the way to completion.

It so happened they had recently acquired a photocopy of the manuscript of *Illusions perdues,* and it was communal contemplation that night of the initial page, and frantic notetaking upon it, that shaped the novel's plot.

They glued the first manuscript page on a larger sheet of Strathmore bond, so that there was plenty of peripheral room 'pon which to jot ideas. They donned their robes, and sat in a circle, meditating over the *Lost Illusions* page, passing it among them, jotting upon the margins, and thus the novel was born. While the jottings are difficult to decipher, an archivist hunched low over it with a high-intensity light and a magnifier, would have translated it something like this:

THE BALZAC STUDY GROUP'S
TRANSFORMATION OF THE FIRST MANUSCRIPT PAGE
OF ILLUSIONS PERDUES:

vol. I

Sophie Belladonna, newscaster for CBS affiliate in Grain Croft, Iowa, is summoned to N.Y. to become anchor for national CBS evening news. With her comes her young lover, Arnold Banañe, a poet who envisions himself as the 1st poet to chant poems on public events to a national TV audience. His hopes are crushed, as Sophie abandons Arnold because of pressure from investigative reporters who quickly discover Arnold, and the tattoo on his left breast, "The works of Genius are watered with tears."

Arnold Banañe is not so crushed by Sophie that he cannot strut forth in the N.Y. literary world -- where he experiments in 3-dimensional poetry utilizing lasers called MEMORY GARDENS. He promulgates a school called INSISTENT POESY -- with its motto, "We Shall Use Violence, If Necessary, to Compel You to Read Our Works."

David Séchard is transformed to Donald Savare, who marries Arnold's sister, Agathe. Donald Savare is the inventor of an ocular-sized TV camera; the unions try to suppress the invention because it allows reporters to operate their own cameras. Savare responds with a brilliant financial takeover of CBS, using the outlaw pushiness of Johnny Vap to help the way.

Vol. III Arnold discovers Sophie's affair with his sister. Heartbroken, Arnold builds a large parachute of SKY GOSSAMER®. He programs a laser love poem to Sophie to (be burned into the parachute as Arnold jumps out over SoHo at 8,000 feet. Too much of the parachute is burned away and Arnold falls to his death.

ROTATING ARNOLD
TRIANGLE

New literary device:
The Rotating Triangle

Arnold Banañe's 1st book:

Laser Burns on
LiPo's Elm Leaf wins
the attention of an entire generation. His attempts to read from LiPo's Elm Leaf on the evening news fail miserably

Sophie
Belladonna, transformed from Mme Barpeton. active in of Lost Illusions; active in

Key Theme of Illusions Perdues transformed to the 3-Volume Genius Hick:
The CONCEPT OF THE BURN

1. Laser Burn.
2. fiscal burn.
3. psychic burn
4. Lake of Fire burn (Guilt-Voyages for self-purification)
5. Cosmology burn-- (All things flow, therefore shall not ultimately all things cold be scorch-ouched by hot?)

Another key theme of Genius Hick trilogy:

ULTRA-SENSITIVITY, the concept of crying

Contemplation of scratched-out lines produced hundreds of pages of dialogue for the Balzac

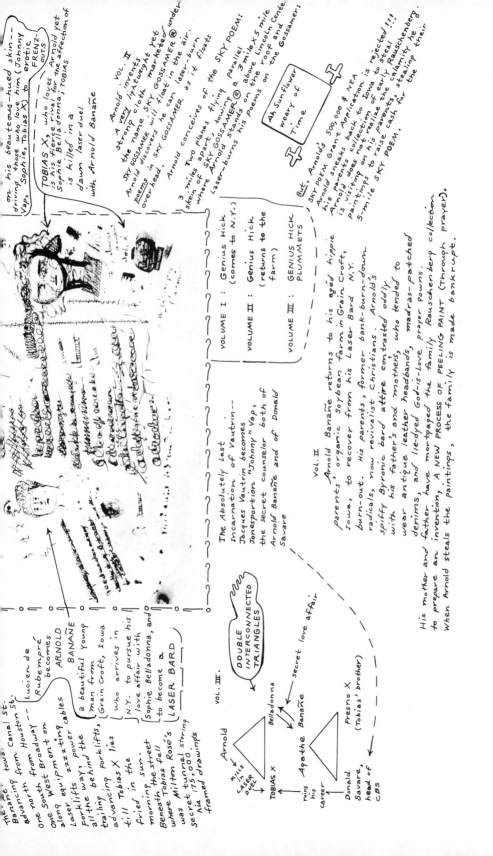

The Ballet tour. Canal St.
Banane advancing from Houston --
advancing from Houston --
one north from Broadway --
one West Broadway on
along equipment on
Laser power cables zzzz-ting
all the behind the
forklifts, trailing forklifts
advancing till Tobias X lies
fried in the
fried sun.
morning the street
Beneath Tobias fell
where Milton Rose's
secret tunnel storing
was $175,000. his
framed drawings

Lucien de
Rubempré
becomes
ARNOLD
BANANE
a beautiful Young
man from
Grain Croft, Iowa
who arrives in
N.Y. to pursue his
love affair with
Sophie Belladonna, and to
become a
LASER BARD

on his beauteous-hued skin --
driving those who love him --
(Johnny Vap, Sophie, Tobias X) to
FRENZ-
OUTS

TOBIAS X, who loves Arnold yet
is his fierce rival for the
affection of Sophie Bella donna,
is killed in a
dawn laser duel
with Arnold Banane

VOL. II
Arnold invents a very
strong yet lightweight yet
Sky GOSSAMER® cloth.
Arnold markets the
name SKY GOSSAMER® under
discovers he can float in the air.
poems in sky GOSSAMER®
overhead. as it floats

Arnold conceives of the SKY POEM:
Two planes flying parallel
3 miles apart, towing a 3 mile 5 mile
skein of SKY GOSSAMER® above Lincoln Center
where Arnold stands on the roof and
Laser-burns his poems on the

Ah Sunflower
weary of
Time

But, Arnold's
SKY POEM is rejected !!!
Arnold's NEA
Grant 500,000 $ Application
Arnold sneaks back to Iowa to steal
is visiting. does not realize
the calamity he
paintings on his parents, stealing their
to raise cash for the
5-mile SKY POEM.

VOLUME I : Genius Hick
(comes to N.Y.)

VOLUME II : Genius Hick
(returns to the
farm)

VOLUME III : GENIUS HICK
PLUMMETS

The Absolutely Last
Incarnation of Vautrin--
Jacques Vautrin becomes
Jonesportion "Johnny" Vap,
the secret counselor of both of
Arnold Banane and of Donald
Savare

VOL. III.

DOUBLE
INTERCONNECTED
TRIANGLES

Arnold

Belladonna — secret love affair

TOBIAS X   Agathe Banane

kills
in LASER
duel

ruins
his
career

Donald
Savare,   Fresno X
head of   (Tobias' brother)
CBS

Vol. II
Arnold Banane returns to his agéd hippie
parents' organic Soybean farm in Grain Croft,
Iowa, to recover from his Laser Bard N.Y.
burn-out. His parents, former bank-burn-down
radicals, now revivalist Christians. Arnold's
spiffy Byronic bard attire contrasted oddly
with his father's and mothers, who tended to
wear antique leather headbands, madras-patched
denims, and lie-dyed God-is-Love prayer gowns.
His mother and father have mortgaged the family Rauschenberg collection
to prepare an invention, A NEW PROCESS OF PEELING PAINT (through prayer).
when Arnold steals the paintings, the family is made bankrupt.

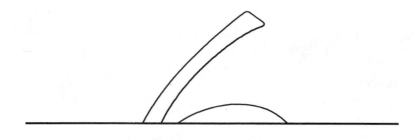

"DELINEATE
THE AGE"

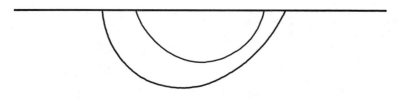

By the end of three weeks, a three-volume work was completed:

Volume I. *Genius Hick* [*comes to N.Y.*]

Volume II. *Genius Hick* [*returns to the farm*]

Volume III. *Genius Hick Flames Out* [*sings the Minus Six Sonata*]

By this initial endeavor, the Balzac Study Group brought back the multi-volume novel, although it was not certain whether writers should have cursed them or praised them.

Ione delivered the manuscript of *Genius Hick* to Barnaby Radither, one of America's leading attorney/therapists, a phenomenon which will be expounded upon more fully in the story of J'Accuse.

Ione was the only link between the Group and Mr. Radither. During its subsequent history, the Balzac Study Group was marvelously adroit at keeping him in the dark as to their identities.

Radither shook his head, lifting the hefty three volumes. "This is just the beginning, Barnaby," Ione said. "We're on fire! This took just twenty-one days to write. It's the finest work since Henry James. We intend to write a book a month for the next seven or eight years; not just hack/whack, but *brilliant* works! We believe that when publishers feel assured they can count on first rate works every month, the paperback bidding wars will sound like the pork belly futures pit at the Chicago commodities exchange before a famine.

"In addition, we want total anonymity. You can tell editors we're a bunch of coca leaf twits in our loft-salons with permanent jet lag from circling the globe 500 times in five years. We're much too rich and highly placed to come out, as yet. When we have a few books on the bestseller list, we'll vent some steam by announcing that some day we'll reveal our identities. Meanwhile, we can plant all sorts of stories in the news mags hinting that so-and-so might be a member of the mysterious writing ensemble. We'll point the finger at everyone from members of the cabinet to Milton Rosé!"

Every reader knows how difficult it is for a client to sow the seeds of enthusiasm within an attorney, much less a noble attorney/therapist like Barnaby Radither, yet Ione was able to spur a hopping excitement in Barnaby. Ione thought she was being unrealistic by announcing, "We want rock bottom ten grand immediately."

"I'll do better than that," he replied. "I'll get you ten thousand each."

After that startling pronouncement Ione was more than a little dazed, and so stood up to leave. "There's only one thing remaining, Ione," Barnaby smiled. "Whom shall I say to be the author or authors of *Genius Hick?*"

Ione paused at the door, embarrassed at slipping on such

an important detail. Feigning nonchalance, but scrambling fast in her mind, she said, "Ava . . . Ava Douzine, yes, *Genius Hick*, by Ava Douzine, how's that?"

"Forty grand in two weeks," Barnaby assured her.

Actually it was just a week gone by when Barnaby called Duct Tape with a contract. The book was joyously to suffer the fate of one of those mysterious books the publishing industry awakens from its yawn to embrace. Like all such books, an immediate legend grew up around it. Somehow, it appealed to publishers that a group of powerful and fashionable types was engaging in secret literature of such high quality. The news mags were suddenly all a-gossip over the secret writing team creating such a stir.

Within a month a paperback sale, and a movie deal, were concluded, and the Balzac Study Group found itself in possession of 500 thousand dollars, which Barnaby handed over to Ione in cash. They met in the iron-fenced kiddie playground in Washington Square Park. Ione and Barnaby both were in deep disguise, to avoid the surveillance of the tax men. Security precautions were tossed aside for a moment at the initial sight of the lettuce, as Ione danced around the merry-go-round, waving aloft the thick wad of the Grover Clevelands of joy. What a dash up Mt. Mooh!!

Their contract called for another book in a month, so they held a meeting to plan it. The first task for a group so suddenly, so opulently, seized from the claws of poverty was to remain calm. They decided for the time being to continue living as though circumscribed by pov. They mailed a large donation to the Balzac Museum in France, and deposited the remainder in a numbered account in the Bahamas.

As for the manuscript due in four weeks, the Group decided on a long term plan which for the next six years they followed with unswerving dedication. The meeting grew charged with tears and overwrought emotion, as they vowed around the Altar of Lost Illusions to translate the entire *Comédie humaine*, including those books Balzac had been unable to finish, into the circumstances of the late 20th century.

Who knows, they speculated, perhaps some similar group

in the 22nd century might translate the Balzac Study Group's *own* COMEDIE HUMAINE into the 22nd century's ethos. And so on. Maybe a great series of transformations, stretching tens of centuries into the future, was being started by this humble group crouched in the back room of the Duct Tape Boutique!

It was still merely a matter of Transformation Equations. Each Balzacian volume would be totally transformed, but the Group decided to leave behind a Transformation Key, so that vignette by vignette each book could be focused on its corresponding action in the Big B's original. Furthermore, the Balzac Study Group realized that archivists and workers of the Data Midden faced centuries of happiness sifting the Group's archives, so filing cabinets and microdot machines were purchased to store their papers.

They knew that the transformations might require as many as twenty years. At the end of it they could announce to the world what they had done, and then could publish their 95 volumes under the title, *20th Century Reflection.* John Barrett was transported with joy, for to have a twenty year work on his hands gave him insight into what Ezra Pound, or Homer, or Dante must have felt when embarking on a multi-decade toil in multi-volume.

Barrett was brilliant at providing historical backgrounds, of the sort the Big B had been so adept in inserting into the flow of a novel. The historical anecdotes provided by Barrett for Balzac Study Group Novels became cocktail party discussion foci all over America. Millions there are who read books for anecdotes, and who has not stood eye-to-eye with someone at a party who is slyly relating to you a tidbit of history or a scientific arcanum culled from a publication he would swear is much too obscure for you to have read?

In addition to formal scholarship and historical anecdote, Barrett brought another important factor to the Group: hatred of journalists. He detested them, a detestation thwarted for years by having to drool upon the shoes of journalism for the sake of his off-Broadway, off-QueensHo, and off-JersHo plays.

George Plyght's area of expertise remained the Stress Question plied among national leaders. Others in the Group would regularly hand him lists of Stress Q's for the next banquet. The Group voted George an allowance higher than the others, to keep his tuxes clean, and his Bentley purring with the proper rich person's perfection. The Group voted tight controls over George, however, lest he allow himself to lose grasp of the Group's high purposes. Once a week, in addition to the regular writing sessions, he was to report to the Group and debrief himself of the various Stress Q's they had given him to ask. George was indispensable to the Group, for all knew that in this data-retentive era, high-level Stress Questioning was the only way to know *now* what the computers might not disgorge for decades or centuries.

Wendy Sark's fields of study for the Balzac Study Group were economics and the Pink Kink, her term for the erotic aspects of the literary/artistic world, especially the phenomenon of the "manizer" woman literary executive. It was her own inclination to absorb herself in the study of the seamy side of scriptive genius. As for economics, she was to become an expert at SoApple techniques of fiscal survival. Such economic studies—formal, footnoted (she was inspired by the scholarly techniques of John Barrett), and single spaced, were eagerly awaited by the Group.

Somehow, Wendy was cunningly adept at breaking behind the barricades of hype, lies, and false prosperity with which the famed often surround themselves, to determine the exact fiscal state of any outwardly prosperous writer or painter. Taking a hint from George Plyght, she asked endless questions everywhere. With her fantastic memory, she could store an awesome array of monetary facts slurped up by a quick eyeball-sweep across a worried artist's desk top. She had a secret compartment in her shoulder bag, in which she held her typed Q-Lists. You might ask why a person with a videotape memory needed typed Q-Lists—the answer is that with a typed Q-List there was no way a screaming, belligerent data-target could sway her away from her questions. So, often in a party's midst she would consult her lists, and then hit the babble trail after zonked, drunken or hypercocaventilating Q-Targets.[6]

---

6. A few words about Wendy's Q-Lists are in order. First, she

Coordinating everything was Ione Appleton. Her role was fourfold: 1. handling business and contracts; 2. chief polisher of word-gnarls; 3. apothegmist; and 4. debriefing grieving lovermen for the novels. At the latter, she had no peer. Just like Balzac had monitored his women friends for their most intimate secrets, Ione debriefed confused modern men of their most love-starred data. Indeed, one of the Group's more successful transformation techniques was to substitute modern men for Balzac's women, and modern women for Balzac's men.

Because of their decision to continue, even with the mon pouring upon them, their normal lives as pov-addled creative New Yorkers, brinked upon ruin, hungry for salvation, keeping up a good face lined with existential dread, they felt qualified to assume the name, *The Cénacle*. *The Cénacle* was Balzac's term for an informal society in his novels of altruistic, idealistic writers, philosophers and people of science.

After this historic meeting, the Balzac Study Group made a second common vow around the altar of *Lost Illusions*, where, attired once again in their clean linen gowns, they placed hand upon fervent hand upon the great open book, and swore to "Get the Data at Whatever Cost," with their

SACRED VOW OF TOTAL DATA

"I, Wendy Sark,   I, John Barrett,
        I, George Plyght,   I, Ione Appleton,

do hereby vow, upon the sacred tome of Illusions perdues, to Know the New Facts Early, and the total details of the old facts, at whatever personal cost. If mountains of steel separate us from our needed data, we vow to scrape our nails to

---

kept a running Q-List on most famous authors, artists, and musicians. They were typed however with a typeface so tiny as to be virtually unreadable. Thus, a list of, say 45 Q's could be contained on an area of several square inches. That way, she could easily carry Q-Lists on up to 500 Q-Targets; plus the small type would discourage anyone reading over her shoulder at the edge of a party as she was preparing for a Q-Assault.

*the bone, and our teeth to the gum, in order to scratch /
chew our way into the Fane of Secret Fact. Whenever hostility, anger, duplicity, or other barriers should arise, we vow
to face such terror with total fearlessness, for the sake of our
noble cause. This I do swear, in the numinal name of the
immortal Honoré, the spirit of whose Cénacle we hereby
adopt as our own!"*

"Together, we shall Delineate the Age!" Ione shouted, lifting her
glass of coca leaf champagne.

"Delineate the Age!" one face nodded.

"Delineate the Age!" one face shone.

"Delineate the Age!" the final face grimace-moaned.

THE
CREATIVITY
BUNKER

Once they had reached the greeny stream beneath the white slopes of Mt. Moolah, the Balzac Study Group ordered the construction of a Creativity Bunker in the apartment directly above the Duct Tape Boutique. The only entrance to the Creativity Bunker lay through a hidden stairwell they built in the Duct Tape back room. The windows of the Bunker, as well as the door leading out to the hallway of the apartment building, were sealed with concrete blocks.

Silence was important. The walls, ceiling, and floors were covered with a Proustcork® Writers Silencing System. Sound from without never penetrated the Proustcork.®

The silent brown of the Proustcork® walls was unadorned except for two plaques. The one, framed in a destruction/construction by Milton Rosé featuring solar-powered replicas of writers' tongues constantly in motion, bore the legend:

The reference, of course, was to the 20 days it took Balzac in June of 1837 to write the first volume of *Lost Illusions*. Some of the most moving struggles in modern literature were the Balzac Study Group's attempts to shave Balzac's two-and-six-sevenths-week record in producing a masterpiece.

Also in a Rosé-crafted frame, on the wall opposite Lost Illusions/20 Days, was:

Hipponakomoiraphobia being the transliteration of the Greek for "Fear of the fate of Hipponax the Poet."[7]

This particular plaque was more important to the Group than one might guess. The majority of them—Wendy Sark, Ione Appleton, and to an extent, John Barrett—had a longing for,

---

7. A sad reminder indeed, o bards, is the life of Hipponax—the *Bard of the Gutter* the professors of classics like to call him. But a reminder to versifiers, playwrights, movie makers, novelists, anecdotists, and historians, of the dangers in hopping the posts of fame to reside on

and a tendency to dwell in, smut and spew-spackled scandal.

The Creativity Bunker bore every accoutrement, every technical aid, to enhance their creativity. Dehumidifiers and machines for producing satisfying tokes of negative ions; a hydroponic coca-bush greenhouse; an exercise room; plus relics once owned by Balzac himself.

The Group was able to purchase at auction Balzac's own porcelain coffee brewer with matching porcelain heating column. On the sides of the heating column were the initials "H.B." beneath a tiny painted crown. Needless to say, hundreds of inspirational pots began to be brewed. They drank so many in fact that Ione sent the pot over to Milton Rosé to have a warning painted above Balzac's initials: "50,000 cups in 20 years!" Scholars had computed that B. had sipped 50,000 cups during the final 20 years of his life, and the reward for those 400,000-odd gulps of midnight Martinique down the deadline-dreading throat was death at 51.

Considerable space in the Bunker was given over to the accoutrements of research. As Apothegm Insert officer, Ione had 300 foreign dictionaries, grammars, and epic texts. Thus, apothegms in Indo-Hittite, Algonquin, Anglo-Saxon, Old Church Slavic, Balochi, Tosk, Frisian, Pali, Gaelic, and a multitude of others, appeared in their novels.

For Ione's 34th birthday, the Group presented her with the

ALPHABETIZED APOTHEGM INDEX TO HONORE DE BALZAC

The **ALPHABETIZED APOTHEGM INDEX** contained some 14,223 maxims, mainly from the *Comédie humaine.* It was computerized, with the

---

Groin Grovel, lampoons, and raillery, no matter how brilliant. Indeed a Bard had better have five feet:

one foot in the Grail
one foot in the glitter
one foot in the gutter
one foot in the grave
one foot in the glory,

to avoid the "everlasting shrine of silence," and to prevent the day when cultists ax down the doors of the library (say in 3050 A.D.) to ray-gun your works.

data able to be presented on the startling Balzac Computer Screen:

THE ALPHABETIZED APOTHEGM INDEX COMPUTER SCREEN

Thus Ione could type a word into the computer, say "journalist" or "journalism," and immediately a slow play-out of quotes rolled upon the screen, as:

1. "I come across journalists in theater lobbies; it makes me shudder to see them. Journalism is an inferno, a bottomless pit of inequity and treachery and lies; no one can travel it undefiled . . ."

2. "Give any newspaper time enough, and it will be base, hypocriti-
cal, shameless, and treacherous."

3. "A spy is systematically shameless and base. There you have
journalism summed up in a sentence."

4. "One by one they drop, some into the trench where failures lie,
some into the mire of journalism, some again into the quagmires
of the book trade . . ."

and a string of several hundred other quotes.

So, when Ione desired an apothegm on a certain theme,
she pondered the samples on the screen, chose an appropriate
one, punched for a typed printout, then re-wrote it entirely,
eager to reap that subtle reward of the apothegmist, to overhear
one's sentences quoted by diverse lips striving to shine in bars,
galleries, and loft-salons, even though the quoters were often
claiming the dicta as their own creations.

Later, the Balzac Study Group added an extremely helpful
stream to the computer: alphabetized psychological assessments
and life-stories (in Balzac's own words) of some 2000-odd characters from his collected novels and tales. Thus, when they were
fashioning their transformations, someone had only to type in a
character's name, say Hector Merlin, Esther Gobseck, Horace
Bianchon, Lucien de Rubempré, or Rastignac, and the screen
would slowly roll with bio-data, from which anyone could jot a
skeleton for later enfleshment.

Standing in front of the Balzac Computer Terminal, if one
looked up to the ceiling directly overhead, one saw a thickery of
brackets supporting long thin metal cylinders with dangling
pull-down rings. These were the famous charts used by the
Group during its writing sessions. One could pull down charts
for a variety of purposes. There were several anatomical charts;
a Periodic Table of the Elements; sub-atomic particle charts such
as for the bonding patterns of quarks and gluons in the neutron.

For descriptions of violence there were grim charts, usually kept covered, of wound patterns from famous murder
cases. The charts whose pull-down rings were the most worn
with use were the so-called Million Dollar Triangles, with idea-
jogging representations such as:

173

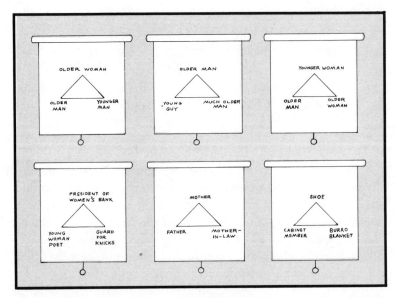

And then, for more complex focuses, the charts of Interrelated Triangles, as:

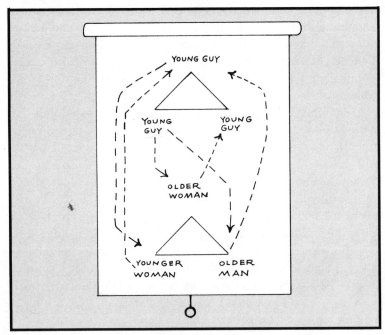

With their first large paperback sale, the Group traveled to all the locations in France where Balzac wrote. The only house of Balzac that survives is the Balzac Museum at 47 rue Raynouard in Passy, situated in Balzac's time on the rural outskirts of Paris on a steep hillside above the Seine. At the Balzac Museum the Group was particularly attracted to Balzac's writing table. One afternoon John Barrett leaned down and began to rub the desk top, and as he held the tangency, an entire novel appeared in his consciousness. John dropped to his knees in front of it, as if he were praying, and spent five hours sketching the novel into his notebook.

While not wanting to hog John's high, the others tried the mystic tome-triggering table top frottage, and all three felt bibliogenetic surges similar to John's. Therefore, they ordered four of the tables to be made, matching the originals pit by pit, burn by burn, coffee stain by coffee stain, down to the nicks on the little brass ring on the drawer beneath the desk top. The I-shaped support frame of the desk, situated near the floor and binding the legs steady, bore scuff marks, which the Group supposed were Balzac's own, struck there in the agitation of fever-write. Naturally they added exactly-copied scuffs to their duplicates.

Once brought to the Creativity Bunker on St. Mark's Place, the tables were arranged in a facing square, and Ione, George, Wendy, and John would each stand behind one, their hands rubbing the shiny tops, pausing now and then to massage a particularly thrilling pit-patch, eyes closed in rapture and then to blink open startlingly with an accompanying quick stamping sound of foot on a floor switching unit to set a dictation machine going, whenever ideas for plot or structure, dialogue and apothegm, should spume into thought. Later when they formed their Business Empire, they marketed a signed edition of the Balzac writing tables, called Baltabe.® The Baltabe® was *the* writing desk for literary America in the last part of the century.

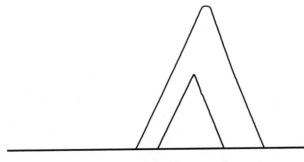

SIDE BAR A
THE BALZAC STUDY GROUP
GALLEYS

The lists on the wall, the pitted writing tables, the negative ion-izers, the white robes, the apothegm computer, the Proustcork® Writers Silencing System, Balzac's coffee urn, all made the Creativity Bunker one of the most prolific and brilliant writing centers in literary history. On the analogy of the desk-frottage, they found one additional mystic influence. One of them discovered that scanning photocopies of Balzac's proof sheets and manuscripts also triggered ideas. Soon Balzac's galleys covered the walls and floors.

It was the hunger for Trance-Scribble. Balzac, via his 18/6 work-to-sleep ratio, oft trance-wrote the first drafts, without

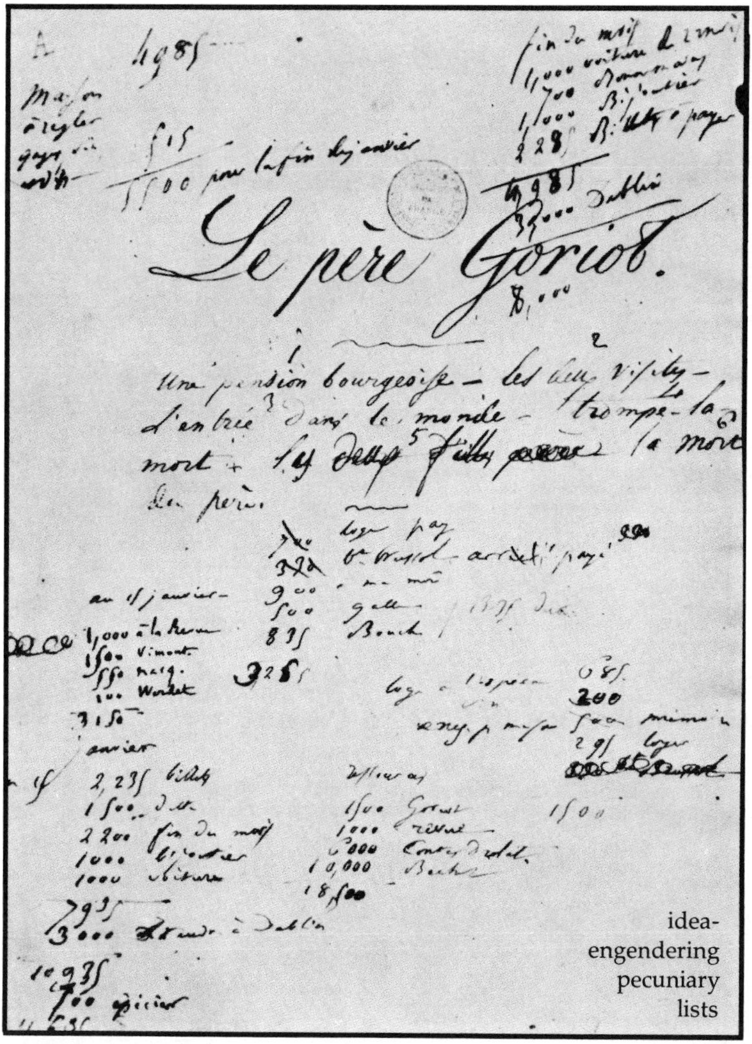

idea-
engendering
pecuniary
lists

knowing exactly what he had written, and sent them to the printer to be set. He then viewed the first, second, third, fourth, fifth, sixth to the tenth successive sets of galleys as mere clear copies, adding to each generation huge plexi of insertions, with hundreds of polishing corrections, all available spaces clogged with the crows of emendation.

That was the Balzac Study Group's goal: the "Inner Pulse

The Search for Coca Leaf Wine

In an old barn, with a sooty ceiling, the ancient posts had been replaced by jacked-up metal columns, and there was an old deer head, one of its eyes missing and evidence of decay in its hairless neck, upon the wall next to the American flag itself tacked with an unauctioned dart set to the paintless planks of the hay loft. There was a viewing stage beneath the flag and the auctioneer's podium apparently from a church some where with chipped decayed ornamental knobs looking like fried eggs smeared with

The two couples from Brooklyn sat, slowly filling the backs of their stationwagons to carry the booty of the houses of deceased farmer families back to their brownstones in BrookHo.

The auctioneer raised his gavel and moaned, "Who'll start me out with five?" while Marcie Margelson squinted her eye to read the writing on the bottle the barker was holding:

"$$$$$$$$$→?$$$$$$"

"C..O..C..A..Wine!" she shouted. And nudged Bernie, her husband. "Bernie!" she giggled, "that's an old bottle of Coca Leaf wine! I bet it's from the nineteenth century. What an idea! Bernie, hey, pay attention. We'd be rich and high all the time! We could market it..."

During the bidding war, Marcie glowered at the dealer in poison bottles holding up his hand against her! He dealt in poison bottles from the last century, the sort with squared edges so that when you reached to the bed table in the dark to

---

Handwritten marginalia:

"Yab-yum," thought Bernie, "I'll be in position on the Marcie or Antonia seat balancing-sitting reversed, driving-coiled spring will sit first on the wire"

at (y), then to slide down to me waiting in the backie "breccia" at (X)

Miso PASTE.

With those words Marcie Margelson opened up the vista of vulturous gentrification. The hollow slacks of bank account computers signaling a falling total. She'd not hear— Leaf lash! leef lash!

receptacks,

EXPAND in next set of valleys

Or, as of the 1302 Or, in China in time of China in-time of China Empress of ruby dropped a tapioca soufflé.

Wei Wang's

the PODIUM SCARRED FROM FIRE

Antonia's hands were

Re: Audience: white haired collectors, solten-pepper fire-plug shaped gens

NOPE

of intermarried valley cousins?

Worcestershire sauce.

Even the cockpits of the minicopters lashed to

in she thought

in poison bottles

STEP

speakers from a battered hi fi off somebody's dead relative.

Bernie was paying attention to an old wagon frame, next to be gaveled, thinking how GENTLY it would look in the bedroom, possibly as a perv-frame for some nocturnal yab-yum, I

The wagon frame once had been owned by the New Delhi, N.Y. grocery delivery man, "He caught a tumor in the winter wind," the auctioneer opined, rasp-coughing a Luck Strike lung in the midst of microphonous misprision-ment....

Someone trapped minicopter-eye.) (eye.)
in a sermonette lashed
Video-loop. to station
wagon roof

(I'm in the back!) (I'm in the back of his office!)

(That is it, it's a "beginning," says the Enigma Ellis says, "on as

R. House.........$350,000
Esquire serial......18
R. Stone...........8
Gorp.........27,500,000
Avon..........8,500,000
Warner.....14,000,000
(cont, please ask Barnaby for all 14 vols)

the roofs of their station wagons waxed packed w/ bric-a-brac, w/ salt & pepper sets marked "occupied Japan," w/ collapsible wine racks, w/ "boxes of contents," w/ Swedish novels from the 1930's, with oily-oozed chair doilies complete w/ the back-of-head outlines of Grandpa Van Wagenen's head at the century's inception

et pluvia plurima

—from Warner Brothers —George

Sandwiches & pickles conc wrinkling brine.
—Get
—Kath
—antonia
—Tandy
—anita
—Lauria D.C.
—Susan
—Sabra
Change name? to 8
Marcie's

Baltabes®
Hammerbank ......116,000 ??
Gallery: shaped foot multiples— 35,000
David Smith, auction, 225,000
Bid on Velasquez --- 1,200,000 ???

MON-FLOOD

Barrett
Barrett
Barrett
Barrett
Barrett

Ego, John, Ego!

THE FRAME of Perv
new title ?
Title of VOLUME 2.?

Hey, Ione!
How about inserting here
New/ ra-wur-ja-jo, LcMycenean wud for Booty?"?

"You shall anoint her breast, arms and shoulders and "with oil "
Bernie quoted,

EIGHT FIGURES!
No, John, nine figures!!!!

Write," the trance-like state in which their master had written. You could see them, holding a Balzac manuscript in one hand, staring at it intently, while writing automatically with the other hand.

Anything written on his galleys by the Big B inspired the Group. Balzac had the habit of jotting lists of his personal debts and lists of incoming mon on the edges of his manuscripts. One such penurious paradigm was found on page one of the manuscript of *Le père Goriot*, which seemed, with each half-hour of study, to engender a plot, a chief character, or a few brilliant pages of dialogue.

When Mt. Moo'-power made it possible, the Balzac Study Group, like Balzac, demanded their galleys printed on large sheets, with at least eight inches of paper on all sides of the printed column. Publishers sometimes sent photocopies of BSG corrected proofs to one another. They begged Balzac Study Group Attorney Barnaby Radither to keep the proofs locked in a safe after publication because of a fear that a grim expensive trend of black-blizzard galleys might roam among the writers of America.

The preceding is an example of a Balzac Study Group galley sheet, the opening lines of the first proof of *The Search for Coca Leaf Wine*. One can see why publishers wanted them locked away forever. Galleys like these are to be ruthlessly extirpated from writerdom!

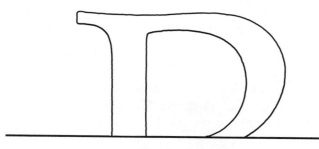

SIDE BAR B
SOME EARLY
BALZAC STUDY GROUP
NOVELS

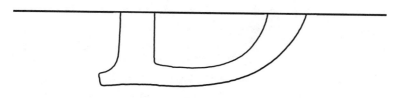

While we cannot list all of the forty-seven novels the Group produced in its first five years, we may select from them a few of the more prominent and stir-creating:

1. *La Messe de l'Athée* (1836) (or *Atheist's Mass*) became, through ingenious transformation equations, *Roman Rinpoche*, the story of a leading Catholic bishop who secretly converts to Tibetan Buddhism, and begins to proselytize in Papal circles.

2. *Louis Lambert* (1832), became *The Philosophy of Abraham Phatter*, wherein progressive computer scientists under the charis-

matic leadership of A. Phatter, foment the creation of 14 million teenaged left-wing Recombinant-DNA-contrived "obedience clones," to force nationalization of the utilities and phone companies and oil/agri-food networks. In the novel the "obedience clones" serve well, and the goal is accomplished by 1999. This book, while a satire, provoked great controversy, and, while hotly denied all around, may have set up the general air of discussion in which The 2000 Society was formed.

3. *Une Ténébreuse Affaire* (1843), was turned by the Group into the ultimate Chain-of-Terror novel, called *Jung Goes Bad*. Briefly, thermal tests in the Pacific by international consortium triggers a huge Fairy Ring of giant volcanoes; Hawaii destroyed; tidal wave ruins West Coast causing a nuclear meltdown at plants in California such that a huge blob of radioactivity is melting through earth toward China; this triggers San Andreas fault— bye bye San Francisco; this triggers nuclear response against Russia by NORAD—missile misattacks: bye bye Portland; national power grid goes black; meanwhile Arabs are sawing off, via "nuke laser," a giant piece of polar ice cap, to tow home to Saudi Arabia for agriculture; when the N. American disaster hits, the iceberg begins to float out of control—the state-sized ice floe smashes into Long Island, destroying it. The CIA disease lab off Long Island is also offed, germs are set loose plus new secret breed of killer bees: N.Y. State offed. The surge of malevolence creates excessive vibrations within the *Jungian Collective Unconscious,* with the result that mysterious cusps of violence erupt all over the globe: world offed, and at novel's end a darkling blob of Jungian disturbance sails out to confront the sun in orbit. The movie from *Jung Goes Bad* was four years in the making and cost 116 million dollars.

4. *Le Recherche de l'Absolu* (1834), (or *The Search for the Absolute*) became the forerunner of another popular modern genre, the "driven inventor" novel. Titled *The Search for Coca Leaf Wine,* it was the saga of Marcie and Bernie Margelson, proprietors of a successful upper Bleecker St. antique shop, who purchase at a Catskill auction an aged Coca Wine bottle, with label intact, from the 19th century when it was still legal. Their search? To

market such a wine, with the ingredients hidden from the feds. In gleeful search, imbibing much of their own product, Marcie and Bernie blow 500,000 dollars in savings, mortgage their house, and waste their children's college money, with mountains of chewed leaves left behind while testing for the ultimate brew, and nothing to show for it but a warehouse of abandoned chemical equipment.

Other titles worthy of mention in their early output included, *Starveling Hacks and the Nobel Prize; Jewish Middle Class Junkies in Rural America and Their Problems; Satisfied Cravings Among Literati;* and *S.T.D.*, the latter being the first of another genre created by the Balzac Study Group, called "initial novels." You were a pitiful specimen at a cocktail party if you did not know the real title of the latest BSG initial novel. *S.T.D.* was, of course, *Suicide Through Debauchery*, a book having the rather lamentable side effect of setting the style for a whole generation of wild youth, much in the way Turgenev had fingered the Nihilists. The generation was called the "Barfists," after the logo, ALL IS BARF, painted on their tee shirts, foreheads, and Duct Tape Capes. What was lamentable about that?—you may ask. Well, in the novel, the Barfists all wore transponders inserted into their hypothalami, or pleasure centers of their brains. The transponders, called Thrill-Ponders,® were sewn permanently within the scalp, and bore on their ends extension cords and outlet plugs, so that for periods of Total Thrill the wearer merely lay down and plugged itself into the nearest wall socket. It wasn't as speculative as the Balzac Study Group had believed, and soon thousands of thrill-starved youths were having illegal transponder implants and would lie around together in transponder crashpads criss-crossed with extension cords, slowly killing themselves via thrills.

Another "initial novel" was their transformation of *Le Lys dans la vallée*, (1836), titled *R.B.O.,* for *Ruined by Obsessions,* the tale of a modest woman overwhelmed by concealed cravings: by sexual desire, by collector's mania and the search for a perfect marriage, so that an obsessional worry about her obsessions ruins a perfect career as a record producer.

183

Secret titles by secret authors! The appeal was nationwide, and those who thrive on advance data—clairvoyants, disk jockeys, and gossip columnists as well—vied among themselves to be the first to announce the correct titles of the Initial Novels.

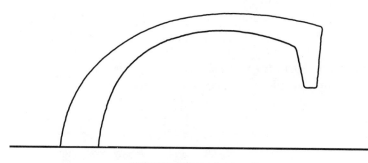

SIDE BAR C
THE BALZAC STUDY GROUP
BUSINESS EMPIRE

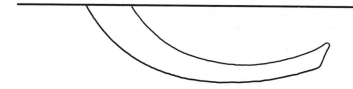

Since it delved so deeply into the desperate economics of the creative, the Balzac Study Group thought it best to set up a Business Empire. Empires were in fashion. It was something rock bands, surrounded by financial advisers eager for action, often tried to do. J'Accuse, for example, owned a disproportionate number of motels in the State of Washington, having fallen for the old "Own 'em all, partner, and then clean up!" scam.

But, did not Balzac cull from his business disasters material for the *Comédie*? The Group had marveled at the Big B's plan once to grow pineapples under glass houses at his country property, seriously planned, but a calamity as far as mon-rake was concerned. Balzac's 1826/27/28 triad of lettuce-loss was a major source of information for *Lost Illusions*. In those three years, he formed a publishing company, a disaster which lost 15,000 francs, then bought a printing company right away, a disaster, and then bought a type foundry, the liquidation of which in 1828 left him in the debt-mire the rest of his life. But what insight he acquired into the mire!

It wasn't just information the Group sought; a Business Empire was an opportunity to put some of its economic theories to work, to set up companies in which the employees owned most of the stock, for instance. Some businesses were formed merely to provide employment for friends. Wendy Sark was in charge of the Empire, and she was determined to set up a balanced conglomerate. While profligate in her private life, like other venture capitalists she was conservative in the life of lettuce. Beyond anyone's expectations, she was successful. Too successful.

After all, you have to fail in order to appreciate the mire of malfiscality. "*Some* of our fiscal projects," John Barrett complained, "ought to sink like a greasy anvil through aspic." Wendy was encouraged to speculate more; to take risks. At that she was successful also. Again, too successful, as we shall see. Their predictions were accurate, for as Wendy set up various complicated business disasters, they marveled at the new seams thus uncovered in the endless N.Y. seaminess-mine, and the plots and story ideas bubbled out of it as out of a giant frontal lobe. Here, then, is the Balzac Study Group's Business Empire:

1. First, there was *SoAir, Incorporated,* intended as a vehicle to get close to the economics of Sigmund Hammerbank and Milton Rosé. As a dash up Mt. Mooh', it was unsurpassed. SoAir solved the problem of gunge-sprinkled air in lower New York. Dirigibles of compressed air floated from the Rocky Mountain Glacier Air Works, situated above a glacier north of Boulder; and when the delicious air was transferred to Air Units on the tops or sides of loft-salon buildings, the last barrier to living in N.Y. was cast into the vale of sneers.

2. *Scythia Restaurants and Hemp Seed Sauna Houses* (in partnership with Sigmund Hammerbank), promoting the culture of Old Scythia, the ancient lands around the Black Sea. Tens of thousands flocked to refresh themselves in the authentic Scythian goatskin and duct tape tents made steamy by pecks of hemp seeds dumped on red-hot stones. There were open hearths, in the Scythian manner, containing bone-fires, and the Scythian skin-care method, a paste of cypress/cedar/frankincense, hued of reddish taupe, covered faces after the hemp sauna and before plunging into pools made of rocks brought all the way from the Dnieper River. There were Glory of Scythia stores attached to the restaurants, selling replicas of Scythian jewelry, hemp-cloth saddle blankets, duct tape yurts, and Scythian face-paste. The apparent habit of Scythian horsemen to tenderize meat by inserting chunks between the saddle and the horse's hide as they galloped long distances was romantically captured by Scythia Restaurants via saddle-shaped hamburger griddles which clamped down on red-hot metal horses' backs.

3. *Privacy Tents, Inc.* There was, in all of N.Y., no place to be cheaply passionate, or to be by one's self for meditation, research, or naps. Privacy Tents were extremely popular, whole streets being closed off for use as sort of Privacy Tent KOA campgrounds. Especially popular was the Wilhelm Reich Privacy Tent line, featuring solar-powered vibrating pillows, mini-showers, and radar to track any minicopter muggers approaching.

4. *Balslag Mining Company.* The Group's first real fiscal disaster, and what a disaster! Here was an example of a Balzac mistake they felt they could correct. In 1838, the impoverished Big B, calculating a profit of over 1,000,000 francs, traveled tortuously by boat to Sardinia, and then by horse to the ancient Roman silver-workings, where he felt that by improved modern extracting processes, he could garner cheaply the silver in the ancient tailings. Balzac had

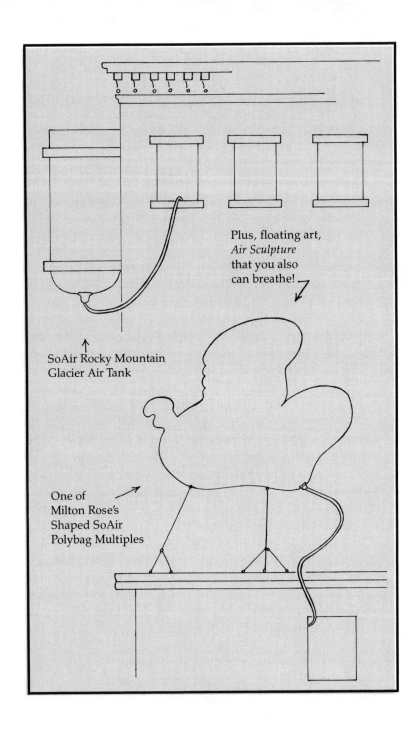

Plus, floating art,
Air Sculpture
that you also
can breathe! ⬎

↑
SoAir Rocky Mountain
Glacier Air Tank

One of
Milton Rose's
Shaped SoAir
Polybag Multiples

blabbed his plan, and a syndicate had already gained the concession, and the million francs went to others. In his role as scientific advisor, John Barrett researched the question of gold and silver mines, and had learned of a solar energy and microwave extraction method, untested, but worthy, he felt, of a try. In conditions of total secrecy the Balzac Study Group, using a million dollar paperback advance, began to purchase tons of old mounds heaped up around abandoned mines above Boulder, Colorado. Wendy Sark, under orders "to take risks," thereupon purchased several huge dirigibles and formed the SoLift Dirigible Delivery Service, which would have hauled tons of the ore to an abandoned subway tunnel in Brooklyn Heights, where the metal would be extracted. The million dollar advance was exhausted in a month, and the Group was delirious with joy over having a Balzac-level business failure from which to gather ideas. They weren't mistaken in this regard, for they wrote a smash novel soon thereafter, *The Lost Hippie Mine,* about a group of exploiters who enslave old Blue Bird buses full of wandering communards and press the communards into underground mining camps for years of manacles, privation, and rock-hack.

5. *H°B°I° (Hypno-Bio Incorporated).* The mon poured in on this one. For 2500 dollars, any citizen could sign release papers and BSG employees would produce a biography of them, by hypnotically regressing the citizen back to diaperhood, and coaxing every event from the brain-files from there forward. The implications in H°B°I° were enormous. No more sleepy boring years at the night stand trying to put the day's events into a diary! Just wait till one's career's zenith, and then hire H°B°I° to suck it out of the pink sphere! Senior citizens, with a few H°B°I° sessions, could produce an autobiography of around 5000 pages single-spaced. The problems mainly devolved around skipping the citizen through the memories of deaths and trauma, always frightfully clear under hypno-regression, but the reliving of the technicolor eros of first loves on hayrides 55 years

ago was worth it to the customers. Ione Appleton and George Plyght were instrumental in creating "H°B°I°-chic," and many a senator, society matron, and corporation executive plunked down the 2500 for a "Personal Roots" job. Fuck the distant past! they seemed to be saying—why grovel in old court records and geneology tables just to learn your great-great-grandmother ran a dog act in a Rumanian circus, when you can concentrate on the living roots of Numero Uno, i.e., yourself, via H°B°I°?

6. *Balzac's Blend Coffee, Ltd.* The Group of course knew that Balzac drank a strong crushed mixture of Mocha, Martinique, and Bourbon, so all they had to do was use a computer to mix the blend that produced the most powerful stimulation while not losing taste. Big bucks at campus bookstores.

7. *Baltabe,® Ltd.* Limited editions of Balzac's writing desk.

8. *Gem Spa.* N.Y.'s ace literary egg cream and chocolate/marshmallow cookie source, located at St. Mark's and Second Avenue, up the street from Duct Tape Boutique. A tunnel was constructed from Gem Spa to the Creativity Bunker, enabling secret 4 a.m. forays for food, sugar flashes, and newspapers.

9. *The Algonquin Hotel.*

10. *Proustcork® Writers Silencing Systems, Inc.*

11. *Days Play,® Inc.* Coca leaf/sesame paste/marzipan chewing plug. The spirit of rural arr!-harr! arrives with energetic vengeance! That nemesis of the foot that accidentally steps into it, the spittoon, once relegated to the American pool hall, became fashionable in loft-salons and galleries.

12. *Literary Secrets Publishing Co.*

    a. Domestic Quarrels of Literati

    b. Project Masticated Spine

    c. The Gug Papers

A few words are in order regarding the *Literary Secrets Publishing Company* and its three publications. Through these, the Balzac Study Group created still another genre of publication, the Literary Quiz Book. All America pretended to be mortified by *Domestic Quarrels of Literati,* a thick tome edited from archivist Art Archives' allegedly abandoned project, *What the Poet is Really Like.* Surveillance chips were placed in the bedrooms and living rooms of 200 of America's foremost writers for a period of three weeks. Before *Domestic Quarrels of Literati* only the FBI, divorce investigators, and intelligence agencies knew the total spectrum of the private disputes of Americans.

Names were left out to protect the garbager and the garbaged both, and to ward off lawsuits. Each Quarrel ended with a short quiz, of true/false, multiple choice, and fill-in-th'-blank. Identity clues had to be provided, for oft the loftiest of literary names had the lowliest of dirt-cheap fights, and one would not have thought such language, borrowed from the operating table and the slums of Colophon, would have been used by such cultured men and women. The book sold four million copies in hardback.

People said, "I'd never purchase such a disgusting piece of trash!"—yet somehow it arrived at their bedside reading shelves. There was something universal about the Quarrels that made all humanity seem as one. Even among Nobel Prize winners and writers with six-figure incomes, there were the commonest, most trite, most prolix, arguments about money, sex, fame, power, jealousy, the attraction of grad students, wills, heirs, *et alia multa*. In Quarrel after Quarrel suspicions were confirmed regarding a sort of Universal Grouchiness afflicting the creative. What a calming ointment such news was to millions, who knew now they were not alone!

In some ways though, literary Hearth-Quarrels were

unique. Angry spouses often demanded to know what the hell happened to disperse that huge paperback advance so quickly. Directed toward male writers, there were numerous fights on the theme, "You're an alcoholic dirty womanizing bum, and all your friends are alcoholics!" Toward successful women writers, the epithets seemed crude pin-pricks to deflate the balloon of haughtiness and overweening id. How shameful it was to hear on the tapes the out-of-style words, "nymphomaniac," "man-izer," and "womanizing bum" tossed around by sneering husbands, wives, and lovers!

The market for *The Gug Papers* was not quite so extensive. A disgruntled poet, rejected seventeen straight years for a Guggenheim Fellowship, acquired, probably by breaking and entering, a fifty-year sampling of letters of recommendation from writers ostensibly urging that certain other brother and sister writers be awarded fellowships. This slender volume, you say, obviously was a collection of hastily-typed hyperbolic puffery of friends writing about friends. Not quite. Not all the letters by far were approbatory. Many august literati might have their feelings badly damaged seeing the callous way their careers and writing ability were handled in alleged letters of recommendation which were drenched in irony, double entendre, and scarcely concealed raillery.

The opportunity to read the letters to the Foundation from T. S. Eliot, Hemingway, etc., created a market for about 100,000 copies, but a 500,000 dollar ad budget insisted on by George Plyght made the project a true venture into the Balzacian debt-mire for the Group.

Most noble of the three books published by the Group's *Literary Secrets Publishing Company,* was *Project Masticated Spine,* a well-planned attempt to break the habit on the parts of poets and poetasters to engage in "bard-stab." And what is "bard-stab"? 'Tis the instant spurts of putdown, cynical comment, deprecation of writing ability, guffawings at physical decay, and the like, which occur among a group of poets in a room whenever one should walk out of earshot, or when the name of someone not present is brought into the conversation.

Let's say we're backstage at the 92nd Street Y, just before a reading, and the bard is sitting nervously with a circle of friends and verse-vultures, awaiting the call from the stage. The bard leaves his chair to retire to the powder room. No sooner is he gone, than: "His hair is falling out," one friend says.

"Yes, his wife is having an affair with my brother,"—another.

"Indeed, his last book was a disappointing piece of worm wax,"—a third.

"Okay, did you catch the expanding stomach?"—a fourth.

"Ha, that's because he's nervous about his silent typewriter," a fifth was quick to add.

"Iggle, iggle," a sixth laughed, "He dreams about a phone call from Stockholm, but the only call he's going to get is from the chairman when they take away his tenure. I know! I'm the chairman!"

And so it goes, until the dear pal returns to sit until introduction time.

A team went out surreptitiously all over America to record thousands of incidents of "bard-stab." Whereas *The Gug Papers* and *Domestic Quarrels* were circumspect, and left most names out, *Project Masticated Spine* trumpeted the names of those chewing the spines of brothers and sisters of literature. Such a scandal it created! The results, however, were magnificent, for those with proclivity toward "bard-stab" were hesitant for years thereafter to drop slime-grime on brother or sister poets, without at least the most careful analysis of the people in the room—asking themselves, "Who has the tape recorder, who is prepared to ruin me, who lurks to shorthand my slime-grime?"

THE THEFT OF
COUNT RASPACHI'S
MANUSCRIPTS

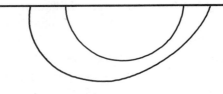

"Psst, George, over here!" Ione gasp-yelled to George Plyght as they crawled beneath a wall of medieval armor in Count Raspa-chi's castle in Milan. Perhaps the pink radio speaker in George's ear connecting them to Wendy and John in the van outside pre-vented him from hearing her, for he continued his disparate crawl down the wrong corridor. Plyght experienced great diffi-culty in his crawl, for the hideous vibrations his knees were en-countering, rubbing and chaffing against the Count's antique Lombard rug, were causing waves of nausea. It was to George what the squeaking of chalk on blackboards is to millions of others. George could stand it no longer, and stood up, albeit in a crouch, causing the Count's alarm beam to be broken, and a "warf-warf!" of spiked-collar mastiffs was heard to start, and a low siren waking the servants.

Luckily they were near the manuscript display cases when George Plyght triggered the mastiffs. Ione cracked the glass with her turquoise canne de Monsieur de Balzac, and pulled the treasures into her Lantern of Knowledge Bookstore tote bag, and the twain hit the bricks in haste. Hand over hand they dangled and bobbed along the underside of a rope ladder tied across Count Raspachi's treacherous moat, and fell into the back door of the van, which sped away so precipitously the rear doors trailed open all the way to the airport.

Ione had left a note on the shattered glass: "Dear Count R.; We shall return the manuscripts in good condition. In celerity, The Balzac Study Group." It was the first time they had publicly mentioned their name, an incident to be regretted as we shall see. Beneath the signature, Ione appended the coat of arms of the Group: silver background with sable printing press, azure chevron, and in the chief: stars gules (red) with dangling coke spoons; tressure of Mystic Initials.[8]

There was absolute jubilation in the back of the van when members began to receive ideas at once from hastily scanning the documents.

---

8. The Sacred Mystic Initials, O.T.I.C.L.A.O.D.I.A.R.S.O.E., for "O that I could live as others do in a regular succession of employment," William Blake lamenting to Wm. Hayley in 1803.

Smump! Smump! Smump! occurred aplenty as George Plyght kissed them page by page. "Dearest Balzac!" spake he, "Thou hast shown us the golden kernel of corn in Demeter's omphalos! Christ! Look at these manuscripts!! Already I can think of questions to ask! Dearth is gone! Conduct me to my writing desk! Smump! Smump! . . ."

Oh reader, what calamity is this we behold—the world's greatest Stress Questioner and its greatest Apothegmist creepy-crawling a castle!? We can assure ourselves with certainty that only the loftiest motives could force a creepycrawl upon great writers. What were these motives? The blame for the lamentable crawl lay on the negative effects of the Indulgence Bunker as much as anything else.

"You mean Creativity Bunker, don't you?" a reader may ask. Unfortunately, we do not. The Indulgence Bunker originally had been the storage area the Group used to satisfy its growing collectors' mania. They rented the apartment above the Creativity Bunker where soon the floor groaned with storage crates of statuary, armor, art, stamp albums, art deco erotica— nearly a million dollars worth. If the reader has ever seen the initial photos taken by Howard Carter in 1923 just after they had broken into the treasure rooms of Tut-Ankh-Amun's tomb, you will capture an idea of how packed with goodies was the Indulgence Bunker.

They assured themselves, "Well, one needs samples of furniture, costumes, and bric-a-brac from many eras if one is to have on hand items to describe in one's historical novels, doesn't one?"

The BSG discovered a secret of collectors' mania, the supreme thrill of tantalizing glimpses of nude white marble statues seen through open crates. Not to mention the inexpressible pleasure of inserting one's hand through the sides of an open crate, pushing aside the shredded excelsior like a bushy coiffure, and then to poke a searching finger beneath a cool marble fig leaf, or to pat a perfect shoulder, kiss an ageless marmoreal eyelid, or to meditate in the morn while softly rubbing a genius-carved buttock, chest, or foot!

In this mode the Indulgence Bunker gradually fructified.

To reach the Indulgence Bunker one entered the back of the Duct Tape Boutique, pushed the button exposing the hidden stairwell, then took the escalator to the Creativity Bunker, walked to the back of it too, pushed another button, and proceeded up a second secret stairwell to the Indulgence Bunker.

The effect of climbing two secret stairwells, with two hidden doors, was to seal them within the Indulgence Bunker. Try as they might to keep them separate, Creativity and Indulgence became as one.

The ambiance was set by an array of gold letters above the door, a quote from the *Comédia*:

OUR LIVES SHOULD BE GUIDED ONLY BY THIS AXIOM
'TAKE ALL THE PLEASURE YOU CAN.'

The Indulgence Bunker had an extremely negative effect on the productivity of the Group. The first five years of the Balzac Study Group had passed so fruitfully! Although not all of their 47 novels during that period had been received warmly by the critics, all had been successful at the ultimate test: units processed through the checkout counters of the world. There had been lucrative paperback contracts for all 47, plus 671 foreign publishing deals, seven movies already made and shown, three underway, six in the can, and another fifteen bought and held in the property departments of major producers.

It was not the hedonism of the Indulgence Bunker that harmed the Group, rather it was the growth of slovenly work habits. In their apartments in SoHo and the Village, they struggled to stay scruffy, and among their friends to keep a worried face on poverty's edge. In the Indulgence Bunker they could lounge about in the languor of lazy luxury. The boredom was exquisite. They took long common afternoon naps even though editors were waiting for texts. It seemed tiresome to continue to mask their names. They wondered if Walter Scott had waxed as bored masking authorship of the Waverly novels as they waxed now in the Indulgence Bunker.

To their credit, the BSG continued their charitable works, purchasing 12,000 replacement barrels for the Brooklyn Bridge

Barrel Generation housing complex. John Barrett had acted on his idea for a secret literary prize, The Balzac. *The 'Zac,* as it was better known, a replica of Balzac's coffee urn with a check for 10,000 dollars inside, had been given anonymously to over 100 needful writers. The Group financed many a left-liberal running for office, and paid for many an investigation into the slime of the robo-right, and the lime of the robo-left. Even so, they felt cut off from their causes.

One fear was that should publishers discover that their huge advances were funding projects like the 15-volume *Encyclopedia of 20th Century War Criminals, Techno-Fascist Profiteers, Evil Scientists, and Robo-Washers,* then the advances might dwindle alarmingly.

Indeed, publishers were concerned aplenty over a certain drift in the tone of the later books of the Balzac Study Group. We are speaking of the tendency toward the trash-job, and especially those trash-jobs directed toward the mores of journalists and publishers. In one lamentable instance (the final Initial Novel put out by the Group, T. L. E. S. W. T. G. O. T. L. P.), when the publisher discerned that the initials were those for The Last Editor Strangled With the Guts of the Last Publisher, a grim adaptation from an adage of Voltaire, the book was very nearly suppressed, and only the solemn promise of BSG attorney Barnaby Radither never to reveal the meaning of the initials saved the project.

The Balzac Study Group did not consider it harmful to become oriented toward the trash-job. After all, is it not the Age of Garbage? But, if garbage of others becomes the Grail, can self-garbage be far hence? Ruinous is a perma-stare into the Ruin. It was as if in paying so much attention to the mire, they became it. After about the 40th book, each member secretly felt they had Slime-Ponders® irretrievably inserted into the sleaze sections of their brains.

The slide toward sleaze was not without its opulent ease. There would always be a movie playing on a screen tacked to the sides of a priceless crate. A dumbwaiter was installed to handle deliveries from Umberto's Clam House. You couldn't walk the tunnel back from Gem Spa to the Creativity Bunker without crushing at least 25 fallen cookies or marshmallow choco-bars, which the cursing unwary trodder would slip-'n'-slide upon to leave a treacherous trail of smeared sienna and rubeous raspberry. Wendy was the culprit, for she had given herself, stomach and soul, to eating and dorking. She couldn't understand why anybody'd bother to dust their face in the cocaine pig trough when one could do it with Wheat Chex and sex. With sauces, with spatters of ink, with crusts of tool drool, her clothes grew tawdry, as she mixed seven meals a day with eleven love affairs "in the name of Information," until she broke eleven demanding hearts, and banned them from her bed, no longer caring to interrupt obeisance at the refrigerator's mouth-must to take showers for the overfastidious men of New York.

As for Ione, she began spending far too much valuable time on another invention, the so-called Laser-Lingus® machine, which combined high frequency sound waves with lasers and alternating cool/hot pulsating water microjets in the creation of a beam/vibration of self-thrill. There were numerous engineering problems, as evinced by the numerous laser burns Ione suffered in the lower extremities in the haste of thrillsome invention. The danger of charbroiling the Venusian V did not deter her one buzz of ultrasound and her workbench grew packed with soldering equipment, tubes, and electronic components. It distracted terribly from the jotting of apothegms.

The Group began conducting shameless orgies of the type you'd have thought to be out of style by now; they descended to the ho-hum land of sadomasochism. The reader can picture the boring patterns of reddened coke-spoon outlines upon bored buttocks from being spanked with the ends of the ceintures on their Balzacian robes. George Plyght set up a roulette wheel and card table by Ione's workbench, and coaxed them all into time-wasting dawns of gambling, with coca-tinged mottlings of mucous all but blocking their nasal passages. Others became druggies. Would you believe elegant Indo-European linguist John Barrett a gluehead? Oh yes, he tried to improve on the image of the staggering dum-dum with its head at the mouth of a paper bag by wearing an ancient Swedish iron-mesh warrior's helmet and squirting the Comet model airplane cement through the

199

mesh against his purpling face. Gluehead is gluehead, John, Swedish helmet or paper bag.

The ugliest sigil of degradation in the Indulgence Bunker was a 17th century silver pig trough with silver porcine legs and silver cloven hooves at the floor, and tiny golden pigs' faces embedded in each silver knee cap. One night they uncrated the silver pig trough and dumped 45 ounces of boring out-of-style cocaine in it. Whenever they wrote thereafter they first lowered their faces to the trough. Why use the coke spoons on the tassels of your writing robes when you can use your face like a pigeon in a dust bath? Piles of rare books served as low stools around the pig trough, the fruit of John Barrett's expensive bibliophilomania. John spent hours selecting a proper collection of books for his own stool, settling on the 1473 edition of Polybius' *History of Rome,* a 15th century *Ars Amatoria* of Ovid, Ezra Pound's presentation copy of *Finnegan's Wake;* and *Four Quartets* (presentation copy to Angleton, CIA counter-intelligence chief).

Gradually the Group had slipped into the Big B's bad habit of signing a contract on a title, or upon the slimmest of outlines. For the first time in their career, the BSG failed to meet deadlines, though publishers remained so confident in their prolificity that a publication party would be announced prior to receiving the manuscript, and the p.r. staff would pack the event with celebrities, allowing the gossip columnists great play at guessing if the real authors were in attendance. Modern speed of publication allowed the Group to use the Hotel Pierre publication parties as their real deadlines, delivering manuscripts only several days in advance, and books would be available only minutes before the festivities.

Closer and closer they shaved the possible time. Nothing seemed to inspire them. Gone were the days when a couple of hours gazing at the Père Goriot money lists could have spawned a trilogy.

At last the Group, walking the sword edge 'tween coma and convulsion, lost out to coma. When the messenger arrived to pick up the manuscript of their latest book, *The Triumph of Guilt,* he could not have known the absolute panic the deadline had caused the Group. Another book, due in one month,

200

seemed out of the question. John Barrett lay asleep on the floor wearing his Swedish glue mask, using a priceless medieval breviary as a pillow.

Ione had passed out sitting up, her head sunk into the silver pig trough. Luckily her face was to the side and she was not smothered in C. On the floor, beamed between her thighs, was the purring Laser-Lingus® machine. George Plyght was curled up asleep on top of his red velvet craps table. The only sound, besides the Laser-Lingus,® was "sluup, slurgle, slashle, sloshle . . ."—Wendy Sark's exploration of mouth noise, sitting in front of an open refrigerator chewing the remains of last night's delivery from Umberto's.

Was this to be the end of the Balzac Study Group? Wendy had so badly neglected the Business Empire that Balzac's worst was matched. Vandals in minicopters had taken to stealing Milton Rosé's SoAir Polybag Multiples on SoHo rooftops, supplying, it will be remembered, fresh Rocky Mountain glacier air to the blackened lungs of New Yorkers. Maf-org was trying to muscle in on the lucrative SoAir business, and had sabotaged the dirigible landing station. Losses were at 500 thousand, and rising.

John Barrett, in what he thought to be the business deal of the century, had fallen prey to one of the oldest rare book scams, the Casket Iliad hype, and lost 750,000 of the Group's savings. All considered, it was absolutely necessary for them to step up productivity. Comas, boredom, and metaphysical distress do not good dialogue produce, as evinced by their latest novel, *The Triumph of Guilt*, which, although a success, made reviewers salivate for the obviously impending moment when brays and guffaws could safely be issued over the decline in powers of the greatest writing team ever assembled.

Unable to sleep, Wendy began out of habit to go over the notes from her last few days of data-gathering. She had been focusing on the strange relationship between Count Claudio Volpe, Sigmund Hammerbank (owner of the Hammerbank Gallery you will recall), and Milton Rosé. Among other tidbits, she unearthed that Rosé was unaware that it was Count Volpe who had not long ago secretly purchased the destruction/construction, *Circles of Paradise*. A promising tidbit. This was the sort of info you use in plying your Stress Questions. Wendy deciphered an obscure note on her pad, a remark from Hammerbank to Rosé at a recent opening, to the effect that a friend of Count Volpe, one Count Emilio Raspachi, a partner in Volpe's rare powder commodities speculations, had just acquired some allegedly unpublished Balzac manuscripts, and was bragging about it all over European cocaine circles.

Wendy knew she'd found the solution to the inspiration problem. At once she slapped everyone awake, and they huddled to plan the caper.

No sooner were they able to drip some perusing drool upon the purloined manuscripts, than restored were their powers! For months thereafter the books poured from their pens. Just in time for the Christmas rush they completed their trend-setting five-volume novel (*Scenes from the Private Lives of Techno-Fascism*), with each of the five volumes as long as *Gravity's Rainbow*. It wasn't long before nascent novelists felt guilt if they couldn't enter the marketplace with a five-volume opener. *Scenes from the Private Lives of Techno-Fascism* made four million dollars in six weeks, and Mt. Moolah was conquered anew!

One of the Balzac manuscripts was a youthful adventure novel written under a pseudonym; another was a lengthy handwritten fragment of a disturbing novel in which the ghost of Lucien de Rubempré (star of *Lost Illusions*) approaches the aged Emile Blondet on the latter's death bed to deliver a lecture in Swedenborgian metaphysics. This fragment greatly upset the paranoid and dissolute BSG in the Indulgence Bunker. So you can guess their relief when, after handwriting analysis, the fragment was determined to have been a forgery. Raspachi had been had.

The genuine manuscript, however, was a great boon to the BSG Business Empire, for it supplied two things: (1) a latent fingerprint of Balzac; and (2) the formula for Balzac's own blend of coffee. You see, the juvenile novel could not provide much inspiration in terms of P&S—plot and structure, but folded inside the pages were a couple of bills from Balzac's tailor Buisson. On one was a genuine Big B coffee spill. This they had analyzed at a lab and were able to find the exact Bourbon / Martinique / Mocha blend for their coffee company. There was a finger smudge on the edge of the coffee spill capturing enough of B's forefinger print to positively identify it. That gave them the idea to dust the manuscript and chits for prints. Then, lo!, or in Egyptian, mek!, they found, using the most sophisticated modern chemical tests, a faint griseous print on the chit, next to the spill, which then was pulled off, photographed, and made into a poster for the walls of the bunkers. Aeternitas!

Eight months passed, and in addition to the quintology for the Christmas rush, they completed three other novels, the so-called Starved Fox series (*The Starved Fox; The Starved Fox and the White Stag of Fame;* and *The Stodgy Buffalos from the Starved Fox's Ashes*). Starved Fox denoted a certain type of journalist then prevalent in the Apple. The novels created great irritation among such journalists, especially among those who found thinly disguised portrayals of themselves in the books.

After the last of the Starved Fox novels had been published, and the fury of lampooned vulpinity had somewhat abated, there came the predictable time when the Balzac Study Group's writing again ground to a halt. They were totally unable to write.

No one bothered to ask George Plyght the results of the latest list of Stress Questions they had given him to ply. Wendy was living again at the refrigerator door, and had given up any form of interview; John Barrett had not read anything on the microfiche viewer in weeks. Ione had developed a duct tape/canvas belt enabling one to wear the Laser-Lingus® around the clock. She lumbered about in floorlength duct-tape gowns with bustles and hoop-slips to hide the cumbersome equipment.

There came the night of the Great Lamentation. Tentatively BSG had decided to have cryptic Thrill-Ponder® inserts cut into their scalps, and a central thrill plug-in console built beside the coke trough. That same night they committed a most horrible sin. They had promised a donation of $10,000 to the National Society of Senior Citizen Proofreaders, but instead, prompted by an evil flash, they had burned the money on the Altar of Lost Illusions and ground the ashes into each other's genitals in a further shameless, out-of-style communal groin-clink. "Let's face it," Ione muttered to Wendy, "The only time I've ever been happy is fucking," and they lay down together on the vibrating Bal-Bed® while by remote switch they lowered two Laser-Lingus® machines into position from the ceiling.

Wendy felt something malevolent, dark and crispy like a tiny bat wing, flutter down upon her face. She screamed, hitting it away. It was a charred bill once destined to aid the golden years of proofreaders. "We're better off dead!" Wendy screamed again, hurling the Laser-Lingus® to an expensive crash. Everyone was shocked. Wendy was never that forceful.

Wendy kicked the Lingus, hating it, her friend of many a night. "Why don't we just turn it up to full power and let it burn out our eyes! We deserve it!" Something, some common energy had been building among them that Wendy's words unleashed. Shrieking grief at a funeral was the sound closest to it. Loud moans, quiet moans, and the dismal chirps of suicide arose among them. Grief poured from life-burnt lips until the fingers of dawn smeared pomegranate juice upon the fetid cenotaphic skyline.

Throughout, the theme was common. "We call ourselves a *Cénacle* when we're nothing but putrid gush in Balzac's bedpad!! We're nothing more than bandits! We do not deserve our success! If publishers knew who we were, we'd never get another advance! We have repeated every mistake Balzac ever made!"

One of them ran to the Altar, seized *Illusions perdues*, and set it afire, tossing the book into the silver pig trough. "We selected the correct book for our altar!" George Plyght screamed, flinging the humming Laser-Lingus® machine into the pig trough on top of the burning book.

Ione ran to retrieve her dearest consolation from the flames. "Nonsense!" she countered. "What's missing from our life," thinking perhaps of the attempted rhinectomy on Mt. Rushmore, "are moments of absolute ecstasy completely embedded in moments of danger."

"Well, you'll not get that in the Indulgence Bunker with a 1,500,000 paperback advance," John Barrett replied. Everyone was shocked over this seeming putdown of the sacred concept of the huge paper contract. "John, go wash out your mouth in the coke trough this instant!" the eyes of reproach seemed silently to rebuke.

Had the Group thus recovered its composure? "If we just stick it out another five years, we may be the first to go eight figures!" Ione shouted.[9]

"No, Ione, we're dead!" John Barrett spoke. "The Thanatophonous Worm cuts off our eyelids and weaves them into gaskets to mend our souls! We all know what we must do! We must donate our money, our name, our scriptive skills to the task of tasks—to that which saves our country as it saves us—to The 2000 Society!" John was weeping.

For minutes there was silence. Ione at last nodded in agreement, followed by Wendy and George. One of them opened the wall safe and dumped a pouch containing 700,000 dollars next to the candle on the Altar of Lost Illusions. Ione beckoned them to join in worship. Together they stood around the pile of green, and spake a common chant—solemn, soft, slow—one of their favorite quotes from all of Balzac:

> "One by one they drop,
> some into the trench where failures lie,
> some into the mire of journalism, some
> again to the quagmires of the book trade . . ."

to which they added the triumphant coda,

> "But Not Us! Not us! Not us! Not us! Not us! . . ."

Always a satisfying chant, and more so on this night of renewed resolve. Suddenly a 1000 dollar bill caught fire! Brightly Grover Cleveland's face made merry as it burned—they swore it seemed

---

9. "The first to go eight figures!" Indeed, the Grail for paperback advances. Perhaps when they were old and hoary, with space colony distribution set up, the BSG could have expected a book to "go Galactic" to trillions of copies, and then, honor of honors, the first nine-figure paper advance!

to laugh and to shout! Its mouth curled up into a perfect smile until a grey tendril of smoke and a wrinkle of rangy red devoured it. John Barrett thrust forth in song, to the tune of *Yellow Submarine*:

We all live in Grover Cleveland's grave
Grover Cleveland's grave
Grover Cleveland's grave . . .

The others also sang.

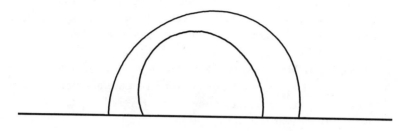

FITZ M^CIVER
TAKES THE CASE

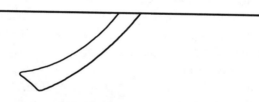

There was great danger of fresh thumbs being flung into Count Claudio Volpe's Etruscan vase. The great art historian and speculator in rare powders was angered to his Etrurio-Druid roots, his great Gabby Hayes mane of hair shaking as he snarled orders into his 24-line telephone console. "Get those manuscripts back, or you'd better put a dotted line around your thumb," he barked at Sigmund Hammerbank in what was as close to a Conceptual Threat as the Count was capable.

Volpe was concerned about his own health, for if Count Volpe seemed lupine in his behavior, his pal Count Raspachi was the type to tie your mom to the stake on dog-blood beach.

Raspachi was a key member of the looney-right Italian group known as Ordine Nero. If Count Volpe took your thumbs, Raspachi was an eye-gouge man. He had no Etruscan vase for storage, but rather used a Waring blender to remove the unsightly evidence. "If ever I see a painting by our dear Mr. Rosé with my friend's manuscripts tacked to it," Count Volpe continued, "I personally will perpendicularly suture four thumbs—yours and his—to the canvas." The gasps and gulps from Hammerbank's end of the scrambler were not from fright *per se*, but rather that his secretary, entering unannounced, should spot the blotch of terrorist micturitions besotting the crotch of his trousers.

Sigmund Hammerbank kept the scrambler in operation and at once called one of America's foremost literary detectives, Fitzgerald McIver, a former OSS officer revered for legendary exploits during War II in Italy, and later with the Missile Protection Agency, from which he had retired over issues of the 1960's war. The security clearance required for participation in the Missile Protection Agency was so lofty that McIver was in a privileged position even though he had retired in protest. The Agency, responsible for the protection of the missiles of America from attack and sabotage, provided Mr. McIver with the circumstances of his proclivity toward "surveillance chip mania." *When in doubt, Surv-Chip® was Fitz' motto.*

McIver gladly took the case. It occupied his time for eight months, and it was the sort of investigation a private eye dreams about—an unlimited expense account. From this case, Fitz put away $175,000 into his numbered account in the Bahamas; not bad for a grouchy 64-year-old archives-shoe from better days. He left a churn of Q's across the United States and every country in Europe. He surv-chipped everywhere, and by the end of three months had 400 chips in place. Stenographers by the dozens typed transcripts of the tapes.

Hammerbank, who had nervously and symbolically taken to biting the skin from his threatened thumbs, rode Fitz mercilessly for results. The case was baffling. The only clue had been the note. But what the hell was the Balzac Study Group? It could have been anything. At first, Fitz felt it might have been a prank pulled off, say, by a graduate creative writing class somewhere, so he spent countless hours calling universities speaking with Balzac scholars, and asking about any informal groups holding high reverence for the Big B.

A few words about McIver's appearance are in order. He had small eyes in large sockets that, jutting, reminded the observer of a flying squirrel. His cheekbones formed curving shelves just beneath the eyes, yet his jaws seemed lumpily gaunt as if he were ever sucking in his cheek meat like a coot with a shifting wad of chewing tobacco. He had the raw, wet, cold hands of a Puritan, unaccustomed to love, yet somehow they were the appendages of a loving soul. His hands aided one of his forgivable vices, his need to listen to erotic taped National Security wiretap babble of the famed and the highly placed. After his retirement, he found that there were no eros tapes so inventive and interesting as those of New York City. You know how to these creative types the sound of a zipper and of snaps unsnapping is sweeter than a tenor singing Burns.

McIver had the habit of monitoring his employers. He had a very thin skin, and wanted to know what they were saying about his performance. He could also check their honesty, or if they'd held anything back about the case. Was there duplicity, or even illegality to it? If so, surveillance chips would tell him.

Surv-chipping Sigmund Hammerbank was very distasteful. Fitz quickly learned all he wanted to know about Hammerbank's cocaine business. His stomach turned, learning that Count Volpe was the secret purchaser of *Circles of Paradise*. Hammerbank was so afraid of Volpe that he'd hired a malnourished artist eager to have her work in the Hammerbank Gallery to come in each morning and paint dotted lines around his thumbs, as a sort of self-C.T.

McIver was horrified to discover the owner of the manuscripts was not Hammerbank, nor Volpe, but Count Raspachi, a life-long enemy of McIver ever since Fitz had encountered him in post-war Italy.

Hammerbank began calling Raspachi directly on the scrambler lines, behind Volpe's back. Hammerbank was planning for the day Volpe cut him out of servicing creative noses with rare powders, and then Hammerbank could go directly to Raspachi for some action. It was a dangerous game, and the thud of thumbs on antique table tops was in the cocacrystal ball.

McIver had that absolute prerequisite of a great private eye, the ability to snowjob a client into believing the case was just about to be solved. To hear him talk, the quarry was panting just out of reach in the dark investigative alley. "Any moment, sir, pant pant, any moment!" Another prerequisite McIver had was great skill in the fashioning of believable expense lists, lists that somehow soothed the client such that he/she paid right away, and that engendered praise for McIver's expertise. McIver had to have that praise in order to get up each morning.

Frankly however, after eight months on the Balzac manu case, Fitz was getting nowhere. His biggest suspect was the chairwoman of the French department at Harvard, whom he had surv-chipped about as systematically as possible. If she picked up one of her fine leather volumes of the *Comédie humaine,* there was a chip sewn in the binding. While he learned much about the private lives of Harvard faculty, there was nothing for the case. Then Jack Barnes of the Lantern of Knowledge Bookstore called him from New York and begged him to come down and check on a rare book deal of which he had a piece of the action. He wanted Fitz to do a background on a possible fake Papal Emissary about to sell the Casket Iliad to a collector named John Barrett.

The typewriter ribbon blushes mystic red to whack such a notice, but John Barrett, scholar, Indo-European linguist, man of letters, fell prey to one of the oldest book scams of the age, the Casket Iliad scheme. When Alexander conquered Darius, king of the Persians, in 331 B.C., he acquired in the regal booty an ornate casket. Alex was wont to travel with a copy of the Iliad in his war train; and when he acquired Darius' casket, he used it to store his Iliad.

The Iliad was published in those days on papyrus rolls, two or three books of the poem per roll. There were eight rolls in the fancy casket which the Papal Emissary revealed to a breathless Barrett one afternoon in the second floor Lantern of Knowledge archives staging area. How beautiful was the papyrus!

There were ornamented rollers for each scroll, with projecting knobs of gold and papal seals affixed to each.

"Aha! Aha!" you'd hear Barrett exclaim, as he tested his Greek ability, scanning the first few lines of book one. It was not only for the honor of owning such an ancient treasure that Barrett was willing to plunk down 1,500 of the Grover Clevelands of joy. For he felt the transaction might signal a papal flood of ancient documents and manuscripts, and that he, John Barrett, had been chosen to become one of the most important figures in the history of classical scholarship. John had long believed that the Church of Rome, and the Vatican Library in particular, had held since pagan times certain allegedly lost manuscripts—the lost books of Aristotle for instance, and who knows, perhaps the lost poems of the genius Archilochus, of Hipponax, of Sappho, and the tomes of Thales and Heraclitus.

"If only the Vatican will keep feeding me manuscripts!" Barrett prayed. He squinted his eyes shut, marquees in mind, picturing his return to the N.Y. stage—this time to Broadway.

AN EVENING WITH THE
LOST POEMS OF SAPPHO

directed and translated
by John Barrett

Yes! To think of producing, one by delicious one, the lost plays of Aeschylus at the Lunt-Fontanne Theater!

So the price of $1,500,000 for the Casket Iliad was not really so outlandish, given the pump-priming qualities of the transaction. The problem was that John had already paid one-half as down payment, a terrible mistake. In the excitement, he had tried to call the Pope to thank him in person, but had reached a stone wall. This did not arouse his suspicions, for he wrote the Pope a nice letter in Latin, and received a gracious reply, he thought, from the Papal Secretary. John meantime examined all sorts of purported Papal documents in Latin authenticating sale by one "Casuus the Syrian" to the 9th century pope, Hadrianus I. Barrett's arrogance was excited by his ability to sight-read the documents. That alone should have been a warning flag. The state of John's Latinity was such that he could chat in Latin back and forth with the Emissary, which further veiled the hype with plies of excitement.

Ahhhk, it looked like a "quick stroll up Buck Flood Boulevard," as Fitz McIver would say. John reasoned he could deal out the Casket in a few years to the Metropolitan Museum at twice what he had paid.

In the meantime actual physical contact with Alexander's *Iliad* might inspire a few novels such as sips from Balzac's own coffee pot had done. John was suffering from what might be termed the "Beatles Break-up Syndrome." He thought, "Why write books with others when I can do it alone, aided by Alexander the Great and the lost plays of Aeschylus? Then the paper advances'll be ALL MINE!!! Heh, heh, heh . . ." It was the mistake the Beatles had made, for, when each member recorded by himself, each was much inferior to the full quartet. The Balzac Study Group wrote with a mystic beauty and precision that a single member could not match, but you could not persuade John Barrett that Mount Mooh' was not conquerable by his own pen.

Jack Barnes was to pick up his 10% from the alleged Papal Emissary at the deal's conclusion. Still, there were certain unanswered questions. Why, for instance, was a stern, austere employee of the Pope staying at the Chelsea Hotel? For this and other reasons, Barnes called his good friend Fitz McIver.

Fitz quickly unmasked the "Papal Emissary" as a notorious former archivist, now master rare book forger, who raced

212

out of Lantern of Knowledge, leaving behind the casket and Iliad both, when Fitz confronted him. Whining cackles of sinuses being cleared in derision were heard all over archivesland. Archivists flocked to Lantern of Knowledge to take pictures of the cunning hype. Art Archives called up long distance wanting to prepare a slide show of the caper for the upcoming convention of the Society of American Archivists, soon to convene at Madison Square Garden.

Before he unmasked the Emissary, Fitz first had the opportunity to break the Balzac case. Routinely McIver placed surveillance chips at Barrett's home residence, a rather seedy flat above the location of the old Cafe Rienzi on Macdougal Street. He inserted a Stare-o-Rooter® into the pad from the hall and found in addition to the normal, cynical, dirty chaos of a New York male writer, the undeniable tracks of poverty—barren cupboards, disconnected phone, skillets crusted with the remains of oatmeal fritters, and the ultimate pov flag: no electricity. John had played his double life well. The question then McIver had to answer was: "Where'd he get $750,000?" Was he fronting for someone? Fitz answered his question easily. First, Barrett was rarely home on Macdougal Street. He was spending most of his time in a boutique on St. Mark's—sometimes staying in the store for days without leaving.

McIver ventured into Duct Tape, where he purchased a fine duct-tape trashcan-liner cape such as was worn by the Diogenes Liberation Squadron of Strolling Troubadors and Muckrakers. During this, he planted surveillance chips. It wasn't long before he determined that the action was occurring on the second and third floors through secret entrances.

McIver raced to the roof, whence he worked a Stare-o-Rooter® insert through the air shaft. By chance the Stare-o-Rooter® dangled down just above the Altar of Lost Illusions, and he knew at once he had a group of sickies on his hands who were possibly worshipping Balzac. How did he know so quickly? By the sound track of the event, which later Fitz listened to over and over in amazement. Next to the Altar of Lost Illusions lay the stolen Balzacian manu's, and the Group just then was performing its *Sacred Forehead Frottage Ceremony*, another desperate maneuver to jog the creative flow. They thought that if they rubbed their foreheads ritually on the actual manuscripts, the mystic creative vibes might again be triggered. "Bonk my brow, o Balzac, bonk my brow!" each spake and lowered their craggy orbs upon the page.

There's nothing like that first moment when one catches the perps! McIver's face always went into involuntary twitches, and his tight, gaunt cheeks were cast into wrinkly disarray as his mouth forced into them with a quaking smile.

McIver's perp-catching jubilation was to be short-lived, however. McIver, even as he was closing down the Balzac manuscript case, had begun the negotiations for his next assignment, to become Chief of Security for The 2000 Society. McIver was in a terrible dilemma. The Balzac Study Group, he soon learned, had just donated 699 Grover Clevelands of joy to the Society. His clients, Sigmund Hammerbank and Count Volpe, would certainly want some arrests made, and some publicity. On the other hand, the interests of The 2000 Society clearly required that the return of the stolen manuscripts be veiled in silence. What to do? Will the nascent Society, growing by the thousands each passing day, be crushed by a literary scandal? Will its own Chief of Security be its undoing?

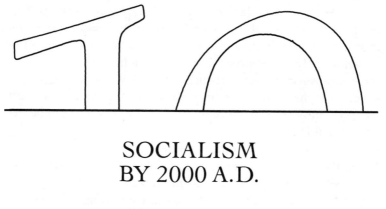

SOCIALISM
BY 2000 A.D.

The 2000 Society's initial meetings were consummated in epochal harmony. Whole generations of partisans were created in a matter of days. People banded together of such disparate styles of life, the convention resembled a Noah's Ark of persuasions.

In order to understand it fully, one would have to coin a fresh word to replace that media-muddied, terrorist-tinged word "revolutionary." The first official acts of the Society were the plenary sessions of delegates from all over America to debate and to vote on what to nationalize, and in what order, by century's end.

The Society, however, did not use the silly word

nationalize. The word was *publicization,* a rather unscholarly concatenation of Greek and Latin components, but suitable for the purposes of The 2000 Society, one of which was to throw off the grousing hounds of right-wing nuttery during the initial phases of the Society's endeavors. Nor did one write *socialism.* The term was now *Public Adjustment.* Again, it was "change the name, confuse the hounds."

The coming together of The 2000 Society was one of those miraculous social events against which all odds were stacked. Cynics, right-center television editorialists, the news mags, and hissing factionists left and right, derided the Society from its inception, but millions arose across the nation to embrace the movement. The media was outraged. Hadn't the nation been informed over and over that such activities were no longer possible? That the scandalous behavior of prior generations, with tear gas forever having corroded their eyes, was never to be expected again?

Scholars pointed to the weakness of the labor movement, the lack of a mass left party, or even of *tendencies* toward mass left action. The task seemed insurmountable. The chief organizing principle of The 2000 Society lay in convincing citizens that the year 2000 loomed as a "Glorious Deadline."

It was a powerful organizing principle. Every American—whether writer, singer, mechanic, teacher, typist, or scientist—realized how their personal success depended on triumph in the labyrinth of chronologic walls. Why not then a Mass Social Movement which also operated under a deadline? The Glorious Deadline.

Polls indicated that 145 million Americans believed the Society's slogan—"If we don't have publicization by the year 2000, we may have to wait 'til 3000." It seemed worth it—millions—rising—joining—engaging in a final struggle to crown a century of gore, the opportunity not to be seen again for another millenium, another stack of centuries, flapjacks of malaise and pain, sliding syrup-coated down the throat of sorrow.

One of the moving forces behind The 2000 Society was rock-bard Jeb Malcomridge, the leader of J'Accuse. This singer and poet seemed strangely unprepared for such a historic role, coming as he did off a decade of ups and downs as leader of one of America's more grotesque bands. But it was he who coined the phrase, "The Glorious Deadline," and he who first persuasively articulated the vision of hidden millions who hungered to work with an organization whose ethics were absolutely pure, whose goals were as sharply known as a hexagonal crystal of quartz, and whose leadership worked in the ranks, and stayed in the ranks.

Jeb had written a famous article for *Harper's*, initially received with great derision, on the premise that retired military officers as well as men and women *now* in high positions in the military and intelligence fields, could be honestly attracted to such a Society.

Ex-intelligence officers admired how neat, orderly, well-financed, and zero bullshit the Society was. It had a clear, unclogged chain of command, with the security apparatus having an important role in the overall program. Security for the Society was designed to be extremely humane, yet utterly ruthless in rooting out right-wing spores. McIver's staff was able to crush networks of provocateurs, to isolate proven double agents, to take secret photos, to stakeout with the best, to interrogate with utmost persuasion, to prepare precise intelligence reports, and to penetrate the opposition.

The plenary meetings of The 2000 Society were not without honest dissension. There was a great drive, narrowly defeated, which would have required all doctors, accountants, commodities brokers, and attorneys to be isolated for one year (2000-2001) of meditative re-education in so-called "zen-zones." Some early achievements of the Society had been successful national campaigns for free pay phone service, the conversion of the electric companies into not-for-profit cooperatives, the placement of a consumer advocate on the National Security Council, a gay chief of the Office of Naval Intelligence, women on the Joint Chiefs of Staff, and a left-liberal head of the CIA. All this occurred *before* the historic convention to decide what corporations were to be picked for publicization. How thrilling it was to a whole generation, the construction of *The List!!!*

Great attention was paid by the media to *The List*. Large

217

companies didn't know whether to sigh with relief or to worry about their stock prices if they should not have been seen fit for publicization. Definitely on *The List* were the grain companies, the coal companies, the overweening phone system, agribusiness, oil, steel, public transportation, hospitals and banks. As to banks, it was the ultimate vengeance of Balzac against his sweaty creditors that the major N.Y. banks—Chase Manhattan, Morgan Guaranty Trust, Chemical, Manufacturers-Hanover, Marine Midland, and Citibank, were to be combined into the *Union de Balzac Consumers' Bank.*

One of the chief questions in any country's publicization is how to compensate stockholders. Should holders be issued nonvoting shares that, while removing them from power in the companies, could be traded on the market? Or, should bonds be issued such that after, say, thirty years, the country would end up with full ownership? The 2000 Society voted to redeem all holdings up to $500,000 per individual; for the rest the pen is proud to jot that the vote was for what *Gorp* dubbed The Grand Burn. The Society opted to approach Milton Rosé to create a series of "Compensation Multiples" to be given to America's formerly wealthy as consolation for seized assets.

European socialists have long felt the frustration, in composing their own lists for publicization, of having so many companies ripe for The Grand Burn. The 2000 Society solved this problem by holding a "National Publicization Lottery."

The Publicization Lottery was staged as a giant media event, with performances by J'Accuse and the Diogenes Liberation Squadron of Strolling Troubadors and Muckrakers. Slips of paper with the names of borderline candidates for take-over were placed in a whirling bingo cage, and drawn in solemn ceremony broadcast to the nation. Thus the Grand Union (no more triple-pricing stickers!) and Winn Dixie food chains were chosen for The Grand Burn, while McDonald's hamburger and the American Stock Exchange were spared.

The 2000 Society invited Fitzgerald McIver to head the security apparatus. The job required protecting the integrity of the Society's fiscal structure, safeguarding its leadership, and preventing insertion of hostile right-wing spores into its echelons.

The invitation to come aboard came just as McIver was breaking the Balzac manuscript case.

He asked for thirty days to finish his other business, including the Barrett/Papal Emissary Casket Iliad case. McIver did not hesitate. He had his probable transplants already lined up. He had genealogied his ancestors for six generations as to longevity, finding the genetic code scheduling a life for him at least a few years beyond 2000 A.D., so he figured the triumph of his old age would be the victory of publicization.

McIver convinced many of his former colleagues in surv-and-snuff (Cold War Intelligence) to join the Society's security team. This was not as surprising as one would expect. The job protecting democratic publicization was a lot more enjoyable than demeaning work guarding toy factories, or running security at rock concerts, or teaching sociology at fourth rate colleges.

In fact, the thrill-level for agents protecting The 2000 Society promised to be as elevated as that for Cold War derring-do. McIver's chilly, pulsing, data-packed mind was ready. Let them sneak into his traps—the spores from South African Intelligence, from the councils of birch-barf, from Exxon Intelligence, from the Scurrilous KGB, or from the Cuban Directorate Generale of Intelligence. Protecting the missile silos on the West Coast from mumbling sickies or terrorists with pry-bars was nothing compared to the task for Fitz McIver protecting The Glorious Deadline.

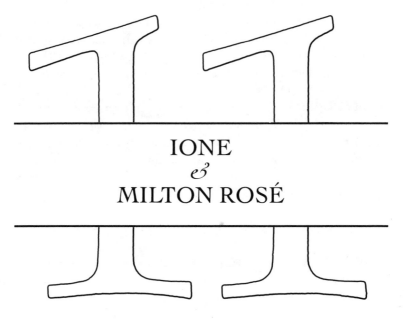

IONE
&
MILTON ROSÉ

The reader might legitimately ask how it was that The 2000 Society was well-funded. Has not the historical weakness of the left been a hutbound poverty? Long before going public, the Society had managed to accrue tens of millions of dollars in assets. It owned its own media and publishing empire, newspapers in key cities, thirty-five television stations, and two major movie production and distribution systems. Access of the Society's programs to the public was guaranteed.

There were many famous names on the list of contributors to The 2000 Society published by the *New York Times*, but strangely none provoked such controversy as the Balzac Study

Group. *Gorp* and *Urge* both devoted cover stories to the mysterious group. Columnists demanded to know who was defaming the great name of Balzac—a monarchist and staunch defender of Christian ideals of wealth and tradition.

Over the years, many articles had been devoted to the famous anonymous writing team, including a list of books believed written by them, but there was nothing to link them to the Balzac Study Group.

One flimsy clue undid them. Early in their career the Group had published its chain-of-terror novel, *Jung Goes Bad*, under the name Damion J. Balstugry.

A Starved Fox journalist one morning was working the morgue clip file looking for evidence to connect the writing team with the Balzac Study Group. He noted that "Balstugry" could represent an elided version of the name of the rich donors to The 2000 Society. The journalist whacked out a front page story, and the chase was on. Other journalists quickly pieced together the 47 books the Group had written during the last five years.

Starved Fox journalists particularly hungered for the pull-down of the wounded BSG deer. Accusations flew. Many famous writers experienced the humiliation of having to say to jostling TV crews, "I am not now, nor have I ever been, a member of the Balzac Study Group."

Ione Appleton was glad to get away from the furor. It was her turn to make the drop of cash into the covert trust account at the Freemon Harbor Bank in the Bahamas.

Following her in deep disguise were Fitz McIver, and an IRS-Intelligence agent named Sean Tooely. Fitz noted to his surprise when scanning the computer passenger list that Milton Rosé also was booked on the flight. "Jesus," Fitz thought, "I hope Milton is not a member of the *Cénacle* too."

There is nothing like mixing a love of the sun with a love of caching the cryptic cash. Whereas Ione Appleton had the final paperback payment for the Starved Fox novels to deposit, Milton Rosé was tossing two sorts of lettuce into his secret salad. First, The 2000 Society had advanced him 200 grand to prepare the Compensation Multiples. He carried a sketch pad on the flight—already he had an idea for a series of giant inflatable barbed wire fences, with a motorized sunflower attached. The sunflower would go into orbit, like the sun, rising each morn on the left and through the day gradually mounting to an apogee above the inflated fence, and then sinking at evenfall to the right. Critics felt that Rosé was proffering the message, "Someday, you'll get it all back," as a consolation to all those who'd lost economic stature through The Grand Burn.

Frankly, Milton wanted to get the Compensation Multiples prototype into production a.s.a.p., so that he could devote full attention to the crown of his life, The Hart Crane Martian Memorial, soon to surface in the media. He was nervous also about his role in the Society—for association with leftists ever tends to thwart the mon-flood to an artist. That was why Milton was glad to have in hand to deposit in his numbered account, an additional variety of lettuce, the remainder of the cash for the sale of *Circles of Paradise* to Count Volpe, bearing the invisible griseous pall of Sigmund Hammerbank's socks. The reader will recall Hammerbank having inserted his feet into the satchel of bills before deciding to purchase *Circles of Paradise* for the Count.

Ione was embarrassed and surprised to see the famous artist across the aisle. Throughout the flight they ignored one another.

Gladly they took leave of one another at the airport, but how uneasy again both were when their cabs halted bumper to rear in front of the Freemon Bank, and they entered the door, one on the heels of the other!

There was an odd assortment of Hollywood types in the bank, mainly attorneys depositing movie distribution skim, but several illustrious names of the cinema were on hand, willing to brave the cameras of U.S. tax agents. Also waiting patiently were some famous rock musicians who did not quite trust their managers truthfully to salt their mon for them, and representatives of that parasite class, the rare powder merchants.

Naturally Ione and Milton chose separate lines, but luck had them reach the tellers' cages at the same time, side by side, and both opened up elegant leather satchels and dumped pleasant assortments of bill bundles, in fact embarrassingly large mottled green ziggurats when they were assembled in front of the tellers to be counted, both depositors breathing heavily, nervous about reproach or indictment, yet thankful that in defiance of certain U.S. laws they were storing some alembic alfalfa against that day when they could purchase a little extra painkiller, a little extra comfort, at the Golden Bard Retirement Colony.

Only at the outer door, after the deposits had been safely counted and entered into their accounts, did they acknowledge one another, "Milton!" "Ione!" and paused for the ritual kiss of the creative. And wasn't it pleasant for both when they each learned the other too had a reservation at The Diamond Sutra Golf Club, a very popular hotel owned by the rock group J'Accuse.

They dined together at Diamond Sutra—as wonderful a meal as ever described in a haute cuisine spy novel—a tofu and mushroom gom-gom served in turtle shells; grape-flavored koumiss (mare's milk wine) served in juniper bough and calfskin flasks; and dessert of sweetened crushed ice from the North Pole.

The Diamond Sutra Golf Club lay at the ocean's edge, and what a beautiful little lagoon it commanded, with a semicircular white beach edged by blue-white bluffs and steps cut into the cliff leading from the hotel to the strand. So it was natural that after dinner Ione and Milton should take a stroll upon the beach. It was natural too that as they walked their shoulders and arms should touch. And the first faint blush of flesh fires arose from such tender unheeding jostling in the growing dark. Both were so experienced, yet tonight so shy. "Why not give it a clink?" both asked themselves silently.

And soon they were facing each other in the moonlight, kissing for the first time. Ione dropped her turquoise Balzacian cane to the sand where it lay atop the tide's wash of kelp. Milton was turned on as never before by her kneecaps shining in the sunset and the patterns of copter-crash scars on her shins. He rained 500 kisses upon the 'caps and the furrowing tissue below. Ione had not felt such desire since with her lover Billie Brigham above Macchu Pichu that horrible dawn so many years ago.

They fucked in the sand up against the wind-hollowed light blue limey rock cliff, the band of drying kelp seven feet away 'tween them and the coral lagoon.

Two hours seemed both like ten hours and like five minutes. Then Milton stood up, his back firm against the cool cliff, while Ione slow-stroked him into Demeter's thrice-plowed numinal furrow. Milton sank to his knees to kiss her, and they edged themselves down again upon the sand. For the first time Milton could take advantage of a new skill brought about by his own secret invention, the Metronomic Cunnicizer,® an exercise machine designed to promote strength and stamina of tongue combined with rapidity plus variation of pattern and pressure of application. The performance was as of the young Liszt at the piano, and at the conclusion, blazing tone poem of lingual flutterings, Ione could stand it no longer, and moan-rolled over, facing the cliff base, hands grasped 'tween her knees, the blue-white stone cooling her chin, her nipples, her knees, her toes in its draining tangency.

A Wraith of Love grew there upon the kelp-studded marge. A Love that rose and twined them both upon the same. "I love you, dear Ione!" "I love you Milton."

It was then, foamy naked in the moon, that Ione Appleton trotted down the slight incline to the surf, and threw her notebook into the looney blue, a very significant act. For love means never taking notes about your lover for use in future books.

Love means never taking notes about your lover for use in future books (unless . . . well, it was impossible to say it . . . unless . . . well, if he, if she, but that's impossible, if s/he hurts me, or leaves, or lies, or . . .). Like all true love, they had life stories to tell; hours were breathlessly exchanged in data disgorgement. At last when they arrived at their current activities, both seemed to stutter, to leave lacunae; for both were bound by current secrets. Milton's was the still-secret Hart Crane Shrine project. Ione's was the Balzac Study Group.

Both plunged. "Milton, I appreciate you telling me about the pain that the detestable *Gorp* and *Urge* have caused you over *Circles of Paradise*. There may be pain for me also. I'm joining The

224

2000 Society, dearest. I have given already, that is, a bunch of us have given, a substantial sum of money to it."

Milton replied, "I too would like to join, but you know, I'm afraid of losing my security clearance on my next project, and . . ."

Ione broke in with the earliest tone of impatience in their nascent love. "Milton, you know, you have to be aware of the 'Drang nach Tory' that afflicts the male artist—keep these names in mind: Southey, Wordsworth, Tom Wolfe, Podhoretz—you see how catastrophic an effect the tory grovel had upon their art."

Milton was so embarrassed he could barely suppress a tear; in fact, could not finally, and his cheek grew gray with a single runnel in the moonlight. "Yes," he responded weakly, "but this project is supersecret. It involves the assurance that the outer space drive will have an artistic tone."

Ione felt a sudden twinge of conscience. "Wait, darling, before you go on. I . . . I've not told you all. Milton, I organized the Balzac Study Group!"

"You!" he thought silently to himself. "Ione Appleton, Queen of the Burnout Brigade! Shaper of duct tape gowns!? Gid-out-a-hyah!!"

"It's true," she continued. "We've written 47 novels together—it's quite an efficient operation. We've voted to give our name and much of our money to The Glorious Deadline! I'm so excited!"

Lucky for them that their hours achatting at the cliff's base were witnessed solely by the moon. Or were they? Oh horrible are the ways of beams, electrons, and tiny circuits! Two sets of ears heard all, o reader; the one, of Fitz McIver, reddened with shame throughout the love, and only whitened again as the lovers' life stories droned onward; the other, of IRS agent Sean Tooely, whose heart rose up and out and down to the beach, where it throbbed in time with Ione Appleton's. A rooftop love attack!?

Agent Tooely lay atop the nearby hotel roof listening through a headset to the whispers of the lovers picked up by a finely tuned shotgun microphone on a tripod. Ione had that

225

quality; men would fall in love with her at a party after a poetry reading. But surely someone could not have fallen in love with her merely by listening to her voice from a hotel roof? Well, there *were* precedents—such calamities were known to have occurred among the boys of national security in their stakeouts. Shucks, Fitz McIver knew a Colonel in Air Force intelligence who fell in love with Jane Fonda's voice on surveillance duty when the antiwar FTA show appeared in Okinawa in 1971. The chap had to be reassigned to less erotophonous cases.

Stakeout infatuations—perhaps there was something about the new generation of surveillance equipment, an unknown electromagnetic factor, as when thousands of N.Y. city males are aroused each time they ride the jiggly BMT subway to work. Having Sean Tooely on the stakeout was a hap of historical weight, for when McIver learned of his presence on the island, he realized he'd have to approach Tooely to monitor his politics. With no effort at all, Fitz turned him! Tooely was very interested in The Glorious Deadline. "There'll be much less subversion and treason after the implementation of the Public Adjustment, and the middle class becomes fully used to it," opined he.

Later Ione worked with McIver on Tooely, and IRS thus was penetrated by the security apparatus of The 2000 Society, an invaluable asset when the tax service was ordered to attack the fiscal structure of the Society with tax audits.

But why was McIver there in the first place listening to the chatter of the surveillance chip? Was he on vacation and merely copping his own kind of thrills? Nay, McIver believed that Ione had come to the Bahamas to stash the stolen Balzac manuscripts.

Down on the beach, Milton was revealing his final secret. "Ione, I have but one secret further. I am preparing the first museum on Mars. We've acquired a marvelous polished seaman's trunk packed with the diaries, poems, and books of Hart Crane! NASA is supplying roving rock-moving equipment, and we're going to hide it in a cave and block up the entrance except for a small opening. Our challenge is to the next five generations to find it. It's my ultimate destruction/construction!"

Ione broke in with an incredulous tone, "You mean the government is helping you hide a literary relic?"

"Yes, it is, Ione. Even the President knows about it. From the point of view of the government, the Museum will comprise an unrivaled public relations endeavor. First, it'll spur exploration. It's species control of a benevolent sort. It soothes the angry intellectuals of earth, and provides the first grand creative interplanetary adventure. You know how they're always worried about the survival of Judaism and Christianity in the space colonies—well, what about poetry and art? This will be Art and Verse's first true voyage!"

There was silence for several minutes, while Ione planned her words. "I have the borrowed Balzac manuscripts—no doubt you've read about them—in my tote bag over there by the kelp. Why don't you think about putting them in The Trunk when you take it to Mars. Hart Crane, I'm sure, would be pleased to have them aboard. Balzac on Mars too! Did they not divide the world between them, Hart and Honoré!?"

That did it. Fitz McIver could stand it no longer. He did something rarely chosen; he reversed the beam, enabling him to send his voice out over the surveillance chip, sewn in the collar of Rosé's jacket. "Milton Rosé," McIver spoke, "When NASA hears, however vaguely, you're mixed up in a Grand Theft Manuscript case, you could lose your clearance!"

"My clearance?" Rosé gasped. Milton was frantic, slapping himself, his clothing, Ione, the ground, trying to locate the noise source. "Who the hell are you?" he asked.

"Chief of Security, The 2000 Society," McIver answered. Hearing the slaps and grating noises of Milton trying to locate the Surv-Chip,® Fitz urged, "Relax Milton, it's sewn in your jacket collar, but you'd better not tear it out; lives depend on what I have to say . . ."

Such words usually calm a subject down. "Ione," McIver continued, "You have to return the manuscripts! If you don't, Count Raspachi will certainly seek to ruin the Society, and most likely kill Hammerbank, Milton, Count Volpe—Volpe's not so important, but the others are; and if Raspachi finds out the identities of the Cénacle, he'll most likely fling an off on you also."

Ione realized that McIver would handle the matter most circumspectly. "I'll leave them at the base of the cliff," said Ione, and tugged Milton to his feet, and both started toward the safety of the Diamond Sutra Golf Club. "Don't worry, darling," quoth she, "You're probably protected by an iron-clad contract. NASA *needs* Crane's trunk on Mars more than you."

Milton nodded. "Say, how'd you know about the 'iron-clad contract?'"

Ione smiled. "Our Group's been researching the matter for the last two weeks. It was to be our next novel."

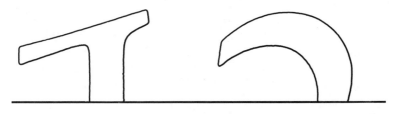

THE
THREAT OF
HECTOR QUEASE

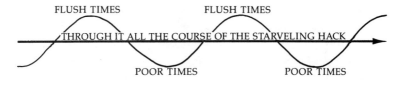

To gauge the hatred of the Starved Foxes for the Balzac Study Group it might do well to present the final paragraph of the famous BSG challenge to the Foxes, in the introduction to the starved Fox trilogy:

Relentlessly the Starved Fox follows his straight, unswerving course through the time-track:

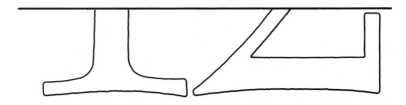

229

We throw down the glove on the table of your sleaze, Starved Foxes! May it bounce into your typewriters and clog their lying keys! Find out our names if you can, stupid beasties! Meanwhile, the "yip, yip, yip" of your pitiful pack, and the "clack, clack, clack" of your unclean keys, will make us happy in our safety.

Who were these Starved Foxes so vilified by the Balzac Study Group? The Famished Foxes comprised a noisy portion of current journalism. The principle rule of Starved Fox publishing and journalism was the age-old "publish cheap/pay cheap." Why pay a few to write for fat fees, when you can train a generation to write ten tiny articles a day, and then give the author twenty dollars, some free theater tickets, and a blow of snow?

By the end of youth, the Hawk of Penury would have clawed their eyes red. The Starved Fox in its middle age would see the world through hard-edged hemic scabs. You could see the desperation of the Starved Foxes in their expense reports—if the expense sheet for the article showed two photocopies at nine cents a page, they'd change it to five photocopies at fifteen. They took subways and charged for cabs; Trailways and charged for Eastern, ever trying for the so-called "triplicate," when three different mags would pay for the same court records or airline tickets.

The lure of Mt. Moolah gave them high blood pressure at age 26. They were careful to emulate slavishly higher paying writing styles. They glued together their magazine layouts according to the sloppiest principles of glue-pot hackery.

They were dandies. The electricity might be cut off in their apartments, and they'd be lunching on Fritos dipped in Mazola oil, nevertheless they would appear on the street wearing 900 dollar tailored suits, diamond cokestraw/tie clasps, and the latest style laser-dried wolf-tongue shoes.

Starved Foxes wrote a lot about nightclubs, movie making, pop music concerts, and the theater. The eyeballs of fans never tire of manic closeups. The Foxes were often banned from concerts and press parties, for they had the propensity for fist-fights with the famed. A fist-fight with a famous entertainer could engender for the Starved Fox at least seven or eight articles, and occasionally a flash of cash from a morning TV talk show.

It was extremely important to know everything about everybody, especially the foibles of brother and sister Foxes. If you had a chance, you would certainly lacerate the posteriors of every colleague whose name came up in the course of a conversation with an editor or publisher. Speaking of editors, becoming one was a temporary method to escape the tribulations of Starved Foxism. For a blessed cycle of time, you were a god, dispensing favors and justice and article assignments. You built up a mound of good will, approving the highly suspect expense lists of friends, receiving flattery and worship, while punishing enemies as only an editor can.

You might even put on a little extra weight against the lean months sure to come when your magazine fails. In the meantime, you burn up the free phone lines, and the unlimited franking privileges, the free food and drink, and all the other perks of puissance *pro tempore*.

Information was always for sale. The boring out-of-style practice of taking money for silence about sexual weirdness of the famed was fervently joined. So was recycling one's data. You built up a file of information, maybe even wrote books on a subject. Then you wrote books from the books, articles from the books, books from the articles. Should you then discover just *one new fact!* you were set. You added the new tidbit of data to the data horde, and you could present new articles, new columns, and even new books!

Starved Fox journalism did produce one important cultural input, the principle that Anything was worthy of review. For instance, Starved Foxes reviewed food service at rock parties—was the catered food at the party for J'Accuse's Christmas Album as good as that for *Eye Bags Blue with Blood*, the Rolling Stones' 123rd production. Nightclub booths were reviewed for their "artistic tension and poetic relief."

Theater groups by the thousands were praised and cultivated by the Starved Foxes. Ditto for cacophonous crooners and dancers barely able to get off the ground. The rule was this: a thousand theater groups and a thousand dance ensembles will

231

provide sporadic employment for about 2500 Starved Fox reviewers. The more productions and dance performances, the more free tickets, the more perks, the more free drinks, and the more fifty-dollar bills miraculously finding themselves in the pockets of reviewers from box office tills.

Gorp assigned the king of the Starved Foxes, a man named Hector Quease, to locate the personnel of the alleged Balzac Study Group. Hector Quease was known among fellow journalists as Sleaze Quease. He was proof that the bottom of the barrel was hard to reach—for his gnarled angry body was already there blocking approach. He smoldered with envy and malice. Sleaze Quease was so hatefully schizoid that he couldn't read his own articles because he grew viciously jealous of whoever wrote them. Nor had he any scruples. He posited, as an ethic: bucks from blood. And then, substituting for character, was the lunge toward the mon, the energy of the lunge, the love of the lunge. He fomented strife, then reaped the mon. He was a huckster of overpriced flashlights in a moral blackout.

He had so many enemies he scoured the world for weak pliant friends to set against the enemy onslaught. He had that salvation of those with many enemies; he loved to be hated. The "Hate Brace" of *1984* served him, but it was two-way. He liked The Giving Hate Brace and The Receiving Hate Brace. Pain turned him on. "Do you have any ethics when you're hurting?" he asked of a victim with a grin.

Unlike George Plyght's renowned techniques of Stress Questioning, Hector's research techniques relied totally on hostility. "If the subject believes it's quite possible you'll kill him, he's more likely to answer your questions," Quease put it simply once at a MORE Convention panel on Interrogation Methods. It's understandable therefore that Sleaze Quease did manage to score a scoop now and then in cases where the pry-bar of fear could be plied.

Quease had devised a trifurcated path to the mon—first as a copyright collector, second as an inventor, third as leader of what was known as Quease's Q-Squad. As a copyright collector, he made his fortune. Such a novel he could have written, had he any skill, on the malfiscality of genius! He was ever on the look

232

out for creative types in weak fiscal condition. He had one very useful ability in this regard; he could spot talent. He'd purchase the copyrights to a bunch of songs from a starving musician in a cafeteria for five dollars, or less. Sometimes a sandwich and coffee would pick him up jazz suites, recording rights, electronic scores. He'd raid their lofts for anything: paintings, signed books, letters, manuscripts, rights to juvenalia. When fifteen years went by, and the formerly starved poet or novelist was at the top, along walks Hector Quease and peddles the novel writ at eighteen, for which he owns all rights, and drooleth he then upon the lower portions of Mt. Mooh'.

He stuffed all copyrights into an old square-topped traveling salesman's bag, with separate vertical compartments that once held the snake oil now holding different types of rights. When after ten years his suitcase bulged with rights to songs, novels, inventions, short stories signed over on the backs of menus or envelopes, feuilletons, suppressed gossip, musicals, and reviews, he sold the bag to an Arab oil prince, convincing him that somewhere within lurked a new *Hello Dolly*. The price? 250 Grover Clevelands of repression.

As an inventor, Hector Quease again profited from pain, through the marketing of his infamous "Curved Punk Pins" of the late '70's. Everyone was startled by the fashion among punk rockers to pierce the cheek and to wear a safety pin impaled through the hole and clipped shut at the mouth. Quease's machine shops stamped out specially shaped and molded pins, which fit body contours so that rockers could bob and groove at concerts without undue pain.

There were several rows of ancient Royal typewriters, covered with eraser granules, and with ribbons so aged there were central barren lines where the keys had chewed the fabric to bits. Nearby was a bank of pay phones surrounded by wall space completely blackened with phone numbers, quickly jotted interview notes, and possible opening lines of stories. Sometimes the Starved Fox would use the phone, scratch the outline of the story on the nearby wall, drag a typewriter over, whack out the column from the plaster, then dash against the deadline to the street for another twenty dollars.

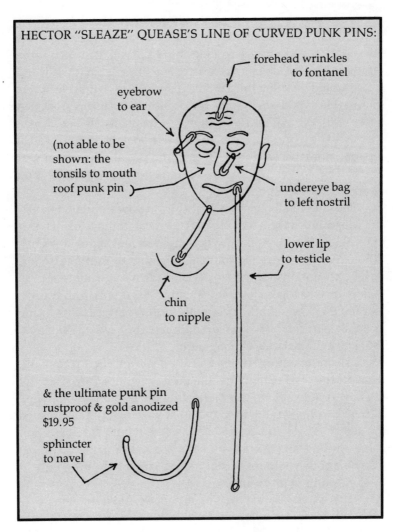

HECTOR "SLEAZE" QUEASE'S LINE OF CURVED PUNK PINS:

forehead wrinkles
to fontanel

eyebrow
to ear

(not able to be
shown: the
tonsils to mouth
roof punk pin)

undereye bag
to left nostril

lower lip
to testicle

chin
to nipple

& the ultimate punk pin
rustproof & gold anodized
$19.95

sphincter
to navel

Key to Quease's task of unmasking the Balzac Study Group was Quease's Q-Squad, a pack of Starved Foxes under his control. The pack lived at several loft/bunkhouses owned by Quease. They did not want to live there of course, but only stayed when they were mired in the trough of pov. Thus, each time they stayed they "owed Quease a night." He kept records of who slept at the bunkhouses, enabling him to know exactly who owed what. "Owed Quease a night" was a phrase loaded with dread, for it meant the Starved Fox in question owed Hector a day's worth of duty, whether research, writing, or thugwork.

The Starved Fox lofts featured tiers of beds four high, and communal kitchens, with dark, vermiform deposits of last year's overcooked spaghetti in every pot's bottom. Coffee grounds covered the floor like brown sawdust in a bar. Women were repelled by the dirt of it, but were not about to perform scullery duty for a bunch of louts, so Starved Fox men were the main inhabitants of the lofts.

The bathrooms at the Starved Fox lofts were strewn with foul linen and underwear, their towels stiff with hasty ablutions. No amount of spritzed Lysol could erase the aura of cooky-toss and diseased colon. The floors, ceilings, walls, and fixtures were caked with a slimy multi-year coating of soap, body hair, shaving lather, bits of paper, skin, urine, blood, and an occasional dry glop of sperm.

Quease charged for everything; for use of the kitchen, for use of the bathroom, for use of the typewriters. In each loft there was a locked storeroom whence Sleaze Quease would sell cheap yellow paper (he bought it at one dollar a ream, and sold it to the starvos at one dollar per 25 sheets), pencils, and Ironword® correction fluid.

Such was the man *Gorp* assigned, at all costs, to track down the Balzac Study Group. *Gorp* had learned of the theft of the Balzac manuscripts from Count Raspachi, who showed them the unfortunate note Ione had left behind, bearing the Group's name, in the Count's castle. *Gorp* thought it quite possible that Milton Rosé lay behind the case. As for Sleaze Quease, none had been so garbaged in the Starved Fox trilogy as he. When it was surmised that the Balzac Study Group of The 2000 Society was the famous writing team, offoidal waxed he. "Off" being to off, "offoidal" being W.O., or Willing to Off.

In his initial rage, Quease assigned a Starved Fox to spray-paint the letters "BSG" on *Circles of Paradise*. Milton had to sacrifice a whole day away from the Hart Crane Trunk project in order to clean the priceless work, due to depart in a few days to its mysterious European owner, Count Claudio Volpe. The initials "BSG" had been sprayed quite skillfully in a perpendicular array, so that the "G" lay upon Beethoven's desk in such a way as practically to outline it. It had a marvelous effect, so Rosé, while totally erasing the other two letters, merely touched upon the "G" and left it on the desk for all eternity to ponder.

Meanwhile, Quease himself broke into The 2000 Society just hours before McIver's security apparatus came into place. Quease found the word "Radither" penciled on the otherwise sterile BSG file. That's all he needed to zero in on Barnaby Radither, the attorney for the rock titans of J'Accuse.

Quease ran with Radither's name to the Internal Revenue Service, not only to urge a tax-ax on Radither, but possibly to collect a 10% bounty on any sums the IRS might be able to obtain. Meanwhile swarms of Starved Foxes carrying clubs were assigned to sleep outside Radither's home and office in barrels. Radither's eyes were blackened and seven of his fingers broken when he finally called McIver to request protection.

Quease paid off some bank officials for a printout of Radither's past five years of checks, but not a dime from the BSG had found its way there. Angered beyond control, Quease personally broke Radither's house windows and trashed his auto. Down in Tribeca an entire Starved Fox loft was converted into a lab for the construction of Conceptual Threats. Starved Foxes had a natural propensity for the C.T. By telegram, by mail, by balloon, by door knock, by record (you haven't lived until a record arrives with a fine barber-shop quartet singing— "Hmmmmm, we're going to kill you, hmmmmm"), by sketch, by skywrite, by pigeon, the threats confronted Barnaby Radither.

Radither was jailed briefly for refusing to divulge the names of the BSG to a federal grand jury. In jail he wrote his famous pamphlet, *Tax Problems for Partisans of The Glorious Deadline*. Meanwhile, Count Emilio Raspachi, as a key gore spore in the international rightist community, announced he wanted far more than the return of the manuscripts and exposure of the culprits. He wanted some chop-chop.

Hector Quease returned from an overseas telephone conversation with the Count, his eyes glazed with happiness. "My first contract!" he whispered to one of his most trusted Starved

236

Foxes. Up to now, Quease had refused all opportunities, say, to kill someone who'd stolen some yellow typing paper from the loft storeroom, or who had stayed overnight without signing in. But *this*, this was a real opportunity! To off someone who has trashed you mercilessly is a forbidden fantasy to many, but now to Quease a fact. The Balzac Study Group and its allies were in mortal danger.

Fitz McIver did not know Raspachi had let out a contract for BSG with Hector Quease, but it was a point of honor with McIver to neutralize Quease—because if Quease could confound the Society so easily, what would happen if Dept. of Agriculture Intelligence (the favorite place now for cover assignments), or Telephone Company Security decided to break up the Society with "disruption engineers"?

McIver hastily gathered from a number of his friends still in government agencies a thick history of Quease's life, looking for something so heinous in the way of personal deportment that Quease might slow down a bit if McIver should show it to him. But what was there to blackmail? For, if you choose the sleaze track as a life path, no blackmail is possible—you just ask them to spell your name correctly, and *please!*, to print it all at once!

McIver had greater success with a scheme to neutralize Count Raspachi. He wanted Sigmund Hammerbank to hear, so he arranged a conversation with the Count over Hammerbank's famous Beatles Scrambler 14, which the reader will recall mixed unused Beatles 8-track outtakes with old WW II Japanese numeric codes in order to conduct his business free from surveillance.

It was an angry conversation—Raspachi viewed his former employee with great hatred, and threatened an off. "Don't take any airplanes, Mr. McIver," he told him. "I'm sure you can conduct the puny security arrangements for your little communist club out of your office."

Around this time, Sigmund Hammerbank began uncontrollably noodling micturitions down his pants leg into the tops of his white boots.

McIver was prepared for his enemy Raspachi. "Dope-dealing dog vomit like you and your Ordine Nero will be crushed. I agreed to return the manuscripts, and if you send one of your men to the Milan airport, you'll find them waiting in the luggage room."

"You should know, Mr. Raspachi," Fitz continued, "we have determined exactly how, and from whom, and at what price, you yourself acquired the manuscripts.[10] Secondly, I should like to focus your attention on a little matter of 39 years ago, in wartime Milan. I was a Lieutenant in the OSS then. One of my operations was the investigation into the Shoeshine Plasma Case . . . ."

Here, McIver paused. "It's been written into a book, Raspachi, with all the names unchanged. Your reputation as a rectitudinous pillar of ageless ethication is in sore danger of being spray-painted with scandal. So, I'd recommend you easing up on the matter of Public Adjustment in our country, and on the role of The 2000 Society in it. Take it away Beatles!" McIver punched in an unused take of *Strawberry Fields Forever*, and walked out of the office.

"Wait, Mr. McIver," Sigmund Hammerbank called with trembling voice, trotting splashfootedly to the door. "What did Count Raspachi do—what was the Shoeshine Case you mentioned?"

McIver masked his disdain for Hammerbank, and replied, "Raspachi ran a group of shoeshine boys in the black market, delivering stolen goods. They were all from war-broken homes. When they resisted or revolted, he drained their blood, sold it to hospitals and dumped them in the sewer. It was a case more disgusting than the one in Graham Greene's *The Third Man*. I suggest you modulate your relationship with Raspachi, Mr. Hammerbank, for you have a great and important artist to protect—Milton Rosé."

---

10. A sad tale for an uncertain occasion, how the scion of European nobility, bravely striving to pay the taxes on the family estates, is thereby forced to form a band, which is in the studio trying to finish a zoo-intercourse concept album, exhausted, sleeping in an energyless heap in the studio floor at $250.00 per hour—so that the scion is forced to deal out priceless family treasures—unpublished Balzac and Victor Hugo manuscripts—to Raspachi for enough coke to finish the ablum.

With Raspachi beaten back for the moment, Quease alone remained a serious threat to the Society. One plan was to hire anti-Starved Fox Starved Foxes to battle the Q-Squad; many held rancor against Mr. Quease. Another was to start an article campaign accusing Quease himself of heading the Balzac Study Group. Both plans were wisely abandoned, for such would have brought sleaze to truth, rather than truth to power.

A way was found, however, for dealing with the Starved Foxes in Quease's employ. For this, McIver inaugurated a sub-genre of the Conceptual Threat, the R.I.C.T., for Relatively Innocuous Conceptual Threat. He considered it great training for his freshly assembled security team. The Starved Foxes normally were edgy, more than a little fearful, so the most circumspect of C.T.'s—postcards bearing a hemic quote from *Macbeth*, say—were more than enough to remove them from the case. Starved Foxes dropped rapidly from his service, leaving only the most loyal in their barrels outside The 2000 Society's headquarters.

Meanwhile, Barnaby Radither panicked when released from the Federal House of Detention. On the sidewalk outside his apartment he found a pile of sleeping barrels. Violating the strictest orders of the Balzac Study Group, Radither took a cab to the Duct Tape Boutique.

"Radither disappeared somewhere in the back of the store for eight hours, chief," Sleaze Quease was told by the head of his surveillance squad. That's all Sleaze Quease needed.

Thoughts of darkling gore captured Quease's mind. Quease had told no one about the contract from Count Raspachi to kill the Balzac Study Group. He wanted no witnesses, so he discharged the entire Q-Squad, giving them an unprecedented two-day vacation. An unprecedented relaxation limberly swept through the Starved Fox sleeping-lofts. In a further gesture of good will, Hector Quease bought a hijacked truckload of Franco American Spaghetti-O's from maf-org, and ordered it delivered with 500 plastic spoons to the lofts. "Eat it in good cheer, my lads!" Sleaze Quease urged.

Then he struck. Four a.m. is the hour of confusion—the hour industrial titans telephone sleeping employees they do not trust to pump them for information, or so Quease had read somewhere. He stopped at an all-night drugstore to purchase some Brut. His shoulder holster, just bought today, was giving forth the fumes of fresh leather goods, so he wanted to dab it with some disguising perfume. His piece was a .22 caliber revolver with the latest mafia silencer, giving the firing the sound of someone spitting a piece of tobacco off their tongue.

Quease stalked the alleyways, the rear courtyard of the Duct Tape building, the surrounding roofs, listening for sounds. Finally he broke into the front door of the Boutique. He figured there'd be no alarm, for the BSG would not have wanted to risk the attention of the police. He went at once to the rear of the store, discovering a cutting room for duct tape gowns, certainly not a place to tarry, as had Radither, for eight hours.

He gauged the distance between the back wall and the outer brick of the building, and nodded with glee. There might be a hidden room or passageway! "These communists are still using tunnels!" he laughed. By luck he triggered the panel, and the door slid open, revealing the escalator up to the Creativity Bunker.

Up raced Hector, and entered the Bunker, experiencing the confusion of any investigator when first wanting to memorize everything at once. The first items to impinge upon his memory were the mottoes on the wall:

and

on the carved planks of antique walnut. He glanced about frantically, noting the computer terminal, the charts on the wall, the million dollar triangle list, the quartet of obviously valuable writing desks strewn with galleys and broken pencils, the sets of bound manuscripts lining the shelves, the Altar of Lost Illusions.

After minutes scanning the room, Hector was still not sure what it was. He ran his free hand—the other was clutching the .22—over the thick Proustcork® walls. Then he knew. "This opulent cave must be their home!" he exclaimed, a shudder of desire spreading throughout his musculature, changing his attitude like a north wind turning south.

He lay the pistol upon the open pages of *Illusions perdues*, and removed his clear plastic surgeons gloves and placed them there too. "I want to join, I want to join," slowly mumbled he. He raced around the room, patting the volumes written by the BSG. "I'll have all these copyrights some day to store in my little black satchel!!"

Quease's happy mood was dispelled at once, when he came upon the hated, the spat-upon corrected galleys, bound in leather, of the *Starved Fox* trilogy! Ugh! Now he knew it was not, "I want to join," but rather, "It's all mine!"

"I hate them!" he shouted. "I'll enslave these writers in a dungeon. I'll torture them in painful thrall!" Then he had a brilliant flash. "Yes, we'll lock them up and force them to continue writing! I'll add an army of Foxes to this little operation. We'll take over a few publishers by force! Next, cackle cackle, we'll break the fingers of the world to read *my* books!"

Luckily the BSG had purchased several buildings on 9th Street directly to the rear of the Duct Tape building. They had already constructed a roof tunnel, disguised as a solar truck garden, leading from the roof on 9th Street into the Indulgence Bunker.

Wendy Sark and John Barrett were on duty in the Indulgence Bunker viewing surveillance screens of the Duct Tape Boutique and the Creativity Bunker, when Hector Quease entered. They followed his activities with great interest, jotting hasty notes, for here was the stuff of fiction! At last, when the screen revealed the revolver residing on the Altar of Lost Illusions, they ran down the steps from the Indulgence Bunker, careful to don patriotic blue hoods; they overpowered Quease, tied him up, and carried him out to the alley.

241

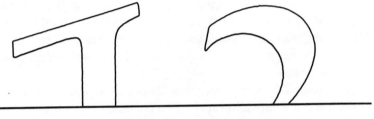

SURV-CHIPPING
THE VENUSIAN
SLOBBER NODULES

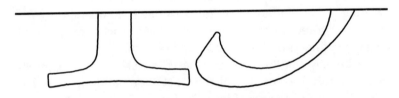

Quease's penetration of the Creativity Bunker seemed to make certain the demise of the Balzac Study Group. When Ione Appleton later viewed the tape of the chuckling Quease walking up to *The Alphabetized Apothegm Index to Honoré de Balzac,* her birthday present!, to chuck each volume along its lower edge, the tears flowed like a harvest, especially when after winding the tape to the same spot several times she deciphered Quease whispering, "I want to join, I want to join."

That night a formal meeting was held, the Group in solemn fresh-washed robes. Emblems of burnout had been tidied away. The silver porcine coke trough had been melted down to provide commemorative medallions to accompany Rosé's Compensation Multiples. Even the coke spoons on the ends of their golden ceintures had been thrown away.

Armed guards sat inside the darkened Duct Tape Boutique protecting the meeting. The Group had entered the Bunker via the roof tunnel on 9th Street.

The list of ideas was long, but the only realistic alternatives were (1) to buy Quease off; (2) to let him into the Group; or (3) the inculcation of a "behavior anomaly" in Mr. Quease sufficient to turn his attention from the BSG. There was a vote on each alternative at meeting's close, when the *Cénacle* walked one by one to the Altar of Lost Illusions and dropped an onyx spheroid into the porcelain coffee urn of Balzac. For alternative three all four onyx spheroids were seen upon counting to be black; none were of the creamy-colored Mexican variety. The vote thus was unanimous: "Robo the turkey."

"Wendy, John," spoke Ione, "You may bring Dr. Goppgunge into the Creativity Bunker."

Dr. Goppgunge was picked up at the Bed of Nails Restaurant, blindfolded, placed in a limousine, driven circuitously to the Duct Tape Boutique, placed there in a trunk, and the trunk then suspended from a long stout pole. The trunk was kept in a slow, dizzying spin as Goppgunge was borne suspended shoulder to shoulder up to the Creativity Bunker.

They op'd the trunk in front of the Altar, unwound the wrappings from the good Doctor, and mek! there he was! one of the most dangerous right-wing nuts in the history of Western Civilization. Dr. Goppgunge had been given nearly a whole volume in the 15-unit *Encyclopedia of Twentieth Century War Criminals, Techno-Fascist Profiteers, Evil Scientists, and Robo-Washers.* The BSG knew even more about the Doctor from researching him for a character in their *Scenes from the Private Lives of Techo-Fascism.* So, to see him in the flesh, as with all enemies, was at first a rush of energy to all, then a room-wide Q: "This dour little porcomorph was a war criminal!? Incredible!"

According to the *Encyclopedia,* Goppgunge had not had his picture taken for 56 years. Therefore, as he was being uncorked, the BSG patted his face down for disguises, removing several national security paste-on warts, some John L. Lewis eyebrows, fake cheekbones, until the prying fingernails finally reached the bare essentials of his ravaged face. Goppgunge stood up in the trunk, his lower legs hidden within, his red, high blood pressure face with dark brown angst-furrows seemed ready to rage, until the Group hastened to soothe him with pliant, worshipful words. "We've heard so much about you, Dr. Goppgunge. We're so honored to have you here with us. Such an illustrious man!"

As they calmed him down, they videotaped him for The 2000 Society files. McIver would never tire thereafter of ordering a private screening of the tape of Dr. Goppgunge, an old nemesis from Cold War days, lifting his leg to leave the trunk, "like a supernatural blob of pizza dough vaulting a wall," as Fitz phrased it. Goppgunge was one of those hyperconfident chubby types that saunter/stagger/swagger like a strutting duck. So much like a bullet-headed duck looked he, and therefore so memorable and unanonymous (sins in the spy trade) that when the Doctor was still working the national security alleys with poison darts, he was usually ordered never to appear in the areas where the snuffs were to occur, but to run the operations out of safehouse motels in nearby cities.

One of the more interesting anecdotes in the *Encyclopedia of War Criminals* described how once they brought Goppgunge to a President who desired to meet a James Bond type. When the courier vehicle arrived at the outer gatehouse of the White House, Dr. Goppgunge slowly surrendered his weapons. Off popped the dissolvable botulism cufflinks. Out of the pocket came the anthrax tabs disguised as 500 mg. Vitamin C pills; the piano wire strangulation noose from inside his Speidel watchband; his neck holster; left-leg holster; right-leg holster; his derrière-crack storage quiver containing C-5 plastique; his .38 detective special snapped to the belt in the small of his back; and finally, his "surreal sumpitan," (a Malay blow-gun) housed in the hollowed-out temple bar of his glasses. When you spotted Dr. Goppgunge at a security meeting innocently and meditatively lipping the temple tips, he was actually practicing the sumpitan rub-out of his bureaucratic enemies.

244

Accordingly, the Balzac Study Group didn't bother to frisk the Doctor when he arrived. What was the use? They were afraid of "frisk follicles," which they had read were sometimes installed in Harris tweeds for the Goppgunge crowd—hairs which, when unduly excited by frisking hands, would spring up, tinged with knockout paste or worse, to innoculate the hands doing the frisking.

Dr. Goppgunge was one of those living legends in the spy field. His esoteric testimony used to enrapture, when that was fashionable, members of Senate Committees responsible for oversight. His expertise excelled in three areas: as scientist-inventor, as technician of Psychological Control / Robo-Wash / Behavior Anomaly systems, and as "activist," i.e., off-oid. Since his retirement, Goppgunge had dropped the off-oid role, and had specialized in creating memory problems in business executives. One computer company would pay well to have executives of rival companies go ga-ga.

His constant fear was the footsteps of other murderers following. Little by little they cut away his stomach when it perforated. He developed a case of arthritis of the neck from years of looking over his shoulder in the darkness. He would back into the entrances of mansions as if he were mugger-warding at the door of the worst slum tenement. He insisted that his wife continue to peroxide her hair at age 67, just so he could grab ultrablonde hairs from her brush to hot-wax along the edges of his auto hood (to see if anyone had raised it during the night).

One might ask why the BSG would approach someone so clearly to be criticized. First, they wanted his services for a noble cause—The Glorious Deadline. And it was rule one of The 2000 Society that no one was so heinous, provided they were sane, as not to be recruitable into The Deadline.

Fitz McIver's security apparatus helped them to locate Dr. Goppgunge. IRS Agent Sean Tooely had tipped Fitz that Goppgunge was trying to arrange bank credit in high six figures in order to upgrade his laboratory facilities, and to outfit a helicopter landing pad, at his home in Golden, Colorado. Goppie was just begging to be hauled out of retirement, so they offered the Dr. a few Grover Cleve's for his assistance. There was an important factor that the cunning Balzacians correctly guessed. And that was that Goppgunge sorely missed the action, and since leftists had supplied the action for him in an adversary capacity for almost 57 years, why not let them hire him now? Goppgunge therefore leaped aboard a chartered copter out of Golden to Stapleton Airport in Denver, and then to N.Y., eager to robo, eager for action, eager for mon, even from partisans of The Glorious Deadline.

Ione wasted not a breath. "We understand you flash-strobe him, drug him, and then erase certain parts of his memory through commands? Is that it?"

"Yes, Ms. Appleton, first we strobe the subject across a frequency band, with median frequency at 680 flashes per minute; and this is an extremely bright-light source we're talking about. The blinding light confuses the subject, both as to the identity of those who have grabbed him, and also prepares him for the robo. Then we inject him with a substance called Quaff-mental-D," Goppgunge lied, not wishing to reveal any secrets. "This effectively prepares his unconscious mind to receive and to obey absolutely the instructions we give him relative to the behavior anomaly."

The Doctor continued. "It's my understanding you want a multi-year period of benevolence and, shall we say, forgetfulness, in the subject Mr. Quease. Fine. I've long felt that we should control the journalism profession more closely."

The others looked away in silent disgust.

Goppgunge felt he knew just what these rich leftists would want to hear—that's why he was cooperating with them in the first place. It wasn't only the mon, for he was preparing the groundwork for his own scheme, called *Project Laid-Back.* That is, instead of programming couriers and on occasion an assassin, why not empower an Anti-Consumerist Strike Force to kidnap and to implant more pliant and laid-back attitudes in those inclined to foment consumerist court cases. "Just think of the money General Motors wasted," Dr. Goppgunge said to the Balzacians, "hiring detectives to look for dirt on Ralph Nader. What they should have done was hire me to strap him down and to restructure that cocksucker's dome! If they had, there'd never have been a U.S. consumer movement in its present form, and we could have robo-commanded Nader to become a nice gentle tax attorney in Anaheim. Heh heh heh!"

Ione suppressed the urge to puke, and replied. "You can appreciate, Dr. Goppgunge, that our views are opposed on most issues. However, we are extremely interested in the installation of a period of robo-benevolence in Quease, and you are the person to do it. We were talking among ourselves how interesting it would be to have him become a member of the Barrel Generation, and actually go to live at the Brooklyn Bridge barrel complex. Is that possible?"

"It shall come to pass, should you deem it," the Doctor replied with a smile and, would you believe it, a click of the heels. "You can insert anything you want. You can make the subject believe he's Donald Duck. Of course, after time, he'll slip into his prior self occasionally, often just when you don't want him to. The best path for a strong insert, therefore, allows for the subject to have a model, or mock-up, experience of the overall experience you want to implant."

"I don't quite understand, Doctor," George Plyght said.

"Certainly, Mr. Plyght. You form the subject's receptivity—usually through a drug, so that his mind is 'thresholded'— as we say—for the prepared conditions. Thus thresholded, you can act out a little play with the subject and thus implant whatever you want."

"Of course," Goppgunge continued, "We do have computer signal implant systems, using which you can beam various program commands to the robo subject. You can develop various computer cassettes for multiple personalities—but I think we want here something untraceable . . ." He paused, searching for the correct word to please the Bohemian leftist-insurrectionists, "What we want here is a *funky* robowash, n'est-ce pas?"

"Doctor," John Barrett broke in, "How about making him into a saucer contactee?" All began to laugh.

"Don't laugh," reprimanded the Doctor. "That's been done many times in the past, usually for purposes of industrial espionage, when one needed to get into an installation, so a security guard was seized, programmed to let certain individuals in without using the fingerprint comparison machine, and then the embarrassing hour's gap was covered by programming an ersatz saucer experience. The security guard usually keeps quiet about it too; you don't start complaining about saucers and keep your job guarding defense secrets."

"Okay," John Barrett continued, "You say that you can guarantee a pleasant experience for Quease that at the same time effectively erases the information we want, and that we can cover for the hours during which you've planted the pleasantness, so to speak, with a saucer contactee experience. But, specifically, how? Just by telling him about it under the influence of the hypno-dope?"

"Not quite," Dr. Goppgunge replied. "As I said, we've found that the maximum strength of the implant is engendered by creating a model of the experience you wish to implant. If you ask me, our biggest problem will be to accomplish it under the deadline you have outlined to me. This will require the concentrated assistance of all of you."

Thereupon Goppgunge reached into his attaché case and pulled forth a cassette lecture detailing a UFO robo system he once developed for the Air Force. The BSG sat around the Altar of Lost Illusions to watch the videotape, while the Doctor went out to a pay phone outside Gem Spa and ordered a courier plane to deliver five extremely realistic poured-rubber Venusian monster suits, which he, Ione, George, Wendy, and John were to don.

Goppgunge made another call and arranged to use a "safevan" with untraceable backstopped license plates, and a walkie-talkie system outfitted with crystals to pick up the broadcasts of N.Y.P.D. Intelligence, the FBI, ATF, the N.Y. office of Dept. of Agriculture Intelligence, and the South Africans.

Thus, art and life congealed once again, and the BSG and a key character in one of its novels formed a team *pro tem*. The Creativity Bunker was transformed overnight into the interior of a spaceship. They purchased an entire recording studio and craned it into the bunker, using the various recording consoles as pretend spaceship controls.

Ione Appleton's skill with duct tape and cloth made it all possible. They emptied the Duct Tape Boutique of feathers, laces, cloth, and trash bags, and Ione spent the night taping together a suitable enclosure around the mock control panels. They remembered the Warhol loft of 1965 and taped sheets of metal foil to the walls.

Within twenty-four hours, the safevan seized a tired Hector Quease outside his home, which they were shocked to discover was in a Long Island suburb. The complete isolation of the target is a prerequisite for a successful robo insert. The only time Quease was alone was when he discharged his honor guard of Starved Foxes and disappeared across the bridge into Queens-Ho to his secret split level, his secret wife, his secret children.

Quease clawed at the masks as he was being dragged into the safevan, snarling, "I bet it's the Balzacers!" By the time he was strapped down, Goppgunge had dulled his sight with the strobe, and had eased the needle into his cheek, and Quease's good guess was jello'd 'neath Quaffmental-D.

Ione read a 100-quatrain poem to the hypno-drugged Quease, describing the mighty fortress space vehicle that had gobbled him aboard. Quease nodded sleepily throughout.

In the craze of an antiques auction someone had once bought an antique tin bathtub of extraordinary size. This they filled with corn-oil tinted with paprika—its surface sprinkled with Cheerios and several hundred circular paper hole reinforcements. Ione maintained her steady chant while Wendy Sark, in full Venusian costume, gently removed Quease's trousers, her molded rubber paws paying careful attention to the wan, tranced membrum virile, which now incredibly bounced to life in the kneading paws. "Hector Quease," Ione announced as solemnly as she could without breaking into laughter, "Thou hast been chosen for The Bath of Eternity."

Thus, they dipped the hypnotized contactee into the corn gush while stroking him lasciviously with long-handled butter brushes.

Quease dug it.

They dried the ithyphallic journalist by passing him closely between a facing pair of steam pants-pressing machines, the type with rollers. With Ione's patterns of duct tape and lace affixed to the rollers, it was quite an attractive sight as the machines were lowered to spin-buff the margarine-drenched Hector Quease quivering with quasi-fulfillment.

Next for Quease was the full Robo-Benevolent Implantation. Dr. Goppgunge signaled to clear the path, and slowly the Venusian Slobber Machine lumbered out of the far corner of the Creativity Bunker, now saucer interior, toward the turkey. Wendy attached earphones to Quease, and a tape began which would structure years of benevolent behavior in the subject.

All night long Goppgunge and the BSG had slaved constructing the Venusian Slobber Machine. Chief ingredients were three milking machines from a Jersey farmer, and a fifteen-foot-high stuffed giraffe from F.A.O. Schwarz toys. The suction of the milking cups was greatly adjusted, for, in applying conjunction with Mr. Quease, they did not want any permanent damage to his tender parts.

Two of the Balzac writing desks were lashed together and topped with a rubber mattress. This was to be Hector's bridal chamber beneath the Venusian Slobber Machine. Roller skates were fitted upon the table legs for mobility. The giraffe's legs were splayed wide, and the milking machines attached to the stomach. The head of the giraffe was covered with one of the Venusian masks. A tiny speaker system was placed behind the mask, to announce at appropriate moments things like, "You are having fun, Hector, fun, Hector, fun, Hector . . ."

The giraffe and the milking machines could be raised and lowered upon the lashed-together Balzac desks. The machines were masked with duct tape and orifice-like cylinders of foam rubber. From a distance, the array of soft tan rubber on the giraffe looked a bit like those nice foam sculptures by John Chamberlain. These, the wrappings of foam about the milking cups, were the "slobber nodules." To decrease the friction of genitalic conjunction, Ione coated the slobber nodules with some of her Festal Cones.

Meanwhile, what was powering the approaching Venusian Slobber Machine? Was it a neat solar-powered battery, or better, one of the tiny insert motors NASA developed that run off a human's heart? Nay, o typewriter, it was an example of how fiercely Goppgunge took up his projects, for 'neath the mantle of metal cloth and duct tape covering the roller-skate-footed Balzac tables resided Dr. Goppgunge, on all fours, providing the motion of the Slobber Machine with his own sweat!

The rubber Air Force monster suits saved the Balzac Study Group's collective arms from the untoward lackthrills provided by their bare arms having to touch the wet, sticky, ithyphallic Quease body, lifting it upon the Venusian Slobber Machine.

This being accomplished, John Barrett walked behind the Machine, and using the hidden crane, slowly lowered the giraffe upon the outstretched Quease, adjusting the modified milking machine vacuum-cups, "sluup, sluup, sluup, sluup . . ."

"Your privies will now be engaged by the Queen of Space, darling Hector," Ione chanted, the others around her bent double, trying to disguise their hissing gasps of laughter.

Then it was Suck City, U.S.A., for the drugged and trancéd journalist.

During the tedious operations on Hector Quease, Fitz Mc-Iver stood in Gem Spa on the corner of Second Avenue and St. Mark's sipping a chocolate egg cream and slowly allowing two chocolate-covered marshmallow cookies, one in each cheek, to dissolve, listening to the conversations then occurring inside the Creativity Bunker down the street through a surveillance chip ear-piece. He could glance down St. Mark's at the growing complex of Quease's Starved Foxes building their barrel living quarters in front of the Duct Tape Boutique. (The so-called Barrel Laws allowed a certain portion of the sidewalk to be used as temporary two-day habitats for members of the Barrel Generation.)

"How distressing it is that memory is nothing but genetic drool," he mentioned to the man stirring him a second egg cream. "But I wonder," he thought to himself, "should I interrupt and save Mr. Quease from the Venusian Slobber Machine?" Fitz McIver's hand was in his pocket fondling the coiled loops of his Stare-o-Rooter.® "Or should I climb on the roof and do an insert?"

"No to both," he decided. The late October weather was

turning chilly, and McIver's cold clammy hands and feet were clammier still as he left Gem Spa and walked south along Second Avenue, glancing at the building that had once housed the wonderful restaurant known as *Ratners,* wishing he could stop for some cherry blintzes and celery tonic. He switched off the Surv-Chip® just as Hector Quease was shouting something that sounded awfully like, "Sock it to me, o slobber nodule!"

McIver was softly singing,

"We all live in Grover Cleveland's grave
Grover Cleveland's grave
Grover Cleveland's grave."

PART FOUR

J'ACCUSE

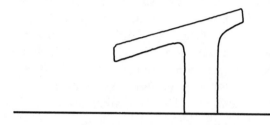

THE
ABLUM PROBLEM

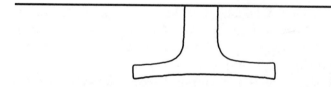

What does it mean to be at the summit of rock & roll, to wear the sacred rock-a-bard laurel, while snapping up motels for your business empire like twigs for a fire? It means your name is J'Accuse, four men—not quite young, not quite old—for whom the unkind glare of bright lights on the wrinkles of biologic phasing is modulated by the distance that fame allows their stage to be placed from the audience.

The career of J'Accuse had led it to roam among the exquisite flowers, deer moss, and licheny rocks of one of those Alpine meadows of fame from which ascension to higher ground could lead rather quickly and painfully to precipitous descension.

"Why should it not last forever?" the men in the band seemed to ask themselves. "Who else but us can aptly enjoy those matterhorns of moolah, lunar peaks of groveling reporters, sheer cliffs of RAW THRILL whence one can perform one's twisting leaps into the waters of performance?" But, have you noticed that however long you're at the top, how little things still loom stupidly large? And so it was that a poll of the band before it went on for the second show at the Milwaukee Civic Arena might well have revealed the single biggest concern troubling them at the moment was the recently discovered "Ablum Problem."

You can determine the rough age of the writer of a fan letter merely by opening the envelope a crack to see if the letter is written on notebook paper with curlings along the left side where it has been torn off the spiral wire. Letters of this type were pouring into the *J'Accuse Revolutionary Transformation Units* (otherwise known as fan clubs), Central Headquarters, at the rate of 5000 per week. Some, to be sure, were eminently readable, but on the whole the quality of letters had dropped off since the late '60's (when each fan seemed bent on a career in psychedelic art and their letters were adorned in the mode of horror vacui, with multi-color eyeballs and deities smiling or glowering from clouds, talking mushrooms, amorphous hearts that upon closer inspection proved to be misshapen guitar bodies, and numerous species of cosmic melt-flowers) or even the smooth-edged '70's and prophetic '80's.

Not only were 74% of current J'Accuse fan letters written on bluelined notebook paper, but during the past seven months the J'Accuse staff had isolated for scientific tabulation the depressingly thick bundle of letters containing misspellings of the word *album*. The letters often began with a sentence like: "I loved your recent _____." The "albums" broke down as follows:

1.	ablum	1643 instances
2.	albem	1471 instances
3.	alblum	1219 instances
4.	ablem	1175 instances
5.	abum	101 instances
6.	alum	16 instances

It is commendable that in every one of the 165,000 letters in the survey, the initial vowel of the word was correct; and the b/l metathesis in *ablum* could perhaps be forgiven, considering the haste of letters scrawled in a boring social studies class. The other misspellings however caused J'Accuse to fear an irreversible drift of the career ship toward the nebbish nebula. What a cause of apprehension! For even the tawdriest of rock wastrel Absaloms know full well that popularity in such a nebula is ever a source of pain and guilt, profligacy and burnout, overdose and selfslice.

Yet, you can go right to the N.Y. Guild of Socialist Copyeditors and ask if many writers of highest repute aren't capable of repeated lapses into dullard spelling. Relax, great writers glancing at this tome, Plotinus could not spell either, and if you couldn't spell Greek, you had a few problems.

So, the Ablum Problem was nothing compared to those looming for J'Accuse, whose career was at what one might call the "cripples at the airport stage." Indeed, there were some bands—but not J'Accuse—such that the wheels of the airplane would have barely—dzert! dzert! dzert!—touched upon the runway when the hot coca-packed nostrils would be blowing steam upon the portholes, hoping to spot a sad line of wheelchairs and people on crutches at the gate eager to be healed by the hands of the famous band. Huge crowds formed wherever in the world J'Accuse traveled, and since two of them, the drummer and the lead guitarist, were so-called Liberated Christians now, there was a sense that the "heal me! heal me!" scene would gather force.

The sacks of mail were already beginning to stack up from the Born Again. Little could the band guess the enormous pressure to come from Christendom to clean up their act and to pull a John Donne suppression on their past. But for now, however, past present future seemed one single Hairy Table, and all of a sudden J'Accuse trotted out of their dressing room, already beginning to sing in harmony as they trotted. There were flickering, suggestive lights, causing a roar in the audience.

There they were! J'Accuse! Donnie Pone, lead guitarist, came racing upon the stage first, holding a perfect, high-low

Persian warble broadcast through a throat mike. Hard on his guitar cord, almost treading it, Jeb Malcomridge, guitarist and keyboard man, also holding a perfect, high-low Persian warble a fifth above Donnie Pone. Next, Wendell Taptap, born again drummer, a gleeful Persian warble issuing from him a harmonic above Jeb Malcomridge! And last, Clayton Feall on bass and perfect soprano warble.

The crowd went nuts at the beauty of the warble.

It was an odd, very diverse audience, one you would have thought very unlikely to go nuts. J'Accuse utilized the only precept of people congregating from disparate life-tracks to form a singing group: "Find out what you can do well together, and learn to do it flawlessly."

All had studied modern dance—in fact could have formed a troupe, and they were exceedingly disciplined. There was a 500 dollar fine for anyone who broke harmony during a concert, and all members could perform a standing backward somersault while playing their instruments and singing. So, they easily sprinted on stage, leaping about, keeping the Persian warble perfect, and then lining up side by side, to sing the opening line of the song, *"The Melody Makers are Mushrooms,"* as beautiful a four-part lyric as found in all of rock.

Tears could have rimmed the eyes of the most avid fans, had they not been bent over in contortions of frenzy, flinging the nascent tears far thence from gyrating visages.

There was pressure at once from diverse factions of the audience for specific songs—during the breaks between numbers the huzzahs and demands sometimes took the form of angry chants. J'Accuse made sure they mixed evenly into the program songs from all seven major phases of their 19-year career. Repeatedly they urged the factions of the audience to blend together, and not to stand coldly apart as at a ballgame.

The Melody Makers are Mushrooms was the J'Accuse theme song, and it always brought the entire crowd together to its feet. As the concert advanced, however, no sooner did they finish a song satisfying one faction, when a second faction demanded one of its songs. So it was then, that a group of several thousand punk nostalgia fans stood up shouting in unison, "Spit! spit!

spit! spit! . . ." The request was obvious. They wanted Jeb Malcomridge to recreate one of his glorious spittle exhibitions from the punk era of J'Accuse, when pitched spittle wars were conducted between the band and its audiences in some of the most prestigious concert halls in North America and Europe. The band had even outfitted its guitars and keyboard instruments with "punk spittle cannons," which peppered the front rows with glitter-spittle.

Jeb Malcomridge finally had come up with a paisley-colored miracle substance which he would chew, and then when its proper moment of salival viscidity should arrive, would ptooh! a gob of it out upon the audience, and the floodlights would trace its trajectory, and it would seem to grow in size, spreading like a fishing net thrown upon the angry waters, until by the time it arrived at a target it would be four or five feet wide, and would wrap itself in full color glory around the head or outstretched arms of a fan. Such was the stuff of the J'Accuse legend, and the audience at the Milwaukee Civic Arena was demanding it, and demanding it forthwith.

It was just as well then that the band began the familiar riffs of its punk phase classic, *Slashing My Wrists Because I Ran Out of Froot Loops,* and the punk faction's delirium needle bounced far red.

The audience could not have seen it, but the band members looked at one another in pain as the song began. J'Accuse felt great embarrassment over its punk rock/glitter phase—an embarrassment not apparently shared by the audience. For instance, there was no embarrassment, only circumspection, in the one-time punk rocker, now sedate banker, who in his limousine riding that evening to the concert had put the smooth suspension system of his Rolls Royce to its ultimate test: he had operated on himself.

Holding an elegant 17th century French royal hand mirror to his face, he had searched for it. It? Yea, it, the wan, faint scar of yore, covered with plastic surgery long since, and over-dubbed with the tan of the sunlamps of the Milwaukee Bankers' Painting Luncheon and Athletic Society. It was the scar, rather two scars, where the painter had once—it seemed so many years ago—pierced his nose and his upper lip, and had inserted one of Hector Quease's "curved punk pins" through the holes just before a punk phase J'Accuse concert.

In the limousine he jabbed himself with a disposable syringe containing a local anesthetic, and then using a tiny battery-powered diamond drill created two perfect round incisions—very unlike the crude borings he had once made with the auger blade of a Swiss army knife! The punk pin on this occasion was not one of Quease's gold anodized sleazies, but rather was a fine diamond clustered edition-of-one, made for the banker by Van Cleef & Arpels.

So, the banker, cleverly disguised in his diamond punk pin, his carefully torn vested suit and his, would you believe it, thigh-high troutfisher wading boots of actual bronze (giving a scrumptious punk-of-yore *draggy* feeling the banker just adored), felt no embarrassment, but felt tears instead, upsetting the purple mascara of his eye corners when the music for *Slashing My Wrists Because I Ran Out of Froot Loops,* the favorite tune of his youth, issued forth from the stage.

Jeb Malcomridge knew it was terribly unseemly, given his position in The 2000 Society, and with the new seriousness of the band, to spit any more paisley punk-hockers into the audience, but he did allow glitter cannons on either side of the stage, which spewed a satisfying cloud of glitter upon the audience at song's end. A poof of sparkling glitter snowed gently and adheringly upon the banker's tear-drenched eyes. He made a note to purchase a vial of the glitter-spittle from the J'Accuse Nostalgia Booths in the lobby.

J'Accuse advantaged itself with its Nostalgia Wear-Out Replacement business—they could supply posters of virtually every concert of the past 15 years, and sold via mail the 32 albums of their career; also tee shirts, caps, Punk Ptooey! Gum, singles, song books, buttons, band bios, belt buckles, and videotapes.

J'Accuse regularly ran ads appealing to fans that grew up in the 1960's and 1970's. It wanted to keep them all, the "ablum"-ites of the present, the allegedly burnt-out radicals of yore, the faded punkers. The tape containing its 19-year computerized fan

260

list was insured for eight million dollars.

Market studies always indicate a nearly total drop-off in the purchase of records after age 30. It was sometimes difficult to keep current addresses of fans who had left New Jersey for Yale Law School and then to D.C., but J'Accuse always tried to send letters on the 30th birthdays of fans begging them not to stop visiting the album counters!

The band discovered one trend which, with the correct advertising, augured a lifetime on Mt. Moolah! Those who'd no longer purchase records could be sucked in with nostalgia. No matter how burned out, how bored with life, how much they deprecated the past, had found a new and better life, had recanted, had reformed, had changed for the better, for the worse, had grown up, grown down, had become religious, had lost faith, had become decadent, had become a Puritan, they *all*, and we mean everyone, could potentially be sucked into a concert, however covertly, by the ageless, age old, and age-targeted, Lure of Nostalgia by Any Other Name or Emblem.

She-of-the-Flowers was her name in '67. She-the-Medical-School-Dean is her name now, her children almost in college, and now she's back at J'Accuse concerts, rocking on her heels: wiser, as voluptuous as ever, ready for action. Without blemish were the wonderful sensations of Remembrance of Freak-Outs Past—the school principal, praying none of his students are in the audience, smoking a 'j' for the first time in 12 years; or the White House Press Secretary who knew President Kennedy wouldn't mind her reliving 15 years later an Ibogene trip with Jeb Malcomridge in an eyeball-painted van in Taos, New Mexico.

Of course there were those who felt depressed at the concert; did not the genius Heraclitus say, "You can't go into the same River twice?" You could sing songs that were as beautiful as Schubert, with lyrics on Shelley's level, yet they'd complain, rightly so, that it had been done much better in the "great funky clunky" of the '60's/'70's. Realizing this phenomenon, J'Accuse deliberately performed certain songs from their past with high energy crudity, letting their voices lapse into atonal masochism. One of these was their classic, *The CIA Made Me Sing Off-Key*, the next song in the concert after the *Froot Loops* punker. *The CIA Made Me Sing Off-Key* was from the protest/chauvo/burn-it-down! J'Accuse phase, and its partisans in the audience went mad with delight.

It might be useful to list some of the principal songs from the six phases of J'Accuse's career prior to the stupendous success of its Christmas album, its involvement in Science-and-Technology Rock, and The 2000 Society:

Songs from the Folk/Folk-Rock/Ban the Bomb/Civil Rights Period:

- ○ Jennie o' th' Braes
- ○ Michael Row Your Boat Ashore
- ○ We are Better Than the Kingston Trio
- ○ Fall-a-diddle, Fud-a-diddle, Fid-a-diddle
- ○ Only A-Heads like A-Bombs

From the Acid/Flower Power Period:

- ○ Flowers Will End The War
- ○ Tim Leary o' th' Braes
- ○ Michael Hallucinate Your Boat to the Moon
- ○ Grope-In After The Be-In
- ○ Then Jesus Came Among the Geodesic Domes at Dawn and the State Police Killed Him Until He Was Carried Away on a Green Frog's Back Rag

Songs from the Protest/Shock Rock/Chauvo-Rock/
Burn It Down Phase:

- ○ (It's so Much Fun) Selling State Secrets to the Chicoms.
- ○ Lyndon Johnson Eats Shit.
- ○ Final Planning Session Before the Revolution.
- ○ Whenever I'm in an Airplane Crash I Reach for my Fly.
- ○ Please Don't Use My Toothbrush After You Blow the Drummer, Little Darling.
- ○ We Are Better than the Beatles.
- ○ The Coitus Oculi Extracti Boogie.
- ○ The CIA Made Me Sing Off-Key.

From the Seventies/Watergate Rock Era
(the nadir of the band's popularity):

- ○ Richard Nixon Eats Shit.

- The Day Chuck Colson Wanted to Drive a Huge, Truck-Sized Tape De-Gausser Past CIA Headquarters in Langley.
- Richard and Henry Got Down on Their Knees to Pray Blues.
- The August Night of '74 Dan Rather Urged Everybody Not to Pour Out into the Streets to Celebrate the Abdication.

From the Glitter/Decadence/Punk Rock Phase:

- You Eat Shit (Or Else!)
- Slashing My Wrists Because I Ran Out of Froot Loops.
- The 1923 San Diego Phone Book Chant-Opera (a 5-record set).
- Let's Get in a Time Machine and Go Beat Up '60's Radicals.
- Never Slap the Face of the President of Columbia Records Until You Have Cashed the Check for $500,000 and the Contract's Signed.
- I Dreamt I Sniffed Coke with Ham Jordan at Studio 54 to Celebrate the Rise in Mortgage Rates.
- Don't Kill Me Until You've Bought My Record.

From Mea Culpa/Repentance Rock:

- I'm Sorry I was so Crummy in the '60's, Hot Mamma.
- Growing Up at 37 Rock Opera Waltz.
- Why Did We Burn That Bank Branch Down? (Now That We've Graduated from Law School and Own It).
- Shame Shame Shame Where I Pierced My Nose!
- While My F.B.I. Files Gently Weep.
- Making a Motion in Chicago Superior Court to Have an Arrest Record Purged for the *Days of Rage* Calypso.
- He Was a Nice Man After All (Blues for Hubert Humphrey).

Repentence Rock lasted for two years, until the band found itself and began to soar upon new wings. *The Wings of Seriousness* was the title of the first album after Repentance/Mea Culpa Rock's conclusion. From that time on, J'Accuse became partisans of History Rock, rock that told stories set in historical circumstances. Mixed with History Rock was another genre, Science-and-Technology Rock. Don't laugh. J'Accuse's educational tunes on detailed scientific themes swept the airwaves. To counterbalance the emerging Christian tone of the group, the remaining agnostics, Jeb Malcomridge and guitarist Donnie Pone, fashioned Nostalgia-for-Camus-and-the-Glorious-Days-of-Existentialism Rock. Indeed, one famous J'Accuse hit from their History Rock period was *The Sartrean Chronicles,* a rock opera featuring a series of story-songs played out by staring at Jean-Paul Sartre's ancient sheepskin flight jacket, the one he wore during War II writing *Being and Nothingness* in Paris cafés. A single, *The Prophecy of Jean-Paul's Leather Coat,* went Moon Rock.[1]

Such was the history of J'Accuse until its Christmas album, issued two years prior to the concert at the Milwaukee Civic Arena. Everybody had expected the album, when it was first announced, to be a cynical mixture of comedy, raillery, e'en mockery, but it was, except for the dance single *(The Roly Poly)* breathtakingly serious. Within six weeks of its release, it sold 45 million units worldwide, and altered the lives of them all.

So, the presence of a group of nuns and priests backstage was understandable, as was a pack of fashionable, money-hungry religious record executives, of the genre BORN AGAIN UNTO THE LORD BUT I STILL USE THE LEAF. The nuns and priests mixed admirably with the punk rockers, the folk nostalgists, and the protest rockers. Their confidence was well-founded. Since Wendell Taptap and bassist Clayton Feall had converted, the attitude was: "We have two of the converted, now all that remain to be grabbed are Jeb and Donnie Pone, and, heh heh heh, we'll have the first international rock group to hoist the banners of Christendom!"

The spotlight blazed down upon an oval in the stage's center, revealing a glorious dancing couple—Milton Rosé and Ione Appleton! demonstrating the new J'Accuse dance single, *The H.C.,* named after Hart Crane.

The campaign to arouse public consciousness about the Hart Crane Shrine of Mars was taking many turns. Ione Appleton had introduced Rosé to Jeb Malcomridge. J'Accuse was in the middle of recording its *J'Accuse for America* album, but Jeb took time to fly with Milton to Florida to meet with NASA officials. J'Accuse agreed to write a tune for TV ads to promote the shrine.

---

1. Moon Rock, a term used in measuring sales of a record, denoting eight million units sold; from the rocks brought back from first trip to moon, sold on the clandestine market at outlandish prices.

In the middle of the meeting with NASA officials, Jeb received the idea for *The H.C.* He jumped upon a table covered with Martian maps and printouts, to give a demonstration of the dance. The startled NASA people were thankful the musician raindancing on their table was doing something creative and not undergoing some sort of artistic "flake attack."

As a dance single, *The H.C.* went Moon Rock in three weeks. The audience in Milwaukee was on its feet to applaud Ione and Milton, and as many as could find room were performing the intricate foot slides and toe-stubbings and hops of the dance rage. Wanna do it too, o reader?

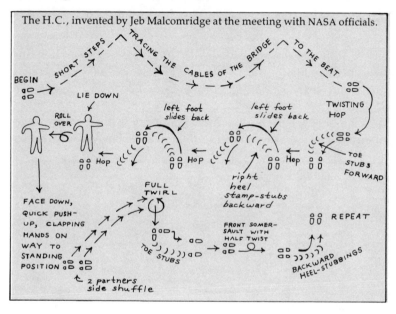

The H.C., invented by Jeb Malcomridge at the meeting with NASA officials.

J'Accuse realized early in its career that if you can associate a popular dance or two with your name, (as of *The Peppermint Twist*, *The Hokey Pokey*, or *The Gobble*), they'll have a harder time stomping your name into oblivion. Just like you can tour a couple of years on the heat of a hit single, a hit dance'll keep you out there in loungelizardland indefinitely. Some early J'Accuse dance singles were:

265

1. *The Vladimir Two-Step*—known affectionately as *The Len'*, named after V. I. Lenin, and of course built around "two steps forward, one step back."

2. *Flower Joy*—tracing the petals of an imaginary acid-induced camellia with the feet, a late '60's classic.

3. *The Frot'* (from 'frottage')—the first of the "rub your partner" dances.

4. *The Shameless*—(from the early '70's, when the band had attempted to "come to grips with California." With a chorus of "Let's be shameless," the dance was performed naked in large redwood tubs of hot grape-pulp.)

Instruction charts were issued with the dance singles. When the band became big league, TV ad campaigns showed political figures and celebrities demonstrating dances such as *The H.C.*, or *The Barrel*.[2]

Later, J'Accuse led the music industry away from the sex-oriented dances of the '60's and '70's, toward formal group dances

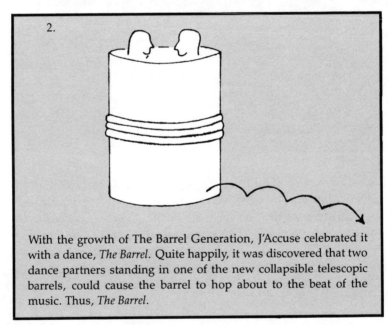

2.

With the growth of The Barrel Generation, J'Accuse celebrated it with a dance, *The Barrel*. Quite happily, it was discovered that two dance partners standing in one of the new collapsible telescopic barrels, could cause the barrel to hop about to the beat of the music. Thus, *The Barrel*.

(such as *The Camus,* the first of the "symbolic biography" group dances, which told the tragic life story of the great philosopher with intricate eight-person footwork.)

There was only one distinct failure among J'Accuse's dance singles, occurring when they inaugurated what was dubbed the "Mimed Punk Dance," to a song called *Zeros On My Scars.* The tune had the rather moronic chorus,

> "I'm just sittin' here adrawin' —yatta yatt—
> I'm just sittin' here adrawin'—yatta yatt—
> I'm just sittin' here adrawin'—yatta yatt—
> zeros on my scars, yatt,
> zeros on my scars."

The instructions innocently called for the dancers to mime zeros on their partners' bodies. The band thought that perhaps some clothing might be torn apart, or some ecstatic punk frottage might occur, but nothing more. How shocking it was then, when thousands of fans who had no scars began to lacerate themselves before concerts, sometimes dyeing the scabs with wild primary colors, and then as they danced, drew real zeros upon each other's sores with wide felt markers. This brought stern reprimands from TV news broadcasters, "No good, J'Accuse, no good!" The band suppressed the single, and called back all copies at double the price.

Like the great entertainer he was, Jeb Malcomridge turned his face in all directions as he sang *The H.C.* Tears were in his eyes noting how all over the hall, all the factions, even the critics, were dancing! As the Quakers say, the spirit of reconciliation is an overwhelming experience.

There was a roped-off "Boogie Croft" in front of the stage for the rock press. These were rock critics?! Gone were the days of army surplus fatigue jackets with oranges in the pockets! Occasionally a searchlight would strafe the rock press, for they were stars now themselves, some as elegantly appointed as a Cronkite, a Kaltenborn, a Severeid, a Walters, a MacNeil, rolling on their footballs sedately, bending over to take some notes when blinding bolts of Eleusinia should boil within their brows. During most rock performances, the critics exchanged cynical witticisms, twisting a shoulder, say, and tapping a foot, say, half to the mood on the stage, half to their own inner melodies. Rarely, there'd be a "quality rock threshold" met, and the journalists would nod assentively to one another, and then go full tilt boogie, no longer merely rolling heel to toe, but slathering at the altar of jog-in-place, sweat, spinal column hypnosis, memories of freakouts past, angst-erasure, spiritual integration, and forgetfulness of the eyes of others.

It was always a joy to J'Accuse to glance down upon the rock press Boogie Croft at critics going full tilt. And so it was at the concert in Milwaukee—staid jotters with fat contracts with *Gorp, Urge,* and *Rolling Stone,* were literally rolling upon the plush carpets during *The H.C.!* There was only one who seemed unmoved, a veritable stele of elegance among them, a benevolent smile on his inscrutable face—Hector Quease!

He stands completely still, in robo-benevolent bliss; his lapel sports a button bearing a full color rendition of the Venusian Slobber Machine. The Balzac Study Group had not robo'd from Quease's personality the urge to dash up Mt. Mooh'. Hector has already peddled expensively a book on his experiences as the first American journalist chosen for "Transuniversal Slobber Nodule Conjunction." The movie of it is being readied for distribution, and Hector is flying around the country doing promo appearances. For the upcoming Christmas rush, Quease's factories, which used to turn out the famous Curved Punk Pins, are bigbucking it with scale model Venusian Slobber Nodule gelbeds for the burgeoning adult toy market.

So, while the other journalists are trying to take notes while at the same time following the intricate footwork of *The H.C.,* Hector Quease stands near the velvet outer ropes of the Boogie Croft, bubbling with benignity. Yet, the words, "Psst, hey buddy!" and "Psst, hey sis!" continually issue from his lips, accompanied by Quease opening wide his bulky canvas raincoat.

In vain one waits for the "Wooo!" that might indicate that Hector were so gross as to be flashing. No, wait . . . do things ever change? Hector is still groveling for mini-mooh'—he has pinned a two-foot array of his old Punk Pins to the inside of his coat to sell to passing nostalgia buffs. Many music critics have cottage or mail box industries to avoid the mallet of pov. You know you have arrived as a critic when you can forgo dealing out your mailbox freebies to your friend who manages a store, and concentrate instead on building a 55,000-unit collection some day to donate to the American Museum of Rock History at Harvard.

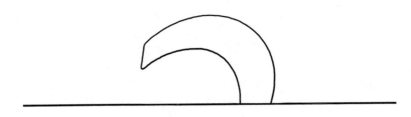

WENDELL TAPTAP'S
SHAME

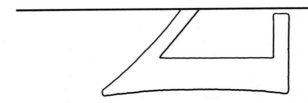

The H.C. came to a glorious conclusion. Images of the Brooklyn Bridge and of Hart Crane superimposed upon it filled the giant arena screen. What a roar! The factions fused in reconciliation. Science-&-Technology rockers danced with punk nostalgia buffs, protest rockers with the Kingston Trio fans, and acid rock formed a cosmic synthesis with mea culpa rock.

J'Accuse spent the last one-half of each concert unifying the factions. So when The Bridge image faded and a fresh image came upon the screen, an even mightier roar was heard from the audience. The image was like a . . . like a box . . . a hat box, it seemed. It was something the crowd recognized and loved. "Put on the wig! Put on the wig!" the auditorium chanted.

Wendell Taptap snapped his fingers, and slowly, from the far heights of the ceiling, a golden hat box, the spotlight chasing its descent, was lowered downward. Indeed, the box contained one of the most famous of all rock costume items, a coiffure once belonging to that golden voice of Sevierville, Tennessee: Dolly Parton!

After a short ballet about the stage holding it aloft, Wendell opened the hat box, and in one of the most cherished rituals of all of music, he placed the hairy sunshine on his head. The roar was painful; the flashbulbs formed a dazzling silver bowl of the arena. And Wendell Taptap, like a wrestler in some wrestling ring in heaven, strutted back and forth in the golden mane.

It had not been always so golden for Wendell Taptap and the Dolly Parton fall. He owned it through direst shame. In the very late '70's, certain culty-wultys stalked American rock and roll bands seeking superstitious, weak-willed targets with fat royalty accounts.

Such was Wendell Taptap, who had to spit, stamp his foot, and twirl three times before he'd even consider entering an airplane. And you know how in a drum case there are those vertical compartments for storage of brushes, sticks, etc.—well, Wendell actually stored holy wafer in Saran Wrap in those compartments, one supposes to ward off possible hemophagic fans on the road.

So it was that Wendell fell in with a shameless charlatan known as Goj-Gorj the Interplanetary. They say the first culty-wulty that floats out of the Astrodome will make the most money. If so, then Goj-Gorj the Interplanetary would have made not much less with the success of his routine. For Goj-Gorj promised, not eternal life, not levitation using astroturf as a launch site, not soul-travel to distant places, not elevation to higher planes nor to bliss city, but the promise of never again to have to go to the bathroom. Don't laugh; rather, think of it, o reader.

Gurus promised everything in the American landscape, but none save Goj-Gorj held out the lure of the Inner Bowel Beam. According to him, each human had a potential Inner

Magick Muck-Muncher Beam of the purest energy. It had only to be activated by the correct regimen, and it would "burn off the waste while still within." The potential for mon was stupendous. Telephone sampling polls indicated that 475,000 humans were ready to sign up in New Jersey alone! An elaborate security force was necessary to protect Goj-Gorj and the secret of the Beam. Goj-Gorj could barely sleep at night worrying about assassins hired by the manufacturers of tufted toilet seat covers and drain-rooters.

Goj-Gorj required, as a first step toward the "fire-up of the Bowel Beam," that Wendell Taptap shave his head, and tattoo an orange blossom on its top. The band begged Wendell not to shave, and his fan mail thereafter dropped off 83%, but his head soon bore a mercurochrome-hued floration. Wendell shined his dome every morning with the guru's expensive "vibe-oil" and a chamois cloth, patiently awaiting that day when the water closet in his apartment should flush its final flush. Wendell performed at J'Accuse concerts with long silken threads attached to the ceiling and leading down to the orange tattoo, enabling the soul as it willed to yo-yo up and down along the silk.

And how did Dolly Parton fit into the predations of Goj-Gorj the Interplanetary? Well, for ten years Wendell had worshipped Dolly Parton—voice, person, songs, stage act, and image. When touring allowed it, he slipped into Sevierville, Tennessee, on the edge of the Great Smoky Mountains, where Dolly graduated from high school in '64. There he sat in the town library weeping over her pictures in the school yearbooks. Dolly at the 4-H Club picnic! Dolly playing snare drums in the band! Quires of verse flowed from his pen thinking of his Dolly.

Wendell would pilgrimage with a backpack to the summit of Webb Mountain, Tennessee, and again lie weeping at dawn listening to her autobiographical songs on a portable player. *In My Tennessee Mountain Home* would e'er produce a gentle rain from his eyes to greet the rubeous sun.

Wendell was much too shy ever to approach her in the flesh. When she became friends with several of his famous women singer friends, he thought he'd perhaps get to meet her then, but somehow the chance was ne'er.

And what was Dolly Parton's allure?—the reader legitimately might ask. Or, to someone who may purchase this book on microfilm in a microbibliothèque used-book stall in some future century, it might be necessary to ask their memory computers, what *was* this Dolly Parton? What was the hold she had on people like Wendell Taptap?

Though to an outsider Parton might have looked totally manipulated, with her haystack coiffure and sequined D's all over her clothes, yet Taptap would have opined that like an Egyptian artist constrained to draw some dumb Pharaoh's baleful prayers on basalt, she found art despite constraint. Songs— emblems of creativity—bubbled out of her lips like a paradise flood.

When we can forgive Sigmund Hammerbank for engaging in whack-whack while sitting alone in the quartergloom of the gallery staring at Rosé's *Circles of Paradise,* can we not forgive Wendell Taptap doing some "closed rolls" on the pink altar while gazing at Dolly?

And what beauty! From the side, her nose had a delicate, nearly straight line, with a finely wrought convexity to make Wendell weep; and the lips were apple-valley full; an evening of kisses in a Time Machine with Dolly at the Sevierville High School Senior Prom was what Wendell hoped to come in his old age, when he felt technology might have made possible reversal of the time-track.

And the mystery of her bosom! Salted ever from sight like secrets in a Victorian tower. There was a Chantress of Amon—a singer of 1100 B.C. Egypt—Wendell saw once painted on a papyrus scroll with breasts the same as hers. Was Dolly Parton, the superstitious Wendell Taptap wondered, descended metempsychotically from the Theban chantress Her-Weben!?

Added to that was the mystery of what her *real* hair, hidden by the flaming bouffant, was like. What was its color, its texture? Maybe she was bald? "Do you have shame of it," Wendell Taptap wrote in his diary, "that you mask it with a mandala of mown sun-shafts?"

Wendell hungered sorely to run his fingers through Dolly's secret, to lick its strands softly with flambant kisses, to pour hot breaths upon it through the burning zero!

Her songs of childhood poverty reminded Wendell of his own pov-hawked youth, when his cousin's galoshes, adorned with ribbons red, once lay starkly beneath the tree on Christmas morn. Her voice was to Wendell a moan of eternity. The effect went way beyond the interesting manipulations of the vowels, *o, u,* and *oo,* in her singing style. In conveying emotion, Parton's tremulous voice matched that of the wonderful Ione Appleton. Wendell wondered if there weren't secret, warbling overtones when she held a note that pleased the ear without registering.

While still in the thrall of Goj-Gorj the Interplanetary, Wendell learned that Dolly had cancelled a 65-city tour because of reflared nodes on her vocal chords, a chronic problem for the genius singer. To keep up the steady scratching sounds of devotees writing checks, Goj-Gorj kept bragging he could cure everything from cancer to the Seven Plagues of Bohemia (hep, strep, syph, crabs, scabies, mono, and gono). Wendell begged the Interplanetary to intercede for Dolly's nodes. Placed in a bind, the Goj agreed to launch at once a long distance curative Beam aimed at Dolly's bedroom in Nashville. Wendell sent her a telegram with the good news that soon she'd be totally cured through Goj-Gorj's noble Beam.

Alas, the Beam did not cure the throat of his love. Wendell began to see the cultic mask aslippin', and once such slippage occurs, one oft sees the culty-wulty under less favorable circumstances. Wendell Taptap was a world famous musician, and he knew that Dolly Parton must surely have recognized his name at the bottom of the telegram. Wendell fell fluttering into the vale of total shame.

How all-consuming is a shame fully conceived! The shame of a famous Vicar caught by the State Police in dalliance with a baa baa while reading aloud Blake's Lamb Song. The shame of a toppled president; the shame of a poet who'd stolen another's secret notebooks looking for ideas and'd been caught. Such was the shame of Wendell Taptap over the orange flower on his pate.

He could not wait for the hair to grow again! "A fig leaf for my pitiful skull!" Wendell cried. "Garb my shame, o duct tape!" With that, Wendell wrapped his head with winding after winding of the sticky gray, covering not only the top of his head, but his face and neck, as if it were a duct tape poultice to suck away the dishonor.

He could not stop thinking about Dolly. One minute he wanted to apologize for the telegram. Another minute he wanted to declare his love. Suddenly, Wendell recognized a path to honor. He knew Dolly had a room in her mansion to store her concert wigs, those famous full blonde leonine puffs of hugeness. Ahhh, thought Wendell Taptap, if only she would give me one to cover my shame!

He pulled a stocking cap down upon his gray tape headdress and flew to Nashville. In a town where obvious is inconspicuous, Wendell purchased a purple Cadillac with a diamond-studded cowboy hat on the radiator and his initials, blinking in neon, W.T., on the doors. He changed his duct tape cap for a ten-gallon felt, and drove back and forth past Dolly Parton's driveway in farm country outside Nashville without the courage to drive up to beg forgiveness, or to ask for a wig.

A coward's path supplanted the fool's courage. At sunset, Taptap parked at the edge of the driveway, looking along the arching path up to the beautiful pillared mansion, and plotted a felony.

By 9 p.m. the house on the hill seemed darkened. All autos had driven away. Quite openly Wendell wheeled his flashy Caddy up to the side of the house. If he were caught, he planned to claim he was merely one famous musician paying a courtesy call upon another. (J'Accuse was in its Punk/Glitter/Decadence phase at the time, and if he were captured illegally inside the residence, he could probably have explained it as some sort of publicity stunt for an album.)

Wendell strolled around the mansion, marveling at its two-story porches and white picket fence. He tried each door. One was unlocked. Tears dropped on Wendell's cheeks thinking of her trust in leaving open a door to the wolverine world.

Wendell knew the location of her bedroom from studying old interviews. Ms. Parton had a habit of talking profusely about her house. The wig room lay to the side of the bedroom, so all he had to do was to open all doors leading out of it. At last, he twisted a knob, pushed the door inward, and highya! the flash-light encountered an overwhelming revelation of blondeness! Rows of wigs on all sides. Wendell's hot palm-perspiring hands rubbed circles all over the formica top of the u-shaped wig counter, not at first daring to touch the wigs on their wig stands.

Wendell glanced about the wig room. A pair of towel bars holding towels monogrammed with large, beautiful D's lay on each side of an ornate gilt dressing mirror. Wendell knew that the Lord might forgive him as he filched a couple of her towels for his Dolly Parton shrine. Then, to his horror, Wendell saw that she had wigs for all occasions, so that it was not going to be so easy to choose. He lined them side by side, testing each against his own physiognomy, his own neck and shoulders, his own skin color. If you borrow a wig from Dolly Parton, you want to make sure it's perfect.

Wendell
braided dreadlocks
and Celestial Corn Rows of Ra
upon one of
the headresses

and placed
a Festal Cone on another.

Few mortals will ever know the initial feeling of Dolly Parton's wig being put on Taptap's shavéd pate. It was eternity! The criss-cross inner lining of starched cheesecloth rubbing ever so lightly lasciviously upon his well-oiled (the reader will recall the administrations of holy Goj-Gorj "vibe-oil") scalp, and then, Elysium! the curlings of blonde hair touching his cheeks and forming a heat-collecting tent at the neck's back! Altars! Grails! Lotophagy!

Samson-like was Wendell's power with Dolly's wig! All at once he acquired qualities of leadership, of esteem, of ability, that before no one had recognized. Briefly Wendell bolted from J'Accuse and released his own single, *Weeping on Webb Mountain*. His career looked golden in Yuk-Yuk Rock, until one night he entered and won a Dolly Parton look-alike contest at halftime in Atlanta during a Knicks-Hawks game, and as a reward was allowed to sing to the crowd. A mistake. When they heard a man's voice from the sun-coif'd goddess, even if it was the hit song *Weeping on Webb Mountain*, a significant part of the audience began to boo and to laugh derisively, so that Wendell panicked and ran in shame from the arena.

Such publicity did not retard his career, but rather pointed it into a definite direction. He was of course willing to perform several numbers in his show wearing the wig, and a kilt-and-tam made from three of her monogrammed towels, but he was not willing to perform entirely in Dolly drag, as certain club owners and television shows urged him to do.

It was not long before Taptap returned to J'Accuse, where he kept his wig and made his Parton-prance on stage a glorious event, working with the grand woman of American Dance Theater, Claudia Pred, founder of the legendary Luminous Animal Theater, to fashion a ballet around the donning of the mane.

GRETA GARBO'S
MOUTH

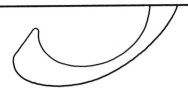

At the end of his ballet, Wendell Taptap stood in the applause as if his body were sensing-paper and the clapping were a chemical to bring out the secret writing on his face—in this case a smile that made a quivering banana of his lips. The applause eclipsed that for *The H.C.* and *The CIA Made Me Sing Off-Key.* Wendell glanced at Jeb Malcomridge and raced back to his drums to begin the roll and flourish signalling the portion of every J'Accuse concert known as GRETA GARBO'S MOUTH.

GRETA GARBO'S MOUTH was a J'Accuse institution, as was the use of glitter-spittle, that caused the band additional embarrassment. The fans however, demanded it. It began during the Watergate/Down-with-Nixon era, and at first merely featured the latest events of the unfolding scandal sung in tight harmony. GRETA GARBO'S MOUTH soon expanded to cover what can only be termed as gossip: data about other rock groups, about politicians, and about Hollywood. By the time of the band's punk phase, there was even something called a "Tryst List," featuring motel and hotel bills of the famed flashed on the giant screen accompanied by a gentle chant of the time, place, duration, and participants.

J'Accuse was now trying, with great resistance from the fans, to convert the MOUTH into a sort of rock and roll news broadcast, with its own investigative team providing text which Jeb and Wendell turned into sleuth-songs. Journalists, while generally decrying the whole idea, stood eagerly stageside with writing pads, listening for story possibilities. No one could deny that it was pleasant, for the truth is that with an active, creative rhythm section, and crisp, accurate four-part harmony, you might be able to sell out halls singing autopsy reports.

With that billion dollar ability to *whisper* in four-part falsetto harmony, J'Accuse began THE MOUTH. The four of them sang "Did you know that?" whereafter two hummed beneath, and the others sang the gossip, one in falsetto, the other in a deep bass, with the vowels held unusually lengthily. They sang the tidbits of data otherwise extremely rapidly, so rapidly that froth-flecks flew in more than normal abundance upon the front rows. The unseemly occurrence of front row rock froth-fleck, by which we mean particles of drool and rapid-lip flippings of foam, brought no change upon the faces of those awaiting the incipience of GRETA GARBO'S MOUTH.

Every few seconds J'Accuse repeated the opening "Did you know that?" And again the humming, and the froth-flow of gossip. The more intimate, the more erotic, the more scandalous the information, the more the audience shrieked for more. Bread and circuses and apertural advertisements.

Sometimes Jeb commissioned The Diogenes Liberation Brigade of Strolling Troubadors and Muckrakers to join them, accompanied by a full orchestra, and performing via satellite hook-up to a multi-nation audience. On these occasions, all of

279

GRETA GARBO'S MOUTH would be devoted to a single "Investigative Anthem" with the texts, usually in rhymed quatrains, flashing on the giant screen while the Brigade sang.

The gossip section lasted about a half hour, guitarists filling in softly behind it with long Grateful Dead-like solos. We can't understand why the Eagles, the Beach Boys, and The Existenz Precedes Essence Tone-Tongs didn't have their own GRETA GARBO'S MOUTH segs in their shows.

Meanwhile, as the marvelous four voices were performing the gossipy froth, an unknown figure in a suit, tie, and vest walked onto the stage, and began to whisper into Jeb Malcomridge's ear. During this, Jeb continued singing and playing his guitar. Jeb shook his head excitedly while the man whispered to him. After the next introductory "Did you know that?" Jeb interrupted to sing, "A good attorney is all the psychotherapist you'll ever need." Jeb meant it.

J'Accuse, like many other bands, saved greatly on psychotherapy bills with the new trend of lawyers as therapists. Some lawyers had gone back to school to pick up M.D.'s. The phenomenon had reached the corporate board room, so that a good barrister, while aiding a multi-national to hide its profits from nosy governments, could concomitantly assist board people with their psychic, nay, even often psycho, crises. Why join a cult when you can hire a lawyer?

With the glut of attorneys in these times, some set aside the scales of justice and concentrated on the culty-wulty. There were unscrupulous lawyer/therapists who would stare-chant rainstorms of mon out of their rock-a-bard clients. Such was not the marvelous Barnaby Radither, who strode onto the stage in the midst of the GRETA gossip to confer with Jeb Malcomridge. For Barnaby the opportunity to branch out as a therapist came none too soon, taking up the slack brought about by the mon drop-off when first the draft ended, and then the dope laws were eased or erased.

Barnaby was just about the most famous of the leftist attorneys. He was an exponent of a Medievalist-Marxist position. The Medievalist-Marxists held that "there had always better be a taste given to so-called 'born adventurers'—the equivalent of the disinherited younger sons of medieval European nobility."

Such psychological types, the lawyer/therapist opined, will always be roaming the world swashbuckling and garnering by whatever device. "They'll just have to be given an extra flash of cash, or else you'll have to imprison them when they show themselves in early childhood," said Radither. "Otherwise you'll have them sneaking all over the surface of Mars looking for Eldorado. They'll use your Crane shrine to store their ore. In fact, that's who'll find Milton's treasure cave, some greedy little Cortez with armpit sweat mottling the inside of his space suit."

J'Accuse's legal fees for some time had been high in six figures per annum, and were lunging of late toward seven. With the formation of The 2000 Society, lawyerly pressure was continuously needed to prevent basketball arenas from cancelling their concerts. Right-wing nuts owned a number of the country's stadia and arenas and were loath to allow the sweet harmonies of The Grand Burn to flow into the aural passages of the young.

Barnaby was allowed access to Jeb Malcomridge 24 hours a day, including concerts. The attorney developed a sort of subdued balletic shuffle, whenever he had to consult with Jeb during a concert. You run a global network, and you have to close down deals around the clock, time zone to time zone. So it was on this occasion that Barnaby Radither dance-hopped across the stage at the Milwaukee Civic Arena, bearing news of great joy.

J'Accuse had just picked up another 21 motels in the State of Washington! Only 23 more to go, and they'd own 'em all. Jeb signaled the news to the rest of the band, and there were smiles and whoops of joy across the stage. J'Accuse made up a song on the spot, *23 More to Go, Lil' Darlin'*. After the spontaneous ditty, Jeb interrupted the concert for an announcement. "Partisans of The Deadline, the forces of The 2000 Society have tonight marched ever closer toward the establishment of the first state in which every single motel will offer a room at prices easily affordable by every citizen! Rates at the Seattle Hilton, and indeed at virtually every motel across the state, are being cut as of tonight to ten dollars per 24 hours. And no more of this checkout at 11 a.m. scam, either!"

A mighty roar greeted the news. "Next stop, the New York Hilton!" Jeb yelled. The last was a ploy. In fact, The 2000 Society was actually preparing to purchase casinos and real estate in Las Vegas, but secretly, and did not yet want the heroin-hooker-gambling-real estate mob to learn of it.

GRETA GARBO'S MOUTH ended, as it did regularly recently, with a quiz on the subject, "Who is in the Balzac Study Group?" The band would sing the question, and the giant screen would flash with answering images say, of Mailer, Capote, Vidal, Joyce Oates, Joan Didion, Faye Dunaway, Rosalynn Carter, Dan Rather, Dolly Parton, Glenn Frey, Hunter Thompson, John Clellon Holmes, Ralph and Huguette Martel, Bob Dylan, George Plimpton, Robert Christgau, Jason Epstein, Milton Rosé, Peter Falk, Shirley MacLaine, Bud Shrake, Al Fowler, Claudia Pred, Barbara Kopple, Diane Wakoski, Robert Kelly, Ed Dorn, Rochelle Owens, Jerome Rothenberg, Miriam Sanders, Ted Berrigan, Kathy Acker, Duncan McNaughton, and Linda Ronstadt (a strong suspect).

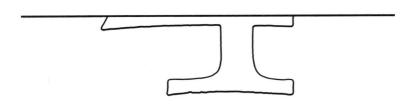

THE THEORY OF
THE CHRISTMAS SINGLE

The concluding portion of the concert was devoted to songs from the Christmas album. The scenery shifted, and a large Christmas tree, a manger, and a glistening multipointed "Holo-Star of Bethlehem" were pushed on stage by electric push-tongues. The Born Again, the Always Been Born, the Methodists, the nuns, the priests, flocked with jubilation. The partisans of glitter-spittle, the partisans of Down with Nixon rock, the partisans of auld lang acid flower piety, of mea culpa/ flagellation melodies, looked none too happy, but lives spent beneath the robo-programs of endless Christmas commercials had conditioned everyone beyond redemption to feel guilty, to

283

spend money, and to smile benevolently at year's end, and so the Christians were allowed by the other factions to grab off the concert's finale.

J'Accuse performed a half-hour medley of Christmas album songs. Whereas the album had sold 45 million units last season, this season the figure was 55. The attention of the media was so intense that a walk down the street was a story. The first song performed was the dance single, *The Roly Poly*; then *Dream of the Southern Road* (a sho-sto-so, or short story song—the basis of their upcoming TV Christmas Special, about which more later); then *The Night the KGB Tracked Santa's Sleigh with a Heat-Seeking Missile*; then *The Ostracized Elf* (story of loner elf later reconciled with the boss); then *Granny's Sleigh Run, Ruined by the Thruway Fence*; then *"Great Pan is Dead! Ho! Ho! Ho! Sang Santa"*; and finally, the most successful single in the history of show business, *Platform 12 Epiphany*, which sold during the last two seasons 175 million units, going Gold to the Eighth Power.

With *Platform 12 Epiphany*, J'Accuse combined rock, religious vision, public service, input into the national debate over space warfare, and national secrets. The strands mixed together overwhelmingly.

Slowly and silently filed on stage the Diogenes Liberation Squadron's 55-unit Investigative Chorus. As the Investigative Chorus assembles, perhaps some information regarding the etiology of *Platform 12 Epiphany* is in order. The story really originated back in 1968-69, when a space engineering student named Morris Margolin had been the highly profligate president of the J'Accuse Revolutionary Transformation Unit at MIT. In time Morris graduated, went on to pick up his Ph.D., and began a brilliant career in space science. He was forgiven his years of rioting, and he became one of those ectomorphic long-hairs with sensitive jobs in military/space science one sees occasionally narrating documentaries on public television.

We have mentioned how J'Accuse took great pains to stay in touch with fans through the years, and also how Science-and-Technology Rock had provided an avenue out of Guilt and Mea Culpa Rock. Morris had become one of J'Accuses paid consultants for Science-and-Technology Rock. Thus, it was while researching a little ditty about metal fatigue in the rotary liquid hydrogen nozzles in space shuttles that Jeb Malcomridge received from Morris Margolin the top secret National Security Agency reports about the Epiphany on Space Platform Number 12.

The Epiphany allegedly happened just as construction was ending on an orbiting solar power station built by the Municipal Power Consortium of New York State. At last New York City was free from the blood-sucking suffocation of the Consolidated Edison Company through cheap solar power owned by all the major cities of the state.

There was a period of several weeks between when the last construction crew had departed and the historic moment when the President should shuttle to the solar platform and ceremonially push the button to start the flow. On Christmas Eve, with just a skeletal guard staff aboard the platform, a team of military officers and military scientists, disguised as construction workers, arrived at Solar Platform Number 12 on a top secret matter. They brought with them some military hardware for secret attachment to the solar station.

Since it was Christmas Eve, one of the men had brought some aluminum rods and strips of green metal foil to make a little Christmas tree. He duct-taped together such a neat tree that from a distance it looked quite real. It floated freely on the edge of the solar platform, and was kept from departing by means of a long red fuzzy garland tied at one end to the tree's bottom and at the other to the platform.

The equipment the military men were attaching was of a familiar genre of high energy death-beam. This one apparently could spit giant hockers of sub-atomic particles down upon a section of earth to kill whatever moved. The scandal was not that this was a typical American secret weapon against the Chicoms or the Russians, but that this represented action against the Yorkcoms. The Yorkcoms? Yea, the military men, with their conservative, rough and ready hands ever upon the arteries of the nation, were deeply concerned over the future of New York City. Would it try to become a state, or set up an un-American socialist dictatorship? One could never be certain, so the death-beam apparatus, like a giant apple-corer, would be in place in case the Yorkcoms should arise, and the flesh-devouring beams from above could be unleashed on the Apple.

The men finished final calibrations for the equipment just before midnight, and were preparing to re-enter their ship, when above them appeared a full-color image of Jesus Christ, his arms outstretched as if he might reach down and grab up the crew. There was a dim chorus of angels, with wings barely visible, behind the apparition. He spoke to the men beneath him. The message was simple. "Don't build any ray guns in holy Space."

The Image ordered the men to remove the devices attached to the Municipal Power Solar Platform. Several were not about to take any guff from an hallucination, and so tried to draw their laser pistols on the putative Jesus, but the pistols melted in the holsters.

"Don't build any ray guns in holy Space," the Jesus Epiphany said again. As further emphasis for His words, the Epiphany, according to the witnesses, caused the death-ray apparatus on the platform also to melt, and with a wave of His hand fashioned a large chalice from the molten metals. The Chalice floated near the crew members, who reported it was filled "with a ripply fluid the color of topaz."

The floating Chalice seemed to pause at the top of the Christmas tree. Then came the Miracle of the Space Drink. The apparent Jesus lifted The Chalice and took a drink, and the scientists at the same moment felt their mouths to be filled with the most pleasant liquid any had ever imbibed. Gulp upon gulp their mouths were replenished. Each gulp was a paperback contract.

The Big J suggested a precipitous departure for the scientists. The voice was so compelling the squad undertook a totally unauthorized early return to earth, taking The Chalice, still containing some of the miracle fluid, with them.

A complete security black-out was placed on the incident. Inspection teams were dispatched to the platform to look for clues of a possible hype having been committed by Chinese,

Russian, or Italian Intelligence, or combinations thereof. National Security specialists felt the incident most likely represented some sort of criminal hologram emission from a nearby foreign satellite, in order to weaken America's will. Sort of the first fake séance in space. But there were many, particularly those who had witnessed what was now termed "The Epiphany on Platform Number 12," who believed in it. The staid National Security Agency seemed divided into factions, the Epiphanists vs. The KGB-holo-scamists.

The documents which Morris Margolin had obtained for J'Accuse alleged that on the trip back to earth with The Chalice, the military men had fought fiercely over the fluid. Instead of saving some for laboratory analysis, they shouted "Skol!" and "Bottoms up!" and drained The Chalice, gracelessly licking the droplets of the Vita Aeterna off the rim, shoving one another aside, and punching each other in the face for extra gulps.

As for J'Accuse, those who were Born Again—Clayton Feall and Wendell Taptap—were able to accept the Epiphany as Real; the others, as Art. The resulting song was a mixture, therefore, of religious fervor and artistic adornment. It had one particular factor which right up front made history. It was the first time in the history of Western Civilization that a voice track, allegedly that of a Deity, appeared on a single.

You see, when Morris Margolin acquired the secret documents he also picked up the tape of the discussion among the scientists at the time of the Epiphany as recorded by a nearby military monitoring satellite. The voice of Jesus, and even the rather fuzzily recorded sound of the chorus of Angels, was able to be mixed at appropriate moments into the song.

Needless to say, J'Accuse commissioned exhaustive scientific tests on the Jesus section of the tape. "Not of known human origin, nor of any known mechanical origin," stated the report. So, who could tell if it was the Big J, or just another KGB hype? And who cared? Did the Brothers Grimm ever turn down a good story?

As it raced up the charts, there to stay for almost a year, *Platform 12 Epiphany* was not without great controversy. First, one of the scientists who had seen the vision sued, claiming it was his "story," having sold exclusive rights to Paramount. It was the sort of nuisance suit that took up the slack from the easing of dope laws for attorney Barnaby Radither. Conservative Christians were upset also, that a group rumored to have 'tock-'too's of Karl Marx graved upon their buttocks, complete with scars where punk pins had once dangled from Marx's eyes, should be wreaking profit from a possibly genuine Epiphany.

For the stage version of the Epiphany, noted artist Joseph Brainard was asked to build a 3-D version of Platform 12. Brainard titled the masterwork *The Holy Holo-J*. And so, at the close of the concert at the Milwaukee Civic Arena, Jeb Malcomridge signaled the stage crew, and *The Holy Holo-J* was beamed into view, the solar platform seeming to hover just above the stage, and then, when the second portion of the *Holo-J*, the rose-hearted Epiphany of the Saviour, came into position overhead, The Diogenes Liberation Chorus began the thunderous hosannahs of the Angels. At the point when the alleged voice of Jesus was played over the speakers, silence reigned in the auditorium; a simple but moving message. Join in, if you will:

And Jesus
shone down upon the warriors
and Jesus
shone down upon the warriors

Don't you build any ray guns
in holy Space
Don't you build any ray guns

in holy Space

And the song ended. A long, ecstatic shriek-moan greeted the bowing band. It was not that the audience was on its feet; each clapper/whistler seemed as a hovercraft floating in joy. "Mutual Forgiveness of each Vice/ Such are the Gates of Paradise," Blake wrote. And such it was, as the factions forgave and one'd. The band could not leave the stage—even the stagehands and road crew were applauding (when do you ever witness that?). A series of encores ensued, ending with *The Dream of the Southern Road*, theme tune of their upcoming Christmas Special.

288

The short walk off-stage after a hugely successful concert, is unique. For a few seconds, neuroses, secret I-Am-Muck psychic selfputdown strands from having been cut from varsity football ten years previous, gomophobia,[3] perennial fears of empty baseball stadia and the band standing in yodeling forlornity on a center stage after blowing 265,000 dollars on the tour's advertising campaign, and other personal problems, melt away in the glow of triumph. Scrubbed youth are huzzahing as if it were a religious event in ancient Attika. Here and there, you can spot a critic bent over scribbling sentences that rock groups pray to the Lord of Vinyl to receive, such as the benevolent Hector Quease, who was covering the concert for *Gorp,* jotting, "Without a doubt the greatest concert in American musical history was given last night at the Milwaukee Civic Arena. J'Accuse has eclipsed The Beatles, The Stones, The Existenz Precedes Essence Tone-Tongs, for musical grit and purity and genius . . . "

The demand-for-attention ratio went to 35 per second, as J'Accuse's musicians ran the gauntlet, gropelet, beseechlet, to the dressing rooms, of old friends, pretend friends, colleagues in music, the beaming president and chief executives of J'Accuse Records, religious leaders, the Balzac Study Group, a sprinkling of elegant wives of liberal Senators, Fitz McIver and The 2000 Society security staff, and benefit beseechers. Of the latter, the reader can understand that benefit beseechers, or "b.b.'s," as the band called them, given J'Accuse's stance of "Publicization by 2000," were a particular problem after concerts. There was also the distant cousin problem; obscure relatives who for years had treated those in J'Accuse like fallen amphetamine toenails, now pushed their way backstage all over the country, promising that they had always loved and respected the particular band member, even when "the rest of the family" had scorned him as a profligate radical ne'er-do-well and atheist.

Hostile snarlers were on hand in abundance also, angry

---

3. Gomophobia, the fear of mouth cancer through repeated burning of the tissues by hot vegetarian casseroles. Such casseroles are known as "gom," or "gom-gom." Gomophobia was a problem to J'Accuse, an all-vegetarian band.

leftist puritans whose spitting, hissing, taut-pressed lips snarled out that sandbags and firing squads were awaiting J'Accuse to a man. "Dirty sellout Swiss bank account crooks!" a bitter face screamed at Jeb trotting past. Jeb was used to it, raising his guitar so as to avoid the spittle and the fist. However often it happened, it was always disconcerting. It's one thing to battle from the stage with glitter-spittle, but to be encountered by an angry, halitosis-halo'd yellow-green splat! on your guitar, well, it makes you forget for a second that they just don't tie prominent partisans of publicization to a sandbag wall.

THE
ROOM TRASH
BENEFIT

The dressing room was crowded with deferential, nearly silent, Benefit Beseechers, of the sort never to have uttered spittle in the names of their causes. There were representatives of the United Way, the March of Dimes, and other well-known charities. There were those representing the Numbers (the DC 4, the St. Louis 6, the Grain Valley 7, etc.). There were questionable types such as beseechers for the Brothers of the Offshore Haven, and The Gnostic Cross Shoeshine Boy Trust. And there were those with whom J'Accuse would never cooperate, such as the Hare Krishna Christmas Seal Foundation.

The praise of a benefit beseecher can be embarrassing.

291

"Not since Nijinsky or Isadora Duncan or Nureyev has there been such a dance as when you donned Dolly's wig tonight," one told Wendell. "Not since Schubert or *Strawberry Fields* has there been such a song as *Platform 12 Epiphany*," another said to Jeb. "Not since the opening riff of *Better Get It In Your Soul* on Mingus-Ah-Um has there been such bass playing," a third said to Clayton Feall.

It was embarrassing. Utterly without humor, to see those bearing press kits or manila folders of information standing all about, ready to speak in the confusing insanity of any dressing room of the plights of the American Indian, of farm workers, of experimental schools, whales, dolphins, seals and oil-free coast-lines; of solar power, food co-ops, underground presses, political prisoners, consumer networks, free dental and medical clinics, free lawyers' guilds, and the threat of rightists drooling for Seven Days in May.

The J'Accuse benefits officer was Susan Bechtel, who strode among the b.b.'s taking names and addresses, and announcing when the next benefits lottery would take place. A lottery was the only way justly to handle such a plethora of noble causes without bankruptcy.

So it was that the exhilaration, the triumph, the banishment of latent I-Am-Muckism, seemed short enough for J'Accuse, and was poofed! in the dressing room by the press of further duty. For it is the night of another Room Trash Benefit, this one to assist the construction of the *Investigatorium*, also known as the *Hall of the Holopoem*, where members of the Diogenes Liberation Squadron of Strolling Troubadors and Muckrakers could perform their choral investigative epic poems in a theatrical setting. What a noble cause! Several leaders of the Diogenes Liberation Squadron, including John and Maggie Muck, are in the dressing room, surrounded by reporters, resplendent in their floorlength duct tape/trash bag capes, their skins a fine leathery healthiness from the pleasure of outdoor living in the Barrel Generation housing complex. They shoot a quick seg with Dan Rather and Roger Mudd, then turn their attention to Jeb Malcomridge for the final preparations for the Room Trash.

There are numerous small personal matters needing attention in a rock star's dressing room, which naturally he or she will want to mask from the curious eyes of any fans, critics, or friends in attendance. Anyone who has toured with a rock band will know that one such matter is the Gunge Trunk Phenomenon.

In despair, in embarrassment, Donnie Pone op'd his wardrobe trunk a crack to locate something to wear. Donnie was an old-fashioned showman, lugging his trunks along into the dressing room wherever they played, even if it were a giant stadium. Donnie slammed the lid shut quickly, in dire embarrassment, for several nuns and the mayor of Milwaukee, were standing next to it. He could tell, as the odor-rays hit his olfactory, that there was nothing clean inside. And there certainly was nothing clean on his bod—for concerts left him grimy, griseous and spackled with glitter-spittle.

The Gunge Trunk Phenomenon seemed devilish, malevolent, as if he were being singled out for haunting by a "gunge hant." No matter how rich and famous Donnie Pone became, no sooner was he on the road more than four or five days, no matter how many trunks of clean and well pressed finery he brought along, everything, every elegant legging of velvet, every ruffled shirt, every vibrating codpiece,[4] was dirty.

It smacked of evil, the Gunge Trunk Phenomenon. It was as if lentuchs or dybbuks had escaped a nearby Isaac Singer story and had invaded his trunk with broken catsup bottles, soot, cobwebs, sperm-oil, rotting garlic, and tincture of jock strap. Donnie wondered if other rock stars suffered from Gunge Trunk.

There never seemed time to have them cleaned on the road, when so much time was spent in airports, at parties, or in sound tests. Donnie had phone bills of 500 a year just calling laundries all across America begging them to ship his aban-

---

4. During its unfortunate punk rock phase, J'Accuse had brought the so-called "vibrating cod" to rock; it trembled beneath the trousers, waxing upon command into "ophidian gnarls," as Fitz McIver would say, of contorted writhing; it even was wired for sound, could groan, could say, like Joe Brainard's drawing of Superman's fly, "Hi, folks!"

doned clothes to him collect. Those one used to call roadies, now organized into the Road Guild of Electronic Craftspeople, contended it was not in their contracts to deal with anybody's Gunge Trunk; for that you had to hire members of the Rock Wardrobers Union. The answer was: secret filth, and carry a variety of spot removers. Like Eskimos chew-softening seal skins, Donnie Pone was ever mouthing his own Finnish head-dresses, or sucking gunge spots from silken sarks, abandoning the filthiest in hotels, or tearing them up on stage and hurling them to the audience. Now you know, J'Accuse fans who so eagerly snatched Donnie's shreds from the air.

The benefit was held in the Grover Cleveland Presidential Suite at the Holiday Inn. J'Accuse paid the Inn for all repairs and the room rent while it was out of service. Participants were required for insurance reasons to wear safety goggles and hard rubber neck-shields to prevent flying glass artery axe-out. Prominent on the wall was the Room Trash Rule Chart:

1. NO BREAKING THROUGH THE WALLS TO THE HALLWAYS, TO ADJOINING ROOMS, OR TO THE OUTSIDE.

2. NO VIOLENCE.

3. NO DROPPING OF FURNITURE OR TV'S OUT THE WINDOW ON LIVING TARGETS.

4. NO RIPPING OUT OF PLUMBING.

Susan Bechtel collected checks, $750.00 per trasher, at the door. For an additional thousand, a trasher was guaranteed a working color television to bash. Susan looked carefully for bulges of contraband in the coats of those arriving. Her first job with J'Accuse had been spotting recording equipment being smuggled into concerts. At Room Trashes her eyes roved for spray cans hidden in mink. Spray-paint was banned, not only for environmental reasons and for reasons of tackiness, but also because the participants tended to get spray-batty and to go for one another's faces.

Formal attire was recommended, since it gave the Trashes in every instance greater energy. Women in gowns, men in

Sprint-Tuxes® flocked to charity Room Trashes all over America. There was to be a Trashathon soon at the Beverly Wilshire Hotel in which the entire hotel was to be torn apart during a three-day benefit.

There was always a hospitality suite adjoining the ripped-up rooms, where people could retire for makeup repair, patching wounds, brushing shards from fur, and for cocktails, chateaubriand, and high energy nut-raisin-date-honey-coca leaf gorp, to fuel further fray.

This particular Room Trash had been booked in advance by a plumbing manufacturers' convention, so there was already a great conviviality among the participants upon their arrival. Boy, were they eager to begin stomping! "I feel just like Orson Welles in *Citizen Kane!*" the matron panted, her pearls already moist with sweat bouncing on her hot, perfumed chest.

"So do I, dear," her companion shouted, putting a metal-tipped toe without further delay through her TV set, the 1000 dollar check in Susan Bechtel's hand not yet dry.

Another minked matriarch ripped down the long line of paneled drapes covering the sliding doors to the balcony, an exquisite thrill, the cloth coming down suddenly, soft, delicate, a settling heap, much of which, added thrills!, fell over her face and coiffure. "So heavenly, so numinal!" her muffled voice tried to shout from the delicate smothering. "Finer than a young lover's hands messing one's coiffure is a curtain messing it in a Room Trash," she thought, then reconsidered, "No, *almost* finer."

Knives were not prevented, nor razor blades, and the room soon flashed with them; the irony of diamond crusted fingers pushing switchblade buttons—snick! snick! snick! One would have thought it a preamble to a rumble in a maf-org disco rather than rich plumbers in platinum.

Sometimes there was a riot, and a group of industrialists would go insane. The authorities would arrive, cash would be proffered, and an intermission held to gentle the cursing crowd. Only once had there been a permaflip, and an interlude in a sanatorium needed for an Illinois congressman.

Susan was excited. One would have expected her, after 40

295

or 50 Room Trash Benefits, to have been glutted with them. There was something lastingly exhilarating about them. Somehow, there was no tonic so sensual as to watch a rock star like Jeb Malcomridge chain-sawing the legs from an armoire at the Delmonico Hotel. To spur the action, Susan Bechtel switched on a Room Trash Nostalgia tape she had spliced together. Oh those sad, sad days of Room Trash long ago—when we were young, of The Doors, The Fugs, The Eagles, The Rolling Stones, and The Webb Mountain Weepers!

"I've waited 45 years for this!" the Saniflush executive exuberantly shrieked, kicking the entrance table, until Susan Bechtel quietly reminded him that the mon-slurp table could not be trashed.

"The Trash is over there," Susan pointed. And the man rushed to the fray, delivering a left hook upon a particularly hideous painting above the bed. There seemed great hostility among room trashers for the paintings and prints common to the American motel room. She kept on hand many extra clowns on velvet, and toreadors on the same, from the Washington Square outdoor art show, to put on the wall to be shredded by rich fists pounding pinkly.

The opening event of a Room Trash was supposed to be the "Glass Storm," so Susan Bechtel urged those who couldn't wait to bash, to pause a moment for a truly exquisite esthetic pleasure. Participants stationed themselves on nearby balconies to view its marvels. And then lucky winners of the "Glass Storm" lottery were allowed to bash out the windows of the room, and a splintery-blizzardly crash would occur, shards of sharpness tinkle-tankling upon the courtyard or roof or swimming pool below. If the outside were illuminated by searchlights, the showering glass shone wondrously for a second, an instant halo-suffused "Air Sculpture" or waterfall of profound estheticity.

Once the Glass Storm was completed, a sort of high stakes game of chance was possible, that is, free-throwing furniture through the open windows, trying to splash the furniture into the pool below. Or sometimes a game of Ring Toss. "Ten thousand says you can't hook this serving cart onto the end of the diving board," he challenged.

"You're on!" And thus a bellhop was ten times sent below to retrieve the increasingly battered cart, bringing it back for further tries.

Some developed instant fetishes. "Henry," the motel manager barked over the phone, "Get some more mirrors out of 6C and 6D, these ladies and gentlemen are still hungry."

Indeed they were, all five of them. Each held a table leg and advanced toward a mirror, grring menacingly, when, just as if they were five gong-ringers in a Grade B Sinbad movie, they bashed the mirror together, and a shower of silvery acute angles fell tinkling. It was erotic, the pricks pushing against pinstripes, the wetness on 25 dollar lace-and-duct-tape undies.

Mattresses floated here and there in the water, sponge rubber guts jutting from slashed striped cloth. Someone was caught throwing ice buckets at the Holiday Inn sign below, definitely a no-no. There were no fires at Room Trash Benefits, although occasionally Susan discovered a society deacon, drool dangling from pyro lips, trying to torch the room. If one wanted to wage one's pyromanic proclivities, one was allowed however to check out from Susan Bechtel a butane welder's torch and to burn artistic patterns into the plastic-fibered rugs.

The president of the American Society of Flush Balls, once the windows were bashed and the Glass Storm fully enjoyed, tied the draw cord from the window drapes around the winding sprocket on the back of the TV and dangled the set out the window to bounce/jog/smash it up and down on the roof of the coffee shop next to the pool. Bored of this, he dashed into a forbidden zone, the bathroom. Trashers were barred from the john because of a benefit at the Beverly Hilton that had flooded several floors. It was too much to expect a plumbers' convention not to trash the bathroom. "Great Jove! I made this in my own factory!" he shouted, crowbarring the toilet off the tiles.

Throughout the action, Susan Bechtel was taking pictures with a tiny camera, not wanting participants to see. When members of J'Accuse arrived suddenly, she hid the camera.

The band had to make an appearance at the Room Trash, but they were increasingly embarrassed at the social phenomenon they had begun. It seemed to them to draw untoward attention to their baleful punk/glitter years. Plus this: not that J'Accuse hadn't trashed a few motels in their day, but once you own some motel chains yourself, you'd be surprised how hesitant you become to toss any TV's out the windows anymore.

"There they are!" voices shouted, as Jeb and Donnie and Clayton and Wendell stepped gingerly over the glass and jumble. "C'mon, be rock stars! Break something, big lads!" someone shouted, handing Wendell a chair leg. With her weapon thus released, she turned to Jeb Malcomridge, "Would you like to come into the bathroom with me?"

"Yeah," a gentleman said, pulling Donnie Pone aside to ask a question asked at least 10,000 times, "What's it like, having all those girls sinking to their knees on the spot?" And why is it that when the drool-lips ask one such a question, they always have to plunge an elbow or at least a couple of fingers into your ribs?

At the end of Trashes, J'Accuse posed with participants for Room Trash Nostalgia photos. There was the opportunity then to arrange the jumbles of broken beds, cracked lamps and shredded drapes into the Art of Chaos. They were destruction/constructions without the latter component. The pictures of the Art on this occasion became the Art. And the Art became, in accretions, the Archives. And the Archives, as it grew from file drawer, to file cabinet, to file wall, to file suite, would become History, offering to future centuries opportunities for doctoral theses, and to the Oxford University Press the opportunity to publish the 11-volume *Archives of the American Room Trash*.

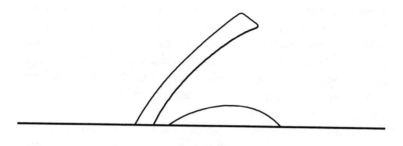

J'ACCUSE
FOR AMERICA

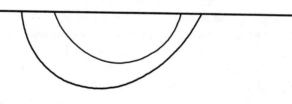

"Even if you're terminally ill, have them carry your stretcher into the recording studio! Punch the knobs with bloody stubs if that's all you have," Jeb Malcomridge advised. "Many groups wait, and wait, and waiting to record break up, or lose what it is they have, or lose nerve, or deny the beauty of early material against the mediocrity of later material. The answer is to record every day, if you can. Sandwich it in between flip-outs, if necessary. Go to bed on a cot in the middle of the studio waiting for a moment of lucidity. Conquer the electrons, or they'll conquer you!"

This was Jeb Malcomridge's advice, and he followed it

faithfully. J'Accuse had recorded at least once a week for seventeen years.

After the concert in Milwaukee, J'Accuse flew to New York to record the next day. The purpose of the session was partly to repair some problems on the sound track of their upcoming Christmas Special. After that, Jeb wanted to lay down an instrumental overdub or two for the next album, titled *J'Accuse for America*. J'Accuse joked among itself how it had never thought it would ever produce a Christmas Special. It was a challenge forced on them by the success of the Christmas album. They noted how television Christmas presentations were increasingly ugly—often with sleazy, mal-formed dolls wobbling arhythmically through ugly frames. Others were crudely drawn cartoons built around an already successful Christmas single. And the situation was worsening.

In recent years there were cartoon specials showing terrorists planting a nuclear device in Santa's bag, and holding Ohio for ransom; there was another, shot with dolls, showing Santa and the sleigh and reindeer going off course in a storm and falling into a Black Hole. Sex was even introduced into specials, with Mr. and Mrs. Claus becoming involved in a torrid triangle with Frosty the Snowman. It was disgusting.

J'Accuse rose up against this new tradition, and brought to Christmas viewers *The Dream of the Southern Road*, based on the song by the same name on their Christmas album. J'Accuse had studied THE CONCEPT OF THE CHRISTMAS SINGLE, with emphasis on how to get inspired with a core idea for such a song. Jeb and Wendell, the main song writers for J'Accuse, isolated two essential factors for successful Christmas singles. First of all you have to "Think Christmas Single." You should take notes whenever the craziest idea should strike. One method, they found, was to allot thirty minutes per day thinking about Christmas. The second factor in successful Christmas singling, was to read the New Testament for song ideas. It was there they found the semination for *The Dream of the Southern Road*.

It was the age-old technique of blowing into focus a minor historical character. In this case it was Jacob, Joseph's father, and Jesus' grandfather. Jeb and Wendell shaped a tale, combining songs and dialogue, describing how Jacob might have aided the Flight into Egypt. In their story, an angel of the Lord appeared in Jacob's sleep and told him his son Joseph and daughter-in-law Mary and the Infant were in mortal danger. A team of goons sent by Herod was closing in as the family tried to escape Bethlehem by the southern route.

Jacob ran through the night from Nazareth to Bethlehem, while a mysterious star of sky light led before him as a guide. Jacob managed to intercept the team of goons, and to confuse them into chasing him rather than Jesus and His parents. Thus the Sacred Trio could escape by the Southern Road.

Claudia Pred's Luminous Animal Dance Company played key roles in the production—serving as angels, as henchmen, etc. The Special was filmed on location in Israel. The critics loved the way that, while keeping Mary perfect, J'Accuse made Joseph an existential poet whose tight philosophical asides were inspired by Jeb Malcomridge's recent reading of Albert Camus' wartime notebooks. Thus, with Joseph "fleshed out," so to speak, the Joseph-Mary-Jesus trio became for the first time a believably real first family of Christendom.

The recording session was held at J'Accuse's own Delacroix Recording Studio, housed in the old Village Voice building on Sheridan Square. Lately there had been great tension at J'Accuse sessions. When your album has just sold 55 million copies, it's difficult, as you begin to record again, to prevent studio personnel from treating you like deities. If Jeb looked as if he were straightening his chair, someone would rush from the control booth to assist him.

Whenever Jeb walked near someone, they tended to stand up expectantly and appear dazed. Jeb was weary of having to tell countless strangers to "relax, and please sit down."

Jeb took pains to assure everyone that he was the same old super-busy Jeb, and J'Accuse was the same old J'Accuse. Indeed, he was the same, and ran the sessions with the same frenzy, pausing to take whispered phone calls by the tens. He had a receiver with a blinking light next to his guitar-stand in the studio for calls between takes.

J'Accuse was giving another benefit that night at Madison

Square Garden, so a number of calls came in giving reports on preparations at the Garden. He talked with Milton Rosé regarding construction of the stage props for the benefit; with Barnaby Radither discussing how to obtain the remainder of the Washington motels; with the U.N. Ambassador on details about the upcoming tour of Russia. Yes, Jeb was the complete phone man. He believed that if you can find some way to pay your $25,000 per month phone bill, you can move the world. "Social Change," saith Jeb, "depends on correct and vehement use of the phone."

The first part of the session was devoted to patching some minor flaws in the sound track of *The Dream of the Southern Road.* The footfall of the henchmen chasing Jacob was wrong. The new track had to be synched with the picture, so the picture was projected on a screen, and the new effects punched in at the correct moment on the tape. Jeb didn't want to use electronic synthesizer sprint-sounds so he rented full Roman soldier regalia, including metal greaves, sandals, helmets, spears, shields, and breast plates. Everyone who happened to be in the studio that day, even the Balzac Study Group, became temporarily Roman toughs. Thus attired, they ran around the studio, directed by Jeb, in role as chasing goons. While invigorating at first, after 47 takes it was coma alley, but Jeb was a merciless perfectionist, whose goal, unknown to the others, was to make his studio goons as tired as the soldiers chasing Jacob must have been.

The recording engineer was Susan Bechtel, in a knitted shawl and floorlength dress, her hair perched most commandingly in a layered bouffant. She found she needed her hair off her neck whenever she recorded. Increasingly, Susan Bechtel has assumed more and more recording responsibilities for J'Accuse. Several years ago she quietly took courses in recording techniques at the New School, and when she learned how relatively easy it was, asked Jeb if she could handle some sessions. It was a long road for Susan, who had been hired years ago, during the Watergate Rock phase, as a bulge-spotter, looking for hidden bootleg recording consoles at concerts. From there, she had become active in the non-profit foundations section of the

302

J'Accuse Empire,[5] particularly Groupanon, an organization to raise the consciousness of self-destructive young men and women fans. Susan Bechtel ran Groupanon with dedicated ferocity.

She was responsible for raising the awareness, not only of hundreds of thousands of fans, but of thousands of young men and women playing in bands. "Their claim of addiction to nameless bodies in the night, 'tis bunk!" Susan shouted. Groupanon made the covers of the weeklies with their demonstrations, as when several thousand Groupanon members stood outside the Piérre, where J'Accuse was staying during their punk/glitter phase, chanting "Wash the dishes! Wash the dishes! Wash the dishes." Such morality! Even though J'Accuse had funded the organization, it spared them not.

Groupanon published fact sheets on the personal habits of rock stars. It sent pretend groupies into dressing rooms, taped everything, and then published the transcripts. It was instrumental in installing under-the-table TV surveillance cameras in rock clubs to discourage bands from taking advantage of oversized table cloths and under-aged fans.

From Groupanon Susan Bechtel rose within the empire until her importance was nearly overwhelming. Her formidability, her moral elevation, aided her rise. She kept to herself when work was over; she seemed totally removed from the tide of lust; seemed a staid member of the growing congeries of sans-sexuality. Yet, she dressed most becomingly, often in an antique Ukrainian shawl, a floorlength dress, and shiny silver boots in which you could see your face.

After the final take dubbing the chasing goons, Susan Bechtel left the studio, not bothering to put on her coat, for she didn't want to be missed. She made a call from a booth on a different street.

"I have what you requested, Mr. Forbes," she said. "I just learned they're going to count and bundle the money in the J'Accuse dressing room. Security will be tight. They figure to begin around one a.m. I have four backstage passes, which I am

---

5. Vide page 304, The J'Accuse Fiscal Empire Schemata.

THE J'ACCUSE FISCAL EMPIRE
DRAW & DRAIN SCHEMATA:

↓↓↓ = mon-out
↑↑↑ = mon-in
↓↑↓ = it could go either way

Electrical Equipment
Development Foundation

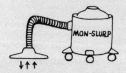

↓↑↑

Road Crew, Bodyguards,
Lighting and Sound Crews

↓↓↓

Accountant &
Office Staff

↓↓↓

Lawyers

↓↓↓

Mt. Moolah, Colombia
Coca Farm & Refinery

↑↑↑

Numbered
Accounts in
Bahamas

↑↑↑

J'Accuse Investment, Inc.,
(owning all the motels
in the state of Washington)

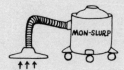

↑↑↑

J'Accuse
Investigation
Foundation, Inc.

↓↓↓

J'Accuse
Concerts
Management, Inc.

↑↑↑

J'ACCUSE ASSISTANCE & BENEFIT FOUNDATION, INC.

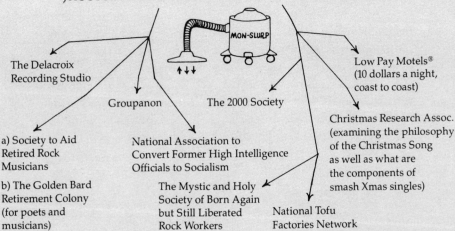

↑↓↓

The Delacroix
Recording Studio

Groupanon

The 2000 Society

Low Pay Motels®
(10 dollars a night,
coast to coast)

a) Society to Aid
Retired Rock
Musicians

b) The Golden Bard
Retirement Colony
(for poets and
musicians)

National Association to
Convert Former High Intelligence
Officials to Socialism

The Mystic and Holy
Society of Born Again
but Still Liberated
Rock Workers

National Tofu
Factories Network

Christmas Research Assoc.
(examining the philosophy
of the Christmas Song
as well as what are
the components of
smash Xmas singles)

taping under the metal ledge of this booth right now. You can pick them up in five minutes . . . "

"Yes, the dressing room is just a few paces down a hallway from the entrance I've marked with blue tape, leading to the underground parking lot you and I drove through the other day. They will station an armored vehicle there, and carry the money from the dressing room. Armaments consist of three of McIver's security staff, armed with revolvers, and whatever the armored car service brings. Uh, Mr. Forbes, are you sure it'll be surgical?"

The voice assured her that the action would be as pristine as ever performed for the good of the nation. "And Susan," the man continued.

"Yes?"

"We've decided that you should compromise Rosé."

"Who?"

"Milton Rosé. We want you, without sacrificing any principles of morality, to cause friction between him and Ione Appleton. We want to split that dangerous little duo right away."

It went without saying—they were not advocating sex. But. "Try to pet with him in front of Appleton," he said. Susan groaned to herself, her face flushing darkly.

"Remember, the safety of the nation is on our collective, er," pausing, hating that word, "our *overworked* shoulders."

"Yes, Mr. Forbes."

They were waiting for her when she returned to Delacroix. Time was tight. It was already late in the afternoon, and Jeb and Wendell wanted to begin cutting an instrumental track for the new record, J'ACCUSE FOR AMERICA, a national anthem concept album. J'Accuse was offering to the nation twelve songs, any one of which they proposed as a national anthem to replace the tired, uninspired, unsingable, bombardment-oriented *Star Spangled Banner.*

Some were songs already written, such as Phil Och's *Power and The Glory.* Others, such as Allen Ginsberg's *Weight of the World is Love,* Whitman's *I Hear America Singing* (with words altered to make it equally feminine), and Emily Dickinson's *The Life That Tied Too Tight Escapes,* were given melodies. The re-

305

mainder were original with J'Accuse.

There was time only to lay down basic instrumental tracks for the Emily Dickinson poem; Wendell on drums; Donnie, guitar; Jeb, piano; Clayton, standup bass. After the fifth take, Jeb called a stable and ordered a thoroughbred horse to be delivered to Delacroix the next afternoon. It was to be another first in world recording.

The poem J'Accuse was offering as a possible national anthem had an image of a horse seeking freedom:

> The Life that tied too tight escapes
> Will ever after run
> With a prudential look behind
> And spectres of the Rein—
> The Horse that scents the living Grass
> And sees the Pastures smile
> will be retaken with a shot
> If he is caught at all—

(Poem #1535, from the *Complete Poems of Emily Dickinson*, published by Little, Brown.)

The goal was to bring the horse into the studio, play the track, and stimulate the horse's heartbeat until it exactly fit the rhythm section of the tune, and thus to add the heart as an overdub.

After the session, Jeb wanted to try some mixes. He had a feeling that today would produce some excellent results. It was the only thing vaguely similar to a cultic belief Jeb allowed himself, his sense of the possibility of mystic communication with recording tape; there was no other way to explain how on certain occasions the mixes were marvelous, while on others, with knobs and levels exactly the same, the results were terrible. Jeb always mixed alone.

Today he asked Susan Bechtel to stay with him, to "work the electrons." In the mores of J'Accuse it was quite an honor to be asked by Jeb to join in the mixing. Jeb was in love with Susan, a love long nurtured, long in growth, and now an inferno. Her formidability had stalled him, but after three years of knowing her Jeb felt surely he could not have been garbaged if he should have stiffly served up some come-on vectors. He was rebuffed! For a while his broken heart threatened to turn the group into a blues band, as a flood of barrel bottom stomp-pain lyrics flowed forth. This was a few months ago.

Jeb became her disciple. He learned austerity from her, learned how to work in deadly seriousness. For twelve years Jeb Malcomridge had believed with all his heart that no one would pay attention to J'Accuse if they "went serious."

It was in this new period of seriousness that Jeb developed the concept of "Grabbing Off a Decade." Commercialism, political struggles, and the exigencies of criticism (critics desperate for something to criticize) combined to force each decade into an organic entity. "Good," reasoned Jeb. "All you have to do is to begin a cunning campaign in the ninth year of a decade, and you can establish the tone of the ensuing decade. That way, you'll have ten whole years to wreak your will!"

Grabbing Off a Decade could backfire, as when Nixon tried to grab the '70's. It was Jeb who coined the saying, "The '80's will trash the '70's for garbaging the '60's."

Thus Jeb developed his vision of The Glorious Deadline. Between concert tours, he helped set up the regional conferences that created The 2000 Society. It was a long way for Jeb Malcomridge, whose career had begun at the very bottom. He could recall J'Accuse sleeping five in a van on top of amplifier cases, waking up two inches from the rhinestone boot, or worse, of a fan; kidney permanently creased by a folded microphone stand, ten degrees outside, the van out of gas, not able to afford a motel, stranded on New Year's morn in a shopping center parking lot in New Jersey after a gig at the Toodle-Doo Lounge.

In those days the young men of J'Accuse were embarrassed just to hear the word socialism. Socialism meant dullness, cronyism among squares, blockheads ranting slogans, queue-ups with buckets for potato soup, and loaves of bread thrown off carts to beggars.

Now Jeb had vastly changed, and he owed it all to Susan Bechtel. Their relationship was one of those in which one partner beams upon the other a nearly unbearable stream of devotion. When he proposed marriage, she turned it aside, but soothingly so, and they remained friends, with the tinge of employer and employee absolutely erased.

Susan could not help but feel happy in the control booth, standing side by side with a man who loved her, talking quietly, their hands working the levers and meters together, the fingers and knuckles as they touched one another by accident, would buzz with excitement.

At the same time, Susan felt a great burden on herself from this first opportunity to mix the songs of a great band. She stood tense and erect, absolutely engrossed in the decisions a mixer must make as a tape plays. She watched for Jeb taking advantage of her, reaching for a sub-ceinture pat, say.

But it was she that, after a particularly successful preliminary mix on Phil Och's *Power and the Glory,* put her arm around his waist.

Jeb did likewise, and they both stood, hands occupied holding one another, listening to the mix play back. Jeb punched the re-wind, and took the album back to its beginning, and the whole finished part of J'ACCUSE FOR AMERICA came from the speakers overhead.

To kiss in such patriotic/matriotic surroundings, with songs honoring America in one's ear—well, could Susan Bechtel have refused a friendly kiss in those circumstances? She didn't. And both hearts beat wildly, as the tape played on.

There was a slight sound, "thwop," as Jeb op'ed a small alabaster jar and shook something upon his fingers. She did not—for the first time—halt Jeb's hand as it dipped to the buttons of her bodice—and opened it. Then—oh no!—Susan's shoulders wiggled involuntarily as she felt an unseemly surge of oleophobia. What was Jeb doing?

He was softly patting a sweet and pleasant gush upon the concavity of her lower throat between the shiny skin-covered knobs of her collar bones. And elsewhere.

Reluctantly Susan removed her attire. When a tremblyfingered man is rubbing distillate of lotus and palm oil on your breasts, you want to open up your granny dress, if only for tidiness.

Jeb stopped on a sudden, squinting his eyes, looking

dazed, barely able to resist the urge to take some notes for a song. Susan took the opportunity to take her diaphragm case to the bathroom. Sixty-four seconds later they were fucking, half leaning, half lying upon Jeb's complex of organs, clavinets, synthesizers in the darkened studio. For some reason, Susan began to shake her head, and whisper, "No! No! No!"

Jeb thought she was ordering him to stop. She wasn't. If you have ever made love on the chilly keyboard and against the patch bay of a synthesizer, you will understand Susan Bechtel's request that they adjourn the tolling of the groin-gong to a more heated surface.

Still within her, Jeb picked her off the keyboard, and carried her out to the wide 48-track mixing board. It was a long, slightly angled panel, with a laminated cloth covering, which somewhat lessened the cold of metal on exposed skin. They spread as best they could in the haste, their clothes and winter coats upon the mixing board. Jeb stood with Susan, her legs still around his lower back. He backed up against the board, and with a little leap found himself and herself, in a sitting position, still fucking, on the board.

Then they rolled upon the knobs, levers, meters, reels and other accoutrements of the mixing unit. As they fucked, the tape of J'ACCUSE FOR AMERICA continued through Walt Whitman's *I Hear America Singing, the Varied Carols I Hear*. It was the word "Varied" that gave Jeb pause, and he lowered himself down the elevation of the mixing board, in order to kiss Susan Bechtel on the upper node of the Venusian V.

"I love you, Susan," he whispered, as he began the fastest flutterings of the tongue in the history of Western Civilization.

"No." she replied, inserting fingers beneath his chin, to lift him away. "You mustn't, you can't, I won't let . . ."

"Please," he begged, "Please."

When she came, all the past was melted away. By chance, just as she came, Jeb was trying to keep her from writhing out of slurp-range, and pushed her several inches up the console's angulation, so that her tailbone pushed the volume lever upward also, and *I Hear America Singing* increased to full volume. Susan was unable to bear more, and threw Jeb's head from her clitoris.

309

She twisted roughly back and forth as if she were lying within a wooden gold-mining sluice, and her hands were clenching the wooden sides, and a torrent of eternity rolled down over her, nuggets of golden pleasure buffeting the tingling red rose of the perfect calling.

"I love you, Susan," Jeb said again, hoping for an answer. She looked long into his eyes, her lips pursing together to keep them from trembling. She seemed about to speak, but suddenly shook her head as if to regain consciousness, grabbed her dress and coat, slid off the mixing board, and ran from the room.

Jeb told them to hold all calls for another fifteen minutes, and began to weep. Susan Bechtel went into the bathroom, to shower, to wash and squeeze Jeb from her skin. She too, for other reasons, began to weep as the sponge-glove lightly slid over her bending muscles.

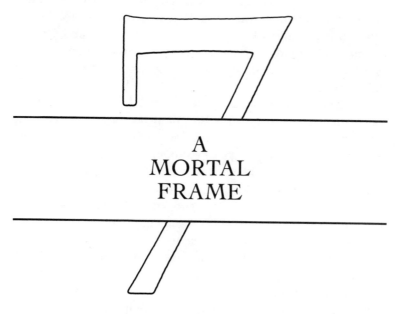

A
MORTAL
FRAME

Even a letter from President Kennedy saying it was fine with him was not enough to give Milton Rosé peace of mind when he finally joined The 2000 Society. A change of political wind might blow the Crane Shrine off the surface of Mars. What if the Balzac manuscript scandal should flare up again?

Milton was beyond the help of the coca leaf, he was so tired of working twenty hours a day on the Crane Museum. It had developed into a vast computerized enterprise even requiring a certain interfacing with the cockle-burr hair styles of the Joint Chiefs of Staff. American Security did not want an unmapped secret lair on possibly hostile turf, so the location of the

Trunk was to be hidden in Space Intelligence Corps computers, just in case it ever needed to be checked for the national good.

Rosé welcomed a break, and when Jeb and Ione asked him to construct the scenery and the Mayflower hovercraft for the benefit, he accepted gladly. Milton transformed the hovercraft idea into a sensational work of art, establishing a method of gathering mon at benefits soon to be copied by culty-wultys, by telethons, by evangelists.

The 2000 Society benefit was being telecast simultaneously to auditoriums in 35 countries. That was what worried Rosé—the controversial hook-up with Poland, Rumania, and Czechoslovakia. He could just hear the generals with whom he dealt on the Crane project pointing their fingers and saying, "Aha! We told you so!"

Fitz McIver, throughout the concert, darted here and there on matters of security. Now and then one saw him trying to pay attention to the music, and he let his knees go wobbly, snapping his fingers to what he thought was the beat, holding his head to the side, like a jazz drummer, his good ear to the music.

The benefit had barely begun when McIver received the full report on Susan Bechtel from the security office. He glanced at it, his heart giving a nervous squeeze like a sponge mop. His suspicions were confirmed, and immediately he assigned staff to follow her around the clock. "Find out where she calls her control. If I judge her correctly, it's the same spot, and the same time, every day. When you find it, Surv-Chip® it."

The preliminary report on Susan Bechtel, issued weeks ago, had predicted a full r.w.n. (right wing nut) analysis on her, but McIver had just too much to do, breaking-in a security staff, setting up proper safeguarded computer facilities (you didn't want r.w.n. computers calling your computer up, and sucking all the data into its own), opening up proper contacts in the law enforcement community, and compiling files on all staff members of the Society. It was just too huge a task for a month's work, and there was nothing so concrete on Bechtel as to warrant requesting J'Accuse to fire her.

As he read the report, McIver whistled with surprise.

Susan Bechtel worked directly under Hunk Forbes of the American Security Command! According to the report, Forbes, one of the most dangerous right wing nuts in the western hemisphere, was currently busy preparing for snowshoe warfare exercises in Northern New York State. Fitz laughed at the concept of para-snowshoe rightists. More often Hunk Forbes' teams could be monitored by law enforcement as they scurried over back roads in the dead of night in pickup trucks, the headlights taped shut to single slits, practicing cyanide dispersal in the event of leftist takeover. But snowshoe warfare? That was new.

The report on Bechtel traced her career. She'd attended a church college in Indiana. On her graduation day, as she stood outside the chapel in her cap and gown, Forbes had recruited her.

Her calm outer demeanor veiled an inner vat of hates handed to her by parents whose mutual hatred had been focused almost entirely on the outside world. Susan Bechtel was ideal for the purposes of the American Security Command. McIver was glad to note in the report that Susan's relationship with Forbes had cooled while she was managing Groupanon for J'Accuse. "She's taking too much of this Groupanon shit to heart," Hunk Forbes was alleged to have said. The implications were obvious—what if she turned Groupanon concepts onto the paramilitary right, and formed something called Rightanon?

McIver continued skimming the document. "Forbes is about to terminate her connections with J'Accuse, though Susan is unaware of it. . . . Forbes distrusts her silver boots and her long dresses almost as much as her work with Groupanon. . . . More than anything he doesn't want her, even in her role as informant, to aid in the production of leftist-inspired phonograph records. . . . He would rather her to have set fire to the recording studio. . . . They are so worried about Susan Bechtel they are giving serious thought to having her killed." Reading this, McIver reached for a felt tip pen to circle it, for it was such information that could help The 2000 Society Security turn Susan into a double agent.

Reading further, McIver saw that Forbes had already thought of the double agent possibility. Susan had flagged-out on American Security Command computers as a "D.A. Proba-

313

bility," so she had to go. What McIver could not guess, reading the report, was that Forbes viewed the Madison Square Garden benefit as a genuine "communist invasion," and intended to pay for the snowshoe warfare exercises with the money from the Mayflower hovercraft. Hunk Forbes had a rule. "Never use your own money; get it from the tennis shoes." By tennis shoes, he meant someone dupable or ripe with mon on the right. Normally he burned someone in a quick oil deal to pay for a paramilitary caper, but the opportunity to grab cash from rich leftists was just too tempting.

McIver personally planted a Surv-Chip® on Susan Bechtel, as she hurried past on some errand or other. He did not have time to monitor the channel continually, but punched auto-record, and from time to time listened in. At the moment his biggest concern was to safeguard the money to be collected at the end of the concert by J'Accuse in the Mayflower hovercraft. The concert, from the sound of it, was succeeding beyond anybody's expectations. Never had such screaming and applause leaked offstage at the Garden. The tumult was just as if one of the major sports teams were winning a championship in the Garden. Compared to this, the Milwaukee concert last night had been a group of hipsters in a coffee shop snapping their fingers at the end of a poem.

Who performed? Jeb Malcomridge spent fifteen hours and fifteen thousand in conference calls, arranging for reunions of groups. In addition to the Diogenes Liberation Squadron of Strolling Troubadors and Muckrakers, J'Accuse, and the Existenz Precedes Essence Tone-Tongs, the following groups were reconstituted, to the crowd's huzzahing amazement: The Drool-Tones (brought back for punk/glitter nostalgia); the original Byrds; the Holy Modal Rounders; Peter and Gordon; Linda Ronstadt and the Stone Poneys; Long Branch Pennywhistle (Glenn Frey and J. D. Souther); The Beach Boys; The Fugs (a story for a separate occasion); the Jim Kweskin Jug Band; The Blues Project; and The Doors (with Jim Morrison's taped voice-track). While not performing live, the Beatles produced a short film for the benefit, a song-medley in honor of the mysteriously deceased rock heroes, Janis Joplin, Jimi Hendrix, and Jim Morrison.

At concert's closing J'Accuse performed standing in the Mayflower hovercraft. While they sang, the Mayflower floated above every section of the arena. In the programs on every seat were small paperclip-like magnets, to attach to checks or bills. As the hovercraft appeared above a particular section, the audience held up their checks with magnets attached, and the pecunia pneumatic grabgelt tube sucked the mon upward, into the craft's pecunia storage bay.

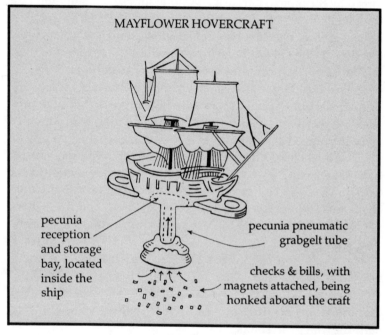

MAYFLOWER HOVERCRAFT

pecunia reception and storage bay, located inside the ship

pecunia pneumatic grabgelt tube

checks & bills, with magnets attached, being honked aboard the craft

Standing in the Mayflower's prow, J'Accuse chanted hypnotically for an hour and fifteen minutes, as if, frankly, the audience were a parakeet being trained to talk. Singing, from the berths aboard the Mayflower hovercraft:

The Glorious Deadline
Don't you want to help
The Glorious Deadline
Don't you want to give to
The Glorious Deadline

How it worked! The money was an avalanche. Pouches containing rare rings and stones, with magnets affixed, slupped upward into the pecunia-pneumatic grabgelt tubes. Searchlights played upon the throng, catching the beautiful lines of pastel checks being sucked aboard, not to mention the dark green of wads of bills also upward slupping.

During the benefit Susan was extraordinarily nervous. Though her clipboard bulged with things to do, much of it she turned over to Ione Appleton and to security chief Fitz McIver. The act of love on the patchboard with Jeb Malcomridge, reinforced by the tape of J'Accuse's patriotic songs, was something, a combination, which flamed into romantic love. She struggled against it. That she should wind up loving a man whose politics she hated! She chided herself out loud. "I must keep my own identity! My own philosophy! No greater enemy of Christendom is there than a Christian on the Left!" And there were deeper, darker sentiments, which she suppressed, and would not even recall or consider—of a communist tongue making her come during a communist anthem.

Nevertheless, Susan Bechtel hugged Jeb coming off stage. "You remember how I couldn't say 'I love you' this afternoon? Oh Jeb, I'll love you forever. I've never felt this way about anyone before. Forever, Jeb, forever!" she shouted, and threw herself against his chest. "Oh, let's go back into the studio right now, Jeb."

Jeb was overjoyed. "Yes, let's go," he agreed. "Oh, how I want to be inside you!"

Susan blushed with a mix of modesty and eagerness. For her, there was no thrill greater than to make love listening to patriotic American songs!

What is to be said, then, when barely after kissing Jeb and softly rubbing his upper legs, playfully pulling his zipper up and down a half-inch, Susan approached the jubilant Milton Rosé and said to him, "Are you coming over to my house tomorrow, Milton? You wouldn't believe how erotic it is to take a bath in a redwood tub full of maté tea mulled with ginger!"

Milton did not notice the inquisitive Ione Appleton across the room, as Susan put her hand upon his belt, and below, while she invited him. Milton Rosé was absolutely suspicious, even paranoid, about the hand and its forefinger which had already worked itself into his trousers to stroke his lignum vitae. Was this woman some sort of agent sent to compromise the Hart Crane Shrine Project?

Yet, had not Fitz McIver himself cleared Susan Bechtel for reception of the most lofty of 2000 Society secrets? Rosé approached the harried McIver and said, "I'd like to speak with you about Susan Bechtel."

McIver knew it's a bad habit to spread intelligence reports among "civilians" but he had listened to enough of Rosé's private conversations, at the time Milton had acquired Hart Crane's Trunk, to trust him completely. McIver handed Rosé the full report on Bechtel. Rosé thanked McIver, turned to glance through it, and put it in his pocket, later to read.

There was one key change in plans after the concert, of the sort that perforates the ulcers of security men. Jeb and Milton wanted to carry the money out to the stage, after it had been bundled, fashion a "ziggurat" of it, then bring the Mayflower hovercraft overhead. All involved in the production would then pose around the ziggurat for a photo.

McIver was upset, and tried to explain to Jeb the dangers. That, plus the overtime rent of the Garden and security personnel would go into five figures. "Just give us 30 minutes, Fitz," Jeb argued.

Perhaps McIver himself had a false sense of security. Everything felt so good! So much love, so much sacrifice! What could ever halt the march toward The Glorious Deadline now? Not even Hunk Forbes and the American Security Command. Not even ten thousand Susan Bechtels trying to stir up trouble.

Over four million dollars were emptied from the mon-bay of the hovercraft—two million in cash. In J'Accuse's dressing room began the task of sorting the checks and bundling the bills. There were magnums of champagne everywhere, and joy as never before. The entire Balzac Study Group was on hand; they can be forgiven their curiosity, for here lay a fit swarm of ideas for their next project—literature's first simultaneously published dodecalogy!

After a few hundred thousand were bundled, Milton Rosé practiced stacking the mon into a photogenic ziggurat. There was an interpersonal matter being discussed while he did this. Ione stood rather jealously above him, demanding in audible whispers exactly what Susan Bechtel was saying as she had massaged Milton's zipper? Ione had pinned a Groupanon button on her label, and occasionally shot a glance at Susan.

Susan's eyes averted in shame. She glanced at her watch, gulped, and begged Jeb to come to the hall with her. Just then, Hunk Forbes and his men kicked in the door, wearing trash bag hoods with eye holes.

Hunk Forbes had misjudged Fitz McIver's seriousness in protecting The 2000 Society. "He just wants a job," Forbes had scoffed, thinking of all the ex-FBI and Secret Service guys now stuck guarding warehouses. He'd not known about McIver's limited edition laser pistols, for example.

McIver received a five-second warning over his earpiece. He bent beside the doorway ready to open fire. Fitz was wounded in the initial gunfire, but three of the trash bag hoods fell dead. Wendy Sark was the bravest in the room, rushing forward to leap on what was seen to be Hunk Forbes himself when she tore his mask away. Wendy received a chop in the leg from Forbes' Black Forest hunting knife, and lay on the floor bleeding profusely.

Milton had been bent over the ziggurat o' green, when the guns began. The shots continued in the hallway, mixed with the clicking zzzt's of laser pistols. Hunk Forbes was able to beat his way out, and escaped in a minicopter.

The room was suddenly silent, except for some weak scratching sounds coming from the stacks of bill-bundles. They were from the hands of Milton as he tried to push himself up into an erect position.

Everybody demanded a return to normalcy. "Is everyone all right!" John Barrett shouted. At once it was obvious there was something terribly wrong with Milton Rosé, as he fell upon the stacks of money and rolled down upon the floor, a few walls of bill-bundles collapsing around him. There was a horrible pulsation of blood pouring from a wound in his chest.

Fast action was needed. Fitz McIver bit his lip, smoothed back disheveled hair-locks with one hand, and with the other brought up the radio to his mouth, ordering an ambulance and paramedic crew at once. Susan Bechtel shoved her way to Rosé's side, wishing with all her being that she, rather than the great artist, were dying on the floor. The tears of deceit poured like weak acid down her cheek, and she pushed her fists against her chest, sobbing uncontrollably, uttering a broken prayer for Milton's soul in between hot-breathed explosions.

Daring to look down at Milton, she spotted her report protruding loosely from his inside jacket pocket, which lay open beneath him. The bullet had penetrated just below the title:

REPORT: 2000 SOCIETY SECURITY
SUBJECT: SUSAN ANN BECHTEL

Susan snatched it hemic-damp from the floor, and ran screaming into the garage past laser-burnt robbers in the hallway.

Without moving him needlessly, Ione Appleton held Milton in her arms, trying to staunch the flow of blood with a swatch of white linen torn from her writing robe, which she had brought by chance in her shoulder bag. In a barely audible voice, Ione was beseeching the Sky to spare her darling's life. She saw that Milton was trying to speak, so she bent her ear near his mouth, to hear him say, "Take care of the Trunk."

Though they made many of the others begin to weep, Milton's words jolted Fitz McIver into action. Fitz forced himself away from the tight knot protecting Rosé in order to supervise another tight knot, that of security men, whom he instructed to form a defensive line, facing outward with drawn laser-pistols, around the ziggurat of money. Others quickly shoved the bundles into pouches to carry to the armored courier cars.

"Milton, darling," Ione answered, "You'll be painting again in a week. But, please remember this—if, God Forbid, anything bad happens to you, all of us,"—glancing around the room as she spoke—"all of us will spend the rest of our lives to finish the Hart Crane Shrine."

Indeed, those standing in the room, their eyes darting from face to face, nodded emphatically, taking a silent two-part vow on the spot. The first, of aesthetics,

To Place The Hart Crane Shrine on Mars,
Or Death.

The second, of morality,

To Meet The Glorious Deadline,
Or Death.

Right then, a team of doctors and stretcher-bearers sprinted through the door, scooped Milton upon a stretcher, and disappeared to a helicopter waiting at the Eighth Avenue curb. It was Jeb Malcomridge who grabbed a doctor's arm, and demanded to know Milton's condition.

"He'll not survive," the doctor replied, and ran to join the others at the 'copter. Ione dashed after them, but was not allowed aboard.

Ione sat crouched on the curb as—whopa! whopa! whopa!—the craft lifted upward, tilted, then sped up Eighth Avenue about 100 feet off the ground, between the rows of buildings. The Diogenes Liberation Battalion of Strolling Troubadours slowly filed upon the sidewalk in front of Madison Square Garden, and formed neat rows in back of Ione Appleton. The men of J'Accuse joined them, along with the stage crew and security staff of The 2000 Society. Fitz McIver stood looking up the Avenue, weeping without reserve. And all began to sing:

Float thou, o soul of the painter,
out beyond the shoulders of slime.

Paint scenery with Rembrandt and Titian
for a Shakespeare-Beethoven opera
or paint with Michelangelo
fair flowers on Sappho's four-string lyre.

And seek thou out, o soul of the painter,
the path of sweet sweet Emily D.,
you'll find Hart Crane there,
                    bard at her side

and look for John Keats, walking

on Hampstead Heath with
    Edna Millay

while we on earth work out
The Glorious Deadline

THE END

This First Edition of *Fame & Love in New York*
was designed by George Mattingly
with Palatino, Cochin, Avant Garde Extra Light,
& News Gothic Bold Extra Condensed types
set by Eileen Callahan & Robert Sibley of Abracadabra,
with illustrations by the author,
& was manufactured in Summer 1980 by
McNaughton & Gunn Inc., Ann Arbor, Michigan.